DEVIL'S SPAWN

MANDA MELLETT

COPYRIGHT

Published 2020 by Trish Haill Associates

ISBN: 978-1-912288-60-1

Cover Design by Wicked Smart Designs

Edited and formatted by Maggie Kern at Ms.K Edits

Proof reading by Melanie Farrow at Professional Writing Services

www.mandamellett.com

Disclaimer

This is a work of fiction. Names, characters, businesses, places, events and incidents are either the products of the author's imagination or used in a fictitious manner. Any resemblance to actual persons, living or dead, or actual events is purely coincidental.

Warning

This book is dark in places and contains content of a sexual, abusive and violent nature. It may not be suitable for persons under the age of 18.

Devil's Spawn is dedicated to my father-in-law, David 'Stormy' Haill who showed us so dramatically that sometimes the impossible actually is possible.

CAST OF CHARACTERS

Officers
Demon – President
Beef - Vice President
Buzzard – Secretary/Treasurer
Thunder – Sergeant-At-Arms
Mace – Enforcer
Sparky – Road Captain

Patched Members
Hellfire
Bomber
Cad
Ink
Lizard
Pyro
Paladin
Rusty
Skull
Judge
Wills

Prospects

Karl

Beaver

Nails

Dirt

Smithy – Failed Prospect

Old Ladies & Children

Violet (Demon's): Theo

Steph (Beef's)

Sindy (Buzzard's)

Moira (Hellfire's): Demon, Kennedy, Samuel

Jeannie (Bomber's)

Jayden (Paladin's)

Mel (Pyro's)

Beth (Ink's)

Sweet Butts

Bella

Breezy

Sheila

Titsy

Tulia

Deceased Members

Blackie – Previous President

Furnace – Previous VP

Ingot – Previous Enforcer

Taser

SATAN'S DEVILS MC

CHAPTER ONE

Lizard

The bright beam of light homing in on my face had woken me. Squinting, I see it's the sun piercing the material of the curtains, successfully finding a gap where I hadn't closed them properly the night before.

Closing my eyes tightly against the annoying dazzle, I repeat the mantra in my head.

I'm Lizard, otherwise known as Norton James. I ride with the Satan's Devils MC and have for the past ten years. I'm thirty-eight years old, and my birthday is... my birthday is the tenth of January. The current President of the United States is... well, who can forget that name? I'm a tattoo artist and I run Devil's Ink on behalf of my brothers. I've no ties, no family and that's how I intend to stay.

All there. All the important details.

Today is going to be a good day.

The uneasy but inexplainable fear that always seems to be there when I awake begins to recede.

Sliding my legs out from under the covers, I place my bare feet on the floor, then look around my room. It's not much but has all the essentials I need in my life. A place to lay my head, a closet for my clothes, and a desk where I can sit and sketch out my designs in peace. With the luxury of an en suite bathroom, this is my home.

I'm more than content to live on the compound of the Satan's Devils MC Colorado chapter based in Pueblo. I have everything that I could wish for, and no desire for anything more. These four-square walls are more than adequate as my personal space. I've no yearning to own an apartment, let alone a house.

Already I hear voices and the heavy stomping of motorcycle boots making their way past my door, my brothers getting ready for the day. The sounds are comforting, reminding me I'm not alone. What would I do without such company? Just take one step outside my door and I'll find men who share my hopes and dreams, and, when I have the need—which I admit is quite often —I can take my choice of the five club girls who exist just to keep us sexually satisfied. In return, of course, we don't leave them wanting.

Hmm. I glance back at the bed where I'd fucked Bella last night. Her tits, mmm mmm. She didn't leave me unsatisfied, that's for sure. The night before that, Mace and I had Breezy and Tulia together. Mace likes to fuck with a partner, and now that Ink's found his one, he'd asked me if I'd like to step up. Suits me fine.

Naked, I glance down at my cock lying flaccid in the midst of my trimmed pubic hair and grin. Fuck me, but I can't understand how my brothers are hooking up with old ladies. I don't have it in me to commit to one pussy for life. What would I do without the variety? Discounting the old-timers who've worn their ball and chain for years, other brothers are now dropping as though Paladin brought some infectious disease up with him from Tucson. First Demon found Vi, then Beef met Steph, quickly followed by Pyro with Mel, and more recently, the confirmed bachelor, Ink, getting together with Beth. Well, whatever they've got, I'm immune to it. Always have been, and always will be.

Best get this day started. Yeah. The sooner my work's done, the quicker I can come home and choose who's going to get the benefit of my cock tonight. Sheila perhaps? Been a while since I've had her. My cock twitches as I start remembering what she can do with her mouth.

Fuck, man. Oh shit, why did my mind have to go there? Now I've got to shoot one off in the shower.

Half an hour later, dressed and my cock behaving once again, I descend the industrial metal staircase which takes me to the clubroom. Already it's busy.

Citizens have this idea that all the members of the MC do is ride around on their bikes having fun and committing crimes, maybe with a bit of murder and mayhem thrown in. While we might do the latter at times, and only ever for good reason, mostly our time is filled with the same shit as other folks, an honest day's work.

"Liz, Theo's got a slight fever. Jay's going to take him to the doctor—"

"Vi," I address the prez's woman and recently qualified tattoo artist, "your boy's ill? You do what you need to do, take him yourself. Me and Jonah can carry the workload for now."

It was the right answer. Vi tosses me a worried smile now tinged with relief. Kids get ill, moms worry. It's just something they do. Blotting out the childhood memory that my own mother wouldn't have given a damn, I just raise my chin when she offers her thanks and hurries off with a fretting child in her arms. I watch her for a moment, thinking how glad I am I don't have kids.

"You around later after church, Liz?" A deep voice interrupts my thoughts.

"Sure, Mace. What's up?"

He leans in. "Got a few goodies from that sex shop on Main. Think they're right up Titsy and Breezy's street. You game?"

Despite the relief I'd only just gotten in the shower, my cock twitches as I slap him on the back. "Sure thing, Brother." I wonder just exactly what he's bought. Something to torture the girls with that will be certain. Then I frown. "But I ain't wearing no cock ring. Uh-uh." Not after last time. Could hardly get the darn thing off when the catch had gotten stuck.

Mace snorts. "Thought it would be the hospital for you that time."

I glare at him. He can laugh, but it hadn't been a joking matter. Turning up at ER with a ring on my fucking dick? No thank you. Relief wasn't a strong enough word for what I felt when the lube had eventually enabled me to work that thing off without having to seek expert assistance. I turn my back on him and walk away before he can see the corners of my lips curve. That shit would be funny if it happened to anyone else, and I can't blame him from getting mileage out of it. It's only what I'd have done myself if our positions were reversed. Hmm, that's an idea. Maybe I can get him to try it.

Still, looks like I've got fun to look forward to tonight. When the club business has been dealt with, of course.

In the kitchen, Jeannie puts my to-go breakfast in my hand, a bacon sandwich with lashings of ketchup spilling out, and pushes a cup of coffee across the table toward me. Various other breakfasts are being prepared. It's like a conveyor belt with men walking in, taking their normal preference, which Bomber's wife knows well, eating fast then disappearing to our various businesses.

"Thanks, Liz." Prez enters and sends me a chin lift. "Vi was worried about letting you down."

"No problem, Prez. Schedule's not overflowing today, and Jonah can get Whale in to help with the walk-ins if there's a sudden rush."

Prez glares at me. "*Weston*," he reminds me, sternly. "Jonah's brother's called Weston."

I'm unrepentant. "Where there's a Jonah, there has to be a whale," I insist, grinning broadly.

"He's threatened not to take the full-time position," Demon warns. "Came to see me himself."

I bristle slightly being the manager of Devil's Ink with full responsibility. I let Demon know. "Whether or not we take him on is down to me, Prez. If a man can't take a joke, well, maybe he's not a good fit."

"He's a fuckin' good artist from what I've seen, Liz."

"I'll reserve judgement until I see him in action, Prez. All I've seen is his portfolio." Which looks fucking ace, I admit, but still, it's more than what ink he can lay down, it's the way he treats the customers, together with his general demeanour. If he goes running over my head for every slight, that shit won't settle well.

Prez eyes me, reading me in that way he does. Then he gives a sharp nod. "I'll make sure he knows that I have full confidence in you, Liz."

In return, I give something back. "I'll curb it a bit, Prez." But it will be hard. Weston must weigh close to three hundred pounds and is only five foot ten. Whale suits him.

Stuffing the last bits of my sandwich into my mouth, I suck remnants of ketchup off my fingers. Then, fed and watered, I go to my bike.

It's not long before I'm pulling up behind Devil's Ink. As I normally do, I take a moment to reflect on how much better located our new premises are. We moved from a shop in a bad part of town a year back, and now attract not only customers who've come to us for years, but a whole new crowd, hence the need to have more hands on board. Business is booming. The amazing designs Vi comes up with haven't hurt at all, and our reputation is gaining ground all the time. That's also got a lot to do with the Instagram page that Vi manages. Demon did the club a solid when he took her as his old lady.

I'm not surprised that Jonah's right behind me when I put my key into the lock, enter, and insert the correct code to turn off the alarm.

"Vi can't make it today," I tell him over my shoulder. "Sick kid."

"We'll manage," he confirms, not fazed in the least. "I'll take a look at the books, see what was scheduled and what I can take from her. Any piercings?" He adds the last with a gleam in his eyes.

"If there are, you can have them." It's not that I mind getting my hand on a clit but prefer it to be in a bed with my dick ready to get some action. Vi normally handles that shit. I'm more than happy to leave that to Jonah—along with the dicks, ears, and nips. Unless a particularly nice pair of tits walk in, that is.

Knowing I've a client booked later for a full back tat, I go to my station and pull the drawings I've already sketched toward me, making a few minor alterations I thought of during the night. It's going to take a few sessions to make this work, but I'll get the outline done today, and start the infill the next time. As normal, when I have a new client coming in, I wonder how they're going to react. Even the biggest man can get scared, and the smallest woman not flinch one bit. Not knowing what this one's like, I select a place where I can start, and still produce something he'll be happy with if he decides the whole piece might be too much. I'd noticed his skin is so far unmarked.

"Walk-in, boss," Jonah's voice calls sometime later. "Can you take it?"

Although I'm used to tuning out sounds, I'd registered Jonah's gun cutting out. Knowing he's obviously in the middle of a job, I respond without concern, shouting out, "Sure, send them on back."

I make one final adjustment to the drawing on my table, before swivelling around on my chair to see my new client is a woman, late twenties perhaps.

I've been a tattoo artist for years and am used to reading people fast, but I don't need the experience to know this customer is nervous. First tat, perhaps? I react accordingly.

"Take a load off." I point to the client's chair. "What is it you're after? Tattoo or piercing?"

She's pretty enough, hair cut in a neat bob, but her eyes are the most remarkable thing about her. They're currently wide in concern and dark. Solemn, as though there's a wealth of hurt and pain there.

"What can I do for you?" I prompt, once more, wondering if she's suffered a loss and wants a remembrance tattoo. I've done far too many of them. My sympathy rises to the forefront.

"I, er..." she starts, then tries again, "Er, do you cover up tattoos?"

Okay, so I was wrong. But it still could be a loss of some sort. Again, wouldn't be a first to cover up a heart with two names which aren't linked anymore. "Sure do," I respond. "Would you like to show me what you've got? Then I can tell you how we can turn it into something else."

She takes a deep breath, then stands, placing her hand on the back of the chair as though needing its support. She turns. Her hands are shaking as she undoes her jeans and pushes them down over her hips until the top of her ass crack comes into view. Then she raises her t-shirt.

As soon as she'd started to rearrange her clothes, I suspected it would be a tramp stamp of some sort. What I didn't expect was what I saw.

It's an intricate design, swirling lines in various colours, not a small or amateur job. No this was inked by an expert hand. And there, across the middle, in flamboyant text the words, "Property of Major."

I stare at it for a moment, then buy myself some time. "You know, the best person for you to speak to is Vi. You see the examples in the window out there?" I'm sure she probably has. "She's got this eye for how to turn an existing tattoo into something else so you can't see what was there before." I can too, but I'm not admitting that.

"Can I speak to her?"

"I'm sorry, she's not in today," I tell her, truthfully. "But hopefully she'll be back tomorrow."

"Oh." She lets her t-shirt drop, pulls up her jeans and refastens them, then turns around. "I was hoping this could be done today."

"I'm sorry. But turning what you've got there into something else will take some work. You'll need to go through what can be done with Vi, then she'll have to book you in. This something you're doing on impulse, sweetheart?" I'm wondering whether she'll rethink it given time.

She huffs a mirthless laugh. "No. But I have been working up the courage to come to you."

Her phrasing and her nervousness start alarm bells jangling. "Well, I'm sorry, but Vi's the best person for you to see. Look, let me get the book and we'll book you in for a proper consultation tomorrow."

I make the appointment for Shayla Yonovich for eleven o'clock the next morning, then as she leaves with a dejected look on her face while my pre-booked client walks in the door. I lead him back to my station and put the morning's visitor out of my mind. For the next few hours, I concentrate on the man lying flat on my table, glad to find he relaxes fast and is easy to work on. The whirr of my tattoo gun and the necessary one-hundred-percent concentration means the time passes fast.

Soon, it seems, my client has gone, and another day, at least for me, is over.

"You okay to lock up?" As I ask it, I know it's a dumb question. I always head off early on a Wednesday as that's the day we have church. Jonah's well used to staying late on his own, or, as I notice tonight, with Whale by his side. I hadn't noticed him come in.

"W… Weston." I raise my chin toward him. "You made a decision yet?"

The big man shuffles his feet. "Yeah, I'll take the job if you still want me."

"No more running to the MC prez." It's Jonah who says this, pointing the tattoo gun at his brother. "The boss," he now points at me, "can call you what he darn well wants."

Weston's eyes darken, but then he shrugs and nods. Seems like he wants this position.

Bending under the reception desk, I pick up some brochures I knew were there and chuck them at Jonah's brother. I might have told Prez I was undecided, but in truth, had already made up my mind. Jonah's vouched for him and wouldn't tell me wrong. "Have a look through for equipment you want to order. Vi will sort it out for you."

As he takes it with thanks and a nod, I realise just how much difference Vi has made to this place. Publicity for certain, and a semblance of order to the routine stuff too. Yeah, Prez did well bringing her on board.

CHAPTER TWO

Lizard

I get back to the compound with time to spare for a beer before heading on into our meeting. I also have a moment to pick up a letter that's come in the mail for me. It's from the VA and gives me an appointment date and time. As I read it, I purse my lips. Fuck knows why they insist on seeing me to offer help I no longer want or need. I am what I am, got my life fixed, brothers around me. Nothing more they can do or that I want them to. I can put one foot in front of the other, ride my bike, fuck, and do my job. What more do I want? There must be many others far more deserving than me.

"You got problems, Brother?"

I'm used to nosy fuckers, and Mace having perused the letter I left carelessly on the bar is nothing new.

"Nah," I tell him without any ire at all. "I'm fine, man. They probably just want to check I'm still alive."

"Are you?"

I thump his arm. "I'm no fucking ghost. What the fuck, Ink?" I snap at the man who's not just giving my letter a casual glance, he's picked it up and is reading it thoroughly too.

"Hey, say's they've got to check your dick."

"It does not!" I rise to the bait, snatching it back in case I've missed something.

"Hope not," mumbles Mace. "Got plans for later. Unless you…?"

Ink laughs and shrugs off the invitation that had been directed his way. "Nah. Happy with Liz taking my place. I'm with Beth now, Brother."

He's been one-hundred-percent faithful since he got together with her. I can't understand it myself. "Surely, you miss fucking the whores?"

Ink slaps me on the shoulder. "Can't say that I do, Liz. Can't say that I do. Beth's everything I want."

"Aww." Mace draws the word out, then stage whispers to me, "Pussy whipped."

After giving a snort to indicate my agreement, I ask, "Heard anything from Beth's mom or brother?"

"Nah." Ink shakes his head. "We won't, either. The only way they can stay safe is to become their new identities and live their new lives. It's hard on Beth, but she understands she can't contact them."

"But you know they're alright?"

"Yeah." Ink grins at Mace. "Lost has a man who keeps check now and again, nothing to link him to us. Least we know they're living and breathing."

"Beth accept that?" Bitches can be tricky. They say one thing but mean another. Sticking with whores means no such complications.

Ink's quick to pick up what I'm putting down. "She knows she has to, but she doesn't like it. The wound's still raw. She misses her mom, but I'm trying to fuck that out of her." He winks. "So far it's working, you know?"

A loud whistle interrupts before I can respond in the affirmative; my view is a good fuck can work wonders. Placing my now empty bottle on the bar, I waste no time following everyone else into our meeting room.

The citizens I was thinking about earlier, who believe our life's all about riding bikes and coming up with nefarious moneymaking plots or discussing how to dole death out to our enemies, would be shocked to sit in on church, I muse, as Buzzard our treasurer runs through the finances as competently as any finance director in a company would. Money's coming in well, so we'll all have a little extra in our paychecks this month. I exchange a fist bump with Paladin, both of us with our eyes on new parts for our bikes. Me, I'm addicted to Screamin' Eagle shit.

As a manager of one of the club businesses, I'm expected to report on how things are on the ground at Devil's Ink. When it's my turn, I give credit to Vi for the increase in revenue, not missing the gleam of pride in Demon's eyes.

"Any update about Weston?" he asks.

"Yeah. Whale's on board." I wink as Demon looks up to the ceiling then down. "He came into the shop before I left to tell me he's accepted the job."

"He's going to fuckin' murder you," Ink grins, "you keep calling him that."

"Smother him more like," offers Mace. "All he needs to do is sit on you and you'd be a goner."

"Don't fuckin' care about the size of his girth." Prez glares down the table. "Weston will be a great addition from what I've seen."

The VP waggles his fingers to get our attention. "Since shit went down with Beth and her family, we still got Dirt and Nails hanging around. We going to give them their prospect rockers?"

"Don't see why not," Mace says thoughtfully. "They've proved they can be trusted to keep their mouths shut."

"I kind of like them," Thunder puts in. "They've got that military experience that works well with the club. I'm happy to bring them on board."

Ink raises his hand. "Been talking to Nails. He suffers PTSD, but that's not unusual." A rumble of sympathy goes around the table. It's certainly not unusual in anyone who's served. Ink nods, and continues, "That dog of theirs is basically a support dog. If they're going to be around more, I think we'll be seeing more of the mutt."

"The dog's probably got PTSD himself," Hellfire states, but not unkindly. The dog lost a leg in Afghanistan in the same incident that made Dirt and Nails leave the Army.

"I reckon Nails and the dog probably support each other," I observe. "We've already got Max. Another dog won't be a problem, will it?"

Beef grimaces. "We'll just have to see how Max takes it." He's referring, like I was, to the seeing-eye dog that belongs to his wife.

"I don't know how Bitch will take it," sighs Prez heavily. "Fuck. When I'm not worrying about you fuckin' lot, it's dogs and cats I have to contend with."

Prez has a good point. Though we pretend to hate her, we've all got a soft spot for the cat who wandered in off the street one day. When she decided to stay, we let her, and her behaviour had earned her that name. Fuck knows what had turned Bitch that way, but that cat hates men with a passion. She doesn't much care for canines either and puts them in their place. One thing for certain, she makes life interesting.

"Right. Quick vote. We bring Dirt and Nails on board as prospects."

Prez counts the ayes and doesn't have to ask who objects. Just like that, we pick up two new prospects. Good timing, as Karl and Beaver will be patched in soon if I'm right. Got to have someone to do all the shit work.

"Ink? What's happening with the gym?" Demon asks for an update, moving on from our four-legged residents, or three in the new prospects' dog's case.

Ink tosses a glare at the enforcer. I smirk. Converting part of the disused factory buildings had been Mace's idea when we thought Ink would be going inside for a few decades. We'd have been doing something for a brother who couldn't be here. When Ink returned, it had become his baby. At first Ink had been excited, then his initial enthusiasm had faded once he realised just what was involved with it.

"Your own fuckin' fault," Mace throws back. "You hooked on to the idea of running it commercially."

"Think that was you, Brother," Ink snarls.

"Well, you ran with it," Demon barks. "Where are you at, Ink?"

Ink's eyes shutter. "If it was just us, Prez, no one would give a damn. But opening it up to the public means getting all the right building permits. Feel like I'm drowning in paperwork and regulations. Health and fuckin' safety."

"Beth helping?" I ask, knowing she is, and for some reason, wanting his woman to get recognition. Of course, as she works in the government offices, she's used to the way officials think.

Ink throws me a look of gratitude. "Couldn't do it without her, Brother. She speaks their language. Anyway, we're getting there. The outside is basically sound now, and we've finally got approval for the number of heads, showers, shit like that."

"Keeping to budget?" asks Buzzard.

"Just about," confirms Ink.

Shit's bandied around a little more, like Thunder wishing Ink would get a fucking move on and Ink protesting that he's doing his best.

Prez signifies he wants to move on and it's then I recall what I wanted to bring up. Leaning forward, I clasp my hands on the table. "Don't know whether this is a problem or not," I start, making sure I've got everyone's attention. "Does anyone here know a man, possibly in an MC, named Major?"

There are shakes of heads, and shrugs of shoulders.

"Why, Liz?" asks the VP.

I like and respect Beef. I answer him directly. "Woman came in today, wants a 'Property of' tat covered up. Fancy work, not cheap."

Cad's looking toward me now. "The woman's name?"

"Shayla Vonovich." I note he's tapping it onto his tablet.

Mace is watching me carefully. "Send her elsewhere," he suggests. "You've got concerns, Brother. Let someone else take the rap."

I inhale, then exhale through my nose. I just fucking love that my brothers have got my back and have immediately gone where I went to when I first saw that property patch.

"What did you say to her, Liz?"

"Prez, I used a delaying tactic. Said Vi was the best person for her to speak to. She's coming back tomorrow. Wanted to have everyone's thoughts on it first."

"Prez?" Cad waggles his fingers. "I can do some searching overnight. If she's local, or this Major is, might be able to turn something up."

"So," Beef sits back in his chair, "covering a property patch doesn't sit right with you?"

"Worried about blowback on us," I respond. Yeah, it worries me. First off, having a 'Property of' patch is more than a wedding ring to any of us, it means a commitment which should last for life. Citizens get divorced, all they need to do is remove their ring. Sure, people in MCs aren't angels, can stray, can have relationship breakups, but a man puts a property tat on a bitch, then she's his property. Of course, he might be an abusive fuck. She could have left him because of it, and I'll stand with her if that's the case. But might be, she'll have regrets. Then on his side, removing his patch may well be something he doesn't want her to do. Depending who he is, there might indeed be trouble for us, especially if she's from a rival MC.

"Leave someone else to do it," Mace suggests for the second time. "Say we don't have the skills to do a good job."

I acknowledge his suggestion, but we can do it right. Some of the other places in town don't have the experience that we do, and I'd be loath to recommend their work. "She's a nice woman, Mace, from what I saw. Hate to have her end up with a bad job."

I breathe in and sigh out again. "It's big." I hold my hands about eight inches apart, then four inches to demonstrate both height and width. "Serious work. I do reckon Vi will come up with a good idea of how to blend and cover it, but some of the other assholes we know around here? She could end up with some of it still showing through."

"Has she considered getting it lasered?"

I nod at the suggestion. "Didn't get that far. I just wondered who this Major fucker was, and whether anyone here knew."

Prez is the next one to sigh. "Vi's got my patch on her. I'd hate if she wanted it removed. Not sure I'd take it out on the asshole doing the job, though."

"But you're reasonable," Hell suggests. "You know Violet wouldn't get rid of your mark without good reason. Liz here is right. If this Major fucker thinks property is his for life, it could come back to us. I agree with Mace. Send her someplace else."

"Of course," Thunder, the sergeant-at-arms puts in, "Major might not be in an MC at all."

"What was she like, Liz?"

I turn to our road captain, Sparky. "Nervous. Scared."

Pal laughs. "So, like most of your customers then."

He's right. I just nod. That she'd had a tat before only means she knows what to expect, and something as big as the one she's got was most probably painful.

Prez pinches the bridge of his nose, then looks up. "Okay. Cad, do your stuff. If you don't turn anything up about this man Major, then I'll leave it to you, Liz. Don't much like the idea of a bitch having a tat when she doesn't want the man anymore, whatever he feels about it. If you go ahead, then we'll be behind you."

"And if we find he's MC?"

Again Prez's shoulders rise and fall. "Then it depends on whether we're friendly or not, and what his position is. I'll maybe talk to their prez and find the lay of the land. If it's going to cause problems, we'll have to turn her away, or persuade her to go back and sort it out. Property is *club* property after all. Pretty serious step to get her marked in the first place, maybe she doesn't realise how serious removal is too."

Yeah, right. Leave the decision to me.

I must have been glaring as Mace raises his hand. "I'll go with Liz tomorrow. See what I think of her too. Could help if Liz and I put our heads together on what's best to do."

I'm more grateful than the enforcer knows. This is why I'd never put myself forward for an officer job, making the right decision is not my forte. I never quite trust myself.

That sorted, Prez brings us back to the agenda. Devil's Pins is under the microscope next. I only half listen to Rusty's report, an image of Shayla's haunted eyes still in my head.

When the meeting ends, Mace claps his hand to my shoulder as we walk out the door, pausing to retrieve our phones. "I told Titsy and Breezy to wait outside my room. You still game?"

"Yeah." I grin. A good session of fucking will clear my head. "Whatcha got, Mace?"

"New handcuffs, spreader bar and a violet wand."

"Yeah?" I repeat, my lips curving more.

"Ginger butt plugs too."

Now I've a vision in my head of those girls squirming when they're on my cock, leg's held open so they can't escape the burn in their asses. "You're a cruel motherfucker, aren't you?"

He chuckles. "I am the enforcer. I like torture, what can I say?"

Breezy and Titsy are leaning against the door to his room. Mace unlocks it and stands aside to let the three of us precede him in, then he picks up a bag by the side of the bed and empties the contents on the comforter. He throws down a handful of condoms for good measure.

I swear both girls eyes brighten as they see the goodies he's bought, picking up the fur-lined cuffs and toying with them in their hands, until Titsy picks up the ginger.

"Uh-uh," she says, shaking her head and inching away. "I am

not into figging." She looks hopefully toward Mace. "Unless this is for you?" She turns to me. "Or you?"

"Nah, sweetheart. All for you. Now, shall we start?" He looks my way and winks. I'm happy for him to lead this show. Mace knows what he's doing and I'm just here to watch, to learn, oh, and to enjoy. From the girl's reaction they're not so sure the pleasure will be theirs tonight.

Did I say Mace is evil and I may have a bit of that streak myself? Hell yeah.

Nodding toward me and then the second pair, Mace takes the nearest set of handcuffs and soon Breezy is restrained to the convenient rails of the headboard on his bed. I'm less than a moment behind him having Titsy imprisoned too. Again I copy him as he takes a couple of pillows and as he tucks them under Breezy's stomach, I do the same to Titsy. Soon the girls are face down with asses up, and we soon have their shorts and panties torn off. Next it's the spreader bars which we attach to their ankles and then fasten to the foot of the bed.

They might be protesting, but their wide-open pussies are glistening with anticipation.

Mace then starts to prepare the ginger. Both girls turn their heads toward him and watch with wide-open eyes as he pares down each root so that it forms a four inch finger. He digs a small channel out near the base to form a ring that makes them look like butt plugs.

I've never played with ginger before. I can imagine the effects, but have never witnessed it. Something tells me I'm going to enjoy this.

Mace wets the ginger thoroughly with cold water from the bathroom sink.

"No lube?"

"No," he replies to me. "Lube is oily and will block the effect." With an evil chuckle he adds, "And we want them to get the most from the experience, don't we?"

The girls both continue protesting as he and I approach. I've played with butt plugs before, so treat this the same. With my fingers, I carefully expose Titsy's rosebud, then, to her objections, start pushing my finger of ginger in. When she clenches, I slap her ass, and she relents.

She sighs a little when it's seated.

"There, that's not too bad, is it?" asks Mace with a knowing wink in my direction. "Liz, come wash your hands. You do not want ginger in your eyes."

Heaven forbid. I follow him and stand by his side at the sink. "How long?" I ask him quietly.

"Not long at all."

"Oooh. Ow. Oh, take it out." Breezy's voice starts sounding from behind me.

"Ow. Ow. Ow. Ow!" shouts Titsy.

Mace is chuckling. "There we go." He walks back into the bedroom and slaps Breezy's ass.

"Ow! Asshole! Motherfucker!" She screeches as she automatically clenches her butt cheeks then releases them when it tightens her anus on that ginger.

Of course, I have to try the same thing. At Titsy's loud protest, I begin to hope brothers in the adjacent rooms have ear plugs.

Both girls now start to writhe. "Fuck me, for fuck's sake," yells Breezy.

"There we go," says Mace. "Makes them feel fuckin' horny. You ready to oblige, Brother?"

Too right I am. Jeans and boots are quickly off and condoms are on.

My cock must increase the sensations. Titsy's, well, I'm not quite sure whether she's trying to get me off, or trying to dislodge the ginger, but she's soon clamping around my cock, coming and coming. I hold off, thinking of everything but the pressure on my dick, practiced at prolonging this.

I hammer and thrust using my hands to push her buttocks together or slap her, making her jump. She's pushing back against me, coming and then again, until her orgasms are almost continuous. Seems the ginger is really doing its stuff. I'm determined not to blow my load before Mace, but I can't hold off. The way Titsy's using my cock is just too much, and that final squeeze… well, I'm a goner.

I'm pleased to see Mace isn't far behind me.

Both girls have now collapsed onto the bed, both groaning and sated, but no longer complaining.

"It's worn off," Mace tells me, grinning.

Well, that was an experience. We get the girls untied and unfigged, then turn them over. My cock is ready for another round, and Titsy's still got more in her.

"You want my ass?" she says, impudently.

I growl against her ear. "Not fuckin' likely." I don't want to burn and risk my dick falling off.

In the end, I come three times before the girls shuffle unsteadily out of Mace's room. Picking up my jeans, boots and cut, I follow them out, closing the door behind me, unconcerned my dick's swinging free as I walk to my room. I shower, go to bed and fall into a dreamless sleep.

Exhausted, I'm lost to the world, only woken when my phone pings the chimes of the morning alarm. I shut it down, roll onto my back and again close my eyes.

My lips move as I mouth, *I'm Lizard, otherwise known as Norton James. I ride with the Satan's Devils MC and have done for the past ten years. I'm thirty-eight years old, and my birthday is… my birthday is the tenth of January. The current President of the United States is… well, who can forget that name? I'm a tattoo artist and I run Devil's Ink on behalf of my brothers. I've no ties, no family and that's the way I intend to stay.*

Today is going to be a good day.

CHAPTER THREE

Vanna

"Hey, bitch, what's up?" Lindy opens her door with her normal greeting, then her face falls when she catches sight of my reddened swollen eyes and blotchy complexion. "Wine. And chocolate. Or vodka. Does this call for the strong shit?"

And this is exactly why she's my best friend. As she steps back, I take her unspoken invitation and walk forward into her apartment.

"I take it he's being an ass again?"

"Oh, Lindy." Shaking my head, I try to get out the words. "It's worse."

"Okay. So he's progressed from ass to asshole. Come on. I'll get the shot glasses."

"Coffee," I correct. "I can't afford to…"

Another look at me, then she tugs at my hand. "Come on, sit down. Tell Auntie Lindy everything."

As I take a seat on her comfortable sofa after kicking off my shoes, I hear her filling a kettle, then cupboards opening and shutting. Soon she's approaching me with a tin of candy in her hands.

"English chocolate. The best kind," she announces. "An English friend of mine sent them."

"You know I love your friend, right?"

"I do. And I've told her." She laughs and pushes the bar of milk chocolate toward me, knowing that's my favourite.

It's a sign of how bad I'm feeling that I don't refuse, even knowing that's the one she likes best too. But like the good friend that she is, she picks up a Milky Way and starts munching that instead.

"Spill. What's happened now?" she asks, licking chocolate off her fingers.

"Hotwiring a car. Driving it away. Rolling it into a ditch." I list my son's misdemeanours. "The police are involved."

"Fuck." Her eyes widen. "Is he going to have to do time?"

I blow out a breath, the strand of hair that's fallen over my face lifting with it. "I'm hoping for probation, but it's only a matter of when, not if, before he goes down." This isn't the first time he's gotten into trouble, and I know it won't be the last.

"Being caught might knock some sense into him," she contradicts. "Having to face up to what he's done might do him some good."

But I know my son. "He'll meet others inside, even in juvie. He'll either be hurt or will get into a gang for when he comes out." As she goes to speak again, I wave her down. "I've got a lawyer, fuck knows I can't afford it, but I wasn't going to leave it to the public defender. She intimated if he's not put away, they might look at his home situation and put him into a foster home if they think I'm an inadequate mother."

"Oh, Vanna." Her hand reaches over and covers mine. "You've done everything you can for that boy. You've lived for him, given your soul for him. You're the best mom in the world. A lot of moms don't do half of what you've done. You've been to every football game he's played in, stood on the sidelines in freezing snow. You've been there for him, helping him with school."

"It hasn't worked though, has it, Lindy? I could never make up for his father not being around."

"Hang on. Let me get that coffee." She gets up, walks off, and returns shortly after, carrying two cups and puts them down. Mine is white with two sugars, just as I like it.

She blows on hers to cool it, takes a sip too soon and winces, then places it on the table. "Lots of kids are brought up with only one parent, Vanna."

"And they do alright," I finish for her. "Perhaps it's me. I've tried my best, but as it turns out, that's not good enough. Nothing I've done has worked."

"Where is he now? School?"

My head moves up then down. "Yes. I'm picking him up. He's not allowed to go anywhere else. I want him under my eye."

"So that's why you're not drinking?"

"First, I'm driving, so yeah. And second…"

She grimaces, understanding what I've not yet said. "You're giving no one any more ammunition."

Exactly. I place my own coffee on the table and lean my head back against the sofa. Castiel, Cas as he's known, is my fourteen-year-old wayward son. He gets into trouble more than he's out of it. Maybe it's because I don't have a man who can help me keep him in line, or maybe I should just acknowledge the truth of it. When things went bad, they affected my son.

"He still has nightmares, Lindy."

"Still?" Her eyebrows arch. "The same ones?"

"About his father leaving and denying him?" My lips press together. "I don't know, but he shouts out at night."

"It's been ten years, Vanna. Surely he can't remember what happened that long ago? He was only four."

"I don't know," I admit. "Maybe it's down to me not handling it properly. I've tried to explain to him, but he's never been able to understand. Maybe if I'd told him his father was dead, it would be easier for him to accept."

"It's not down to you, Vanna. You always expected him to come back, it's just that he never did. You never wanted to close the door and kept it open."

She's right. I did. I never stopped hoping. "What am I to do?" Sitting forward, I put my head in my hands, rubbing my eyes then drawing my fingers down my cheeks. "Cas is going through his teenage angst, and all this just adds to it. I can't remember him ever being a happy little boy, despite everything I tried to do. I don't know what's going to happen to him, but something has to change. We can't go on like this. Lindy, I'm scared I'm going to lose him." To jail, to a gang, or to a foster home. "What am I to do?" I repeat.

"Get married again."

I hold up my hand with my wedding band still on my third finger of my left hand. "I still am."

But that doesn't put a dent in her stride. "Divorce his ass and take him to the cleaners while you're at it. You've never asked for a penny, have you?"

I haven't. That's down partly to pride, but also for the sake of the man I promised to love forever. It's meant I've been a working mom and Cas a latch-key kid when he was old enough to be left on his own.

"I don't want another man," I tell her, my mouth quirking slightly. "I can't get involved with someone just so he'd be a good influence on my son."

"You can't go through life moping after a man who doesn't want you, Vanna." Lindy picks up her coffee and starts drinking now that it's cooled. "What are you going to do when Cas is grown and moved away? He's going to one day, you know?"

"For now, he needs me. He's only got one parent. I've got to be there for him. How would I have time to go on dates anyway, and I'd need to, to meet a man? It's not like I can pop one into my basket at Walmart." After all this time, I might entertain the idea if it was that easy. I've been on my own for far too long. Sex I can probably take or leave as long as I have my trusty vibrator and a few inspirational books on the side, but it's the comfort of someone else being there, someone to share all the joys and tribulations that I feel I'm missing out on. But Cas would see that as another betrayal, and he's had far too much of that already in his short life. He needs me, whether or not he wants to. I know him too well. He'd be suspicious if I brought home a man, and would probably rebel even more.

Lindy's staring into her cup as if trying to find the answer there. "Why don't you let his father have him for a while?"

"You know why not. That's an impossible idea."

"Is it? How long since you've seen him? Since you've spoken with him? Maybe everything's changed now."

Maybe it has. But it wouldn't be for the better. If it were, he'd already be here. I frown. "If it's changed, then why hasn't he been in touch? No, he's moved on as he said he would. He wants nothing to do with me or our son."

Perhaps I should divorce his ass as Lindy had suggested. After all these years, desertion would be easy to prove.

I glance up at her clock on the wall, drain my coffee and stand. "I better run now if I'm going to catch Cas when he comes out of school."

"If you're not by the door, he'll take off." She knows me, and him, only too well. "Look, why don't you bring him over at the weekend. We'll do something, I don't know, the zoo?"

I roll my eyes. "Zoos are long in his rearview, Lindy, though I wish they weren't. Stock car racing or motorbikes are now far more his style."

"Have you thought about that? Getting him into driving lessons or something after school? If the kid's got an interest in something, it may just focus his mind."

It's a good idea and I'll see what's available. My husband might not have had a hand in raising my son, but he's turned out to be a motorhead just the same.

I do feel better for coming here and speaking to my friend who knows my whole story and who offers support without judgement, or, not too much of it anyway. I'd had to cut my own mom out of my life when she couldn't understand what had happened, and why I was left to raise my child alone. Her outpourings when Cas was around hadn't helped him adjust, and his repetitions of *Gramma said* would undo all the progress I thought I'd made. Of course, her absence hadn't helped either. She was just another person who seemed to have abandoned my son.

Christ, what a mess I've made of life for me and Cas.

I hug Lindy and thank her, then drive to the school where I park well in time to collect my boy. As predicted, his face falls, and he grows sullen when he sees me waiting.

"You didn't have to collect me, Mom. I could have caught the bus. Surely you're supposed to be at work?"

"I took a personal day. I had to go and see your lawyer," I explain.

"Well, fuck me. It's my fault. I never expected that."

I don't know what gets to me most, him swearing, or his sarcasm. But it reminds me what a failure as a mother I am. I try to bite my tongue, but I fail. "Yes it is your fault. No one else persuaded you to hotwire a car and steal it."

"I hate you, Mom."

Sometimes I fear he really does.

"I need to get some groceries." I wait for the explosion that's surely to come.

"And you couldn't fucking do that before picking me up? Dammit, Mom. Drop me at home first."

I'm not stupid. If I do that, he'll be gone by the time I get home.

Pick my battles, I remind myself. What would seem bad for anyone else is par for the course between me and Cas. I have to tread carefully or else I risk him storming off, not returning, and becoming just one more statistic. So I smother my temper. "No, you can come and help choose what we'll have for dinner. After, we can get ice cream."

"Ice cream?" He turns to me with a scowl. "I'm fourteen, not four. Anyway, I've got plans. There's a girl I was going to see later."

Girl? Christ. This day just goes from bad to worse. Of course I've had the chat with my son, the one he should have had with his father. But I'm not sure how effective it was. My fourteen-year-old boy is tall, six feet even now, and even though I'm seeing him through biased eyes, know he's a handsome fella. Apart from the trouble with the law, I've visions of him getting an underage girl pregnant.

"You are grounded, Son. Remember?"

I swear I hear him say, *we'll see about that.*

It's at times like these when I really do wish I had the support of a man.

Lindy had reminded me I had one. Would things be different if I stepped up and went to see how the land lay now? Could, as she'd suggested, things have changed? Would he now be prepared to step up and accept his responsibilities?

How much would it hurt to try?

I'd broken once when the only man I've ever loved walked out of my life, but managed to pull myself back to some semblance of stability. Seeing him again might send me back into the depths of despair. Could I take that hurt again?

Just one more look at the sullen boy sitting beside me and I know, for his sake, I have to try.

CHAPTER FOUR

Mace

"How's the ass?" I wink as I ask Titsy when I bump into her in the kitchen. Her mock glare makes me grin.

"Hey, Mace. Wanna have some fun later?" Breezy seems up for more.

Well she is until I call out, "Jeannie? You got any ginger root around here?"

"No ginger," says Breezy firmly. "Unless it's going up your asshole."

I nearly spit out my mouthful of coffee at her suggestion. Then I notice the time. "Later, girls. Got places to be."

That place is Devil's Ink where I'm going to take a look at the girl who wants her property tat removed. Something has gotten the normally unflappable Lizard spooked about it, which was the reason I'd offered to help check her out.

So far, we knew Cad hadn't managed to locate a member of an MC that goes by the name of Major. Well, he'd found one, but on checking, that man was as single as me. Of course, motorcycle clubs don't have the monopoly on property patches, some BDSM folks are into that shit too, but it was a good idea to check. Don't want to give a rival club the opportunity to come in guns blazing, accusing us of stealing their women away.

It's a nice spring day as I ride the short distance to the strip mall where the tattoo shop is located. The feeling of warm sun on my face has put me in a good mood, I realise, as I roll the bike into a spot reserved for us to the rear, then walk in the back entrance and make my way to the front.

I greet Vi who's sitting behind the reception desk. "Hi, Vi. How's Theo?"

She rolls her eyes. "My little man is fine. In fact, he was right as rain by the time we got in to see the doctor. Still, she checked him out and said he's all good. Just one of those kid things."

Nodding sagely as if I know what she's talking about when I don't have a clue, I glance around. "The boss here?"

"Lizard!" she calls.

The man appears. "Mace." He throws me a lift of his chin. "Anything new?"

Cad had told me he'd already given Liz all that he'd found out, so I simply shake my head.

The shop bell dings behind me.

I glance at the woman who's walked in, then at Liz. Liz raises an eyebrow, and I give a small nod back.

That one glance had shown me three things. One, that the woman had an ethereal beauty, two, she was terrified and I wasn't sure why, and three, that if Liz had designs on her, he was going to have to take a step back. *I want her.* Well, not for good. But for one night and I won't want to share. My cock is definitely interested.

She's got a property patch on her back, I remind myself. *That's why she's here.* She belongs to another. Or, at least will, until that shit is covered up. Any ideas I have will just have to wait.

Vi seems bemused that neither Liz nor I have said anything. She stands and smiles warmly. "It's Shayla, isn't it? I'm Violet. You've got an appointment with me so we can see about covering your tattoo. Do you want to come this way?"

She nods shyly at Violet, then her eyes come briefly to mine before looking down. As Vi walks off, she makes no move to follow. It takes me a second, then I realise the way Liz and I are standing, she'd have to brush past us to follow the prez's old lady, so I take a step back. Shayla takes advantage and making herself as small as possible, almost runs off in the direction Vi had taken.

I tilt my head questioningly to the side.

"I spoke to Vi, explained I'd like to know more about her old man before she proceeds. Vi might be able to get more out of her than we could."

"She relaxed when she saw she was going to be dealing with a woman." I stare at the closed door Shayla's now seated behind. "You could be right, Liz. She might talk to Vi. She's a looker though, isn't she?"

"Not bad. Could do with a little more meat on her bones. But her eyes, man. You see those?"

I nod. I had. "Seen more alive ones on a corpse," I agree, knowing exactly what he's getting at. Perhaps it wouldn't be so easy getting her into my bed after all.

We shoot the shit for a while, then the bell dings again, and Liz, seeing Jonah and his brother both occupied, gives his attention to the man who's arrived. As Liz takes him on back, I settle down, flicking through a tattoo magazine, getting some ideas for a new tat I'm planning for on my chest.

I look up at one point and get a smile from Vi as she goes to the copier, puts paper in, gets paper out, and disappears back to her station. A short while later, Shayla reappears. I go to stand, but stop as Vi catches my eye and shakes her head.

"We can start Monday," she tells Shayla. "Any particular time?"

They sort out times, then Shayla asks, "And you can work with my friend, too? Can she come along then? She's, er, nervous."

"Sure, no problem. We'll see how we go. I'll put aside enough time to do the outline for both. But discuss it with her, she might want something different to you."

"Thank you so much." Shayla seems to sigh with relief. "You don't know how much better I'll feel to have this gone."

"Happy to help." Vi smiles at her. "I'll see you soon. Have a good weekend."

The door opens, dings, then closes again, and then, she's gone. I notice Vi standing, staring at the now empty doorway.

"You get anything out of her?" I'd wanted to question Shayla myself, but know my normal methods of interrogation probably wouldn't have gotten results. At least I know when she'll be here again, if I'm going to have to bring my enforcer skills into play. Hopefully, I won't have to. I raise a quizzical brow at Vi.

She nods. "Yeah. I need to talk to you."

At that moment, Liz walks out, giving instructions to his client about aftercare. When the man's gone, he looks at Vi, unknowingly repeating my question. "You get anything out of that woman?"

Vi jerks her head toward the small staff room at the rear, and Liz and I both follow her.

She busies herself putting the coffee machine on and gets down three cups after querying me with a look.

"There's something odd there. I'd say that tat wasn't wanted."

Lizard snorts. I roll my eyes. Fair bet if she wants that shit covered. Vi shakes her head. "I don't mean *that*," she starts. "I mean, that it wasn't her choice to have it in the first place."

"She say that?" I ask, the hairs on the back of my neck rising.

"Not in so many words. But she's very eager to see it gone." Vi presses her lips together. "I'm going to do this, Liz. I know you've got concerns, but if I'm right and that tattoo was put on without her permission. If she was forced, well, that's abuse, plain and simple."

"I don't disagree, Vi," Liz tells her. "If she needs it covered 'cause she didn't want it there, then we'll do something she does want instead. Did you talk about removal?"

Vi nods. "Yes, but I think she's looked into laser treatment.

She's worried that that might show something had been there. People will always know she had a tramp stamp removed. She wants it to look like something she always intended."

"Did you find out anything about this Major?" I ask.

She shakes her head while pouring coffee into the cups. "I did start to ask whether he was a biker, but she clammed up. I didn't want to press her too much today. I thought she might give me more when she comes back."

"She liked your ideas?"

Vi smiles. "Of course she did. It's not going to be easy hiding that script, but I'm sure I can do it."

"What are you planning?"

As Liz asks, Vi goes to get her artwork, and the two bend heads over it. Feeling like a third wheel, I drain my coffee and take my leave. To be honest, I'm not sure they noticed me go.

I take the long way around back to the compound. Actually, I detour from the route quite a way, enjoying my day off that Pyro, the manager of the auto-shop had given me. Why waste it when I can get the wind in my hair and some pavement under my wheels? I ride with no particular destination, eventually arriving home with a clear head, red windblown cheeks and a smile on my face.

When I ride up to the gates, I notice the commotion. Leaving my bike at the side of the road, as Dirt, one of the new prospects we've only just appointed, seems intent on not opening the gate. Wondering whether he's being overly cautious or proving his worth to the club, I slip down my bandana, tuck my Ray-Bans into my pocket and am pulling off my gloves as I approach the car and its driver standing beside it. My smile gone, I now wear my best enforcer face.

"What's going on?"

Dirt sends me a look full of gratitude. "This woman wants to see Lizard."

Unashamedly, I blatantly check her out. She's in her early or mid-thirties by my estimation, but not past her prime. Red hair, either naturally sleek or artificially straightened, reaches down her back. As she turns, I notice stunning green eyes and full lips which draw my attention. Her figure is hidden by her jacket, but her legs are encased in a pair of tight denim jeans. *Nice ass.* If she was younger, I'd be jealous she was asking for my brother and not here for me.

"What do you want with Lizard?"

She's also examining me, and her lips press together tightly. A wave of something like pain shutters her features as she thinks on whether to enlighten me as to the reason why she's here. I don't leap to the obvious that Liz has gotten a town woman pregnant. I've never known him to go with a woman other than the whores we keep for that purpose.

Instead of explaining her presence, she asks a question of her own. "How is he?" She looks like she's holding her breath for the answer.

The enquiry takes me unawares, and automatically I reply, "Same as he's ever been. Now answer me, what do you want with him?"

"That's between him and me," she replies quickly. "Look, is he here? Or if not, where can I find him?"

"Who are you?" We don't give information about brothers lightly.

"Evangeline James," she replies with no hesitation. A slight lift of her eyebrow suggests she's querying whether I've heard her name. "Vanna?" She then offers what appears to be a shortened version.

"Are you a sister?" She shares his surname. It's odd, Liz has no family of which I'm aware, and my senses become heightened.

She huffs, looks at the ground, then stares blankly into the distance.

"Cousin?" I try again. That might make more sense, Lizard mightn't have mentioned extended family.

Now she turns back with something akin to a look of scorn on her face. "I'm his wife."

I bark a loud laugh and add a snort for good measure. "Don't know what your game is, but it's not going to work. Lizard is single, has always been single. Ain't no bitch in his life and never has been." I'm firm on that. Lizard would have mentioned if he'd ever entered into matrimony. He shares my views that life is best lived as a single man, and never hinted there was a time he'd thought otherwise.

I expect her to look disappointed being caught out in her lies, but she slumps as though completely defeated. *Had she really thought that ploy would work?* Well, whatever business she thinks she has with my brother, with that untruth, she's not getting close to him now.

"I still need to see him. To try..." Her eyes flick away then back. She looks like a woman at the end of her tether when she adds now sounding desperate, "Is he here? Or if not, what time will he be back? I'll wait..."

No she fucking won't. "I think you need to leave," I state firmly, noticing Dirt listening intently, his body language taking its cue from me.

"I can't leave until I've seen him," she says firmly. "Not until I've at least tried."

"Tried what? What do you think you're playing at? What are you trying to get over on Lizard?"

Neither my enforcer's snarl nor my threatening step forward, work. Instead of cowering, her back straightens. "Whether or not he acknowledges it, I'm his wife. And he needs to know about his son."

Lizard has always been firm about not wanting children. He's never knowingly sired a child. My voice comes out in a growl. "Are you trying to say you had his kid and kept that fact from him?" Dirt I noticed has stiffened as well. If, in the unlikely event, Liz had fucked a town woman, or someone he met on his travels, he should have been told about the outcome. "How old is this fuckin' baby you're trying to blame on him?"

"Fourteen."

Four-fucking-teen? The reply shocks me. This is ancient history, before Lizard joined the MC. It must have been while he was still serving as a Marine. Maybe there is something in his past he hasn't shared with me. I start to think there could be something to her story. But fuck it, she's admitted Lizard didn't know he had a kid. That shit doesn't sit right with me. You do not hide a kid from a man, even one who doesn't want one. What bitch does that? Then has the fucking nerve to turn up out of the blue as she wants something. Money probably, that must be it.

While I'm filling with disgust, she's staring at me. Her head coming up as she seems to read what I'm thinking.

"I'm his wife," she insists. "He's never divorced me, and I haven't divorced him. I can prove who I am, and what I am to him."

"Prove it, then," I challenge.

CHAPTER FIVE

Vanna

I suppose I should have expected I'd not be able to walk straight into the MC's clubhouse and demand to see my errant husband, but my hastily devised plan hadn't involved much more than trying to find Cas's father. At my wit's end, I didn't know what else to do.

Lindy had offered to have Cas with her this evening. By now she'll have collected him from school and probably fed him all the types of junk food he likes eating, but as a good Mom, I restrict access too. Then she'll get him playing on her Xbox and he'll be having fun. He likes Lindy, sometimes I think a lot more than he likes me, which left me free to drive down from Denver.

Now that I'm here, I'm not giving up without at least getting the chance to talk to the man I'm still legally tied to, and who the law says is bound to me.

Prove it, he'd said. The man who's confronting me hasn't introduced himself, and neither has the one refusing to open the gate. But I can read, and the name on his cut says Mace, and under that there's a patch saying he's the enforcer. I've no idea what that means, but deduce he probably enforces the rules. Right now, he's protecting Lizard from me. I actually feel a warmth that Lizard has such support, but the main emotion is anger that he's preventing me from seeing my husband, and that, in turn, is doing nothing to help Cas.

Delving into my bag, I pull out a crumpled piece of paper and unfold it. Then, I show him the marriage certificate, unwilling to completely let it leave my hand.

"You know him as Lizard," I explain, "but his legal name is Norton James. And that's proof he married me."

"I know what my fuckin' brother's citizen name is," Mace snarls. "This could be a fake."

My eyes widen. "Well the original in the courthouse in San Diego will prove it's not."

"We'll be checking," he warns me. "But for now I don't fuckin' believe you."

Enraged I turn, pull up my jacket and ease my pants down a fraction. I don't show him all of the tattoo—well, Lizard was the last and only man, except for my doctor, who's seen all of my ass. But it's enough for him to read, "Lizard."

"That's not a property patch," he sneers. But I can see by the way his eyes have widened that the tattoo's registered with him. He tries to dismiss it. "Our tats read 'Property of'."

"Lizard was Lizard well before he joined your club," I tell him, wondering why I've the need to justify myself. "As you'd know if you really did know him. He got his name not long after he joined the Marines and preferred it to Norton. Lizard has been Lizard to me since we met."

He almost flinches as I give him the explanation he must recognise. But still he hesitates, gesturing again at the paperwork and checking the date on the certificate. "You're telling me you married just after he enlisted?"

I nod. "I met him when he returned from his first tour." I feel my eyes glaze as I remember those happy days. "When he came back from his second, we got married."

"How did he get his name?" Mace snaps.

"He could remain still like a lizard basking, then go from

being a statue to moving fast and pouncing." It was lame, but most of them had picked up nicknames for barely any reason.

It's at that moment I hear the sound of a motorcycle coming up the road. Mace's face tightens, then he says, "Well, I guess you're going to get the chance to see your old man, if he really is that to you."

My gut clenches, realising the enforcer's somehow recognised the sound of Lizard's bike. My hands sweat and my body starts shaking. *Don't expect much,* I tell myself. *Or better, don't expect anything. Nothing may have changed.*

But it's been years since I've seen him, and I'm here out of desperation and hope that something has.

The bike draws closer, then slows, then pulls over and the engine stops. I get my first look at the man who the years have treated kindly. To my eyes, he's more handsome than ever before. His hair has grown longer, and I like that change.

As I'm drinking him in, studying him intently, he gives me no more than a quick glance before turning to Mace.

"What's going on? Why is this car blocking the entrance?" At last his eyes land on me, leering as he regards me from head to toe, then with a knowing smirk he turns back to his friend. "Who's the bitch?"

My heart breaks all over again as I hastily take back possession of the document that proves he's my husband and push it into my bag. When Mace's eyes catch mine, I give a violent shake of my head and send him a pleading look with my eyes. Luckily, Lizard's attention is on the other man and not me. *Don't confront him,* I try to signal. It doesn't work. I've tried before with disastrous results.

Mace's eyes narrow, and a thoughtful expression comes over his face. "Nothing to bother you, Lizard." I let out the breath I hadn't known I'd been holding. "She's someone I want to talk to." He turns to the man who's on gate duty. "Open up, Dirt. Liz, you get on in. And you," his intense stare comes back to me, "you drive inside and park. We're going to have a conversation."

It doesn't sound like a conversation I'm going to like. *Could I make a run for it?* For a moment I think about jumping into my car and getting the hell out of Dodge. But if I leave now, I've again given up. *Cas needs guidance, and who better than his father?* A father who doesn't recognise his son's mother, and has, for so long, refused to acknowledge his son.

I can't leave.

It's clear Mace thinks I'm lying and wants to know why I'm here, and what I expect to get from hounding a man who has so clearly shown he doesn't recognise me at all. In fact, after one curious glance as though wondering what Mace wants with me, as soon as the gate is opened, Lizard gets back on his bike, starts it, and drives through and onto their compound.

"You." Mace is regarding me sternly, without an ounce of sympathy on his face. "You've got some explaining to do."

"I'm happy to tell you everything." My eyes go back to my man, who's now backing his bike expertly into a parking space. "But I'll have to get back to Denver to collect my son later. My friend's only got him until ten. It's his bedtime…" I stop, realising I'm rambling.

"If you tell me what game you're playing, I'll make sure you leave in time to get your son." It's a threat and a promise. If I don't answer to his satisfaction, they'll, what? Keep me here against my will? Surely not. But whatever risk there is, it's negated by me seizing this one chance to get back my man. Maybe not as a husband, but at least, as my son's father.

"I'll tell you everything," I repeat. "There's no reason and nothing to gain from me telling you lies."

"Dirt. Drive her car inside."

I'd left the keys in the ignition, so when the prospect does what Mace demands, I've no option but to walk through those gates as he goes to his bike. But I wouldn't run anyway. I've already decided that's not an option for me.

I catch up with Mace after he's copied Lizard's actions and manoeuvred his bike into a spot left vacant. Idly I wonder whether they have assigned parking spaces, and whether it's because he's the enforcer that his is closer to the main door. Not the closest, but about fourth in line. Then I realise, it really doesn't matter whether or not that's the case.

"Come." Mace stands back and indicates I should precede him inside.

I enter what is obviously a clubroom. The air's tinged with cigarette smoke and beer, and men are standing around with drinks in their hands. I notice it's pleasantly painted and there are matching sofas, tables and chairs. My eyes spot Lizard and I turn away quickly, having spied a woman he's got his arm draped around.

Oh no. I bang the heel of my hand against my forehead. *Of course he's moved on and has someone else.* Deep down I'd acknowledged it as a possibility, but being faced with it hurts, really, really hurts. I'd stayed lost in the past while Lizard has found someone else. *Why should he have waited when he couldn't remember he had a wife?* My steps falter as I reconsider my decision to come to the club. *Can I deal with the pain of seeing Lizard with another woman?* Gritting my teeth, I remind myself I didn't come here for me, I came here for my son.

That he's with someone new shouldn't stop him stepping up and being a father to Cas. Maybe Cas will get on with his step-mother? Maybe she would get through to him more than I can. But looking back, my eyes narrow. The woman with her arm around my husband looks more like a hooker. Is she really someone I'd want to spend time around my son?

"Move." The snapped instruction gets my feet moving, then I pause, wondering where I should be headed. Mace waves his arm. "This way." Now he's in the lead, and trailing in his footsteps, I'm led across the clubroom and down a short hallway.

Raising his hand, Mace raps on a door.

"Enter."

"Wait here," Mace instructs, and his eyes catch those of a man behind me and some sort of silent conversation goes on.

Swinging around, I see another biker who's appeared at my rear and is standing with folded arms. Guess my escape route has been blocked. Though I wasn't going to take it, the fact I haven't one does unnerve me. But as well as fear, I feel anger. The one man here who should have my back doesn't acknowledge me. Not for the first time, I'm reminded of a saying Lizard used to use. It describes our situation exactly, *FUBAR*. We are certainly fucked up beyond all recognition.

Time ticks past, and I wait. I take out my phone to check the time, my guard growls, and I put it away. *Six-thirty.* I've a two-hour drive ahead of me and need to leave at the latest in an hour and a half, if I'm to make it back to Lindy's.

Christ, I wish they'd hurry up.

Five minutes later, and at last the door opens.

"Come in." Mace's voice is no less stern than it was.

There's a man sitting in front of the desk and another behind it whose dark unwelcoming eyes glare at me. "Heard you're here to cause trouble for our brother."

"No, I'm not." Well I am, of a sort. Cas could certainly fit the definition of trouble. I hate that they're not introducing themselves, and there's no name plate on the desk to give me an indication. "Sorry, you are...?"

"Demon, President of the Satan's Devils MC. Next to you is Beef, our VP, and you've already met Mace." He sprints through the niceties. "Let's cut to the chase, what do you want?"

I wonder where to start, and whether I should first appeal to his better nature. "Have you got children?"

He's surprised by my question, but pride makes him answer. "A son, yes."

"How old?"

Again, a parent's automatic response, "Eighteen months."

I give a quick smile. "A nice age. Mine's fourteen and he's not such a bundle of fun."

"Enough about fuckin' kids, what are you here for?" Mace snarls out behind me.

"I know you're going to question every word coming out of my mouth," I begin, "so I'm going to ask that you hear me out without interrupting. I need to get back to my son, and this will take forever if you refute everything I'm telling you."

Demon stares at me for a moment, then gives a sharp nod of his head. "We'll play it your way. For now."

"The reason why I'm here is that I've stayed faithful to my husband, Lizard. I've not wanted another man, well, maybe I have needs, but I've a son to raise, and my focus has been on him. I've tried to do everything right, but Cas is… difficult. My father is dead, I have no brothers, or sisters come to that. No family at all really, since my mother and I fell out. No, I'm not looking for sympathy, but my son needs help. Cas has no male figure in his life, and I think now he needs one." I hold up my hand and turn around fast as I hear Mace's intake of breath. "Cas is pushing boundaries. First it was mischief, what all kids do. Sneaking candy without paying for it. But it's escalated. He's fourteen years old and last week hotwired a car. I'm doing all I can to keep him out of jail."

"You do realise you're in a one-percenter club, darlin'?" I look to my left and notice Beef, their VP, has a twinkle in his eye.

I turn back and address the president, "I've been a good mom, or tried to be. Yet the choices facing my son are either juvenile detention or being taken away and put into the system unless I can get him back in line. I'm at the end of my tether. So yes," I nod at Beef, "I know what you are. But at the very least, if you break the law, you know how to hide it."

"We don't break the law," Demon snarls, his eyes seeming to flare, and he sends a warning look to the man sitting beside me.

"Bit late to come looking for a dad for your son if you hid him all these years," Mace snarls. I don't even turn to look at him. "Should have thought of what might happen when you decided to keep that shit from him."

He's so far off the mark, I ignore him. Not having finished, I continue now. "I hoped Lizard might have recovered, thought time might have healed him. Thought perhaps now he'd acknowledge he had a son and would step in to help him. Cas needs a man, needs someone he can look up to."

"Lizard didn't even recognise you," Mace remarks, almost spitting the words out. "You say you're married—"

A knock on the door causes him to stop speaking and step away from it. When he pulls it open, yet another man steps inside, this one so pale he looks like the sun never touches his skin.

Entering, he nods at Demon. "All checks out, Prez."

"How did we not know this?" Demon's hand slams down on the desktop, so loudly, it makes me jump.

The pale man shrugs. "Before my time, Prez. Lizard joined what, ten years back when he started prospecting? I was a bit later. Buzz did the background checks before me, and probably didn't have access to everything I have. He would have checked his service record, but seems he didn't dig deeper."

Demon's eyes burn into me. "Why didn't Lizard recognise you?"

Three men's heads turn to face me.

I take a deep breath, having already decided Cas is more important than invading my husband's privacy and sharing what, obviously to these men, is his secret. "Because he's got retrograde amnesia."

There are four audible gasps at my answer.

"Amnesia?" Mace scoffs, being the first to recover. "That man remembers everything. Talked to him enough. Over the years I've heard everything about his home life, his training in boot camp, his tours, particularly the first which is the only one he wants to talk about. Of course he can't remember the incident that got him invalided out of the service, but that's common enough. He'd remember if he had a wife and a kid."

Tears fill my eyes, and my voice weakens. "Yes, there was an incident. He was standing next to a truck when it was hit by a rocket grenade and exploded. He had a brain injury, it was severe. He was in a coma, and I... I sat with him. Cas was just two years old. I prayed and prayed he'd come round. He coded a couple of times, but they managed to revive him. For weeks I sat at his bedside, refusing to give up hope. At last, one day, he opened his eyes." I sob, loudly and then once again continue, "His first words to me were, *'Who the fuck are you?'*"

I'm not aware I'm crying now until I get a tissue placed into my hand. I dab my eyes, blow my nose, and then thank the VP.

"Did he get therapy?"

"Yes." I pull myself together and respond to Demon's question, asked in such a level tone it helps me to pull myself together. "But it didn't work. He remembered, as you say, growing up, joining the Marines, even his graduation ceremony. He remembered his first tour, then, blank. Nothing after that until he woke up in the hospital. Me? He didn't recall. In fact, he was suspicious of me." A sob makes me shudder, but I try to swallow it down. "When he met Cas, he didn't believe he was his son."

"You split up, then?" Beef's shaking his head. "You gave up on him and left?"

I give him a *what do you think I am?* look. "No, I did not. I spoke to his therapist who suggested once he was well enough to leave the hospital, that he come home with me. The idea being that back in his home with his familiar possessions it might help his memory. But it didn't." I pause, lost in the past for a moment. "He couldn't remember the house we'd moved into, could only remember living alone on base. He'd been overseas when Cas was born, came home to see him, but we didn't have any photographs to prove it. I just hadn't thought to take any. Pictures of Cas and me, but most without him there. I did manage to find a couple, but he couldn't remember. He... he used to get angry, and he accused me of photoshopping them."

"He violent toward you?" Beef asks.

I shake my head. "Never raised his hand toward me. He was angrier that he couldn't remember." My voice drops to a whisper. "He wasn't comfortable at home, his memory wasn't triggered by things familiar. It made him worse, he kept berating himself. Worse, he kept denying that Cas was his." My eyes close and I draw in a loud breath. "As well as retrograde amnesia, he had short-term memory problems. Each day was a new one for him. Each day he'd wake up unable to remember what had happened the previous one. He was stuck in the past, unable to learn new things. We tried for a year and a half, and then we had an argument. He told me I wasn't his wife, and Cas wasn't his son. Cas was four..." My breath hitches. "He pointed at Cas and said that kid is not mine. Cas still has nightmares about the day his dad walked out."

"Fuck," Mace says from behind me.

"I think I made it worse. I was, still am, proud of his dad, and I let Cas know that. What happened to Lizard wasn't his fault. I didn't want Cas to feel he'd been fathered by a bad man. So I'd tell him stories. But the memory of that day is lodged in his head. He even asked when he was older, if Lizard had been such a good man, why had he left? I think he blames me, and questions himself."

"You think that's the reason your boy's acting up?" Demon asks.

I shrug. "I think it's linked. Cas can't understand how Lizard has forgotten, and why he can't remember."

"That why he still goes to the VA?" This from Mace.

He still goes? I nod my head. "If he's still attending his appointments, yes. But early on, he decided he was their experiment, to see if he could remember things he'd lost from inside his head. He thought they were treating him like a guinea pig, and for all I knew, they were."

<hr>

CHAPTER SIX

<hr>

Mace

Christ. I don't know what to think. Vanna's finished her heart-breaking-if-true story and is now quietly sobbing but also making an effort to compose herself. I go over the way Lizard was today, giving no sign he recognised her. But if what she said is true…

"Vanna," I address her directly. "You said you lived together. So he knows you from after the explosion that fucked with his head. Why did he blank you today?"

She shakes her head. "Who knows how the brain works? That was the short-term memory loss as I said. Each day seemed like a fresh start. Each morning, I was greeted as though I was a stranger. It's as if he couldn't keep a memory of me or Cas in his head. As if a tape was constantly being rewritten."

"Just you?" I ask.

Another side-to-side movement of her head. "Memory is a strange thing. As far as Lizard knew, he was twenty-two. They got him a job as a mechanic when he recovered enough, he could do that, remember a trade, but couldn't remember the way to work. He could drive a car, but not remember a route. Other things he never forgot, like how to draw. He was always a good artist."

"He functions normally now. Wouldn't have gotten past his prospect patch if he had problems with remembering shit."

Now her head moves up and down. "He improved. I kept tabs on him via his therapist. I suggested going back and confronting him again, but I was told he was getting to a good place and perhaps I was somehow bad for him, was holding his recovery back. I always hoped he'd return, so just settled back to wait. I knew gradually, he was beginning to learn new things and remember them. But still, his doctors thought I should stay away, make a clean break. Eventually he moved and I lost track of him."

"But you knew where to find him today?"

"He left San Diego, and I didn't immediately know where he'd gone. Then a year later, I learned he'd come to Denver to stay with his friend, Hatch. I, er, I know it sounds stalkerish, but I moved there too." At the mention of Hatch, my eyes meet Demon's.

"Go on." Demon chooses not to enlighten her.

"I hoped one day he might remember. If he saw me around, saw me with Cas… but it didn't work. By the time I'd completed my move, he'd disappeared again. I went to Hatch's address, found the place locked up and for sale. The realtors said they didn't know where the previous renter had moved. I couldn't uproot Cas again, so we stayed in Denver. A couple of years back some paperwork caught up to me, it had been chasing me halfway across the country. It had his current address on it." She breaks off and looks at each of us in turn. "This MC in Pueblo."

"But you didn't come to find him then?"

"I was scared. Scared of exactly what happened today, that I'd come, and Lizard wouldn't recognise me anyway." Her hands gesture around. "Nine years ago, I might have tried. But it's been ten years now. Eight before I knew where he was." She shrugs. "I'd made sure people knew where I'd gone, so if Liz wanted to find me, he could. That he hadn't come knocking meant one of two things. Either he'd remembered and moved on, or his memory hadn't come back." She pauses for breath, then carries on, "It wasn't until I thought I had no other option if I was going to help Cas that I made the decision to come and see whether anything had changed. As you know, it's been a wasted trip." Her shoulders slump in defeat, and she makes a weak dismissive gesture. Then she lets out a sigh. "Look, I've got to get back to Cas. You know I haven't been lying, so please, let me leave. I'll just have to think of something else to do, some way to get my son's life back on track."

From the look on her face, she's at her wits' end. I exchange glances with Demon. We know only too well what happens when someone gets onto the wrong side of the law. Some pull themselves back up, we've got examples of that in the club, some continue the downward spiral, never learning from their mistakes and end up serving a long sentence or dead.

Demon picks up his phone. "Vi, can you come to my office?" Then he puts it back down. "When my wife comes in, I want you to go with her, Vanna. Give us a moment to talk about your situation."

"I've got to get back to Cas," she protests. "I'll be late if I don't leave now."

"Your friend okay with him staying a bit longer?"

"She would be, yes, but it's a school night…"

"Not going to do the kid any harm to stay up late for once. Give her a call and sort it out. We'll be as quick as we can."

She's got no choice, and she seems to know it. Vi comes in, and Demon calls her over and whispers to her quietly. Vi nods her head and smiles Vanna's way.

Vanna stands. "I'll clear it with Lindy, but I might as well leave. Lizard's not going to be any help, there's nothing more you can do." Her lips purse. "I'm sorry I laid that all on you. Please, don't think any the worse of Lizard. He can't help what he doesn't know."

Prez nods. "Vanna, I understand. But please, give us a

moment to talk." He regards the woman who looks like she's carrying the weight of the world on her shoulders, staring her down until she nods and turns to go with his old lady.

When Vi guides her out, I plop down in her now vacated seat. "What do you reckon, Prez?"

"I was going to ask you that," he unhelpfully replies.

I don't try to pretend I don't know what he's asking. I'm longing for a smoke, but in deference to the prez and VP, refrain from lighting up in his office. Well, to be honest, I don't want my ass kicked. But nicotine levels low or whatever, I try to think.

"Liz gets headaches, sometimes bad ones. I know he's going to the VA, thought it was just for that. Knew he'd got a bang on the head, didn't know it was so serious."

"You've known him since he was a prospect, Mace. Her story add up? I'm wracking my brain and I can't think of anything to either support or disprove it, but you were closer to him than I was."

He means, until I made my promotion to officer, I was just a lowly member like Liz. I speak slowly, gathering my thoughts as I do so. "He's spoken at length about his first tour but wouldn't go into the others. That's not unusual for someone who's served, some things you don't want to remember."

"He was quiet at first," Demon says, his brow creased. "He didn't come out of his shell until he was patched in."

"He can speak without thinking at times," Beef contributes. "Even I've noticed, just thought he was being an ass, but some of the things he comes out with..." He shakes his head. A fleeting smile crosses his face but disappears quickly.

Yeah, Lizard can be quite a laugh. But what if the inappropriate things he says aren't deliberate, but unintentional because of injuries in his head? Doesn't affect the way I think of him but is worrying instead. *Has my brother been struggling and I haven't fucking noticed?*

"If we accept her story at face value, I don't like that she needs support, and the man who should give it can't step up and provide it. Christ, if I wasn't around for Theo, I know everyone here would help."

"She's a brother's woman. She's got his name on her back. That shows at one time he was fucking serious about her."

Demon nods at me. "It would appear so. But why does he block her out now? She's a good-looking bitch, but you say he didn't look twice at her?"

"Maybe he doesn't fancy her?"

I bark a short laugh at Beef's suggestion. "She's got tits, an ass and a pretty face. When have you seen Lizard want more? No, anyway, what I meant, there was no recognition there at all."

"Fuck." Demon lowers his head into his hands. "What happens when a brother cuts an old lady loose? Never experienced it, so don't know. Do brothers step up if they just grow apart? If she'd stepped out on him, it would be different, but if we're to believe what she says, she's been faithful to him all these years. It isn't her fault the man who made vows to her can't keep them himself."

"Are you saying, Prez," Beef starts, "that we've got responsibility for her?"

"I think," says Demon slowly, "that we need to handle this with kid gloves. If Lizard is still recovering from a serious brain injury, I think we need to step carefully. Confronting him with the truth might do more damage than good. But I don't want her to leave thinking we're not going to help her. This is Lizard's kid we're talking about. What if one day he remembers, and he discovers his boy in juvie, jail, or worse, six feet under when it could have been prevented?"

Put like that, I agree with Demon. What do we do when a brother isn't around to do what needs doing, or, in this circumstance, can't cope? We step up.

Demon raps the table twice. "We'll get her to bring him here, tomorrow after school. They can stay for the weekend."

"Er, Prez, it's party night tomorrow and Saturday. I'm not sure that's suitable for a kid."

"Oh come on, Mace. You can keep it PG when he's around. The kid will have to go to bed at a reasonable time. Vanna and Cas can have my room. Vi and I don't use it much, it's easier with Theo to stay at the house."

"So he stays for the weekend, what then?" Beef sounds confused.

I, too, look at Demon, interested in where his thoughts are on this. I'm listening as he replies to the VP. "Sounds like the kid needs to learn a few home truths which his dad isn't in a place to share. So, we take him under our collective wing."

How the fuck do we do that? Well, hopefully Prez has got some ideas even though his lad can only just walk. I suppose we were all Cas's age once, guess we'll have to fall back on that.

A quick text to Vi brings Vanna back to the office. When we tell her the plan, she's at first overwhelmed, then thankful when we give her our reasoning, then her face falls.

"Lizard might not recognise Cas, but Cas will recognise Lizard. Or will when he hears his name. Demon, this will not go well."

We hadn't thought of that.

"Mace." At my name said in that tone, the words following bound to be an instruction, my eyes snap to Prez. "You go to Denver, tomorrow. Speak to Cas, explain about his father, then bring the boy and Vanna back here."

"Me?" Christ, I'm no child whisperer. I know fuck all about talking to a kid.

"Yeah, you, Mace. You know everything. You've met Vanna. You know Lizard. And you because you'll lay it on the line for him and won't speak down to him. Kid who's hotwiring cars and looking at juvie? He needs to hear it as it is and not with sugarcoating."

Vanna's face has hope written there for the first time since I met her a few hours ago. She turns to see my reaction. What can I say but raise my chin and give them a yes.

As Vanna gets up to leave, Demon asks, "You okay to drive tonight?"

A fleeting smile. "Roads will be quieter so, yes. Lindy said Cas wouldn't mind waiting up for me, he's playing *Call of Duty* right now." Her face twists as if she's not too happy with that. But hey, he's a kid, and like any others ignores the eighteen-only label.

She leaves, Demon indicates I should stay. He's quiet, thoughtful for a moment, then he says, "We can't risk mentioning any of this to Lizard. Fuck knows I don't know how to handle someone who's got such a huge fuckin' hole in his memory. I'll get Cad digging into his medical records, see what he can find out."

"Do you reckon his therapist would talk to us?"

"No, but he might talk to Vanna. Lizard won't be seeing the same one as he's not in the same area."

"Fuckin' therapist told her to stay away."

"Might have been the right advice for his patient, Beef."

"Yeah, but not for his kid. It's all fucked up, Prez. Sounds like that kid needed his dad in his life."

"Kid's got us now, Beef." Suddenly, I'm determined to help.

"Cad knows and the three of us." Prez's eyes rest on me, then Beef's. "Let's keep this to just us four for now. Liz won't want his business spread around the club, and I don't want people treating him differently or making allowances for him. To us, Liz is the same man he's always been. We'll see how this plays out, and see how we can help this Cas, whatever way the cards fall."

My thoughts have gone from thinking Vanna was playing some game to get, I don't know, support for her kid that maybe wasn't even Lizard's, to agreeing we'll step up and do what we can to fill the void that Lizard can't.

She seems a decent enough woman, one who's cared for Liz

from a distance all these years. Could we somehow thrust them together, even if he never remembers the past? Get this family unit mended?

Problem is, I just can't see it. Lizard has always been adamant he doesn't want a wife or a kid, so how can we push both onto him? A grown kid at that, who's trouble by the sounds of it.

I walk out of Demon's office and the first person I spy is Ink. I'm halfway over to him with the greeting of *Leatherneck* on my lips, which will garner the response of *Ground Pounder* as I was in the Army, and he in the Marines, when it hits me. Lizard was a Marine, yet I've never been tempted to tease him in the same way. Why not? Probably because Ink and I discuss our service and are proud of the time we served. Liz is far more reserved about his tours. *Because he can't fucking remember.* With new information in my head, I realise a lot of things suddenly make sense.

The next day I take my truck which I use more often in winter and try to avoid for the rest of the year, and drive to Denver, the GPS guiding me to Vanna's house just as she's leaving.

"I'll be back soon. All I've got to do is pick him up from school and bring him here, probably having some argument on the way. Make yourself at home, there are the makings of coffee in the kitchen—"

She's rambling again, I cut her off. "You go get the boy. I'll be fine, okay?"

I stare after her car as she drives away. Shows how much she's worried about her kid; she's just left a strange man in her home. Her reaction to the Satan's Devils is warming, most civilians run a mile from us. I think it's a sign of the regard in which she holds, or held, Lizard. That even changed as he is, if he's a part of this MC, we won't bring trouble to her.

I take the opportunity to look around. If I'm going to help the kid, learning his environment can only help. I immediately see she's doing her best with the little she's got. Nothing looks new, but everything's clean and tidy. The television in the living room is old, but probably functional. The sofa is comfortable and the room has a welcoming vibe. The kitchen cabinets are stocked, but with cheap unbranded products. The boy's fed, at least. All these years she should have been getting support, but I doubt Lizard has paid any. She could have proved their relationship like she had with me, but at first, I suspect she hoped he'd come around to accept it, without DNA tests and the like. Then, she probably just became resigned that it was her on her own. Still, it looks like she's done the best for her kid.

The latter thought comes when I step into a different realm, Cas's bedroom. He's got a good monitor and a fairly new model Xbox with games galore too. Any money she has, it seems to have been spent on him. Kid probably doesn't appreciate the half of it.

I try to remember myself at fourteen. I, too, was a little shit, I'm certain of that. Maybe Prez choosing me to come here and deal with Cas is the universe's form of retribution.

I'm drinking a coffee by the time I hear Vanna's car pull up in the driveway, grimacing at the bitter taste of the cheap brand. I lean back against the counter, in line of sight of the front door.

It opens.

"I don't understand why you took another fucking day off. It wasn't fucking necessary."

"Don't swear," Vanna says tiredly, and I suspect this conversation's been going on since she collected him.

"You call in sick? And you tell me not to fucking lie!" Cas's half turned to speak to his mother and hasn't yet noticed me.

"I took leave," she tells him. "I don't lie."

"Fucking hell."

"Watch your language," I snarl, causing Cas's eyes to snap to me.

They widen, his eyebrows rise until they meet his hairline. I suppress a grin. He's six foot and the image of his father, well, when he was younger that is. Any doubts I may have had over his parentage immediately disappear. His hair flops over his forehead and is redder than Lizard's. He probably gets the colour from his mom, and, like her, his face is freckled. But it's his features, his nose and his cheekbones that are all his dad's.

"Who the fuck are you?"

He might be tall, but I'm taller. I'm also a heavily muscled man, from the neck down covered in tattoos. I'm probably not who he'd expect to find standing at the kitchen counter in his mom's house.

Wisely, he takes a step backward which brings him up against his mom. I notice her hands rise and clasp his biceps as if comforting him.

"I asked who the fuck you are, and what you're fucking doing here?"

"Watch your language," I bark again. I may not have risen to Sergeant-Major during my time in the Army, but I've been at the other end of enough orders to mimic the tone. "If you ask again properly, then I'll tell you who the fuck I am."

"You're swearing," he challenges.

"I'm a fuckin' man," I respond. "But I'll do you a deal. What new game do you want?" He stares at me sullenly, clearly unable to understand, so I make myself clearer. "You got an Xbox? Come on, there must be a game you want to get your hands on?"

His eyes grow even wider until they resemble saucers. "Er, the new *Call of Duty*?"

Tugging at the chain that attaches it to my belt, I take hold of my wallet, open it and take out three ones, slapping them down on the counter. "I swear, I pay. You swear, you pay. You don't swear? I'll buy you the game, anyway."

He swings around to look at his mother, but she's relaxed and unconcerned. In fact, I see her mouth twitching at the corners as if she's trying not to smile. Then his gaze returns to me, and his expression is guarded. "You still haven't told me who you are."

I nod, as he's asked without punctuating his statement with profanity.

"Are you a friend of Mom's?" Now he looks suspicious.

"No," I reply, noticing how he steps slightly more in front of Vanna, and he takes a small move up in my estimation. It's a protective gesture, whether conscious or not. "I'm not a friend of your mom's. But I am a friend of your dad's."

CHAPTER SEVEN

Vanna

Oh no!

This is so not how I expected this to go. I thought Mace would ease Cas in gently, not drop this on him all at once.

I was impressed when Mace had given Cas a reason to stop swearing—the equivalent of a swear jar. Why had I never thought of that?

Now I'm totally horrified. So yes, if Mace had said he was a friend of mine, Cas would have gotten all the wrong ideas, but coming straight out with he's a friend of his father's will immediately make Cas's hackles go up.

My hands are still on his arms, no longer reassuring, but ready to hold on should he try to get out the door. Not that I'd have much chance at physically stopping him, but I'd make a darn good attempt.

While Cas stands stock still, and I stand stunned, Mace leans back comfortably as if he's used to propping up the kitchen furniture in my home. When Cas moves, it's not to run, it's to move closer to the stranger in the room.

"A friend of my dad's? Then you're not welcome in this house. Tell him, Mom, tell him to go." My son makes his desperate sounding appeal without turning around.

"Cas," I make do with addressing his back, "listen to him, please."

"He's not saying anything I want to fucking hear."

"I'm keeping count," Mace says, mildly.

"And I don't give a fucking damn."

Suddenly Mace stands. He's taller than Cas, and far more heavily built. As he pushes away from the counter, my son takes a step back. I don't blame him.

"Stay right where you are," Mace demands.

Christ. Is that man's voice loud? And commanding. He might not have been speaking to me, but I'm rooted to the spot.

"I want to talk to you man-to-man, and you're going to listen. You old enough for that, or do you want to go play with your toys?" He sneers the last word.

"I'll listen if it's anything I want to know." Cas tenses but replies. I suspect only I can hear the sliver of nervousness in his voice.

"Not the way this works, boy," Mace sneers. "Men listen to facts, then make up their minds. Filtering out the unpleasant shit," he pauses, opens that wallet and slaps another dollar down, "means you'll remain ignorant all your life. You want to be treated like a man? You sit and have a discussion."

"Why should I when I already know what you're going to say? Mom's obviously asked you to talk to me, so I can guess why you're here. You're going to tell me I shouldn't have hotwired a car. That I shouldn't have crashed it—"

Mace snorts. "You shouldn't have gotten caught, and before you steal a car, you should learn to fuckin' drive."

As a dollar slams down, my lips curve. *Cas is going to have his new game in record time.*

Cas, though, is stunned. "Who are you?" he says at last, almost in a whisper.

"Name's Mace. I'm the enforcer for the Satan's Devils MC."

My feet now under my control, I walk further into the room so I can see my son's expressions. He's looking confused.

And disbelieving. "Where's your cut and motorcycle?"

"I came in my truck for reasons I'll tell you soon. And even if I was on my bike, I'm based out of Pueblo. Wearing my cut out of area is disrespectful unless it's been cleared that I can fly my colours in your town. Respect is a code that I live by. You give me respect, I give it back. Disrespect me or mine? Then you'll soon wish you hadn't."

I may not agree with everything Mace is saying, especially when he essentially told my son hotwiring a car wasn't wrong but that getting caught was, but this conversation is exactly what my son needs. Getting told what's what by a man. A man who's demanding respect.

I've tried, but I'm Mom.

Suddenly Cas grins and asks hopefully, "You gonna show me how to drive?"

"Nope," Mace replies, popping the p. "Not if you're going to steal cars. Something you shouldn't do, or only when absolutely necessary. You know who you stole that car from?" When Cas shrugs, Mace continues, "What if they had a sick kid, or a sick ma or pa? What if a friend called, needed his or her help urgently? What if they couldn't work as they had no transportation? What was your need, Cas? Was your need greater than theirs?"

Another shrug, but this one not quite so certain.

"What was your need?" Mace asks again.

A pause then, a defeated, "I was bored. Just wanted to see if I could do it."

"Happy to teach you how to hotwire most models of cars, Cas, but only if you promise to only ever use those skills when it's life or death. Deal?"

Well I'll be damned. As Mace steps forward holding out his hand, Cas steps forward and shakes it. "Deal."

"Few things for you to agree to, Cas, if you're going to be my friend. You never, ever take a man's ride. You never even touch a man's bike without permission. You never put your hands on another man's cut, even to move it so you can sit down. You understand?"

Cas nods. He looks serious, taking it all in, but curious as well, not understanding why Mace is telling him this.

Mace raises his chin and then jerks it in my direction. "You, me and your mom are driving back to Pueblo soon as you're packed. You're staying the weekend on the Satan's Devils' compound. I'll show you the bikes, take you on the back of mine if your mom's agreeable."

"What?" Cas looks to me, his eyes shining. "This for real, Mom?"

I look toward Mace. Cas hasn't put two and two together yet. Not surprising, I hadn't told him Lizard is a biker.

Mace points to the dining table and the four chairs that came with it. It was a thrift-shop find, but I sanded then varnished it so it doesn't look bad.

"Let's sit down. Gotta explain some things to you."

Without argument, my son sits. Mace goes to the chair opposite him, I take the seat in between.

Mace clasps his hands on the table, looks down, then directly at Cas. "How old are you, kid?"

"Fourteen."

"Fourteen," Mace repeats. "Grown out of a boy, but not quite into a man. Though I suspect you've been the man of the house for a very long time."

"Since… I was born." Cas substitutes the last for *since Dad left* remembering Mace's initial introduction.

"So I'm going to speak to you as an adult, and I expect you to consider things without simply dismissing them."

Cas's chin lifts then falls.

"So, Cas. You gonna listen without fuckin' interrupting?"

Instead of answering, Cas nods toward Mace and tilts his head to the side. With a sigh and a shake of his head, Mace extracts another dollar and puts it on the growing pile behind him. I wink at Cas, and he…? He winks back.

"Right. Here's the thing. I said your dad was my friend, he's more than that. He's my brother. Not by blood, by choice. He's a member of our club. All the members are my brothers."

Cas has gone tense with just the mention of Lizard. He glances at me, then back to Mace.

Mace's face darkens as Cas opens his mouth, and he says fast, "I said, hear me out." He waits for Cas to relax before he continues, "Your dad got a serious brain injury, you know that? Well, I did and I didn't. Only just learned how bad it was. The man I know is good, brave, would give his life and all he owns to the people he loves."

"He doesn't love us," Cas spits out, a wealth of emotion in his voice.

"He doesn't know you, Cas. He doesn't know your mom either. He knows us. You know how to become a member of a motorcycle club? No? Well, you need to prospect for a year or more. For that time, you do all the… bum jobs. You clean up shit, puke; you wash bikes. If a member asks you to clean the heads with your toothbrush, you snap to it and do it with a smile on your face. If you do that, you earn the club's trust. When we know you'll do absolutely anything, you're patched into the club."

"Do you kill people?"

Mace glances at me, then back at Cas. "I won't lie and I ain't going to admit it."

Again, Cas glances at me to see how I'm taking it, but I keep my face impassive. If Mace gets through to my son, I don't care how he does it.

Mace takes up his thread once again. "Lizard prospected for us, earned our trust and his patch. Became a brother. We judged him for the person he presented to us, not because of anything he'd done in the past. Yeah, he loves us, and we love him back, but it's been earned, not gained just because we wear the same colours on our backs."

"Are you saying he doesn't have to love me because I'm his son?"

"Nope. I'm saying he doesn't love you because he doesn't know who you are. He did, before his injury, but kid, that fucked with his head. Way I see it is, if two hangarounds, that's wannabe members, walked into our club and said they wanted to join up but not prospect, we'd laugh ourselves sick. That's not the way this works. I expect you already know there's no such thing as a free lunch. Lizard can't remember being married, he can't remember having a wife. He can't remember fuckin'—that's a verb not swearing—your mom, nor putting you inside her. He can't remember you being born or any of that shit. You turning up expecting him to have a come-to-Jesus moment and suddenly fall in love ain't going to happen. Because he doesn't know who you are."

I've tried. Tried to explain it. But nothing I said ever made sense. Of course, I didn't paint the picture that Mace has, nor had the full attention of my son or not when he could keep a hold on his temper.

And I'll be darned if Cas doesn't turn to me and hold out his hand. Dubiously, I put mine into it.

He stares at me, his eyes suddenly looking older than his years. "You never stopped loving him, Mom, did you? That's why you've never found another man." He shakes his head. "You're hurting too, aren't you? He doesn't know you either."

Tears prick at my eyes. He doesn't know the half of it. When Cas squeezes my hand then releases it, my fingers curl into my palms, remembering not only doesn't he know me, but unlike myself, he's moved on.

My son's attention has switched back to Mace. "So, how do we prospect for his attention?"

Mace laughs loudly. "Fuck. Yeah, okay, I'll put another dollar in. In fact, I'll put in two. 'Cause, fuck me, that's the way of it. Not sure we've got much of a plan, but we'll approach this from two fronts. I want to see my brother right, and if possible, you and your mom back in his life. But I'll warn you both, Lizard's brain got scrambled up, that's obvious. He might want things now he didn't want before, and those things he used to want, hold no desire any longer. So perhaps all we can hope for is that he'll do right by you and your mom, even if he can't be a husband to her."

"I know that, Mace," I tell him, remembering what I'd witnessed. "I wish I didn't, but if he wants a divorce, I'll give him one, no hassle, no problem. All I want is for him to acknowledge his son and have a relationship of some sort with him."

Mace nods. "May not know you myself yet, Cas, but what I've seen, I like. You're protective of your mom, sit and listen when you need to. I'd be proud to call you my son. And I think Lizard will, once you've 'prospected'." He winks. "Now the other front is the medical one. Not sure how far we'll get, but we'll make sure Lizard's getting the right treatment he needs, and the right therapeutic support."

"If, if his brain's fucked—verb not swear word," Cas giggles, then grows serious again, "could it cause him damage if he's confronted by me and Mom?"

"I'm no doctor, Cas, but yeah. There could be a risk. Might also mean he'll never accept you or come to terms with it. But I'll tell you this—club is not going to turn its back on family, and that's what you and your mom are, however this plays out." He holds out his fist and Cas bumps it with his. "You're club."

We're club.

Dare I hope we're not alone any longer? Can I believe this man? Will Cas get the male influences I've always wanted for him?

Not sure I want him to hotwire any more cars or to learn more about such things, but hell, it's better for him to know when and when not to and how not to get caught. I can't be picky and say a bunch of bikers wouldn't be good for my son.

Their core values—respect, love, family, and support for each other—well, if Cas learns that much, it can't do him wrong.

Cas looks at me, then at Mace. Then he stands, his hand resting momentarily on my shoulder. "Well then, I've got to go pack. Come on Mother, you've got to get your glam on."

My glam?

Mace winks at me.

"Vanna," he says, as I start to get to my feet. "It may take a while. I've been thinking. I'll introduce you as a friend of mine. Just a friend," he adds fast, "no funny business. But I think it's best for Lizard to be able to get to know you again, no pressure."

I ask the question I should have voiced way back, saying tightly, "That woman I saw Lizard with. Is it serious? Will I be stepping on anyone's toes?" Again, my hands clench. "Introducing me as someone to you will sounds right, if," my voice catches and I try to tamp down the anger I know it's not right for me to feel, "Lizard is happy with someone else..." My voice trails off as I find it too hard to complete my sentence.

His face tightens and he glances in the direction that my son had gone, making sure he's out of earshot. "Vanna, I can assure you Lizard hasn't got a girlfriend, fiancé or wife. But I have got to warn you, the club has girls, they're there for one thing only. Sex. Sex without strings or emotions."

I widen my eyes then close them, picturing the girl who'd had her hands on my husband, then I open them again, having prepared myself, and ask for the confirmation I'm certain I'll hear. "Lizard... Liz goes with them for sex?"

Mace's eyes meet mine. "Yeah."

Yeah.

I stand, walk to the counter and lean over it, feeling my body vibrating with rage. *Lizard goes with whores.* The good news is that he isn't taken. The bad? Whether or not he knows it, the fact is, he's fucked around on his wife. For the first time ever, I have to ask myself, *If I get a chance to win Lizard back, do I still want him?*

"He doesn't know you exist, Vanna," Mace reminds me, correctly interpreting my tense stance. "I promise you that he's never taken to a particular woman. The girls are there, we use them."

Him as well? I take it if I asked the question, he'd respond, yes.

My husband has lost his memory, he doesn't know he has a wife. I know the person he left has changed, and I hope for the better. But the man who left me, has he changed for the worst?

Guess I'm going to find out.

I remind myself, I never set out to regain the man who'd been so sincere the day he said his vows. What I need first and foremost is a man who'll step up and be a dad for my son.

CHAPTER EIGHT

Lizard

"Do you have to get them, you know," Wills bumps my arm with his, "hard?"

"Nah. So," I try to get back to my story I'm relating to Sparky and Wills.

"How do you do it then?"

Rolling my eyes, I explain, "You stretch it out and wrap it around your fist or over a block."

"Ew."

Seems I've shut him up for the moment at least having planted that visual in his mind. "So, I asked him if he was a shower or a grower." I chuckle, thinking back.

"Does that make a difference?" Wills interrupts yet again.

"Yeah," I explain as patiently as I can. "If he's a shower then what I draw will stay basically the same erect or not. If he's a grower, that shits going to stretch. Think of a three-hundred-pound Marilyn Monroe."

"I'd rather not," Sparky butts in. "So, what was he?"

"Well he looks down and says he doesn't know. I glance at his goods myself and can barely see a bulge in his pants. So I surmise and tell him he must be a grower. Then, I have to explain that means it gets bigger when he's about to fuck."

"And?" prompts Wills.

I chuckle again. "And he says it stays the same, hard or soft. He wanted me to adorn his three-inch dick."

"Oh, man. So he's got something to impress with?"

"Not just that." I struggle to get the words out, the chuckles streaming from me. "He'd brought in a pic that wasn't going to fit, no matter how much I resized it."

"Did you tell him there wasn't enough of a cock to tat?" Sparky's roaring with laughter. "What the hell did he say to that?"

"I thought he was going to punch me in the mouth until I suggested a piercing instead. Thought it might give some poor woman a bit of pleasure at least."

"Hey, Nails," Wills shouts out to the prospect who's bartending at the moment. "What would you have tatted on your dick?"

Quick as a flash he responds, "A nine-inch nail of course."

I think as one, we all lean over the bar and peer over and down.

"Grower," Nails says smartly, before moving off with a wink.

"So," Wills prompts.

"So what?"

"Did you pierce his dick?"

I crease my eyes having lost the thread of this conversation. "Sorry, I was distracted by Nail's nine-inch dick."

"So *he* says." Sparky starts, looking around. "Hey, Dirt!" When he catches our other new prospect's eyes, he yells, "Has Nails got a nine-inch dick?"

"How the fuck should I know?" Dirt calls back, the sack he'd been using to collect empties dangling from his hand.

"You live with him." Sparky's unrelenting.

"Yeah, but we don't compare dicks."

"Hey, I'm a grower as I said. Dirt doesn't get me hard."

"Prove it!" Beef slaps a twenty down on the bar top. "That says it's not nine inches. Come on man."

Nails is a prospect. If he wants his patch, he'll do whatever is asked of him. It's always a good laugh teasing a newbie.

We all start slapping our money down, Beef starts recording bets which currently go from three to ten inches. The longest was a joint bet from the club girls who I think are just optimistic. I stare at Nails, trying to read the man, before placing down my own two tens.

"Nine," I say, hopefully, thinking of a shit job I can give him if he's lying. Shittier than taking down his pants and getting himself hard in the middle of the clubroom.

I can tell the man's reluctant as cries start to go around of 'drop 'em, prospect', and 'does that man want his fuckin' patch', and 'who's got a ruler to hand'—the phrasing of the latter causing a few laughs. Beaver, I notice, is smirking at the other end of the bar. As a prospect who's been here a while, he'll be appreciating the heat is on someone else now.

With a sigh and a glare at the VP, Nails comes around the bar, and starts unzipping his pants.

"Hey, I'll help."

"Prospects don't get whores' hands on them," Bomber snarls at Breezy. "Let the man handle himself."

Again, we all crack up.

But Breezy does help, though in a hands-off way. She lowers her top so her tits are hanging out and fondles them, while licking her lips. Nails pulls out his cock and starts tugging on it, then fists one hand around it, fondling his balls with the other.

"Don't you dare come," yells Dirt. "I ain't cleaning up your shit."

Nail's head goes back and fuck me, well that cock swells and lengthens. Quite impressively actually.

"Is that it?" Rusty asks. "Here, Liz."

As I turn, he hands me a fucking ruler. "Why me?"

"'Cause you're used to handling dicks. Come on. Go measure it."

With a grimace I step forward. "Don't you dare go off, Prospect. You get cum on me and you won't get your patch."

"Well for fuck's sake hurry," Nails gasps.

I place the ruler against his dick, pressing it against the root making him gasp.

"Hurry up!" His voice is tense.

"Nine inches!" I announce in delight, seeing the size of the pile on the top of the bar.

"Hey, let me check." Beef comes over.

"Man, *hurry the fuck up.*"

"Hold it there, Nails. Yeah, Liz, I think you're right. Good call, Brother. Anyone else want to take a look?"

Seems they all do. Nails is going red in the face. "Jeez, I'm—"

"Don't you fuckin' dare." Thunder's loud voice booms.

Eventually Beef takes pity on the man both fighting to maintain his erection and trying hard not to come. "Okay, put it away now, Nails."

Then we all stand watching him try to get his very erect and reasonably long cock back inside his pants.

"Can I take five?" he asks, sounding desperate.

"Who's serving fuckin' drinks?" Judge bangs the bar top. "I want a beer." He shakes his head at Beaver, warning him to stay where he is.

As a result, Nails doesn't get his five minutes, instead he has to hobble stiffly back around the bar to pour our drinks.

I'm just reaching to collect the pot of money lying on the bar when the main door opens and I automatically swing around to see that it's Mace, with a woman and teenage boy in tow. It's the bitch who was here yesterday, and I wonder why she's back. The boy is staring at me as I count up the money. I turn away, not knowing him from Adam. Not my business, or nothing more than idle curiosity as to why we have strangers in the club.

But as they walk past, I hear the boy ask Mace in a loud voice, "Do they swear a lot here then?"

Mace snorts and looks over at the money I just picked up.

"Just a bit, little bro," he answers the kid. "Yeah. Just a bit."

Then he's taken them over to the stairs which lead to the bedrooms. Has Mace picked himself up a woman? If so, she's quite a pretty-looking bitch, though older than the ones he usually goes for. Wonder if he's going to share her? Hmm. Probably wouldn't mind that. Would have to ditch the kid though.

Well I had me some entertainment at the prospect's expense and earned myself a hundred bucks to boot. Good times. I stand with a beer in my hand, wondering which sweet butt I'll get to warm my bed tonight, thinking once again this is the fucking life. I've got everything I want and need here. There's nothing missing at all. Nothing at fucking all.

For some reason, I think of the kid who just walked in. He reminded me of me for some reason. Strange to think I was once a pimply brat his age. Christ.

As usual the blast of pain hits me by surprise, coming on with no warning. I place my elbows on the bar and put my head in my hands, trying to massage my temples.

"You okay, Bro?"

I breathe in deeply, let it out slowly, then do it again. Then again. After the third time, the pain's receded sufficiently for me to speak. "Fuckin' headache, Mace. Must have overdone it today." While I'd been bent over with pain, Mace and at least one of his visitors had obviously come back downstairs.

"You know what causes them? You're getting them more often it seems."

"Yeah. Pretty certain it's my age. Reckon my eyesight's going. All that close work I'm doing, concentrating and shit. Probably eyestrain and I need glasses. I'll go see the optometrist when I get time."

"My mom sometimes gets migraines when she has a period." The voice isn't one I recognise, it's squeaky as if half-broken.

I raise my head to see the young boy standing next to Mace. "Yeah? And how do you know about fuckin' periods, kid?" *Did I know someone who got bad when they were bleeding?* Can't place it if I did.

The teenager standing next to Mace eyes me sympathetically but answers my question. "I live with a woman, they can't hide shit."

Mace leans down, but I can hear what he's saying, "Just because your mom isn't here doesn't mean you won't get fined." He taps his head. "I'm keeping a tally, lil' Bro."

The kid rolls his eyes.

"Hey, Lizard, meet Castiel. Castiel, meet Lizard. Or Liz as we call him." Mace now addresses me. "His mom, Vanna, is an old friend and they've come to visit. They're going to be staying for the weekend. She's up getting settled in Demon's room."

So they're not sleeping together? Or probably that's where the kid will be while his mom warms Mace's bed.

"We've just come down to grab a couple of sodas."

"Your visitors want something to eat?" Nails asks as he grabs the drinks and puts them on the bar. "Think there are some leftovers."

"No," says Mace.

"Yes," says the kid at the same time.

"We stopped for food on the way here," Mace challenges him.

"So?" The kid, *Cas*, shrugs. "I'm a growing boy, what can I say?"

Mace laughs. "You're the devil's spawn, that's what you are." He ruffles the kid's head. "Come on, let's see what these fuckers left."

"Language!" the boy admonishes him.

As the pair walks away, my eyes follow them, and I shake my head. Mace seems really friendly with that kid. Strange he's never mentioned him or his mom before. Even stranger, yesterday I'd have sworn she was a total stranger to him. But what do I know? Ruefully I rub my head where the pain has now dimmed to just a dull residual ache. Can't trust this brain of mine to know whether I'm imagining things or if they're real.

"Head bad?"

"Not great." I give a half-smile at Tulia's obvious concern.

She takes hold of my hand. "Come on, how about I make you feel better?"

That sounds fucking good. I already know she gives great head massages which have worked a time or two before, and when my head's eased, well, there are other things she can do with her hands. And her mouth.

Tulia does indeed make me feel better. When she leaves having provided me with a variety of her services, I fall asleep fast. Waking, I'm sweating with the gunfire and explosions from my nightmare still ringing in my head. My body shaking, I go to the bathroom and take a long piss. I look into the mirror, noticing my bloodshot eyes. Christ, that dream was a fucker. I haven't had one so bad in a long time. I wonder what brought it on.

Returning to my bedroom, I eye the bed with distaste, not trusting the nightmare not to return if I close my eyes again. Moving to the window, I pull up the blind and see the night sky lightening. Suddenly an early morning ride looks a more attractive option than sleep.

The clubhouse is deadly quiet when I leave. When I return several hours later, it's a hive of activity. Breakfast noises of the clattering of plates are coming from the kitchen, accompanied by the glorious smell of bacon. *Can anyone ever get fed up with that?* Not me, that's for certain.

I grab a plate, thanking Jeannie, and to annoy her man, Bomber, plant a kiss to her cheek, then getting out of his way, head to the clubroom to find myself an empty seat. I spy the woman, *Vanna, wasn't it?* who Mace brought in last evening sitting alone, but no sign of my brother or the kid. The wind therapy having done wonders, I feel sociable today, I decide to go over.

She's got a cup of coffee in front of her, and her nose in a book. Or eyes on her e-reader, the modern equivalent.

She looks up as I near. "Good morning, Lizard."

"You remember my name?"

"I met you before."

Yes. The day before yesterday, of course. Mace had told her my name. Hadn't he said she'd come to find me? I shake my head. Must be getting muddled, it must have been him she'd come to see.

"Where's your boy?"

"Cas," she gives me his name. "Mace has taken Cas to your auto-shop. He had to go down to check something out, and Cas loves anything to do with cars and bikes, so he tagged along." The way she bites her lip makes her look worried.

"What's up with that?"

"Nothing wrong with what he's seeing, it's how he's getting there that concerns me. He's gone on the back of Mace's bike."

"First time?"

"Yessss."

"Well, don't worry. Mace is a good rider. He'll take extra care with a passenger."

"Thank you for that." She seems genuinely grateful for my reassurance.

I'm burning to ask why she's here, but I don't think it's my place. She proves herself a mind reader.

"You're probably wondering why we're here. Cas, well, Cas has had a bit of trouble recently, and I'm on my own. Mace thought he and you, his brothers, might help steady Cas a bit."

I nod toward her left hand where I've just noticed a wedding band rests. "Your husband's no help with that?"

"My husband's gone."

The way she's spoken makes me surmise he's dead. "I'm so sorry for your loss."

She shakes her head. "It's a long time ago now."

"But you still wear his ring?"

"I still love him."

Her simple words both impress and dismay me, that she can remain true to a man who's in his grave. Or at least, in some ways. I'm driven to check. "So, you and Mace?"

"Just friends."

For now, I think to myself. Knowing my brother and how unusually patient he seems to be with her son, I think that change might be on the horizon for her.

I chuckle, remembering last night, and being unable to stop myself messing with her, I lean in. "You know what Mace calls the kid?"

"Er, Cas?"

"Nah," I tell her, a smirk on my face. "Devil's spawn."

Her hand covers her mouth as she gives a tinkling laugh. "Oh my God, he's right. That's exactly what he is." As she continues chuckling, I'm thinking it wasn't as funny as all that, but it seems to have appealed to her. I'm wondering exactly what this Cas did to earn such a title. But hey, aren't all kids trouble? That's why I never want any myself.

A reminder goes on my phone.

"That's my cue to leave, I've got to get to work. I run a tattoo parlour, and Saturdays are the busiest days of the week. Hey, you want any ink, you come to me, darlin'."

"Thank you, I'll remember that."

I start to stand, and for some reason am driven to ask. "You got any tats already?"

She blushes red. "Just one."

"Oh?" I don't know why, but something makes me want to know more. Call it professional curiosity, I like checking up on another artist's work. "Can I see it?"

"No," she tells me. Then adds, "Only my husband has ever seen it."

Oh fuck no. I rise with a semi hard-on imagining exactly where it is. Quickly I leave and escape to Devil's Ink.

It's a busy day and I hardly have a moment to myself. We

end up turning away a lot of walk-ins even with Jonah, Whale and Vi all working alongside me. But we don't waste the opportunity, trying to book those who're not members of the *must have it done today* brigade into the quieter times during the week.

When I finally close up and return to the compound, word reaches me that Demon's issued a command, *no public fucking while the kid's around.* As I presume he'll be gone tomorrow, that's not going to be too hard. Particularly as I'm exhausted, a nice gentle fuck in my room is probably all that I'm up for.

I eat, drink, socialise. I notice Mace and the kid playing pool while Vanna looks on. I watch Mace get beat, then, can't resist wandering over to see he's getting slaughtered by Vanna too. I linger as he tries a rematch, finding my eyes drawn to her delicious ass as she leans over the table to take her shots. The table that she'd probably be disgusted to know the other things that it's used for. But the prospects do clean it.

I'm pushed away when Vi, Jay, Steph and Beth gather around to cheer her on. Vanna goes on to beat Rusty and Sparky, then no one else will play her. At one point she notices me watching and looks straight at me and winks.

Wondering whether it was her late husband who taught her to play as expertly as she does, I take myself off to find Breezy to ease the sudden ache in my dick.

That night I have another fucking nightmare. Fuck this shit. I thought I was done with it. It's the type of dream you can't catch hold of when you awake but are just left with that lingering feeling of helplessness and terror making you afraid to chance anymore sleep. I'm tired as hell though, so I try to drop off, but keep jerking back awake. I don't rush to get out of bed the next morning, just lazing and thinking. Remembering.

I'm Lizard, otherwise known as Norton James. I ride with the Satan's Devils MC and have done for the past ten years. I'm thirty-eight years old, and my birthday is the tenth of January. I'm a tattoo artist and I run Devil's Ink on behalf of my brothers. I've no ties, no family and that's the way I intend to stay.

When I finally rise, I just grab a bacon sandwich and eat it on the way to my bike.

I work Sundays, letting Vi and Jonah have the day off. Whale and I handle the trade well between us, him impressing me with his standard of work and how tidy he keeps his station. So much so, I even call him Weston a couple of times and ordered in pizza for us both at lunchtime.

By the time I get home, Mace has gone and so have Vanna and Cas. Tits are out, well those of the club girls at least, and gloves are off as anything goes again. The place is back to normal and I can relax.

Funnily enough, I think to myself, looking around the crowded room, I didn't even have much to do with him, but I miss that little shit. Devil's spawn indeed. Sounds like Mace came up with a good name.

I even catch myself wondering whether he'll be visiting again.

CHAPTER NINE

Mace

Once Cas had returned from his second trip upstairs to collect yet another thing which he'd forgotten to pack, I'm at last able to put the truck into drive and start the journey back to Denver. I'd enjoyed watching the interaction between mother and son, realising how much there was to all this parenting shit, and how having the patience of Job was essential.

"Have you got everything, Cas?"

With an exaggerated eye roll he'd replied tiredly, "Yes, Mom."

"Phone charger?"

Cas had stared, then turned, and reaching the stairs, took them two at a time.

"Toothbrush?" she'd asked when he'd come back down, sending him running back to the bedroom again and descending with his bag of toiletries in his hand. She hadn't commented, just thrown a wink my way.

But her moment of parental satisfaction hadn't lasted long. I didn't miss the look of longing and regret she'd sent in the direction of the clubhouse when we finally got on our way and wasn't surprised that the drive started in silence.

Glancing to my side, I see Vanna with a pinched look on her face. Her eyes are directed forward, but I suspect she's not taking much notice of what she's seeing. Not surprising, she's got much to contemplate. For a start, spending a weekend on a biker compound where something is always going on is probably very different to how she normally spends her free days. The noise level for a start, music, talking, laughter and there were even a couple of brothers getting rowdy and pushing each other about. All good-natured, of course, but to an outsider, it could be disturbing.

She'd handled it in her stride as I suspect she does most everything else, her reaction fuelling my growing admiration for her, together with a better understanding of how well she's coped bringing up Cas alone.

Apart from the general atmosphere, she'd stayed for two days in a place where her husband lives, the man who doesn't recognise her, or acknowledges their relationship.

It had been last night when Lizard had led a giggling and expectant Breezy up the staircase, clearly heading to his room, that I'd caught her staring, her hands clenched at her sides. Mixed emotions crossed her face—anger, betrayal, longing, desire, disgust, and finally defeat. Immediately, I'd crossed to her side and spoken quietly to her.

"You use a vibrator, Vanna?" The shock on her face had me swallowing back laughter.

"None of your business, Mace."

She tries to turn away, but I don't let her escape. "I bet you do." I nudged her with my elbow. "Got a fancy rabbit one, or a G-spot stimulator?"

"None of your business," she spitted out again, her eyes widened in horror. "This conversation is over."

"Hear me out," I snapped. My commanding tone got her eyes on my face.

I nodded toward the staircase where Liz had just disappeared. "Men and women have needs. You've probably got a BOB that you're friendly with. Me and my brothers? Well, we've got the whores. Means no more to us than a session with your vibrator."

Her eyes narrowed and moistened. "How the hell can you say that, Mace? Lizard's gone off with a flesh and blood woman, not one who's battery operated."

I tapped my forehead. "It's in here that matters. Breezy, Tulia, hell, any of the girls could leave any time, and we'd miss them about as much as if one of your toys broke. New girl comes along? Well, she'll do instead. What I'm saying, Vanna, is that there's no emotional commitment. None at fuckin' all. Lizard's not stepping out on you, he's just using her for a sexual release. You feel guilty using your vibrator?"

"Of course I don't. But—"

"Lizard doesn't either. Add to that, darlin', he thinks he's a free man."

She was quiet for a moment. I watched as she considered my words. I know it's hard for someone who doesn't live in our world to understand our relationship with the club girls.

"Don't judge Lizard for what he can't remember," I pushed once again. "If he knew he was married and still stepped out on you, your anger would be justified. Lizard's got no reason to think he's being unfaithful. Again, I tell you, it's just sex. No emotion, no loving. No attachment. A mutual itch scratched, nothing else."

Finally, I seemed to get through to her, the tension in her body receded slightly. "It still hurts, Mace. Knowing that doesn't make me feel much better."

Putting my arm around her, I gave her a much-needed hug. "I know, Vanna. I know."

"I hate that Cas has seen too. He'll never understand."

My cheeks actually started to burn. "I, er, may have had a similar conversation with the kid."

Again, her eyes widened, her brows rose to meet her hairline. "You what? Mace!"

"Hell, darlin'. You wanted him to have a male influence, well, I spoke to him, man-to-man."

Her head was shaking, turning one way then the other. Her movement continued for a few seconds. "He was okay with it?"

"He'd rather his dad was fuckin' his mother, but yeah, he's okay with it."

"Please tell me you didn't use those exact words, Mace?"

I think she was worried I had traumatised her son forever. "Not precisely." I didn't admit I'd come damn close to it.

But fuck me, Vanna having Liz's infidelity right up in her face must be fucking hard. I wonder whether she'd ever be able to forgive him, even if Lizard woke up one day and remembered her. Or whether Liz would ever be able to forgive himself. *He doesn't know what he's doing,* I remember.

I check in the rearview mirror. Cas's brows are drawn down, and his hands are clenched in fists.

"How did you think it went?" I ask, in general. My question directed at whoever wants to answer.

"You were right, Mace," comes a voice from the back seat. "I didn't understand until I saw my father." He pauses for a moment. "He didn't leave because he wanted to, it wasn't Dad who abandoned us. It wasn't his fault. I was holding onto my anger as I didn't have anything else. So I'm not the only kid at school being raised without a father, but it hurt, Mace. I wanted him to be there and cheer me on when I got a home run or a good grade."

"Cas," Vanna starts.

"Mom, I blamed him for not being there. Now I've seen him… I don't know. It made sense. I don't like it. I'm frustrated as hell I can't get through to him, but, yeah, it's all making sense."

"How about you, Vanna?"

She's quiet before she speaks. "I'm glad Cas saw his dad. I'm glad he's getting a chance to know his father, even if it's the man now and not who he was. But for me? It hurt, Mace. It hurt."

"You want him back." It's a statement, not a question. Anyone watching her can see she still loves him. Despite all his faults and the substitutes he uses for a vibrator.

"He's not right, is he, Mace?" Cas speaks again. "Those headaches…"

I don't know how to respond. Lizard is convinced he just needs glasses to sort himself out, and last week I would have thought that was the answer. Knowing now how serious his brain injury was, that it had almost killed him, the headaches which seem to be increasing both in intensity and occurrence are beginning to worry me too, making me think there might be something very wrong with my brother.

"He's got an appointment with the VA doctor soon. I'll make sure he goes, Cas."

"He's been staying away?"

"Yeah, Vanna, he has. He thinks he's fine and doesn't need to see anyone."

"Do you think he knows that he can't remember? That there's a huge hole in his life?"

I give her question the weight it deserves. It's something I'd never have thought to ask myself until I knew Lizard's background. Little things I missed now begin to add together, forming a picture of my friend which I'd never previously considered.

I flick the turn signal, swing past a slow-moving truck and trailer, and then when I'm back in the lane, answer, "I'm pretty sure he does, Vanna. But as the things he needs to know are the things he remembers, he's living with it and coping." I'd actually been talking about this with Demon and Beef. The gaps Lizard has, hurt her and his son, but not the man himself. Or not on the surface. It had made us more determined to help her and give Cas that male influence that was missing from his life. I issue the invite Demon had extended. "You're welcome to come back next weekend, if you want to."

I hear Vanna's indrawn breath but can't predict her answer. Cas though, he needs no time to think.

"I had a great time. Mace, I loved being on your bike. Seeing the shop. Playing pool with the brothers. Mom, can we come back?"

I try to persuade her. "Think we did the boy some good, Vanna."

She's quiet for so long, I'm not even sure she's going to respond, then I hear a quietly spoken, "I think so, yes. Cas and I need to talk, and I need to think. I don't want to do anything to hurt Lizard, but is being in his face or staying away the answer?" She shakes her head. "I wish I could talk to his therapist."

The last one had told her to keep her distance, and I'm not convinced that had been the right solution. But hell, I'm no expert.

To be honest, I don't know what the correct course of action is. Lizard, for all intents and purposes, is a confirmed bachelor who doesn't want kids. He's settled and happy in his life. Knowing the truth and believing it and still feeling the way he does? It would fuck with his head. He'd have to deal with being presented with something he's certain he doesn't want. On the other hand, if I could pick a woman for my brother, it would definitely be someone like Vanna. And Cas as a kid? He's a handful for certain, but also an intelligent boy who, if pointed in the right direction, could have a bright future.

I settle for telling them, "Let me know what you decide. I can come pick you up…"

"I'm perfectly capable of driving us to Pueblo, Mace."

I hide my grin at her declaration of independence and suppress my dismay that Lizard has no idea what a good woman he has. "Well, just let me know. I'm happy to make the trip or not. Whatever you decide."

By the time we finish our conversation, we're approaching Denver. Vanna tells me a shortcut which doesn't show up on the GPS. In a few minutes sooner than the device originally predicted—and who doesn't take satisfaction from that?—we're pulling up outside her house.

I get the bags and carry them to the step. She invites me in, but I cringe at the thought of that cheap coffee, and decide I'll pick something up when I top off with gas on the way back. I wait until they're safely inside, then return to my truck and start it.

My lips curve as I drive away. I'm the fuckin' enforcer. Never in a million years did I think I'd get involved with a woman and her kid, even if I'm standing in as proxy for my brother. Truth be told, if Lizard hadn't a prior claim on her, I might have been interested in her myself. Though to be honest, it doesn't take much to excite my dick.

Two hours later I socialise, drink, fuck, then when I've tired myself out, go to bed. Just a normal Sunday night on the compound. I switch off completely. With no thoughts lingering to disturb my rest, I sleep soundly until morning. Then I rise and get ready to start my week.

"Mace. That bitch is coming in again today. Vi's going to start working on that property tat."

Lizard's talking about Shayla. With Vanna here, she'd been put right out of my head. Now I remember the good-looking woman who'd interested me last week. I raise my cup of coffee toward Lizard. "Cad find anything more out?"

"Nah. No one's heard of any other Majors, not in an MC anyway. He's asked our other chapters and the Wretched Soulz. He's widening his search, got his contacts on the dark web looking."

Of course, he has. The way Cad gets his info is a mystery to me. "You going to try to speak to her?"

"Vi is. She's going to probe who this Major fucker is. Demon's happy we cover the tat, but if there's anything she can tell us, he wants to know. Just in case."

I smirk. "Want me to have a word?"

Lizard chuckles. "Not sure we need your enforcer skills just yet. But you're welcome to hang around if you want to try out your charm on her."

"What fuckin' charm?" I bark a laugh.

"The charm you were using on that bitch this weekend." His eyes narrow. "What's she to you, Mace?"

"She's the wife of an old friend." I don't even have to think about my explanation. Little does he know it, but it was the truth that came from my lips. "That's all, Liz. She's not for me."

"Yeah." He stares off into the distance for a moment. "Noticed she still wears her ring. Faithful to a man who's gone."

"She is," I confirm.

"He die in service?"

I might be happy stretching the truth, but I can't outright lie to my brother. Seeing Pyro, I avoid answering, calling out instead, "Wait up a minute, Ro!"

The man I've called, turns. I pat Liz's shoulder then leave him and join the man who, today, is not only my MC brother but my boss, the auto-shop manager.

"What's up, Brother?"

"That girl we spoke about in church. The bitch with the property tat. Vi's starting work on her today."

"You need to be there?"

Again, I can't tell an untruth. "Not really, but if you can spare me…"

Pyro taps his fingers together, his brow creasing. "Ink and the others will probably be enough for today. And put it this way, Mace, if this is going to cause trouble for us, Demon would have my hide if I could have done anything to prevent it. Yeah, you go talk to the bitch. You never know, your newly discovered charm might get more out of her than even Vi."

He laughs at the scowl on my face. Second person today to mention the word charm in connection with me. Not a good rep for an enforcer.

"Hey, Ro?" I shout to his back. When he pauses his pace, I make an exaggerated pout and follow it up with, "I'll show you my fuckin' charms later." When he laughs loudly and resumes walking to the door, I show my middle finger even though he can't see it. Shame that fuckin' gym's not up and running yet. I could demonstrate my charisma in the ring, starting with rear-ranging the face of any fucker who thinks I've become charming.

I stomp off toward the kitchen, my annoyance fading when I see Mel unpacking tubs of what I know will be confectionary perfection, she's clearly just brought in. First, I turn and look behind me.

"What's up?"

"Just saw Pyro walking off in the other direction."

Mel laughs. "He ate so much at home, I've sent him away. I threatened to make him get on the scales."

I love Mel for my brother. He's been so much happier and more settled since she's been in his life, as though he'd found a part of him that had been missing. Mind you, anyone would be lucky to have Mel for a wife. If I had someone who'd cook such delicacies for me, I'd never want to leave home. Just sit, eat, get fatter and fatter, until my time came, and they'd have to take apart the door to get me out of the house.

"Mace?" Mel's standing with her head to one side. "Are you okay?"

"I'm fine, darlin'. Just thinking about women who can cook, and where I might find one."

"Thought you weren't a one-woman man," she chides, opening a tub of cinnamon buns and waving them in front of my nose.

Taking one, I agree. "Perhaps one who can cook, one who can clean, one who can f—"

She places her fingers over my mouth. "Keep that thought to yourself, please." She rolls her eyes. "Hey, what's with your friend, Vanna? You really just 'friends'?" She puts the word in air quotes.

"Sure are," I confirm, the words slightly muffled, spoken as they are around crumbs.

"I noticed something odd about that son of hers."

"Yeah?" I take another bite.

"Is he related to Lizard by any chance? He looks like him."

Crumbs fly out of my mouth as I choke. *Fuck. Fuckity fuck.* When Mel finishes slapping my back, admonishing me for stuffing too much in my mouth, I respond as nonchalantly as I can, "Nah, must be coincidence," adding, "Poor fucker."

"Poor, why?"

I wink. "Well, if you think he looks anything like Liz's ugly mug."

She bats my arm.

"How's the pregnancy going?" I distract her with her favourite topic.

Like expectant moms do, my words cause her to hold her hands to her stomach, pulling her top tight over it to emphasise the still small, yet obvious, baby bump she has going on. "I felt her move last night."

"Really? You know it's a girl?"

"No. We decided we don't want to know. But this is so different to last time, I think it will be."

I think of starting a book, especially as it appears, I have inside knowledge. Out loud I reassure her, "Everything's different this time, Mel." I catch her eyes and hold them. "You've got a good fuckin' man by your side."

She doesn't have to say a word to let me know she's in total agreement.

In the end, I consume three cinnamon rolls and two muffins before getting on my bike. While the sugary taste has lifted my mood, Mel's words about Cas cause me to worry. Yeah, he very much resembles his dad. I wonder whether anyone else has noticed? Lizard hasn't, or, at least, he hasn't remarked on it.

CHAPTER TEN

Mace

When I arrive at the tattoo parlour, it's just before eleven. Vi and Liz are out of sight, presumably working with clients, and Jonah's manning the reception desk. He looks up and raises his chin as I enter, then addresses the woman who's sitting stiffly waiting on a chair.

"Violet will be with you soon. She's just running a couple of minutes late."

The woman is Shayla. I notice again what a pretty face she's got, won't be any hardship to keep her company for a few. I take a seat opposite, avoiding sitting next to her as I don't want to spook her. Sitting back though, when I stretch out my long legs, there's not much space and my feet touch hers. She jumps and quickly pulls back feet, which look half the size of mine, tucking them under her chair.

"Sorry." I resituate myself, bending one leg, and resting my other ankle on that knee.

"You're fine." Her voice is sweet, quiet and soft.

"Here for a tattoo?"

She seems surprised I've spoken again. She looks around, her gaze pointedly landing on the examples of tattoos done by the artists here, then a quick smile comes over her face. "Er, duh?"

I nod at a poster advertising piercings. "You could be here for that."

She shudders. "No way."

"Not even ears?" I turn my comment which could have been interpreted as lewd into something more innocent.

"Oh, I had those done years ago." She relaxes a little, as if she had indeed thought I was being suggestive.

"So where are you having it? Your tat."

Her mouth presses together. Then, she turns the tables. "What about you?" She gestures toward my arms already covered in colourful depictions of almost every design you can think of. "I can't believe you have any more space."

I place my hand over my heart. "I've got room here."

"A woman's name?" she takes a stab.

"Nah. Not found my one yet." I don't add, I'm not looking.

"Right, I'll leave you with Jonah and he can settle you up. You've got your instructions about aftercare?" Vi's voice reaches us. She drops her client off at the reception desk, then turns to the woman I've been speaking to.

"Shayla. Good to see you again. Sorry I overran. You want to come on back?" As she steps aside, she glances down at me. "You okay, Mace?"

"Yeah," I tell her. "I'm waiting on Liz."

As the two women disappear, my eyes seem locked on Shayla's ass. Bit skinnier than I'd normally like, but hell, the way her hips sway when she walks goes straight to my cock.

I flick through a magazine, help myself to a coffee in the back, stand and stretch, then study some of the work Liz produces. Hell, no wonder this place is doing well, he's a fuckin' ace artist. As for Vi, seems she's just getting into her stride. Wouldn't surprise me if she turned out even better. Jonah's no slouch either. Hope Whale turns out as good.

"Hey Mace." Liz puts in an appearance, jerking his head toward the back. When I approach him, he turns and leads the way into his office.

"I spoke to Shayla for a couple of minutes."

"Yeah?" My statement has captured his interest. "What's your impression?"

I've been thinking about that. "Jumpy, nervous. Of course, she might not enjoy anticipating needles going into her back." The sound of Vi's tattoo gun whirring reaches us. "Couldn't tell much more than that." Of course, I hadn't been able to come straight out and ask her about the tattoo she didn't know I knew she had. "Seems quiet in here today?"

"It's Monday, Brother. Sometimes I wonder why we open at all. Don't get much walk-in business. The hairdressers next door is closed, so we get no business from that."

I nod. "How long is Vi going to be?"

"Depends on the tolerance of her client. She's booked her in for a four-hour stretch. Fancy a smoke?"

I do. In deference to the clients rather than any citizen law, we step out the back. The sun is shining as I take out my cigarettes and pass him one. I flick my lighter, then cupping my hand around it, hold the flame to his, then to mine. I breathe in smoke, feeling the nicotine soaking into my lungs. I know I should give up and have been cutting down, but hey, a man's allowed at least one vice. *Hmm. Got a few more than that.* Shit, riding my bike is dangerous for my health, but who the fuck cares? You only get one life, might as well enjoy it.

We stand and enjoy our cigarettes in a comfortable silence.

"Appreciate the company if I'm honest, Mace."

I raise my chin in answer. "Can you take off? If Shayla's going to be tied up with Vi for a spell, and this place is dead, we could go and get some lunch."

"Don't see why the fuck not." He brightens and stubs out his cigarette in the receptacle provided for that purpose. "Let me just check with Jonah. If there's been no sudden rush," his mouth twists showing he doesn't expect it, "want to go get tacos?"

"Yeah." I could definitely eat, my sugar-filled breakfast

already forgotten. I suspect Liz will suggest a food truck which has surprisingly good offerings.

Jonah's good, so we go get ourselves fed. When we return, Vi's at reception. She turns when we walk in.

"Shayla's gone, but she's coming back." Unusual for the prez's woman, she seems tense.

"You're doing more work today?"

Vi shakes her head at Liz. "No, but she's bringing a friend with her." She inclines her head toward the back and stands. Following, I once again find myself in Liz's office.

"So?" Liz queries as soon as the door is closed.

Vi looks at me, then her boss. "Her friend also has a tat she wants covered up."

"More business," Liz observes, while from the look on her face, I'm wondering whether there's more to it than something which, on the face of it, doesn't seem strange. We often get more clients from personal recommendations.

"She give you any info about this Major?" I throw in.

"No." Vi's lips press together. "She's not very chatty. I did try and probe a little, asking if a relationship had gone sour. From her reaction, it certainly had, but she didn't give me any details."

"Is that usual?" I ask. "Do people normally shoot the shit while you're working on them?"

Vi shrugs. "It depends. Some will hold a conversation to take their mind off what I'm doing, some get lost in the sensations. I'm sorry, but I really couldn't read much into it."

"What's your view of her, Vi?"

Another rise and dip of her shoulders, and that worried little frown appears again. "She's not from here, has recently moved to Pueblo, that much she did tell me. She found us online, came to us because of our reputation and good reviews."

"She know the shop's owned by the Satan's Devils?"

"I think so, yes."

A lot of nothing. Apart from some very acceptable tacos, on

the surface, a wasted day for me. But Vi does seem unusually agitated.

"What are you worried about?" I ask her directly.

She shrugs again. "I don't know, Mace. Something feels… wrong."

There's a knock and the door simultaneously opens to reveal Jonah. He jerks his head at Vi.

"Your client's back. She's got a friend with her."

"Why that face, Jo?" Liz queries, having picked up something's not right just as I have.

"If that girl's eighteen, I'll eat my fuckin' socks," Jonah tells us.

Lizard leans forward and starts banging his head on the desk.

"If she's got a parent's consent, she can get a tattoo done. No lower age limit in Colorado with permission," I remind Liz.

He points up to the list of the shop's rules on the wall. *No tattoos under the age of 18.* Yeah, we set our own requirements. I know Liz's reasoning, should someone point the finger at us, all those parental permissions are just one more set of paperwork he needs to have and keep straight.

"It's not a tat," says Vi. "It's a coverup."

It's a reminder that someone, somewhere, has already given an underage girl a tattoo. One she now regrets from the sounds of it.

"Boss." Jonah looks awkward. "What do you want me to do?"

Vi stands, using her hand to push herself up. "Let me handle this. I'll take her back to my station, have a look at what she wants done. Ask her, her age, then report back."

Unlike me, the prez's woman couldn't appear less threatening if she tried. Certainly, a good idea to let her handle this.

"Might just be a small heart with a boyfriend's name," I tell Liz. "If she's that young, maybe it wasn't even professionally done. If she can get the right paperwork, maybe we can make an exception this once."

"I don't like this Mace. I don't know what it is, but I've got a funny feeling about Shayla." He taps his nose. "There's a smell I don't like."

I know he doesn't mean he's taken exception to her perfume.

Lizard might have forgotten a lot of his time with the Marines, but he still retains his training to his core. I, too, am constantly on the outlook for trouble. You don't spend time in the sandbox without looking over your shoulder and being aware of the slightest thing out of place at any time.

He fidgets, I pace. I'm hoping my innocent suggestion was right and we're looking for problems where there are none. But when Vi returns, just one look at her face tells me I'm wrong to be optimistic.

Liz stands fast. "What is it?"

Vi looks stunned. "She's young. Fourteen, fifteen? Sixteen at a stretch. Shayla's trying to tell me she's an adult," she huffs. "No damn way."

"The tattoo?"

I know something's very wrong when Vi looks straight at me. She's gone pale. "It's exactly the same one as Shayla's." And in case we had any doubts, adds, "Same man."

Fuck. Two identical tats? Two women wearing the same property patch? That sounds more like a fucking brand.

"Okay," Liz starts, drawing out the word.

"It gets worse," interrupts Vi, her eyes filling with tears. "She's a nice girl. Pretty to look at. She's quick to smile. Easy to scare—I moved too fast and she jumped. She's also, she's… mentally impaired."

"Oh fuck no. We can't do it, Vi."

"Please Liz, please. Just talk to them. Please." Vi's close to begging. "There's something really wrong, and we can help sort it out."

"What's up, Liz?" Ignoring Vi for a moment, I focus on him. His firm refusal sounding alarm bells.

My brother meets my eyes. "It's against the law to ink anyone who's not all there."

"Since when do we care what's legal?" I scoff.

"Since we run a legit tattoo business. Since we've moved to a good part of town and attract a better clientele. Since we have 'nice' women coming in from the hairdressers next door. You think they're not suspicious enough when they see brothers around? They come because we're good at what we do. They come because they dared themselves to walk among men like us. They come because they'd delight in finding we don't walk the straight and narrow. One step out of line and we'd have the heat coming down before we could blink."

I'm not fazed. "So, we do it off hours. Let's at least talk to them."

At his reluctant nod, Vi turns. Moments later, she's encouraging Shayla and the girl into Liz's office. I've positioned myself just in front of the door so she doesn't notice me until I've shut it, and now stand with my back against it so she can't run.

Shayla's still talking to Vi. "I'm not sure this is necessary. I'm prepared to pay the full price for both. I don't need a discount, so I don't need to see your boss." She sounds nervous. When her wary glance around the room shows me in my stance by the door, she pales. "Look, we'll go somewhere else."

"Sit down," barks Liz.

CHAPTER ELEVEN

Lizard

I didn't mean to snap, just need to get this situation under some semblance of control. Jonah and Vi were right. This kid, now sitting in front of me, isn't even close to the age of consent.

I take a moment to steady my voice, needing first to stamp down the rage which had risen inside me. "Hey, honey, would you like some candy? I've got some in my desk outside we can get for you."

The girl puts her thumb in her mouth and nods shyly. Vi goes to the door, Mace steps aside to let her out, then retakes his sentry position.

"What's your name?"

The girl looks at the woman now seated beside her. The woman mouths something. The girl shakes her head. Then it's Shayla who provides the information I asked for when she says, "Esme."

"Esme," I say, keeping my tone as gentle as I can. "That's a nice name."

Vi had told me she was pretty. When she smiles, it could brighten a person's day. I'm not sure what it is, there's such a look of innocence and joy about her. My hands clench. Only one reason a man puts a property patch on a female, and it's not because she's his daughter.

I move my gaze onto Shayla. Without preamble, I get straight down to what I want to know. "Who's Major?"

A whimper draws my attention away.

"It's alright," Shayla reassures Esme, more confidently than I expected, as though she's being strong for the girl. "He's not here, okay?" Her face grows fierce. "I'm never going to let him hurt you again."

Just my enquiry has upset the kid. She's drawn up her legs so her heels rest on the chair, her arms are wrapped around her knees and her head is bent with her face hidden. At that moment, the door opens, and Vi walks back in. She sees Esme and glares in my direction, then spares another for Mace.

"Vi," I decide fast, "can you take Esme back to your station? Perhaps she'd like to help you draw something?"

Shayla looks my way, summing up the situation fast. "No, no talking." She starts to stand. "We'll be on our way. I'll pay you for what you've already done—"

"Sit," I tell her again, almost surprised when she does. "Sounds like you and the girl both need work completed. I suspect you came to us as you thought we wouldn't ask too many questions, and maybe you're right. We give a shit about what we do and running a good business, but we also give a shit about keeping women and kids safe. You're free to go, we ain't gonna stop you. Just think about this. Any tattoo artist prepared to work on her," I point to Esme, still rocking in her chair, "won't be worth shit. Anyone good enough will be too concerned about the authorities."

"But you aren't?"

"We are," Mace's voice booms. "But we can work in devious ways. Do this shit off-site or off hours if need be. You think you can find anyone else willing to do that?"

Shayla's voice shakes slightly, and her glances in our direction show she's clearly unnerved by being faced with two, let's admit it, overbearing men. But she stands her ground which makes her go up in my estimation. "I don't understand. Why is it such a problem?"

"Can't hide what she is," I say, bluntly.

I'll give her one thing, she cares for that kid. It's obvious as Shayla bristles. "She's—"

"A lovely girl," I put in fast, softening my voice again and making an upward curve of my lips. "Pretty as a picture," adding, "Ain't you, sweetheart?" when I see her peering at me through her fingers. "Bet you're pretty bright too. Just, you've got something different to bring to the table than most other people." I doubt she understands me, but her rocking ceases, and that smile reappears.

"They'll help, *we'll* help," Vi tells her. While Shayla doesn't know it, Vi means the club, not just the men but the old ladies too. "But to do that, they," she points first to Mace, then indicates me, "need to know your story, that of Esme too. I'll keep her amused so you can go into details, I guess you may not want her to hear."

"You're free to go, Shayla. We'll not keep Esme or you here if you'd prefer to leave, but I'll hazard a guess you've got yourself into something you need help getting out of. Something isn't right, that's fuckin' obvious." Mace's voice thunders out again, making Shayla jump and turn around. I indicate with my hand; he should calm his tone down. Shayla's like a cat on a hot tin roof, and she'll run if we don't keep things quiet.

He takes my cue, and offers more gently, "You don't know us, darlin', but we know the half of it now. We've seen the name..." He doesn't repeat it, knowing how it set Esme off before. "Now we know it, what happens if we start asking around?"

"You can't!" comes her horrified objection. "Please..." Shayla draws her hands down her face and looks at the girl by her side. When her eyes meet mine, there's defeat in them, but she nods. "Esme?" She waits for a moment until she gets the girl's attention. "Why don't you go with Violet? Violet draws pictures. You can show her what you can do if she has a pencil and paper you can use."

Esme looks around at Vi who's smiling and holding out her hand. "What do you like to draw, Esme?"

Esme checks in with Shayla and mouths something.

"Dogs. Cats. Any animal really," Shayla answers for her. It's clear she's making an effort to hide her fear from the girl. "Go on, Esme. Go show Vi what you can do."

"I like drawing animals as well," Vi tells her. "Shall we both draw unicorns?" Vi puts her arms up to her forehead. "They've got two horns, haven't they?"

Esme shakes her head violently, and holds up just one of her hands, with her forefinger pointed straight up.

Vi giggles. "I'm silly, aren't I? Unicorns only have one horn. I must be thinking of a cow."

Esme seems comfortable to go off with the woman who clearly wouldn't recognise a unicorn if she met one.

As soon as the door closes behind them, I ask, "Doesn't she speak?"

Shayla draws in a deep shuddering breath, then her eyes find mine. "I'm scared. Scared of talking to you, scared of not in case I'm turning help down. I'm scared to get up every morning, scared to breathe. I'm scared for Esme... Scared all the time."

Resting my hands on the desk, I try to gentle my features. "We can help you, Shayla. Or we'll give it a fuckin' good try. Reckon you need someone on your side."

Shayla looks like she's having an internal battle. Sitting back again, I fold my arms. The ball is in her court now. It's her decision whether to trust us or not. I see the moment her shoulders slump, as if the offer of having someone to share her burden is too much to turn down.

She speaks so quietly, I struggle to hear her. "Esme can talk, but she won't. Not now. When... when I first met her, she was chatty. Too talkative. Well, let's say she was told to shut up one too many times."

I hear Mace's growl. Then he finds his voice. "Who's this fuckin' Major?"

Shayla's eyes glisten.

Mace moves away from his place by the door and instead takes the chair Esme had vacated. "Darlin', I can think of only one reason why two women have the same 'Property of' tattoo, especially when one is a minor." I watch her face as he speaks and know we've got one part of our answer by her expression. He continues, "What we don't know is who this motherfucker is, and whether you're still in danger. So, here's one question for you. You come to the end of your journey, or are you still on the run?"

She seems relieved we've supplied our own answer. "We don't stay in one place long, if that's the answer you're looking for. I don't even know if he's still looking, but I can't risk him finding out where we are. The less anyone knows, the better for us."

Mace nods and looks thoughtful. "Satan's Devils understand property patches all too well. If one of our brothers finds a woman he intends to spend his life with, and she's of the same mind, she gets his tattoo. She's proud as fuck to wear it. You know why?" When Shayla looks incredulous and raises and lowers her shoulders quickly, he continues, "Because it shows he loves her and so much more. She's protected, not just by him, but all of his brothers. They'd die before anything happened to her. Anything happens to him? They'll be there for her. It's more than a wedding ring in our eyes, it's more of a commitment."

She stares at him for a moment, her eyes wide and disbelieving. "Does Violet have a property patch? She said she was married to your prez."

"She does," I reply. "She designed it, I did the ink."

She looks dumbfounded that anyone would wear such a tat voluntarily. "My experience of property patches is different."

I place my elbows on the desk, and my chin on my clasped hands. Watching her carefully, I tell her, "Vi loves her property patch as it shows she belongs to her man, and her man, as he wanted her to wear it, belongs to her. She's got a leather cut with the same words on it. So, any fucker can see who'll he'll have to take on if he lays so much as a hand on her. Now, if someone wanted to remove or cover her tattoo, Demon would shred him to pieces."

"Vi would probably help," Mace puts in, to lighten the mood.

I throw him a quick grin before continuing, "A property patch is important shit. That's not to say they're never covered or removed. Relationships break down in all walks of life. A man might die, his woman might move on. But if a man still regards a woman as his, then the removal of the tattoo is as fuckin' serious as a heart attack."

"Why are you telling me this?" She's gone tense. "Are you telling me you're not going to help after all? That if Major has marked me as his, you think I should return to him?" Her hand goes to her mouth. "Oh, my God. Are you going to send us back?"

"No, no," I say firmly and fast. "Mace told you what patches mean to us, as wanting someone to wear their name is a big deal and not done lightly. We view property one way, as something to be cherished, cared for and protected. Major obviously uses the word to show ownership. I will cover your tattoo, hide it completely, no ifs or buts about that, Shayla. But we do need to know who Major is. Helping you might bring trouble to our door, and we need to be prepared to face it."

Her shoulders slump. "I'm sorry, I didn't think about what it might mean for you. We'll go—"

"Hey, hold up." Mace waits for her eyes to come to his. "Trouble is what we live for, sweetheart. We just need to know who we're dealing with. You think you can get your tat covered," his hand waves toward the door through which Esme had disappeared, "hers too, then disappear into the night. What if Major finds you? Gets out of you where you had the work done? What if he's circulating your picture around and someone has seen you coming in and out of here? Lands us with a heap of problems, trouble, and we don't know where it's coming from. So one, we need information to work with and two, I want to help you. I've got a feeling all of the club will have your back when you finally tell us what's going on."

She stares intently at him, then turns those eyes with such hidden depths to me. She shudders, an action which shakes her whole body. Then slowly, she nods. "I worked on the outskirts of Vegas. I went into town to drop off some paperwork for my boss. I knew the accountant, and when he asked me out for a drink, I went. By the time I walked back to my car, it was dark—"

"He didn't escort you?" I butt in.

"No." She seems surprised. "It wasn't a relationship, just two colleagues socialising. I wouldn't have expected it." She shakes her head as if dismissing the very notion while I inwardly seethe. Doesn't matter if the woman means something or not, she shouldn't be walking the streets alone at night. A glance at Mace's tense face shows he's of the same opinion.

"Anyway," she continues, "it was dark. Suddenly arms were pulling me into an alley, then something was put over my nose and mouth... When I woke up..." her eyes close, and Mace reaches out his hand to take hers. When she startles and pulls hers away, he holds up both palms toward her in apology.

"Sorry."

"No, it's me, I..."

"Just tell us the rest." Her reaction needs no explanation.

"When I came to, that's when I met Major. He said I was now his to do with what he wanted. It was only the next day I was forced to have this tattoo. They restrained me, held me down, I couldn't move. Then, he and his men raped me."

She says it so coldly, so matter-of-factly. Rage boils inside as I crease shut my eyes, trying to avoid even thinking of the picture she's painting. I'd imagined the worst and I'd been right to do so.

"Fuckin' hell." Mace's hands are clenched as though ready to beat someone to a pulp. I watch him fight to hold himself together, eventually doing so enough to spit out, "He's a pimp, and you were an unwilling part of his stable." His tone is chilling, letting me know if he ever comes face-to-face with the man, Major will be in a world of pain he would be unable to imagine. I'll be right there behind him.

Shayla sobs. "I didn't make it easy for him. I fought, I was punished. I tried to escape, no chance, I was brought back. I kicked men in the balls, they retaliated." She shakes her head and winces. "They used tasers so my skin wouldn't be marked." Her flat tone of voice as she pronounces her final words make goosebumps break out on my skin. "He broke me."

Mace is likewise affected. Standing and turning, he bangs his fist against the wall. "Motherfucker," he snarls.

Now she's started, Shayla's going to complete her story. "Once I was totally compliant, he put me to work. He's a pimp, yes. A high-end one. He'd dress me up pretty, send me out with some of his men to pre-arranged appointments. Sometimes alone, sometimes with another woman. We had to do whatever his clients wanted. I was his property, as he told me time after time. I belonged to him, and being marked as I am, I could never escape him. I'm surprised he didn't add his phone number and a 'if found please return to' address on the tattoo. Of course, I didn't suggest that to him."

"I can fuckin' understand why you want that tat gone," Mace turns and states, his face taut with rage.

"All his girls were tattooed?" It's an obvious statement though I'd intoned it as a query.

She nods. "Yes. To show we belonged to him."

"Was Esme already there?" I'm barely holding on to my rage at the thought that sweet girl had been through the same things as Shayla.

Her face twists. "No. She came later. I begged him to let her go. I said she was special, he called her stupid. She cried and cried because of the pain of the tattoo but didn't understand what he'd done. She didn't realise why all the men would tell her, *you're Major's*, but they just continued until she believed it. It broke my heart when she told me she was his. *I'm Major's,* she'd say. And then, when she wouldn't stop talking, she was tasered. Again and again." She looks up and her eyes meet mine. "I begged him to let me take her punishment for her." Again, that full body shudder as if remembering the prongs hitting her. "He took me up on the offer, but that meant if she spoke, we were both tasered... She does talk a little, but only to me, and only when no one's there." She looks up and meets my eyes. "He said it didn't matter she had nothing between her ears, his clients would only care what was between her legs."

Mace kicks the chair he'd recently been sitting in. "He's fuckin' dead. But he's not going to go easy. I'll kill him, revive him, and kill him all over again. He'll beg to die before I'm finished."

I let my eyes fall on Shayla. Mace is so angry, his rage coming off him in palpable waves. I'm concerned how she'll be taking it and expect to see her cringing in her seat. But she's not. She's staring at him wide-eyed in wonder, as if he's some kind of hero, truly comprehending for the first time that he and I are nothing like Major.

Although my wants and desires are the same as my brother's, I'm trying to keep calm so as not to frighten her. I get her attention back to me. "How did you escape, Shayla? From what you said, it sounds impossible. So how did you get free?"

Slowly she blinks, as if having difficulty switching between Mace's fury and my patient questioning. She provides her answer. "Esme was special. She was so clearly innocent. Major was waiting for the right time, the right man. I suspect he knew he'd get good money offering up her virginity. I hoped he'd never find someone so twisted..." Her face fills with pain.

"They'd broken me. I'd given up searching for a way out. I'd become this obedient slave that did whatever I was asked to do. My life was over. I didn't have the energy to try to escape anymore. I knew one day, one of the men I was given to was going to kill me, but even that was okay, and I hoped it would come sooner rather than later. Then Esme came along." Her eyes flare as her mind takes her back in time. "I knew I had to try to get her out, even if it meant sacrificing myself. I couldn't see how, but I was determined to do it. But no opportunity presented itself. I'd left it too late. He'd found a man who wanted her."

"Did he have her?" Mace sounds like he's hanging on by a thread.

"No." A small smile crosses her face. "Major thought he had me in the palm of his hand by then, and Esme would do anything I told her. So he paired me up with her, explaining that I go with her. I think he thought I'd tell her to do whatever the man asked. He didn't regard me as a flight risk, or not so much as he'd done earlier. There were two of his men with us, but they didn't come into the bathroom I'd told them we had to use. Oh, they'd checked it and thought the window was too small, too high to get out of." Her face twists, half in triumph, half in something remembered that wasn't so pleasant. "Desperation makes us do anything, doesn't it? A busted leg had to be better than what was planned for us, *for her*. I went first, landed winded but not broken. Major was right. She did whatever I told her. She jumped too. Landed on me, but she was unharmed. We ran." Another twist to her face. "Well, she did, I hobbled."

I exchange a look with Mace. Fuck, but they were lucky. I'm relieved Esme had been saved from the worst, but gutted what happened to Shayla, and more than a little impressed at the fortitude she'd shown.

"They must have searched for you," Mace rasps. "How the fuck did you keep out of their clutches?"

"We hid, in a dumpster, both of us clinging to the other. Esme knew, somehow she knew to keep quiet and still. We stayed there for two days. There were rats, food rotting around us. But still, she stayed mute, clinging to me, knowing enough that she shouldn't move or give us away. Not even when a drunk pissed on us."

Mace is pacing, when he reaches each wall, again he bangs his fist against it.

"When I thought it was safe, we emerged. My posh dress was discoloured and torn, Esme's hair ratted and her clothes unrecognisable. Under cover of darkness, I moved us to the worst part of town. We were so disgusting, even the dropouts avoided us. We lived rough. I pretended Esme was my daughter. I managed to scavenge food and scrounge some clothing from a charity store. Cleaned us up and knew we had to put distance between us and Vegas. So we hitchhiked. Got dropped at a truck stop, and I... I did what I had to do to get us a long-distance ride out of Nevada. We stopped off in one place then another and eventually ended up in Colorado."

"You still living rough?" She doesn't look like it, but then, she's resourceful.

She shakes her head. "No, I managed to get a job waiting tables, enough to get a dump of a one-room studio, but it works. All I wanted was to save up enough to get rid of this tattoo, firstly because with it, there's always a chance the wrong person might see it. Secondly," she looks up and meets my eyes, "I won't ever belong to a man again. I'll never be property. Ever."

"You safe?" Mace suddenly swings around.

I wouldn't need to be a mind reader to know what he's thinking as his thoughts are probably along the same lines as mine.

Her quick look down gives us the answer neither of us like, but then she straightens her back. "The diner's not too bad. Andy, the owner, keeps a shotgun under the bar. The apartment is cheap, and not in the best part of town, but it's better than living rough."

Her eyes that I thought were so haunted now also seem tired.

Mace looks like a taut elastic band to me, as if he's going to snap any moment. I can read the signs, so I'm not surprised when he mumbles something about needing to be somewhere, then opens the door and walks out.

CHAPTER TWELVE

Mace

I left Shayla with Liz for two reasons, the main one being I couldn't stand to be in that room anymore. What I'd heard about her was enough by itself, add a cute kid like Esme into the mix and it becomes so much worse.

I don't know who this Major is, have never heard of him before. That's what had gotten me so uptight, that I couldn't jump on my bike and go deal with him myself. I've an enemy to fight, and I've no idea who he is or where he's to be found.

It angers me that there are men of his ilk who think they can steal women and own them. I'm not naïve. I know it goes on all the time, but to come face-to-face with someone pulled off the street just because they've a pretty face and a body that men would like to fuck is abhorrent to me.

I'm also annoyed at myself. While I can't put myself in the mindset of a man who'd fuck a kid like Esme, what was it I thought when I saw Shayla for the first time? That I wanted to sink my dick into her. After hearing her story, I hated that I, too, had seen her not as a person but as a body. The only difference between me and Major is that I like my women willing.

It's pulled me up and made me think twice. Most women to

me mean little more than having tits and asses which turn me on, exactly what I'd thought when I first saw Shayla.

Shayla's story had gotten to me. Sure, she had the assets which made my cock stand to attention, but as I listened, it wasn't her physical attributes that had me listening to her. It was her bravery, her loyalty. She had stood up for that girl, offered to take her fucking punishment, and risked everything to save her from the future Major had planned for her. She'd done what she had to, to keep them both safe. Her resilience in simply surviving was admirable.

I've never thought of giving a woman my property patch, but I live with men who have. It's in our bylaws that we mark our women, but I've never seen anything wrong in that. To us, our property is something to treasure, to love and protect. Any of my brothers would be fooling themselves if they thought ownership worked one way. I'd often joked, the old ladies had their men by their balls, but it's true, when brothers fall, they go down hard. If anything happened to the woman who wore their patch, they'd be devastated. We all know Heart's story, the man in the Tucson club whose old lady was murdered. He very near followed her into the grave, such was his desolation at her loss.

Some clubs might treat property differently, but not us. Some clubs pass their women around, but again, not us. For a pimp to kidnap and hold women against their will, that thought fills me with disgust.

I pause for a moment outside Vi's station. What fucked up kind of man would take a girl like Esme? Who the fuck would destroy that kid's trust, seeing her not as a sweet child, but as an opportunity to make money? It's way beyond my imagination, which brings my thoughts back to Shayla. She's fully grown, but just thinking about what she's been through makes me feel physically sick. I may torture the sweet butts, but only sensually, never, ever, would I use a woman who didn't want it, or said no to anything I proposed and meant it.

Hitting the heel of my hand against my forehead, I realise it's only my refusal to force myself on an unwilling woman that separates me from Major or his clients.

Shayla's reactions, her nervousness around me and Liz, showed how greatly she'd been damaged. I've no idea what she was before, but suspect she knew of the darker side of life only from stories in the newspaper, never expecting to be living it herself. Men were viewed as potential boyfriends, maybe future husbands. Now she knows intimately that there are men who take without giving, who hurt, just because their innate strength means that they can. She was denigrated as something less than human, her own thoughts and feelings meaning nothing at all.

How does someone come back from that? How can Shayla live with what she was forced to do? *She gave up.* But wouldn't we all, if every escape attempt failed and was followed by punishment? When it mattered, she proved she's a special and resourceful woman. She got away and took Esme with her.

Is she really safe now? Or is Major still trying to find her? Property. For the first time ever, I think of that word with distaste, the meaning of her property patch one hundred and eighty degrees away from what we believe it stands for.

I want to find Major, kill him, and make sure she's out of his clutches forever. It's become my nightmare, as well as hers, to think he might ever take her back.

"Mace?" Vi's standing at the doorway that leads to her station. She jerks her head, inviting me in. It sounds like it hasn't been the first time she's called me.

"Yeah?" I cough and try again when only a strangled word comes out. "Yeah?"

"Are you alright?" The prez's wife steps forward and looks up at me, her eyes dark and concerned.

I shake my head. "Their story, Vi. It's bad."

"Kind of guessed that from the tat they're both wearing." She would. She's seen the dark side of men herself. "Will you come here a moment, Mace?"

I don't know why she wants me, but not many people refuse

Violet anything. I follow her back to her station. She stops by Esme whose head is bent over a piece of paper.

"Esme, will you show Mace your drawing?"

I hate that the girl shrinks into herself when she sees me hovering. Fucking hate it. I stay quiet, knowing I should leave Vi to do the talking. Esme's learned men can and will hurt her. She needs to be treated like a piece of fragile glass.

"Go on," Vi encourages. "I know he'll like it a lot."

Composing my features into the complete opposite of my normal enforcer's snarl, I take a slow step closer, as though approaching a wild animal, not wanting to make any sudden moves to spook the nervous girl. I prepare myself with platitudes and false praise for when I see what she's produced.

Esme looks at Vi, Vi gives her an encouraging nod. Then shyly, she pushes a piece of paper across, withdrawing her hand fast to avoid any touch between hers and mine.

I pick it up and study it. Then look twice. Raising my eyes, my brow furrows and I toss Vi a questioning look. Vi must have outlined it, and Esme coloured in between the lines.

Vi interprets what I'm asking, and answers before I use words. "All her work," she confirms with a smile full of respect and pride targeted toward the young girl.

Wow, just wow. This kid has some talent. It's a perfect unicorn. Vi couldn't have drawn one better herself.

"Esme, you are one talented young lady." I'm still staring at the paper in my hand. "This is amazing, sweetheart." My reaction is totally genuine, and something of that conveys itself to the girl who gives me a tentative smile. I go to give her the picture back, but she shakes her head.

She mouths something, I can't translate it. But then she gestures with her hand.

"For me?" I check to make certain.

Her energetic nod says yes.

I have two emotions. Pleasure that she's sharing something with me, and a doubling of hatred for the man who took away her voice. Every protective instinct rises inside me. Immediately, I know I'll do everything in my power, so nothing ever hurts her again.

"Thank you, sweetheart, I'll treasure it. Tell you what, I'll get a frame and hang it in my room."

She understands me. Her face flushes red, and that quick sunny smile comes to her face. I know right there and then, I'd do anything to make that permanent.

"I'm going to ring your old man," I tell Vi, tightly, not looking forward to the conversation I need to have. Then I address the girl who I'd love to reward for my gift with a hug, but refrain, knowing I'll scare her. "I'll see you soon, okay?"

I step out, walk through the reception area, slipping my already treasured drawing into the desk drawer as I pass. I proceed out front, then around to the alley at the side, and then act on the second reason I'd left Liz and Shayla in his office. I take two objects out of my cut. I light a cigarette first, fuck, I badly need one, then I call up the first pre-set number on my phone.

"Prez, we've got a fuckin' problem."

"I suspect I know what you're going to tell me. Cad's just found some info. Major isn't a biker. He's a fuckin' high-class pimp out of Vegas."

I'm not surprised the tech guy found out. He always gets there eventually.

"I've got Red's guys looking into him," Demon continues, his voice booming down the phone. I turn down the volume a little. What he's told me is good news. Red's the prez of the Satan's Devils' chapter in Sin City. Hopefully he'll find Major and it won't be too long before I can get my hands on him.

"Shayla brought a friend to also have a tattoo covered." I fill him in on what he doesn't know. Proud that I'm keeping myself more or less under control. "She's fuckin' underage and has some kind of mental problem. She's got the same tat as Shayla. He fuckin' marked a kid as his property, Prez." I slam my fist holding the cigarette against the wall, making ash drop off. *Okay, not so much under control.* I draw in a deep breath before continuing, "He intended to pimp out a mentally retarded girl," I stress, so there can be no misunderstanding. "Just fuckin' lucky Shayla got her out before he found someone to pay a high enough price."

I hear Prez's sharp intake of breath. "How old is she?"

"My guess is fifteen or so, could be a little older I guess."

"They living safe? Well enough hidden if Major's looking for them?"

"They're living cheap, so no would be my summation. Shayla's been scrimping to get enough money to cover their tats." That's not hard to understand. With that on their backs, it's a direct link back to the man who believes he owns them.

"No charge for them," Demon shoots back quickly. "Liz comfortable doing the work on the girl?"

"I think so." I haven't had a definitive answer from him as yet. "But if he does, we'll need to keep it quiet, Prez."

"I hear you, Mace. Need to keep our public face clean."

"Prez." I try to find the words to formulate the suggestion that's been growing in my mind. "I don't know the risk she's in, but I suspect Major may well want to reclaim his property. She doesn't think she's run far enough, and my gut feel tells me she's right. Until we know more about this motherfucker ourselves, I think we should treat them as being in danger."

"Fuck." Demon goes quiet while he thinks. "You're suggesting we bring them here to the compound, aren't you? What the hell has happened to my enforcer, Mace? I expected you to fuck it up with Vanna and the kid, yet you didn't. Now you're falling for a sob story from a couple of strays."

His tone is gently mocking, and I don't take offence. In some ways, his chiding is helping me get my head back into the game, to lock down my rage and turn it into something worthwhile, such as dealing with the situation we've been handed. "It is what it is, Prez. How these girls have been treated goes against everything we stand for. I haven't spoken to Liz, but I'm pretty sure he'll be feeling the same. And then there's Vi. She's been looking after the younger one, taken a shine to her if I'm not wrong."

"Christ. If my ol' lady's gonna be on my back, I'll have no fuckin' chance. Okay, bring them in. Luckily, we've still got Skull's room vacant. They can squat in there until we work out what to do. I'll call everyone in later. You know what they're like. Nosy fuckers won't want to be kept out of the loop."

"One problem, Prez. Esme's terrified of men for good reason, and Shayla's jumpy as fuck herself."

"Make my life easy, why don't you?" He's quiet for a moment. "You sure here's the right place?"

"No," I reply, honestly. "But I think we'll have to try to make it work. Unless you can think of anything else?"

Demon's quiet for a couple of moments. "Wish I could, but I can't. Brothers will just have to wear kid gloves around them. Maybe show this Esme that there are men who can be trusted."

My bet is that Shayla will need to relearn that as well after her time in Major's hands.

When I return inside, Vi and Esme are no longer at her station. I head on back and find the four of them in Lizard's office, open soda cans in front of them, and more candy has magically appeared. Leaning over, careful not to touch her, I swipe a bar that's in front of Esme.

I'm rewarded with a glare, followed by a frightened look. But that fades at my wink, and she gives a tentative grin.

"Thieving asshole," Liz rebukes me.

"Language," I tell him. Having spent the weekend with Cas and Vanna, an idea comes into my head. I turn my eyes on the girl. "Liz said a rude word. I think he owes us a dollar, don't you, Esme?"

I'm not sure of her level of comprehension, but she seems to understand at least that. Lizard's forehead creases, then he gives me a chin lift, takes out his wallet and passes over a bill. Esme stares at it.

I chuckle and instruct, "Take it. It's yours."

She glances at Shayla who gives her a nod, while shooting me a curious glance. Suddenly, I realise all the brothers are going to hate me for starting this up. But hey, if Esme gets the confidence to start demanding payment when they swear, maybe it will do her some good.

"You spoke to Prez?"

I nod, then turn to Shayla. "We've told you we're about respect, family and keeping women safe. The club would like you to come to stay with us on the compound while we work out what danger you're still in from Major."

Her eyes widen in horror. "Stay with you? With bikers? No, we couldn't do that." She looks between me and Liz, blood draining from her face. "Come on, Esme, time to—"

It's Vi who steps in and interrupts. "Hold up a minute, Shayla. The compound is secure and can be protected, far safer than being out on the streets. My man is the prez, and what he says goes and," she leans in conspiratorially as if Liz and I can't hear her, "in turn, he'll do anything I say." I smirk at her suggestion, but there's probably some truth there. Especially if she uses sex as a weapon. "No one will touch you or harm you, I can promise you that. Once Devils extend their protection, well, you can be assured you'll be safe. The last place Major will expect to find you is living with us."

Shayla studies her, as if estimating how sincere she is.

Seeing an in, Vi enlightens her, "I've got an eighteen-month-old boy, the bikers all love him. It's not all men either, there are other old lady's too. Jayden is a nursery nurse, she loves kids, and I bet she'll take to Esme. Steph is our VP's woman, she's blind and is amazing with it. She's got a lovely guide dog. Beth, well she's a giant who's with Ink, and then there's Mel. She's pregnant and we're all treating her so damn carefully as she miscarried last time she was expecting. She bakes, and oh, the cakes she makes. They are to die for."

I find myself licking my lips at the reminder. "Don't forget Jeannie, she's been around the club for getting on forty years. And Mo, the ex-prez's old lady. And Sindy who's... with Buzzard." I nearly said *who's Buzzard's*, but at the last moment remembered to change the wording she probably would object to.

Shayla's not at all certain. Her face tightens. "What will the men expect for payment?"

"Nothing," I say fast, wondering if I should explain why. She's going to find out pretty soon if she comes back with us, so might as well get this out in the open now. "We're not in need of unwilling women, Shayla. Got girls of our own who live at the club and cater to our needs. Oh, no." I hold up my hand to stop her at that twist of distaste. "They're there for mutual satisfaction, stay because their needs align with ours. They choose to be with us, can leave at any time, but bikers hold a certain attraction for them."

"Whores?" she says with not a little concern.

I shrug. It is what it is.

Vi's lips press together. "Can't say I'm enamoured of them, Shayla, but the thing is as Mace has said, they *want* to be there. In your position, I wouldn't understand it either, but they enjoy the... loving they get." She too tempers her words in front of Esme. "The fact is, no one needs to pressure you because they've already got willing girls."

Shayla still seems unconvinced. It's Lizard who comes up with a suggestion. "Why don't you come back with us, see what you'd be getting into? I swear on the lives of my brothers that you will be free to leave at any time. Not swapping one captor for another, Shayla. I fuckin' assure you of that." Proving he learns quickly, a dollar passes from his hands to Esme's before I can prompt him.

Seeing Shayla's wavering, I add one final word on the matter.

"We don't know who Major is and whether you're with us or not, we won't stop digging. The info we find, you'll want to hear first-hand. Maybe you're right to keep running, maybe Major stays in his own turf and has given up looking for you. Whichever it is, I swear to you we'll find the answer."

Shayla looks at him, at Vi, then finally those haunted eyes land on me. She nods toward the money that Esme is holding. "You're about as far from Major as anyone can be. I think I trust you, Mace, and you, Lizard, too. But it's hard to believe there are more like you. If you give me your word we won't be held against our will, we'll come back with you and see if we'll fit."

Leaning down, I untie the sheaf on my ankle, take out the knife, and press it into her hand. "Keep this on you, darlin'. You won't have to use it, I promise. But you're not unarmed or helpless."

I've surprised her. Taking advantage of her capitulation, I waste no time, summoning Dirt with the truck and texting a few extra instructions.

Half an hour later when we've drunk our sodas, demolished the candy, and Liz and Shayla have admired Esme's drawing she'd done, which I'd retrieved from the drawer and brought back to show them. Suddenly, there's a knock on the door. Dirt walks in, accompanied by a three-legged Chesapeake Bay Retriever.

Esme's eyes go large and she can't seem able to focus anywhere else. Bagel, apparently named because of the light chestnut brown colour of his wavy coat, seems likewise to be drawn to her. With a tail that's wagging furiously, he limps his way over and plonks his head in her lap.

And fuck me, she giggles. It's the first actual sound I've heard from her.

"You sure about this, Mace?" Dirt sounds anxious.

"Yeah, Prez has already said you could bring him around. I'll let Beef know so he can manage Max." Max, Steph's guide dog, has been known to object to canine interlopers in the clubhouse, but on that occasion, it was a sniffer dog accompanying cops who were ripping the clubhouse apart. I suspect he'd picked up a vibe from us.

Dirt and Nails were both injured when their Army jeep hit an IED. Bagel had been in the truck with them, and only the three survived. They'd formed a strong bond between them. I knew Dirt was worried about bringing his dog to the club, but I thought as Esme enjoyed drawing animals, it was a fair bet she liked them, and having one with her when she entered a strange place full of men might ease her mind.

Dirt holds out the looped end of the leash. "Want to hold on to him, sweetie?"

Esme's wide eyes suggest she very well might. Being a well-trained ex-Army dog, I suspect he doesn't need much controlling.

CHAPTER THIRTEEN

Lizard

I'm not sure whether my brother might have grown a vagina. Just this weekend he was being supportive to a kid and his mom that he said he was no more than friends with, and today he's taken Shayla and Esme under his wing. I'll give credit where credit's due though, getting Dirt to bring his three-legged dog was a stroke of genius. The girl had seemed entranced from the moment she'd met him.

On our bikes, Mace and I arrive back at the compound shortly before Dirt, following more slowly in the truck. We find Prez has already summoned the brothers in, most of whom were already in church awaiting our arrival. When I see Prez hovering in the clubroom, I suspect he's got the rest out of the way, so Shayla and Esme aren't overwhelmed at the start.

"They're coming then?"

At his question, I cup my hand to my ear, hearing a sound of an engine and then it cutting out. "That's them pulling up now."

The three of us turn to look expectantly at the entrance. Dirt opens the door, then steps aside so Shayla can enter. She looks nervous, even scared, but Vi is right beside her, an encouraging touch on her arm. Bagel, seeing Nails coming out from behind the bar, steps forward, bringing Esme along with him at the other end of his leash.

Prez waits where he is, allowing Shayla to come inside at her own speed.

"This is it." Vi flourishes her arms around her. "It might not be much, but it's home."

Shayla turns to her. "The gates shut behind us." She sounds almost accusing.

"Gates keep people out as well as people in," Demon's voice booms. "You are welcome to stay here as long as you need to, or free to leave at any time." He steps forward, but before he closes the gap between him and the newcomers, he pulls Vi into his arms, lowering his head and taking her lips, as one hand moves protectively over her belly making me wonder whether they've got news they haven't yet shared. "You okay?" he asks, quietly, when he ends their demonstrative kiss.

"I'm good," she replies. Then turns to the females behind her. "Ladies," she includes Esme in her description, "this is my husband, Demon. He's the prez of the Satan's Devils."

I notice Shayla relaxes slightly at Demon's evident care for the woman at his side, an almost envious look crossing her face as she bears witness to their obvious love for each other. More tension fades when a shrill voice screeches, "Mommy!" and little Theo comes into sight, barrelling toward Vi.

Intercepting him, Demon swings him up into his arms and the big stern MC prez tickles his son, making him scream and laugh. When he wriggles, he puts him down.

"Max! Max!" an annoyed female voice sounds.

I swing to see Max galloping across the clubroom, screeching to a halt just in front of the strange dog.

"Max!" Steph shouts again, but for once, her dog ignores her.

"I'm sorry." Nails moves up beside her.

"My fault," calls Mace. "I told them they could bring Bagel here. To help settle Esme."

"Bagel? Esme?" Steph sounds completely confused.

"Long story," says Vi. "But Max and Bagel seem to be getting along."

Well, I suppose if dogs mutually sniffing rear ends while moving around in a circle is anything to go by, they are. At least no hackles are raised and there's no growling.

Vi walks over to Steph and takes her arm, then glances back to Shayla and Esme, the latter seeming entranced by the two dogs who seem fast on the way to becoming friends. "Come with us. The women will be in the kitchen. It's our own private space." Once the two start to follow her, I hear her grumble, "I keep on at D to build us a proper place out back, a living room, TV area just for ourselves but their gym takes precedence for now. But he'll get around to it one day." Her voice fades as she reaches her destination.

"Will he?" Mace asks, a smirk on his face as he regards Prez.

"Probably," Demon responds, fondly looking in the direction his woman disappeared in and gives a resigned shake of his head. "Come on. Everyone's waiting."

The conversation dies down quickly as we enter our meeting room, brothers all dying from curiosity, wanting to know why we've yet more strangers on the compound, female ones at that.

Thunder looks across the table at Mace. "You got a new habit of picking up strays?"

"First one wasn't interested, Brother. See how soon he's moved on to the next?" Pyro thinks he's a barrel of laughs.

"Alright, zip it." Demon bangs the gavel. "Who's going to start? Liz or Mace."

Pressing my fingers to my forehead, I let Mace carry on. I've got another of my fuckin' tension headaches that's starting to build. Knowing the punchline, I concentrate on fighting back the pain, content to let him bring everyone up to speed.

"Liz?"

When I look up, it seems like it's not the first time someone's been trying to get my attention.

"Headache?" asks Mace, his voice carrying both concern and sympathy.

"Here." Paladin shoots a packet of Advil down the table. Gratefully, I swallow a couple dry.

"What d'you need?" I say at last, hoping the tablets work quickly.

"We were talking about Esme's tat, whether at her age, it's better to get laser treatment to remove it." Prez's words are spoken tightly, and I glance around, noting all my brothers' faces look thunderous. Though I'd zoned out of the discussion, I take it they're as fucking upset by the situation as I am.

When I place my head into my hands this time, it's not just to ease the ache, it's because I'm thinking. Finally, I respond. "That shit will take multiple treatments, and the tats coloured as fuck. The writing is black, so they'll be able to get rid of that, but the likelihood is they'll only be able to fade the rest, and something of it will remain. It's best done by a professional, someone who knows what they're doing. Removal is not without pain and can easily get infected. I don't know if she'd be able to look after it well enough, even with Shayla's help." My hands clench as I think of the bastard who's the reason we're discussing removing a tat from an underaged and mentally challenged girl. "I'd prefer to cover it."

"I wonder where she's from?" asks Pal. "Surely, a kid like that would be missed? It's not as if she's an unruly teenager likely to run off." He pauses. "Unless she was already being treated like shit."

Cad nods. "I've been thinking that myself. You're right, Pal. It seems unusual for a girl like that to just be walking the streets and be picked up. The woman got any idea how they took her?"

Mace answers, "She didn't say. Esme just appeared one day. I don't know if she was able to tell her. Right now, she's not talking, so it's hard to know what her level of comprehension is."

Cad nods at him. "I can discreetly start looking to see if

anyone's asking questions. If she's got a loving family, she might be missed. Even a care home would be looking for her."

"She might have shit parents who sold her for cash because they couldn't be bothered to fuckin' look after her."

"Don't have much faith in the human race, do you, Rusty?"

"Seen too fuckin' much, Brother," the older ginger-haired biker responds to Judge. "She could have been with foster parents who found her too challenging."

"Do you think Shayla will take responsibility for her, long-term?" Prez asks Mace, then includes me.

"Don't know much about either of them," I reply. "Just know I don't want Major to get his hands back on them. He needs to be removed before they can think about a future."

Beef says determinedly, "Only thing that man's getting his hands on is a fuckload of pain and six feet of earth over the top of him."

Growls, stomps of feet, and fists bumping on tables shows he's just voicing what we all think.

Prez taps his fingers together, then gives us his thoughts. "Shayla looked nervous as hell when she came in. You're the kid and woman whisperer, Mace." He looks at the enforcer with a smirk. "Got any hints for how we should help them settle in?"

Mace rolls his eyes but sits forward looking serious. "I think her first thought was we might want to use her for ourselves." He waves his hand in a downward motion. "Simmer down, told her that wasn't the way of it, but she's not going to trust easily. Not just her, the kid doesn't want to talk in case she gets fuckin' tasered or hit. Keep your distance, don't touch, don't crowd, and no mention that she's got boobs or an ass, or not in her hearing."

"Has she?" asks Sparky.

"She's a bitch, what do you think?" Hell bats him around the head.

"I fuckin' know that," Sparky defends himself. "But are they nice?"

Mace groans. "That's precisely what I'm saying. That's not

the way you should be thinking of her. Look, treat her as you would your sister. She's out-of-bounds. And before you say you haven't got one, Sparks, I fuckin' know you have."

"Sure wouldn't want to fuck *her*." Sparky puts his fingers in his mouth and pretends to retch.

Mace glares at him which shuts him up. "As far as Esme goes, she's got this amazing talent. She can draw, really well. I think we ought to encourage that. Praise her, hang her fuckin' pictures up. Show she's worth more than what she was sold to provide. And," he narrows his eyes again, this time his fierce expression includes all of us, "she's a kid, so if you swear in front of her, cough up."

"What?" Various people ask in various tones of astonishment.

"She's already had me for five dollars," I admit. "But Mace has got a good point. Men have been abusing her, not treating her as human. If you do swear, apologise and pay up. Putting a bit of dough in her pockets will make her feel valued."

"A bit of dough? She'll fuckin' bankrupt us," Bomber groans.

"Won't do any harm to start watching your language when she's about," Prez remarks. "Theo's starting to talk now, Mel's expecting. Can't reprimand kids if their role models use foul language."

Bomber gasps. "We've got to pay them all? Christ, Prez, you'll need to increase our wages."

"Kids will end up richer than us," Wills mumbles.

"Too fuckin' right," moans Rusty, to my mind sort of proving the point.

On that note, we break up.

"You okay, Brother? How's the head?" Mace sounds and looks worried as he waits for me to leave the meeting room.

"Not good," I reply honestly, touching my hand to my brow. "Think I'm going to lie down for a bit."

"You made that appointment to have your eyes checked?"

"Yeah. Going on Wednesday," I admit.

I never expected to end up wearing glasses, not until I was middle-aged, and I don't feel I'm close to that. Isn't that like when you're fifty? But it's probably down to the work that I do, always concentrating. Two things my job needs are a good eye and a steady hand. He pats my shoulder as I walk off toward the stairs.

After a couple of hours lying down in a darkened room, my head feels a lot easier. The rumbling of my stomach reminds me I've not eaten since the tacos I had with Mace at lunchtime. As I open my door, I find Steph leading a procession to the room next to mine. The one that used to belong to Skull, *God damn his black soul.*

"Okay, this is you."

Shayla catches my eye and mouths, *How does she do that?* I shrug. I have no idea. Max isn't even leading her, he's sticking close to Esme's side. I reckon Steph has counted the steps, and the number needed to reach any of the rooms and has them stored in her mind. Sure, being blind does hinder her in some things, but not as much as you'd think.

"Hi, Liz," Steph greets me, and I've no idea how she knows I'm there. I manage to refrain from sniffing my armpits. She ignores me after that, opening the door to the empty room and gesturing inside. "Prospects were told to get this place ready, but I can't tell if they have or haven't."

"You're spidey sixth sense doesn't tell you?"

"Liz," Steph admonishes with a laugh.

"Looks like they have." Shayla gives a smile as she glances inside. "This will be great, Esme. Where's the… oh, there's a bathroom as well. It's a palace, isn't it?" She forces a smile as the girl beside her nods vigorously. I'm so full of admiration for this bitch, it's unreal. But maybe caring for Esme helps her bury her own trauma to some extent.

"I'll leave you to get settled. Come, Max."

I watch, shaking my head, as Steph unerringly walks back to the stairs, holding my breath until her hand's on the bannister.

Then I turn back to Shayla, catching her before she follows Esme into the room. "You coming back down?"

Shayla shakes her head. "To be honest Lizard, I'm exhausted. I think we'll just stay up here."

I translate what she's saying. "Shayla," I start forcefully. "Nothing is going to happen to you here. I know it's too early for words to make you believe it, but you can trust us."

She offers a weak smile but betrays herself by glancing down and noticing the lock on the door. Then she catches my eye. "I'm not sure I'll ever be able to trust anyone again."

There such desolation in her voice it's like a punch to my gut. "How long?" I ask, gruffly. "How f… damn long, Shayla?"

She doesn't pretend to misunderstand. "A year or thereabouts for me. Thankfully less for Esme." Now it's her changing the subject. "Everyone's been so kind to Esme, the women, and also the men." She gives another one of those half-smiles, making me wonder what it would take to put a full one on her face. "Esme's made a fortune already, haven't you, Es?" Esme nods seriously, then looks around her new home, trying out the bed by jumping on it. I turn to go, Shayla stops me. "I can't thank you enough, Lizard."

"No thanks required." I don't need her gratitude for something any of us would have done.

"Yes, they are. And Mace who started that dollar for each swear word business? Pure genius to get Esme on board."

I was quite impressed with my brother myself. Though I expect I'll become much poorer for it.

Before she can fully close the door, there's a streak of fur down the corridor and I'm not fast enough to grab the door handle as a very large cat missing an ear runs past me, jumping onto the bed where Esme's now sitting. The girl grins, holds out her arms and that darn cat snuggles right into them.

"Er," says Shayla, seeming not sure what to do.

"That's Bitch," I tell her. And fuck me, but Esme glares at me and holds out her hand. "Nah, not swearing, sweetheart, well not really. That's her name. She hates men, none of us can go near her, but tolerates women and kids okay. She's wormed and has no fleas so she's fine if you want her in here with you."

Shayla eyes the cat. "I'm not really a cat person, and I don't know much about Esme at all, except that she loves animals big and small. So, if she's not allergic, I think having the cat here will be good for her, if that's okay?"

"Okay, darlin'? Keeping her out of our way will be doing all us men a favour." I chuckle as I, at last, make my escape, and go find something to eat.

CHAPTER FOURTEEN

Vanna

"Hi, Mace, it's Vanna." I kick off my shoes and walk into my kitchen.

Mace's voice thunders through the phone. "Hi, Vanna. You made your decision yet?"

"I think so, yeah. How's Lizard?" To be honest, I'm still undecided whether to return to the compound or not, but Cas wants to go, and it's worth suppressing my own hurt to see him smile. He's also behaving better this week, and I'll take that, even if he's just doing it to persuade me to return to Pueblo. I'll have to accept I'll have to watch my husband being unfaithful. Maybe it's time I dropped that label, when he seems perfectly happy with his stable of girls instead. *Younger, prettier…*

I force myself to concentrate on what Mace is saying.

"Lizard's the same as he always is. Had a couple more headaches but he swears he's okay."

Now I stop thinking about me, but about Liz instead. "Has he had more since seeing me?" *Am I doing him harm?*

Mace is quiet for a second. "Not that I'm aware of, but I'm not with him night and day."

I make my decision. "Okay. We'd like to come down at the weekend if that's alright with you and everyone else there. I just didn't want to come if my presence caused Lizard pain." I'll just have to suppress my own pain for Cas.

"Of course, you'll be welcome. How's Cas dealing with everything?"

Turning, I lean my ass against the counter. "He's been a different boy this week. We've actually been talking without one of us wanting to throw something. He's been thinking about the weekend a lot. We've discussed what it would be like if Lizard never recognised or acknowledged him, and he's decided he still wants to come back. I think the bikes are a big draw, but so's getting to know his dad. He says it's good to find out about the man who is his father, whether Lizard knows that or not. I think it's a comfort, understanding he didn't intentionally leave him. If Lizard is half the man that he was, Cas will find a man he can respect." I didn't mention the little matter of Cas seeing him go off with different girls.

I've been doing a lot of soul searching over the past few days and have realised I need to let Lizard go. We're only tied together in my head and on that piece of paper that makes it all legal.

"He's certainly that," Mace agrees. "But what about you? What are your expectations?"

"I've been thinking about that too, Mace. I can't have any. Whoever Lizard once was, he's not that man now. As you told me, the last thing he wants is a woman with a kid in tow. When we met, I was twenty, with a pre-pregnancy body. I'm now in my mid-thirties, and not the girl I once was. He won't be magically attracted to me—"

Mace's annoyed growl interrupts. "Don't put yourself down."

"Just saying it as it is, Mace. No, I can have no expectation of anything except closure. At the back of my mind, there was always the thought he might wake up one day and remember, but there's not much chance of that now. Even if there was, me and Cas may not be right for him anymore, and I'd hate to force him into anything when it's not what he's after. All I want for him is to be happy and healthy. I think seeing him now is going to help me move past it. Maybe even move on and see if there's someone out there for me."

"You giving up on him, Vanna?"

"Never, no. But Mace, the last thing I want to do is hurt him. He's reached a good place and he seems happy. Yes, I want Cas to get to know him, but I don't want to screw his life up."

Mace is quiet for a moment, then says simply, "You want me to come get you?"

"No, I can drive as I told you. Maybe we'll come down Saturday morning, instead of Friday night?"

"You don't want to come for our party?" A chuckle reaches me down the line.

I snort. "I think Cas might get fed up with going to bed early. Saturday will be fine, we'll be there mid-morning, if that's okay? I've been chatting with Mel. She's going to do some baking and I said I'd help." I'd gotten on well with her. Hey, look at me. Making friends. I smile to myself. Sure, I know some of the parents of the kids Cas is friendly with, but the only real confidant I have is Lindy. I frown slightly, of course, I can't be completely open with any of the women at the compound. None of them can know the real reason I'm there.

"That's great, you getting on with Mel. How did you find Beth?" The way he asks, I take it he's got a soft spot for Ink's woman.

"Good. She's great, even if I get a crick in my neck when I'm speaking to her."

He barks a laugh. "I'll expect you on Saturday then. Want me to take Cas to the shop for a few hours?"

"He'd love that Mace. Thank you."

"No problem, sweetheart, I'll teach him how to hotwire another car." When I shriek, he chuckles and says quickly, "See you soon," then ends the call.

I put down the phone, grinning and realising I'm looking

forward to the weekend. It's something to look forward to after the hell of a week I've had. Turns out my boss really wasn't impressed with me taking leave on short notice, even if I'd had a good reason. I'm now on warning not to do that again.

Monday had been bad. I was called into the manager's office as soon as I turned up for my shift. It was true, as he'd seen fit to remind me, I work hours to fit in with my son. Again, as he'd reminded me, my office skills weren't exceptional, and I could easily be replaced. I suffered through the whole lecture, biting my tongue, reminding myself I needed this job to keep a roof over our heads.

Tuesday he'd tested me. Sending far too much work my way so I struggled to complete it in time. I hadn't complained, he was just pointing out that work, which had piled up while I'd been off. It still had to be done. That any of the others could have done it was not the point. I'd suffered in silence and simply hoped things would settle down again.

Today had been slightly easier, but the lunchtime meeting with the social worker had been fraught when she'd asked if Cas had been in trouble again. I didn't enjoy my capabilities as a mother being brought into question. I'd left her office, concerned that despite everything I'm doing, the decision may already have been made to remove my son from my care. It all hinged on whether they were going to give Cas a custodial sentence or probation. I hope for the latter and dread the first.

Surprising me, Cas had enquired about my day as soon as I'd gotten home. It hadn't been concern for the outcome of the meeting I'd had, he didn't know where I'd been. But unusually. he'd noticed the stress on my face.

"Mom. I think it's a good idea if we go to Pueblo this weekend."

I ruffled his hair, and he jerked away. "You liked it that much, huh?"

"Well, yeah," he replied as if I was dumb, but then added, "You seemed relaxed there. I'd heard you laughing and genuinely smiling which you haven't done for some time."

That pulled me up. He was right. Knowing Cas had so many of Mace's brothers watching out for him had enabled me to relax, and despite having to cope with seeing Lizard again, I had had fun.

"You worry too much," he'd told me.

Well, of course I do. I'm a mom with sole responsibility for a son. A son who's been a lot easier to live with this week. That must be down to getting to know Mace and the other men.

"What did he say?" Cas comes into the kitchen, making a beeline for the fridge. He opens it, frowns, then shuts the door and goes to an overhead cupboard instead. In a moment, he's got a packet of cookies in his hand.

I swear he eats me out of house and home. There's no point in reminding him dinner will be soon, whatever he stuffs down now, he'll be hungry again then.

"It's fine, Cas. We'll drive down Saturday morning."

"Cool. Hey Mom, can I go round Jordan's tomorrow? I'll go straight from school."

My immediate reaction is to say no. Cas still hasn't let on whether any of his friends were involved when he stole that car. I suspect they were. But just who, I've no idea.

"You can't stay the night," I tell him firmly, watching his expression as I do. His face starts to tighten as I go for broke. "I'll pick you up at nine."

His breath whooshes out. I tense, waiting for the explosion that I'm sure is about to come. "Mace told me men prospect for his club to earn the members' trust," he reminds me. "Takes about a year, sometimes more. Some men never make the grade." His eyes find mine. "I've lost your trust mom. Look, I know I did a stupid thing. I want to have the freedom I had before. I want to go around a friend's house without a curfew. But, I do understand why you're worried about me. Words won't cut it right now, will they? So, I won't make you a promise you won't trust I'll keep. I won't fight you on this, Mom."

If I ever needed proof going to find Cas's dad was the right thing to do for my son, I've got it now. Tears prick at my eyes.

I'm not stupid and know this new version of Cas may not hang around forever. Angry hormonal Cas may reappear at any time, but that it's had some impact is incredible, and I'll make the most of it while it lasts.

"Aww, Mom." Cas steps forward and gives me a hug, then asks, "How long until dinner? I'm starved."

The next day, having an unexpected free evening, I go to visit Lindy. She barely lets me get in the door.

"*Now* I'm going to get the whole story," she says, sparing a moment to pull me into her arms, then lets me go just as fast, standing back expectantly.

Rolling my eyes, I tell her, "I've told you what happened on the phone. Lizard doesn't recognise me and is living it up as a single man."

"Yeah, but I can't see your face on the phone. What you didn't tell me was how that made you feel?"

She's made dinner for us, some kind of chicken stew which smells great. I follow her into the kitchen as she prepares some sides, and I hop onto a stool.

"It's as hard as ever, Lindy," I admit. "Half of me expected him to recognise and greet me in some way. I know we'd never just pick up where we left off, too much water has gone under that bridge, but hoped we could be friends for Cas's sake. But there wasn't a flicker of recognition at all. It's alright. I'm happy enough that Cas has a chance to get to know his father."

She points a wooden spoon at me. "You're a bad liar, Vanna." When I shrug, she continues, "You haven't seen him for ten years. Has he changed? I mean, physically? It would help if he had a pot belly."

I chuckle. "Unfortunately, no pot belly. In fact, I hate him for how good he looks. He's matured well, like a fine wine. He's always had muscles, they look even more defined now. More delicious tattoos. No signs of grey in his hair which has grown longer. He's as attractive as ever."

"Delicious tats, eh? You want to lick him all over?"

The trouble is, I do. "He wouldn't look twice at me, Lindy." I frown and try to explain. "There are club girls, girls who live at the club. They like sex and are not shy about taking what they want."

"Whores?"

"They are, but they clearly enjoy what they do. They're young, pretty. They've got great figures…"

"Probably from all the workouts they get."

I grin. She could be right, there. "And all the protein in their diet." As I add that, Lindy gives a startled snort. I wait for her to stop laughing. "Thing is, with that on tap, why would he want a frump like me?"

"You are not a frump." Turning, she places her hands on her hips. "You haven't had your hair trimmed in ages. You could do with updating your wardrobe. You just don't make the best of yourself."

"I can't afford new clothes and have you seen how much a haircut costs? Every time I think of going, something else pops up, like having to get a new tyre for my car."

Dinner ready, she starts plating up. "I've got some clothes you could borrow. We're about the same size. And as for your hair, I'll treat you."

"Lindy, I can't ask you to do that!"

"You're not asking, I'm telling. See, here's the thing," she passes a plate to me and hops up the other side of the counter, placing her own in front of her, "I want to do this for you. I've a friend who works in a salon in town, she does discount rates for me. I'm sure she'll do the same rate for you if I ask her. You've lived for that boy of yours, Vanna. Now's perhaps the time to start thinking of you." For a short while she's silent, and all I do is utter appreciative sounds. It's always nice to have food cooked by someone else. When she's halfway through, she pauses, and winks. "So, Lizard isn't the man for you. Are there any other hot bikers?"

A laugh is startled from me. "Oh Lindy, if only you knew. Hot bikers? Well, duh, yeah."

"Well, smarten yourself up and perhaps one of them will be for you."

But I need to remain faithful to Lizard. Ignoring her, I finish my food, then help her rinse the plates and stack the dishwasher. It's when I'm drying my hands, my eyes fall on my wedding band. *Could I ever see myself taking that off?*

My husband might as well be dead to me.

If he was, would I have mourned him all this time? Would I be able to put him behind me after ten years? Of course, I'd never forget the man that he was, but that's all he'd be. A memory gradually fading over time. That he's alive has meant I'd held onto a hope that one day he'd wake up and remember.

Closure I'd told Mace. Last weekend, my talk with Mace, tonight's talk with Lindy have helped me to start thinking straight. Even if Lizard regained his memory, he's built a new life for himself. We may no longer have things in common. Perhaps how he lives now is what he wants out of life. If I spent time with the man I met last weekend, would I still like and admire him? For a start, I don't like his approach to casual sex. The man I'd married would never have stepped out on me. But would he even be able to be faithful again, now that he's experienced variety? I couldn't share a man, and maybe it wouldn't be so easy to forget the years when he's been with easy women, while I've satisfied myself with my BOB.

Could another of those gorgeous specimens of men be one for me? Mace? I like the man. He'd be good for Cas. But while he's handsome and well-built and probably wouldn't disappoint in bed, when I consider sleeping with him, it does nothing for me. Not compared to my thoughts about Liz.

Closure.

Well remembering my man's cock and the magic it could perform is doing nothing to get me closer to that.

Twisting my wedding band, I wonder if I should take it off

and swap it to the other hand. Still wear it but make a statement to myself and others that I'm free, no longer shackled to any man. *But his tattoo is still on my back.* I'll never do anything to remove that. Lizard had been so proud when I'd agreed to carry his name. A small smile curves my lips as I remember the first time after I'd gotten it and he'd made love to me. Doggy style, of course. Hmm. What was exciting and a tremendous turn on for him had been very beneficial for me.

"Have you made a decision?" Lindy asks, sipping her coffee and indicating the one she's brought in for me.

I snap out of my reverie, realising what she's talking about when she waves toward my hair. "If you can get me a discount, I'll pay for the cut myself," I say in a voice brooking no argument. "As for clothes, if you've got something suitable, I'll borrow it."

She grins. "Compromise, huh? I'll go with that. I've got Shauna's number. I'll give her a call and see if she can fit you in tomorrow after work. You go upstairs and raid my wardrobe. I'll be there in a sec."

An hour later, when I go to collect Cas, the back of the car has a selection of clothes piled on the seat, including a fetching butter soft leather jacket that fits as though it was made for me. Leather-looking leggings, that I don't think I'm brave enough to wear, not with the size of my ass, and a selection of tops, some lower in the front than any that I've ever bought.

"You have fun at Jordan's, Cas?"

"Yeah. It was okay. Mom, what are these?" He points over into the back seat.

"Lindy lent them to me. Oh, and I'm having my hair trimmed tomorrow." I glance at him, seeing by his expression he's put two and two together as expected.

"Uh-huh. Mom's dolling herself up," he tells me in a singsong voice. "Going on the prowl, Mother?"

I punch his arm lightly.

"Mom." His voice returns to normal and, at the moment, is

gravelly deep, a suggestion of what it will be like when it breaks completely. "If Dad never remembers, then you deserve to be happy again. Try and get to know the other bikers."

"Cas…"

"No, Mom. Seriously. I like the club, like the work they do on the bikes and cars. It's fun being there. So do it for me. Hook up with a biker, will you?"

What?

Stunned, I start to smile at the knowledge my son thinks I could have a chance attracting one of these sexy men.

"I heard Rusty's single."

My smile slips completely away. Rusty has to be sixty, if he's a day.

CHAPTER FIFTEEN

Mace

"F ... Damn thing."

"I think 'damn' is technically swearing, Brother." I laugh when I see Pyro just save himself from having to put a dollar in the gallon jar that's now sitting on one end of the bar. There's another the same size at the other end. Already, Esme's money is racking up. "Look at it this way, you'll have cleaned up your language by the time your kid is born."

"Can't change the habit of a lifetime," he grumbles. "Don't see how it matters. Kid can't repeat what she hears as she doesn't speak." His eyes follow Esme as she walks into the kitchen, followed by the two dogs who've taken to escorting her around.

He's not being cruel, just frustrated. Try as we might, she still refuses to say a word. Really, she needs to see a therapist of some sort. Fuck knows what's going on in her mind, but we're being cautious, the last thing we want is for Major to find her. Red's still no closer to finding out more details of exactly who the man is, or the length of his reach.

Pyro signals for Karl to bring him a beer, then raises an eyebrow at me. When I nod, he raises another finger, and Karl places two bottles in front of us. Having four prospects is benefi-cial, there's always one around to tend the bar.

"You know who I admire in all of this?" He turns to lean back against the counter. "Shayla. She got them out. Kept that kid safe, provided for her. Couldn't have been easy lying low when she had her to look out for, but she didn't abandon her."

He's right. "With that tat on her back, the wrong person seeing it could have meant she'd be stolen back by Major. I can see why Shayla kept the kid with her." But like Pyro, I'm impressed by everything she'd done. "I wish Cad could find something out about where Esme comes from. Surely, someone, somewhere, must be missing her?" I can't allow myself to think her family had been pleased to be shot of her. Sure, Esme has issues, but she's a delightful kid, and no bother.

"All we've got is a first name, and that she's got problems. Don't even know if there's a name for what she's got, or whether she was born that way, so he can't search medical records. Like finding a needle in a fuckin' haystack."

I nod toward the jar.

"She ain't even here," he hisses when he turns back around to see where I'm indicating. Then laughs. "You getting a cut out of this, Brother?"

No, I'm not. But seeing the way those dollars are mounting up, I wish I were. There are even a few IOUs in there as well. Reckon come payday, the levels in the jars will rise.

Suddenly both of us lurch forward.

"Hey, what you two ladies gossiping about?"

"Ink," I cough as I recover from the hard slap to my back. "Asshole." I give him one of my best glares. Then relent. "Actually, glad you're here. What do you think about this?"

I place a coloured drawing in front of him. He picks it up, then whistles through his teeth. "One of Esme's?"

I nod. I glance at Pyro, wondering whether he's going to mock me or not. Then at Ink, not certain he might not do the same. Nothing ventured, nothing gained. "I was wondering about having that on my gas tank."

It's a picture of a rearing stallion, his front hooves raised, his eyes blazing and angry breath coming from his nostrils. How the fuck Esme can conjure something like that up, I've no idea, but it's nothing you'd expect from a childish sketch.

"I'll tell you what I think, shall I?"

I look up then down. I thought it was his opinion I'd just asked.

"I wish I'd fuckin' seen that first, Brother." A wide grin spreads across Ink's face, which slips when I nod toward the jar.

"She'll be pleased," Pyro observes. "Fuckin' over the moon I would think, Mace. With a talent like that, doesn't matter what other drawbacks she has." He sees my glance and shakes his head. Oh well, he's right, Esme's not within hearing.

Fleetingly I wonder how she'll grow and develop, whether the two women will stick around somewhere locally so we'll find out. My eyes go to Shayla who's currently playing a game of pool with Beth. It had amused me as Beth had very carefully inspected, then wiped down the pool table first. Uh-uh, now they've caught my eye, I can't look away. Shayla's just bending to take a shot… That ass! A little more padding as she puts back on the weight which I'm assuming she lost, and it would be perfect. As it is, I wouldn't complain if I was pounding my cock into it…

I swing back around fast. That woman's been objectified by men enough. Doesn't need a man like me leering after her. While I suspect Beth was probably responsible for dragging her down, it's progress that Shayla's ventured to the clubroom without Esme as a buffer. Last thing I want to do is chase her away.

"Any idea when the gym will be completed, Ink?" I ask to take my mind off of the woman I shouldn't be having lewd thoughts about, discreetly adjusting myself in my pants.

"Nope. I'm beginning to wish we'd never gone with the idea of opening the place to the public. If it was just us fuckers using it, we wouldn't have to be so fuckin' particular. Now it's all got to be built to code. Apparently, it's not cool to have walls falling down on customers."

I look at him out of the side of my eye. "Not sure I'd be too keen on that myself."

For a response, all I get is a shove with his fist, then he calls out, "You ready, Beth?"

His woman mimes finishing her game, and he nods back. Seconds later, I wish she'd been ready to leave as he starts on me. "So, that bitch of yours is coming back at the weekend, then?"

I'd mentioned it as an aside last night in our normal Wednesday church in case anyone objected. No one complained, though a few groaned and mentioned they couldn't afford having kids around. Which, predictably, got another mention of Theo, followed by a few comments about how all kids should have naps and go home by five so the men could let loose. I'd grinned, just imagining what Cas would have to say on that matter.

"She's only a friend," I tell him, yet again. "It's Cas she's coming here for. I've told you and everyone else this, Ink."

Pyro then starts in too. "It's how it starts, Brother. You think you're just supporting them, then they worm their way under your skin and voilà. They've got you forever."

"You love Mel. Always did."

Pyro snorts and shakes his head but doesn't deny it. "Didn't allow myself to think it while she was with Skull. Could be similar to you, Bro, though there isn't another man in the picture, or not one who's breathing that is."

He doesn't know the half of what's wrong with that statement.

"Hey, that kid of hers. Anyone else notice he looks like Liz? Could he be a relative or something?"

I still at Ink's words, feeling blood drain from my face. "Haven't noticed," I tell them, trying my best to sound convincing. "Kid's got red hair, just like his mom."

"They've got the same nose though, and the same sulky look to their mouths. Hey, I might ask him."

"Leave it," I tell Ink fast.

"Why so defensive, Mace?" Ro asks.

Sorting through my thoughts at lightning speed, I come up with something that's not quite a lie. "I've known Vanna for ages." *Well, almost two weeks.* "You can see for yourself, Liz has never met her. And Cas has no cousins so I can't see how there can be a connection. Maybe way back there's a link in their DNA but hell, heaven help me, I'm probably linked to you two if I look far enough back on my family tree. We're all probably related in some way."

Pyro stares at Ink, and murmurs, "Thanks for that thought, Mace."

"Shut it," Ink growls, but laughs.

Finished with her game, Beth wanders over. Leaning in, she gives Ink an open-mouthed kiss. Now there's one brother I thought would never get caught. There's no doubting how happy he is with her though, despite the troubles they had to go through to get together.

"See you later, Ground Pounder."

"Later, Leatherneck," I respond, as he at last lets her go, and hand in hand they walk out the door together.

I notice Shayla's tidying away the pool cues and racking the balls for whoever wants to play next. She's doing it hurriedly though, as if without female company she's going to escape back to her room.

Deciding to go over, I approach. With eyes that have learned to be aware of her surroundings, she notices me as I draw close. Hoisting my left buttock onto the pool table, I fold my arms and face her.

"How you doing, Shayla?"

Her shoulders move up, then down. "Good?"

"Are you asking or telling me?" I chuckle softly, while examining her face. Her eyes still look like there's no life in them.

Another shrug. "It's hard for me to feel safe anywhere, Mace. My gut tells me I can trust people here, but I've time on my hands, especially as Jayden's taken Esme under her wing. I think I'm only just beginning to process what happened to me."

I can understand that. Like a soldier in a war, she's been doing what had to be done. It's only after the bullets stop flying, you check to see what damage there is. As for thinking time, we've made her give up what really was a shit job. I'd ridden past the dive where she worked and wasn't comfortable with her being there at all. A suggestion that it was best if she kept out of sight was the only persuasion it took for her to tell Andy and his shotgun a final goodbye.

"If time's hanging on your hands, why not help Jeannie out in the kitchen?"

An almost there smile appears. "I tried, but Jeannie hates me."

She's not exactly right, but I remember now that she allowed a pie Jeannie asked her to watch out for burn when she'd left it too long in the oven. Thereafter, her offers of help were turned down. Prospects clean and tidy, so there's not much else for a female to do.

"Jeannie's okay." I defend Bomber's old lady. "She just likes to be in charge in her domain. Perhaps you could help by peeling vegetables or something?"

She holds out her hand with a Band-Aid wrapped around one finger. "Tried that. Failed. Blood on the potatoes is apparently worse than a burned pie."

I have to laugh at the crestfallen look on her face. "Can't you cook at all?"

"I can open a can and pour it into a saucepan. I can put bread in the toaster, er," now there's an actual grin, "some of the time without burning it. And I can microwave. When I remember to remove the tinfoil first."

I snort. "Thought women were born with the cooking gene."

"Obviously my genetics are wrong. I must be partly a man."

My eyes view her up, then down. "Well that part must be in your head. You look all female to me."

Damn. Fuck it to hell. Why did I go and say something like that? To cover the moment of awkwardness when I realise given her situation I shouldn't have been looking, and she, clearly linking my statement to how she's been objectified for the last year, bristles. I make a swift change of subject.

"What are you good at?"

"Machinery."

Well fuck, I didn't expect that. The expression on my face must show my surprise, as she nods sharply. "Give me something mechanical that doesn't work, and I can usually fix it."

Well colour me surprised. "You work on bikes? Cars?"

Her hands move a foot apart, then widen. I frown, then realise she's indicating bigger. "Tractors?"

"Large farm machinery, yes. Oh, I could find my way around a smaller engine, but I'm more used to something larger with the torque to drive a combine harvester."

"You trained?"

"Graduated in mechanical engineering, so yeah."

My eyes widen in admiration. But before she can latch on to that, I shake my head, forcing the corners of my mouth to turn down. "Shame it doesn't make up for the fact you can't cook."

She stares at me. Just stares. Then, when my lips twitch, she snorts a laugh, then another, then she's doubled up laughing. When she straightens, she wipes tears from her eyes. "Asshole," she tells me.

Four days ago, she wouldn't have dreamed of calling me that, or anything like it. *Progress.* I have a warm feeling inside that it's me she's growing more comfortable with. Rather than analyse why I should feel that sense of pride, I nod to the pool table.

"This one of your talents?"

"That would be telling."

"Want to be beaten?" *Poor choice of words.*

But she's got a sly look on her face. "I've got nothing else to do. I don't mind standing bored while you work the table."

Huh. Minutes later, it's me standing looking on as she expertly sinks ball after ball, eventually getting a short turn which, I completely fuck up, then, for the second time in less than a week, my pool playing ability is brought into question by a woman. *Aren't women supposed to know their place?* Which is, of course, allowing the man to win. But she certainly doesn't, and I find I don't care at all.

I love the little jump of triumph she makes as the final ball sinks into the pocket. Without thinking, I place my arm around her.

"You're a ringer, sweetheart."

I'm a big man, my arm, like everything else about me is muscular. I'm totally unaware I've trapped her until she goes stiff by my side.

"Let me go." There's desperation in her voice. "Let me *go!*" she repeats.

Immediately my arm drops, and I look down to see her shaking, her face white. "Oh, baby," I tell her quickly, "I'm so fuckin' sorry. Deep breaths, babe. Deep breaths. Look at me." My gentle voice has panicked eyes staring my way. I take a deep breath, hold it, then exhale. Then I repeat my actions. "Breathe, babe."

She looks like she's struggling to do that simplest of action, but tries, eventually inhaling sharply, and then, mimicking my movements, holds it before letting it out. She copies me again and again until finally I see her relax and her shoulders slump.

"Come and sit down." I indicate a couch, and when she sits, putting her head into her hands, I take a chair opposite.

"I'm sorry." Her apology's offered in a low weak voice.

Dismissing her words, I tell her, "Shay, you were forced to do things you didn't want for the past year. No wonder you don't fuckin' want a man's hands on you. It's me who should apologise. I didn't fuckin' think."

"I'm fucked up, Mace. I don't think I'll ever be right again."

"Darlin', you'll get there. May need some help, but you'll get through this."

"Help?"

I nod. "Yeah. You and Esme both. I think you need some therapy. What I saw just now was a classic PTSD response, and Christ knows you've been through trauma." As her face tightens, I wave my hand around the room. "If brothers here haven't got it themselves, they know men who have. The way you reacted is nothing to be ashamed of."

"How come you knew what to do?"

"I served, babe. I've seen things no man should have. Yeah, I know a bit about what you're going through."

"I'm scared I'll never get over this. That I'll always panic when a man gets too close."

I fucking hope not. "It's about learning coping mechanisms, babe, and that's why I think therapy could help."

She's quiet for a moment, then she says, "I was surrounded by broken women. Each time a man would enter the room, it was to torture us, or take us to get dolled up so we could go service one of their clients. In my head, I equate men with pain, or being forced to do something I don't want. Just telling you this, hurts, Mace."

I wish I could wave a wand and wipe away her past, but I can't. "You won't forget. But you can learn how to deal."

"After my panic attack just then?" Her eyes open wide. "I can't see how."

"You've been free of him, what, three months? All that time you've been running on adrenaline, looking over your shoulder, doing your best for you and Esme. Fuck woman, have you any idea how strong you are? You got out and stayed free, and all with a disabled kid."

"If I'm as strong as you say, why do I feel so weak?"

"Because we've taken the load off you, baby. You've got a roof over your head and food to eat. You're protected and safe.

That adrenaline that built up inside you, now has nowhere to go, but your body's still programmed to fight or flee."

She flops back on the couch and brushes both hands down her face. "I suppose that makes sense. I still feel responsible for Esme."

"Where is she now?" I ask, although I already know.

"With Jayden in the kitchen. She's helping her draw. Or, just watching while she does it. She's trying to get Esme to say something."

"She's such a good kid, Shayla." Hoping to put a smile on her face, I tell her of my plans. "Esme's fuckin' talented. That picture of a stallion she drew? I'm having that airbrushed on my bike."

"Mace!" The delighted grin shows I've startled her, but now in a good way. "She's going to be so proud of that. When are you doing it?"

"When Ink can get around to it. He's our airbrushing expert. I'd attempt it myself, but don't want to fuck it up."

A critical humph sounds from behind me. Shayla's eyes rise over my head, and I swing around to see Esme standing there with her hand held out. And fuck me, in a soft, sweet voice with a scolding tone, she takes a breath, then says, "Pay up."

There's a gasp from Shayla, and I'm feeling as though I'm on the top of the world as I give an exaggerated huff and reach into my wallet, but I wink as I hand the dollar over. I watch as the kid walks across the bar and drops the bill in with the others in the jar.

CHAPTER SIXTEEN

Lizard

As she wouldn't be here if she hadn't walked into my shop, I feel some responsibility for Shayla and Esme, so when I return from work and see the woman sitting alone, I at least feel I need to check in with her.

"Hey, Shayla. How's it going?" Some responsibility, not enough to cater to any of her possible whims, so her nod gives me all the answer I need, and I hardly break step as I continue my walk toward the bar.

Once again, I've left Jonah to close up. Tomorrow, being Saturday, will be one of our busiest days, which means I'll have to go slow at tonight's party as always on a weekend. No one wants a tattoo artist who's bleary eyed with a hangover working on them. Of course, I'll have a few beers, but will resist the urge to overindulge, and concentrate instead on my other method of relaxation, sinking my cock into any available whore.

Tonight, there will also be girls up from Pueblo, wanting to dip their toes into the wild side of life, but I tend to avoid them. I'm not in the market for a woman, and some of these girls want to attract a biker of their own. Club girls know the score and just want a good time.

"Lizard."

My name makes me turn. Shayla's followed me to the bar. "Want a drink?" I nod at Beaver and get his attention.

"No, I'm fine. I, er, just wanted to know when Vi could do some more work on my back."

I grin. I happen to know she's already been pestering Vi. "Week after next, babe. Sure, we can put the sessions closer together, but it's best that the outline is properly healed before she continues." A thought occurs to me. "You are sticking around, aren't you?"

She shrugs. "I've been in Pueblo a month now."

I take it she's getting itchy feet. I turn to face her, so she knows I'm being serious here. "No one knows where you are. You might have noticed we keep ourselves to ourselves and don't go divulging our business to strangers. You're safest where you are, doll. Where else would you go? You got family or friends you can stay with?"

She huffs. "I do, but back in Vegas, and I'm not going anywhere near there."

She's right to steer clear of anyone from her old life, of course. If Major's looking for her, her known contacts are the first place he'd go. Means she's totally alone now, though.

"Well, you've got us now. You're welcome to stay as long as you want, and if Vi is going to complete your tat, that's one more session at least."

"Lizard."

I lift my chin to the man who's just joined us. "Ro."

"Just who I was looking for." But he's not talking to me, he's addressing the woman by my side. "Mace says you know your way around engines?"

My lips press together. Now that's something I didn't know. I raise my eyebrow toward her.

"Big ones, yeah," she replies.

"What about cars and bikes?"

For the first time I've seen, she becomes animated. "They work on combustion?"

"Well we're not talking electric ones. Not yet."

She frowns. "Lots of mechanics are going to be out of work when those get more popular."

Pyro grimaces. "Tell me about it. A completely new set of skills will be required. Mechanics like us will be relegated to swapping out tyres. Might need Cad to replace us with his knowledge of computers as we won't know how shit works."

"Can't you retrain?" I ask, interested.

It's Shayla who replies, "For electric cars it will be all about the electronics. Some people may be able to learn a new trade, but engines won't be the same anymore. Mind you, it's already getting increasingly more computerised. Which is why I like working on farm machinery."

"But you do know your way around gas engines now?"

"Yeah, I can fix them. Why?"

"Because Mace is a fuckin' pain in my ass and he wants Ink to paint his tank. Spring's here and everyone wants their bike serviced now. Don't like turning work away, so an extra pair of hands would help."

Shayla's eyes have more life in them than I've seen so far. "Sure, I'll help. I, er, don't have access to my qualifications..."

"Don't give a shit. I'll tell you what I want doing and supervise, at first at least. The way you work, darlin', will tell me all I need to know. Get Mace to bring you to the shop on Monday, and I'll show you around. We'll talk rates then, dependent on what you'll be capable of doing."

"No," she says fast. "You're housing and feeding me and Esme. I don't want anything more than that."

"You ain't working for nothing, babe, and that's final. Mel?" Pyro's already walking off toward his wife.

As Shayla's mouth drops open, I laugh. "I wouldn't argue with him. If he wants to pay you, why turn it down?"

Her reaction to Pyro offering her work that she was trained

for seems to have given her back a spark that she'd lost. We've been tiptoeing around her, but perhaps this is exactly what she needs, something to occupy her and get her out of her head.

"Lizard? Shayla? Can you come to Demon's office now?" Cad yells out, and waves frantically toward the room he'd suggested.

"Oh shit," Shayla breathes. "Is it Major? Has he found us?" Just like that, her pleasure in Pyro's offer disappears.

"Don't borrow trouble," I warn her. "Quickest way to find out is to go and talk to Demon, now."

But when we reach Demon's office, he waves us out with the explanation. "Gonna get a few heads in on this, we'll use the meeting room instead."

It's been a while since a woman has entered our hallowed room where we hold church. Shayla walks in and stands for a moment, taking in the leather-seated chairs and the table with the Satan's Devils' insignia carved into it. She shivers as though she finds it intimidating.

Demon follows us in and points Shayla to a seat. She sits, perching on the edge, looking uncomfortable, as well as nervous.

The door keeps opening and shutting. Mace enters, followed by Beef and Hellfire. Cad arrives carrying his computer, and Thunder takes his place to Prez's right-hand side.

Demon flashes a glance toward Shayla, taking in her shaking hands, and starts, "Won't draw this out. No need to worry, Shayla. But Cad's got some good news, or at least, we think he has."

When Demon gives Cad a nod, he takes over. "Found this out and brought it to Prez. He wanted to make sure it checked out, so I've dug as deep as I can." He pauses and opens his laptop. "Pretty certain I've found Esme's parents. In Flagstaff of all places."

"Flagstaff, Arizona?"

"Is there another, Beef?"

He shrugs. If the VP doesn't know of one, I certainly don't.

"Their kid disappeared on a shopping trip," Cad continues.

"One minute she was supposed to be with them, next it seemed she'd wandered off. They searched for her, involved the cops, but nothing ever turned up. That was four months ago, which tallies with your timeline, Shayla."

Shayla's head nods vigorously, but her brow is scrunched as though she's trying to process this information. "Major took her from them? What was he doing in Arizona?"

Cad looks blank. "I've no fuckin' idea. More likely to be opportunist rather than planned, or maybe he did target her, who the fuck knows? Esme's a pretty girl." He grimaces. It's easy to see why Major thought she'd be worth something. "I don't take anything at face value, and neither does Prez. A kid like Esme is bound to be challenging. I wanted to check that the parents weren't involved, that they genuinely lost her and want her back. I've checked their bank accounts and recent purchases, and nothing suggests they came into money at the time. Quite the opposite, in fact. Once the cops turned up nothing, they re-mortgaged their house to fund private investigators."

"So they've been actively trying to find her?"

"She's still listed as a missing person, and from the police reports, the parents haven't given up. They're still pestering the cops on what is now a cold case for them. No one saw Esme being taken away, so the snatch was done cleanly and efficiently. The only CCTV available shows her looking at a window display while her parents hadn't noticed her stop, then, she walks out of sight. No one else in the footage."

"Major picked his moment and was clever about it," I suggest.

"Doubt he did it himself," observes Beef. "Probably one of his minions."

"If she got lost," Shayla adds to the conversation, "she'd have trusted anyone who said they'd help her."

Of course, she would, and someone had taken advantage.

"It's a mystery how she got from Flagstaff to Vegas, or how

she came into Major's hands, but it appears she did. It's Esme from photos the parents posted. They're all over social media."

Shayla's hands form fists. "Major had books with our pictures in there, a brochure of sorts. He showed me once." Her face twists. "If her picture's been plastered around, people who saw that would have known she was missed. Not one of them did anything to stop it."

I refrain from telling her it wouldn't have mattered a damn to men who preferred their women unwilling, or young.

"Are you on social media, Shayla?" Cad asks.

She shakes her head. "I was… before. But I've avoided it and any digital footprint since I got free."

Sensible girl. She hadn't given into temptation in case Major used it to track her.

Demon takes over. "Cad brought this to me first thing today. I asked the Tucson boys to check the home out and then called this meeting when Drummer reported back. From what they said, the house is in a nice neighbourhood and the family's lived there for years. Lady posed as a journalist, and the parents were only too willing to talk to him to get her name front and foremost in the news once again. Obviously, the story had died over the months she'd been gone, the initial interest fading. He saw her bedroom left untouched, her drawings pinned up in the house, some framed. Her mom was upset, but proud of the work her daughter had produced. He also talked to the neighbours and heard stories of a happy, loved and cared for girl." He pauses and looks around. "From what he said, it sounds like they're genuine."

"I agree it sounds kosher," says Beef, and Thunder nods.

"So what are we going to do about it?" Hellfire asks.

"That's why I've called us together," Demon states. "If there's a fuckin' sniff of a chance they had something to do with Major, I wouldn't for one second countenance handing her back. But Cad's found no link with him anywhere. Looks like this is just how it sounds, an abduction and grieving parents who've no idea where their daughter disappeared to." He glances at the only female in the room. "You know her, Shayla. Your view is important to me. Did she ever mention her home or family?"

Shayla's lips purse and she doesn't give an immediate answer. Then her mouth opens. "She used to cry for her mom and her dad. I got the impression she had no siblings?" Her intonation rises, and Cad interprets it as a question.

"She's their only child," he confirms.

Shayla nods. "Crying for her mom was one of the things that got her punished, so in the end, she stopped. Then, of course, she wouldn't talk at all. Before that, I'd tried to ask where she came from, but all I got was 1601 River Street, which was probably useful if you knew the town or city, but..." her voice trails off and she shrugs.

Probably why she hasn't mentioned it before.

Cad's eyes brighten. "That's the address," he confirms.

"What are we waiting for?" Hell snaps. "Let's get them here. Esme wants to go with them, she can. She indicates otherwise..."

"One sign that Esme's uncomfortable with them, I'll take her away." Shayla sounds firm. "Not allowing Esme near Major again."

"No one wants her back in his hands," Demon growls. "Not taking any chance of that."

"Is there a problem here?" I've been quiet up to now. "If Esme was going to be making Major money, and fuck knows I hate to think it, but I can understand how he could have from some twisted motherfuckers, but might he try to take her back? He might have eyes on her parents, just in case she returns if she's that valuable to him. He was never able to cash in on his investment."

"She can't go home then." Shayla sounds alarmed. "I agree with Lizard there's too much risk."

Beef wipes his hand over his head. "Esme has needs, and God help us, we're trying to provide them, but she needs serious therapy. She won't say a fuckin' word. That's not good for the kid."

"She spoke yesterday," Mace puts in. "Told me to pay up when I slipped up and swore, but she hasn't said a word since." He catches Shayla's eyes.

She shakes her head and confirms it. "I tried, thinking that was a breakthrough, and I think it was. But she needs time and patience, and, as you say, professional help."

"So how do we swing it?" Thunder's face is taut.

Demon thinks for a moment. "Shayla did nothing wrong. All she did was free Esme and kept her safe for the last few months. Esme wasn't talking, so how did we know where to return her?" Fuck me, he sounds like he's talking about a stray dog. But relocating her might have been easier if she was. Some dogs are microchipped. As we learned to our cost, Max is. When Beef took Steph into hiding, Max's chip led the bad guys directly to them. "We tell them the truth but ask them to keep us out of it."

"I'll have to move on," Shayla tells us. "If her parents see me here and let slip where I am, Major will come to get me. I know he will." Her voice has gone soft, scared, but also determined.

I see Mace tense. "You're going nowhere, Shayla. We just need to make fuckin' sure you're left out of it. As far as they'll know, you've already moved on and left Esme with us."

"That would work," Beef agrees. "We've got enough women around to make this a safe place for Esme to be left, her parents would buy that."

"Settled." Demon picks up the gavel and bangs it, the noise making Shayla jump. "I'll ring her parents. If I'm right, they'll be here first thing in the morning. We'll check Esme's reaction, and if she's happy to go with them, the handover shouldn't take long. We'll say the woman who saved her has already left and we've no idea where she's gone. We don't even have to mention Shayla's name."

"Warn the parents to be on the lookout for Major." Beef's looking concerned. "They've got to understand the risk they're taking. Soon as she reappears at her home, he'll know where to find her."

Fuck it. I hope we're making the right decision and that sweet girl will soon be back where she belongs and out of the clutches of men like Major forever.

CHAPTER SEVENTEEN

Lizard

I'm Lizard, otherwise known as Norton James. I ride with the Satan's Devils MC and have done for the past ten years. I'm… thirty-eight years old, and my birthday is the tenth of January. I'm a tattoo artist and I run Devil's Ink on behalf of my brothers. I've no ties, no family and that's the way I intend to stay.

Before I open my eyes, I hear the tapping of rain against my window. Guess I'm not going to moan at having a busy day ahead in the tattoo parlour, whereas some Saturdays, I do end up envying my brothers with a day off instead. From the sound of it, today's not going to be great for riding.

I sit up straight as I remember what else should be happening later. If Demon contacted Esme's parents and they were as loving as we hoped, I doubt they'll waste any time coming to collect her. I'm only assuming he made the call last night. When I'd left the meeting, Bella had been available, and I'd made good use of her for a couple of hours. Then one of my blinding headaches had come on suddenly, and I'd dismissed her, turned off the light and slid into bed.

Sleep gradually gave a release while the pain still assailed me. Luckily, this morning, it's gone.

I throw off the covers, eager to discover whether Demon's

call was successfully made. I feel invested in the outcome, though God knows why. I haven't had a lot to do with Esme since she came to the compound, apart from stuffing dollars in that overfilled jar. But I was the first to know of Shayla and the young girl's problems and was happy my brothers stepped up and gave them refuge.

That I'd stayed clear since then hadn't been surprising. I've never been interested in having kids of my own, did everything I could to prevent it. Always used my own condoms and not one a girl conveniently had in her purse. It's rare I ever go with anyone other than the club girls who were all on some kind of contraceptive to ensure no slipups were ever made. A couple of times I'd been with hangarounds, but not often. Young dizzy girls are not my style.

I shower, dress, slide into my cut and attach my wallet to the chain on my belt, then descend the metal staircase. The first person I see is Mace. He's pacing by the door. During the time I've walked from the top step to the last, he's taken out his phone and checked it twice.

I cross the room to him. "The family coming?"

"Yeah, Vanna and Cas are on their way. I'm expecting them any moment now."

I thought he'd been getting on well with Shayla this week. I hadn't missed how patient he was being with her and far from his normal enforcer self. I'd actually thought he was getting close to her, and fuck knows, that girl needs someone on her side. Now I find he's waiting on the other bitch and her son? What's the fucking man want? Both women? He's greedy as fuck. I roll my eyes. "I was actually asking about Esme."

"What? Oh, yeah. Her parents are on their way now. Shayla's already said her goodbyes to Esme, not that the kid understood. Now she's gone with Pyro, who's dropping her off at Mo's, to keep out of the way until the kid's gone, or, not as the case may be." I nod, knowing there's no way we're going to let just anybody take her. "I'm waiting on Cas. Then I'll be taking him to the auto-shop."

"What about Vanna?"

"Oh, she's arranged to do some baking with Mel. Seems they're getting on like a house on fire."

As if he's summoned them by magic, the front door opens and the woman and her son come in, both of them already dripping after just the walk from the car to the clubhouse. The boy looks like a dog as he shakes the rain off him.

Vanna wipes her face with her hand and pushes back her damp hair. To give her credit, she looks amused rather than worried about the damage to her style. As her hand draws my attention to it, I notice her hair looks different. Just as long but seems to hang better. Fuck, if I was in the market for a civilian woman, I'd be happy to give her a try. She's an attractive bitch for one in her thirties. No wonder Mace is sniffing around.

He shouldn't be.

Shaking my head, wondering where the hell that thought came from, I start to turn around, my intention to get some breakfast before going to work.

"Cas, you okay to head straight out? Pyro needs me at the shop now."

"Sure," I hear the kid answer excitedly.

"Hey, Liz. You got something you've been keeping to yourself?" Judge calls out, then walks closer, looking between me and the boy standing next to Vanna. "You and the kid look like two peas in a pod. He's got your nose."

He looks nothing like me. Red hair and green eyes, whereas I'm a dark blond and mine are hazel. "I ain't got a monopoly on my nose, Brother," I bark dismissively. "You trying to stir shit?"

Judge is now close enough to bump my arm. "Just saying, there's a resemblance."

"There's no fuckin' resemblance, and no fuckin' chance." With a leer, I give Vanna the once over, and scoff. "Haven't ever been there, nor have any inclination." Realising too late how that might sound, I throw the woman a look of apology. "Don't mean anything by it, darlin', but you're not my type."

Her face gives nothing away, not even a twitch. Cas though, well the kid goes white. Makes me wonder if he knows who his father is, and if not, whether he'd be worried if he was a biker. Have to admit, his mom seems pretty comfortable in this environment. Well, whoever fathered him, it certainly wasn't me.

I do notice Cas had bounced in. Now with what's probably a teenage mood swing, he looks sullen and his smile's been replaced by a frown. That right there, I remind myself, is why I never wanted a kid.

"I've got your helmet here." Mace gets between me and the boy, reaching over to a table and picking it up from where it's been hidden on a chair. "We've got to get moving, Pyro wants me there yesterday. Best put that on inside." As he hands the kid the lid, Mace's face morphs into a grin. "It's raining out."

"We're not going in a car?" Cas asks, his voice dripping with scorn.

"Nah. Little bit of wet never hurt anyone. Hey, Karl! You got some wet-weather clothing Cas can borrow?"

The prospect yells back that he has and is soon approaching with a waterproof jacket.

Cas looks at it but doesn't take it. "I don't want to go, Mace. It's bucketing down out there."

His sulky tone gets to me. Mace is doing him a favour taking him to the shop, and the kid doesn't want to go because it's fucking raining? As my eyes open incredulously, I swing around. *What do they make kids of nowadays?* "You won't fuckin' melt, kid, now go and get on Mace's bike," I snarl.

Surprised I've entered their conversation, Cas's angry eyes snap to mine, something in his expression making me take a step back.

Christ. Pain slams into me as though I've been hit around the back of the head. I stagger slightly, then straighten again.

"Who the fuck do you think you are to tell me what to do?"

Trying to deal with the pain, my mouth opens and shuts and I'm at a loss for words.

"Cas," Vanna says loudly. "Where are your manners? If you don't want to go on the bike, I'll drive you…"

Now I'm glaring at her. "Kid does what he's told, or he's not going."

Why the hell do I care?

"You okay, Liz?" Mace asks me, his face appearing to shimmer through my unfocused eyes.

"Bad head," I rasp out. "Don't let the kid get away with it, Brother." Then I turn and walk away toward the kitchen, letting them sort it out themselves. Perhaps having some food might ease the pain. The thought flits through my head that maybe the kid hasn't anything to do with me, but he's got the same mile-wide stubborn streak.

Shortly after, when I'm tucking into some pancakes, eggs, and bacon, with a cup of coffee next to my hand, Vanna walks in on her own. She seems agitated.

"What did the kid decide to do in the end?" I ask, my headache having receded a little.

She looks down, before meeting my eyes. "He went with Mace. I'm sorry, Lizard. He's not always that way. It's coming here…" I notice as her words trail away.

"Coming here… What?"

She looks away. "He finds it hard is all."

Hard? Thought the boy enjoyed being on the compound. But maybe he doesn't like being told what to do. She probably lets him get away with shit that wouldn't fly with us. But if he doesn't want to behave, there's a simple answer for that. "Well don't bring him, then."

As she inhales sharply, Mel shoots me a look and crosses to her. "Kids, eh? Guess this is what I've got to look forward to." Her hand smooths over her rounded belly.

"Fuckin' kids," I say to no one in particular and pick up my fork again.

"P-p-pay u-u-up," a little voice sounds. It's one I've not heard before.

Despite everything, I break out a smile. "Well, of course, Esme, sweetheart. Here, take five. I'm sure to f- slip up again."

She grins, takes the bill, and skips off out of the kitchen, returning a few seconds later. I shake my head and chuckle to myself. *I hope she does get collected, else I'm going to be broke.* Still, it was good to see for myself that she's starting to recover her voice. Even if she only uses it to demand money for her fucking swear jar.

Suddenly, I hear a commotion from the clubroom. I push my plate away and stand, checking my gun is in my cut and at hand if I need it.

"Where is she?" comes a shrill voice. "Where's my baby? Where is *she*?"

Esme, I notice, has gone still as stone. Her head tilting as though she's computing something.

"Esme! Essie?"

I go out through the door to find Demon facing two people down. Suddenly, I'm pushed forward as someone bumps into me, physically clearing me from the doorway.

If Demon had had any expectations of how this reunion was to be handled, his plans are having to undergo an unforeseen and very swift change. Esme doesn't falter, just tears across the room and throws herself into the arms of the woman who's clearly her mother, she even looks like her. Her father's arms swiftly surround them both, and all three are crying.

"That went well," I say to no one in particular.

The man is the first to straighten, leaving his wife and child sobbing and hugging, then he, wiping his own eyes, steps toward Demon. Due to the frown on his face, I also move closer.

"I'm Dave Black, otherwise known as Demon." Prez holds out his hand.

"The man I spoke to on the phone," Esme's father states. Joy at the reunion being replaced by concern.

Demon nods, though there's no need to confirm it.

"You said you wanted to fill me in, in person." There's an imperceptible straightening of his shoulders as if in preparation for a weight he'll be asked to bear. Any hope that there's an innocent explanation for the four months his daughter's been missing, is not there.

Demon raises his chin. "There are things you should know that are better discussed face-to-face. Would you come to my office?"

"I, er, Maisie?" he calls out to Esme's mom.

Demon puts a hand on his arm. "Why don't you let Esme and her mom have some time together." His eyes flash, signalling something which the girl's dad picks up on, and his face becomes grimmer.

"Here, D. I'll get them some refreshments." Vi, who I hadn't noticed, steps up, holding onto Theo's hand.

Looking at her fondly, Demon says to her, "Thanks Vi," then to the man, "This is my wife, Violet, and our son, Theo."

"I'm Brett. Brett Waterman."

As he introduces himself to Violet, I notice his eyes linger on Theo, then they rise to nod at Demon. Seems something about her having a young child has reassured him.

Prez notices. "Well come this way, Brett. Vi will make sure your wife and daughter are looked after, while I catch you up on what you need to know."

Vi, with Theo toddling along beside her, approaches his wife, Maisie, tapping on her arm to get her attention. Then she gesticulates in our direction, then toward Demon's office, clearly telling her where we're taking her man, reassuring her he won't go far.

Brett relaxes slightly, but his face becomes tight as Demon raises his chin toward me. "Join us, Liz?"

Why me? *Because I'm the one who started this.* If I'd simply refused to cover a 'Property of' patch, we'd never have found Esme.

I sigh and taking out my phone, send off a short text warning Jonah I probably won't make it to the shop today, then follow Demon and Esme's dad.

As soon as we're behind the closed door, Brett asks even before sitting down, "Where's she been? How did she come to be with you?" His eyes narrow. "Did you take her? Did you have anything to do with her disappearance?"

"I told you on the phone, we discovered her only a few days back. Kept her safe while trying to find out who she was."

Brett's eyes focus on Demon's, then after a moment, he gives a slow nod. "Sometimes words settle better when you can see the man who's uttering them." He pulls out the chair, and at last, sits. "Esme means the world to me, Mr Black. I…" he pauses to wipe moisture that's again leaked from his eyes with no embarrassment. "I still can't believe she's out there with Maisie. I…"

Demon pushes the jug of water toward him, along with a glass. "If I could spare you this, I would, Brett."

"Give it to me, Mr Black. Tell me what I'm dealing with."

Prez gives him a moment to wet his throat. When Brett replaces the glass on the desk, Demon waves in my direction. "This is Lizard. He runs our tattoo parlour. Best we start from the beginning and tell you how Esme came to be with us."

Then, with a deep sigh, Prez starts talking. As he does so, he identifies the part I played as the man who first raised suspicions about a woman with a 'Property of' tattoo.

I've seen Mace use torture before to break men, but I've never seen a man so hurt and destroyed by mental pain. When Demon mentions Esme's tattoo and the significance, he's openly crying, weeping into his hands. Demon and I give him some time to get his grief under control. Brett goes up in my estimation as slowly he fights for that inner strength inside him.

When at last he stops sobbing, Demon emphasises, "She wasn't molested, Brett. The woman who helped her escape got her out in time, but she will need therapy. She's not even talking.

How much she knows of what might have happened, no one can tell."

"Oh, she's said a couple of words," I correct, trying to lighten things up and give him some hope. "She tells people to pay up." Or at least, she has me and Mace.

"Pay up?" Brett's eyes narrow suspiciously.

Demon chuckles. "We've been trying not to swear around her. If we do—and we fuck up a lot—we give her a dollar. There are two fuckin' swear jars out on the bar, probably close to overflowing by now."

Which he now owes two dollars to, but I hold my tongue, thinking it's probably best not to point that out.

Brett tries to process this information. "You're saying you've been trying to make her more comfortable around you? Fuck, she must hate men now. I don't know what to do, Mr Black. She's already damaged. I don't know where to start getting the help that she needs. What do I do?" It's a rhetorical question which he doesn't expect us to answer, I can already see wheels turning.

"Why's she the way she is? Has she got some kind of condition?" I ask.

Now Esme's father's eyes harden. "She wasn't born this way. We had been given the gift of a beautiful, healthy baby girl, and we wanted to bring her up and help her thrive the best we could. She was normal, if you want to term it that. Trouble was, there's a history of congenital immune system problems in her mom's family. We were advised that Esme shouldn't be vaccinated because of that history, that there was a risk if we did, that she'd have health problems. We wanted to do the best for our girl, so took the doctor's advice. He said the incidence of her catching something was low to non-existent, as the US was mostly clear of mumps and measles."

"She caught something?" Demon's face has gone dark.

"Seemed a couple of the parents at her playgroup were anti-vaxxers. Of course, we didn't know, and it still shouldn't have been a problem, but one of the kids brought something back from a visit to see Mickey Mouse, and it wasn't a toy. It was a virus which was passed onto Esme. She was three years old when she caught measles." His brow creases in remembered pain. "Measles. Such a simple word, yet no one understands just how devastating the complications can be. Esme's brain swelled. We were warned we could lose her. As it was, we had to watch while she was having convulsion after convulsion. I wouldn't wish that on any parent. She lived, and I thank God for that every day. But it left her disabled intellectually." His eyes rise to Demon's. "You've got kids, for heaven's sake vaccinate them. For the sake of kids like Esme, if not for themselves. Esme was fine before she got ill. After..." he waves his hands as though there are no words to describe it.

Jeez. Never having had kids, I hadn't come down on one side or the other of the vaccination argument, but hearing Brett? Must admit, I didn't realise how what I thought was a simple childhood disease could have such disastrous consequences.

My eyes rise to Demon's who confirms, "Theo has been vaccinated and any other babies we have will also be."

"What happened didn't change how we felt about her. She's everything to me," Brett says sincerely, challenging us to say Esme's worth any less than anyone else. "Damn near broke both of us when she went missing. It's only hope that she was out there somewhere and would be home one day that kept us putting one foot in front of the other. We never gave up searching, even when the police stopped actively looking. We haven't any other children, not because we'd be taking the same risk, but because we made a conscious decision to ensure she was the centre of our universe. She's special in so many ways. Happy, chatty..." he stops when he realises she's not talking now.

"She's fuckin' talented. My brother's currently having one of her drawings painted on his gas tank," I tell him.

"She can draw," Brett agrees. He looks from me to Demon.

"Art is the way she expresses herself. Is the woman who rescued her here? I'd like to thank her. I owe her so much."

Prez shakes his head. "No. She wanted to keep moving, she's worried about Major tracking her down and taking her back with him. She left Esme in our care. We've several old ladies here who've been caring for her. My wife, for one, as you saw just now."

"Is Esme in danger from this Major?"

"Not going to lie to you, Brett. Short answer is, I don't know. Long answer? You got a gun?" When Brett nods, Demon continues, "I'd keep it on you and don't let Esme out of your sight. Oh, go to the press, get them to print a story about how she's back. Also, go to the cops. I don't know what the law is in Arizona, but in Colorado, it's illegal to tattoo anyone like Esme. That, for a start, with no other evidence, is enough to have them searching for Major. May make him go to ground, or at least make it too hot for him to try and get his hands on her again."

My fear is that he'll want his property back. But all we can do is impress on Brett the need to take precautions, and hopefully they'll be enough. We can't keep Esme away from her parents, she needs more than we can give her.

Brett's head is dipping up and down slowly. "I'll talk to the cops. See about getting her some protection. As you say, making a noise about her return may keep this Major at a distance. I doubt any prosecution will stick, though. Esme, well she's not a credible witness."

"We're not giving up searching for Major." Something passes between Brett and Demon, acknowledged only by lifts of their chins.

"What about this fucking tattoo on her back?" Brett looks toward me. "Can I get it removed?"

I give him my advice. "It would have to be done professionally. Not by some quack. Will take ten or twelve sessions in my estimation, or she could cover it up. Vi can show you the design she did for Shayla. I know Esme liked that."

Brett's head falls into his hands. "I don't know what's best to do, but I know I hate it and I've not even seen it." He thinks for a moment. "If I go to the cops, will it cause trouble for your club?"

Demon shakes his head. "They're welcome to talk to us. We run a legit tattoo parlour; we've got nothing to hide. We didn't touch her tattoo ourselves, so we're in the clear. But there's not a lot we can tell them. Our tech guy traced you through public records and the noise you made about Esme on social media."

"But you didn't go straight to them to tell them you'd found an underage girl who's been abused. Fucked up badly enough she refuses to talk."

Demon leans forward, his hands clasped on the desk in front of him and his eyes flare. "Didn't know who her parents were, Brett. Could have been some sorry fuckers who sold their own kid. Cops could have passed her back to her family who'd simply give her to the likes of Major, again. No, we couldn't risk that. Not until we'd checked her home situation out."

Brett stares at Demon, then huffs, and proves he's not stupid at all. "The visit from the journalist on a motorcycle? I thought it odd the press was resurrecting the story, but at this point we'd clutch at any straw offered so we talked to him."

"She's got a lovely room, I'm told." Demon smirks.

Esme's dad is quiet as everything sinks in. "Thank you," Brett says suddenly, his eyes filling with tears once again. "You did your best, I can see that. Others might just have wanted shot of a disabled girl, but you, you helped her. Thank you on behalf of all the Esme's out there. I'd like to thank the woman who helped her as well. Between her and you, she's had some angels watching out for her."

Not angels, I mentally correct him, or maybe the one. But it's Devils who been looking over her this past week.

"Just sorry we weren't there earlier," replies Demon.

Brett wipes his eyes once more and noisily blows his nose. "This is going to kill Maisie. How the hell do I tell her?"

"She's got her daughter back," Demon says confidently. "It's devastating, I know. But the what-ifs are worse." He means she had so narrowly escaped being raped and ending up dead or never being found. Not much but he's right, Brett needs to be grateful for small mercies. "What you've both got to do is help Esme get through this. Focus on her. One thing I will say is, she seems resilient."

CHAPTER EIGHTEEN

Vanna

"What's going on?" I ask Mel, when there's shouting coming from the clubroom.

I'd noticed a young and strangely quiet girl, but assumed she was the daughter or relative of one of the members. But the way she'd left the kitchen with such a look of disbelief and hope on her face made me think it was something more.

When Mel fills me in on her story, I have to find a chair. Mel said no one knew for certain, but they thought she was fourteen or fifteen, and I agree, she didn't look much older. *She's the same age as Cas.*

Boys could be pimped out the same way as girls, I know that of course, but I'd never dreamed I'd have to fear him being taken. Just the thought is unbearable, and Mel has to put a tissue into my hand as I consider it. Cas has been sneaking out at all hours, when he's staying around his friends, and I'm never quite certain what he gets up to there. What if one day he just never returned? I don't think I'd be able to bear it.

"They haven't seen her for more than four months?" When Mel nods, I think what a happy reunion they'll be having, but then realise that will be tinged with grief. From what I've been told, Esme has retained her virginity thank God, but must have lost her innocence and bore witness to the depravity of men. How does a parent cope with that knowledge?

Vi appears in the doorway, one hand on the doorjamb. "Demon's talking to Esme's dad, I'm keeping Maisie, her mom, company. Can we have some coffee and some of your muffins if they're ready, Mel?"

"Yes, I'll bring them out. I've got those cupcakes Esme likes too."

"Thanks, oh, and Demon's explaining everything to Esme's dad. I think he should be the one to update Maisie. She's just happy that Esme's safe and well." Vi gives a sad smile. "Well, I think she's happy, she's not been able to stop crying yet."

At least she's got her partner to lean on, I think, perhaps a little waspishly. Then want to slap myself around the head. What that poor woman's going through, I wouldn't wish on my worst enemy, and she doesn't even know the worst as yet.

Not wanting to crowd her, Mel and I stay in the kitchen and continue baking. Mel explains that she loves cooking here as the equipment's much larger than what she and Pyro have in their house.

The men who aren't working today pop in from time to time and that tub of muffins Mel baked start to disappear. I help her prepare another batch. The simple chores of working alongside her help me come to terms with the words Liz had thrown at me earlier—his justification why Cas could in no way be a son of his. It had hurt. Guess I had my answer about whether he and I had a chance of getting back together. None.

Obeying her instruction, I take Mel's next batch of muffins out of the oven, acting on autopilot, while thoughts race around my head. There are worse things than being a single mom with a wayward son, as Esme had proved. What if Cas was taken from me? I don't think I could survive it.

I should be thankful of what I've got and accept miracles don't happen.

So deep in my thoughts, I'm not sure how long it's been

before Esme comes into the kitchen, dragging her mom and dad along.

"Er, we're going now. Esme wanted to say thank you and goodbye to everyone."

Mel brushes flour off of her hands. "You got a hug for me, Esme?"

Apparently, she has. And one for me as well, though we've not met. Max and Bagel who've snuck in and are lying under the table hopefully waiting for crumbs to drop also get hugs and kisses, and Esme gets her face licked by two lolling tongues in return.

"Bitch?"

When Esme asks, Mel covers her mouth. "You spoke," she comments delightedly.

Esme's mom's face has tightened. "Not sure that's a good first word," she remarks.

Mel enlightens her. "Inappropriate for certain, but that's the name of our cat. You want to go find her, sweetie? I think I saw her going up the stairs.

"She's here, Mel," Vi calls out, coming in with a wriggling bundle of fur in her arms. The cat seems to settle when Esme reaches out and takes her, and when she nuzzles her face in its fur, it purrs.

Still sniffling and wiping away another tear, Maisie gives a weak grin. "I won't ask how she got her name."

Mel rolls her eyes. "That's easy. She hates men and scratches them when they go near her. Women she tolerates, kids, for some reason, she loves. Oh, and not dogs…"

Esme's put the cat down. Bitch gives a loud hiss and arches her back. Immediately Max and Bagel slink away and disappear into the clubroom.

"Well, we'll be off now. Thank you. Thank you for finding her." Maisie shrugs as if those are insufficient words. When Esme follows them, Maisie backs out of the kitchen keeping her daughter well in sight.

As she's still thanking anyone and anybody, Lizard walks over to the bar.

"Nails? Beaver? Amalgamate her fuckin' money will you? Put it all in one jar." He then turns to her dad. "Reckon she's got the makings of a college fund here."

My eyes widen when I see how many dollars are in the jars. They really do swear a lot.

"Er, what do you want to do with the IOUs, Liz? Half the brothers aren't here."

Lizard sighs as he replies to Beaver, "Tally them up and I'll make good on them. Brothers will owe me instead. I'll make sure they fuckin' pay." His eyes close. With a sigh, he shakes his head, takes out his wallet, and another couple of dollars joins the growing pile.

In the end, the prospects have to use a garbage sack, which Beaver hands to Esme's dad. When he takes it, I notice the man's movements are jerky. I take it he's unsure what to make of the bikers and their generosity.

Then, Esme and her family are gone, and the clubroom falls silent. From the little I've heard, that family will have a long way to go before they get back anywhere near normal. Still, Esme going home with them must be a good start. A blind man would have been able to tell how much she is loved.

"I'm going to start making pies to go into the freezer, Vanna. Want to come keep me company?"

"Yeah, Mel…"

The clubhouse door opens, banging back on the hinges loudly. The sound makes me spin around, and there's my son, followed by Mace whose face looks as black as thunder.

What the hell has he done now?

Cas comes stomping over to me with that sullen expression on his face I know only too well.

"I didn't *do* anything," he gets in first.

"He put his hands on a brother's bike without asking permission," Mace snarls as he reaches his side. "Started the fuckin' engine."

"I wanted to know what it sounded like." Cas has a strange look on his face, defiant and challenging.

"Mace told you not to touch the bikes." I remember him telling him the rules that day in my kitchen.

I know exactly what Cas has done. He's pushed over the line to see what he can get away with. It's something he's done with me time after time. I sigh heavily, uncertain as always how to deal with him. *Ground him? Take his Xbox away?* I know only too well that only increases his resentment and worsens his behaviour. I thought he'd been making progress this week but being back on the compound has set him off, and I suspect it was the earlier altercation between him and Liz.

For the moment, I ignore him. "Mace, I'm so sorry…"

"Who's fuckin' bike was it?" a low voice growls. The voice that still has the power to send shivers through me.

Mace looks over my shoulder at the man standing behind me. He stiffens slightly before he replies, "Yours, Liz."

"I left it there to have that fuckin' rattle looked at, not to have grubby hands all over it. He fuckin' started it?" Liz now directs himself to Cas. "You dared to touch my ride?"

It's worse now I know it's Lizard's bike. In an instant, I realise Cas isn't so comfortable with the fact his father doesn't acknowledge him as he'd implied. It was his dad's bike he dared touch, and in another life, he'd probably have been encouraged and not denied. But there's no relationship except unbeknownst to Lizard, they share the same blood.

I can see Cas vibrating with rage and perhaps something else. Disappointment, as though he's realised however he tries, Lizard won't give him any special treatment because he doesn't know of any reason he should. I let my eyes flash a signal to Cas, *Keep your mouth shut.* I'm crossing my fingers he doesn't blurt out the truth.

Lizard looks tired and drawn, but then he had just sat

through what was probably a very difficult meeting with Esme's dad. No wonder he looks pale. It's a similar look to how he'd often returned from a tour, exhausted and drained. Of course, back then, I'd pandered to him, ran him a bath, given him a massage, my hands easing his pain and tension away until he started to relax. Then tension of a different sort would arise, one that was easily dealt with when we fell into bed, or, as many times, Lizard's need for me had become so urgent, he'd taken me up against the bathroom counter, the bed proving too far.

Now I've no right to touch him. I'm unable to show my vested interest in easing his pain, but he's in no state to have the truth thrown at him.

Freckles are darkening as Cas's face reddens. *He's going to blow.*

"Come on, Cas. Our bags are still in the car." It had been raining so hard, I'd told him we'd get them later, and so far, I haven't had a chance to bring them inside. Stepping forward, I take his arm. "We'll go home." I turn toward Mace. "I'm sorry." Once again, I'm apologising for my son's behaviour. It's something I do time after time.

"Yeah, get out of here. You're not welcome here, kid."

Cas pulls out of my hold and swings around. "Who do you think you fucking are?" he shouts at Lizard.

Oh God, no! I throw a pleading look toward Mace.

Stepping between Lizard and my son, Mace's voice belts out, "Go with your mom, now."

For the first time, I hear him use the voice he must bring into play when being the enforcer and keeping everyone in line. It's a half bark, half snarl. A command that must be obeyed. Luckily, it pulls Cas up, shocking him. His attention now turns to the enforcer, and he stands with his mouth gaping.

Like a light going on, I think it dawns on him what a spectacle he's making, and how he's taken things too far. His lip starts to tremble as he glances at me, then looks at Mace.

"Can... can we come back?" he asks.

"No, you fuckin' can't." After that pronouncement, Lizard storms off.

"I'll walk you out." Mace's voice has dropped to a more reasonable tone.

Now it's stopped raining, the sun has come out and the pavement is steaming. Really this weather should be the other way around, black clouds would better match my current mood.

Mace sees us into my car then stands with the driver's door open, bending down to talk to us inside.

"I'm sorry, Vanna, Cas, but this isn't working. Hear me out, Cas." Mace hardens his voice as my son starts to voice an objection. "Lizard isn't ever going to recognise you. You can see the place he's in now. He's happy with his life, and anything you tell him wouldn't be appreciated." He pauses, and sighs. "I know my brother. If Liz knew his responsibilities, say you took a DNA test and proved it to him—and believe me, that's what it would take—and you removed any doubts he could have in his head, you'd fuck him up more. He'd step up, give you money. But hell, Vanna," his eyes go to Cas's and he gives it to him straight, "right now he doesn't even like Cas."

"He's my dad," Cas says quietly, a sob in his voice. So alien from my boy who tries so hard to pretend he's a grown man.

Without looking in that direction, Mace waves his hand behind him. "Every man here chose this family. Blood counts for nothing. Told you, you had to work for his respect, Cas. Well, you've lost it now."

Cas wipes a tear from his eyes, then looks at the wetness on the back of his hand as though he can't believe what it is. I can't remember the last time he cried.

"Look," Mace continues, "I hope it works out for you. If Cas needs a lawyer, Mel's dad is an attorney who lives in Denver. He can perhaps find one to help you out." I go to tell him I'm all set for that, but in the end I don't bother. The offer is a nice gesture and I shouldn't be throwing it back in his face. But I can't take any help from the club, especially when he continues, "It's best that you don't come back. Best for Lizard and best for you." He glances at Cas, then focuses on my face. "It's not doing you or Cas any good, Vanna."

I can't tell him that's a lie.

He closes the door, a jerk of his chin replacing the word good-bye. Then he nods at Karl who opens the gate, and I start the engine and drive out.

Cas leans around, watching the compound fade in the distance behind us. We're a few miles away before he speaks.

"I fucked up good this time, didn't I, Mom?"

Fighting back my own tears, I don't reply. Not even to admonish him for swearing. Mace was right, it's best we keep away from the compound. Lizard had said it himself; he doesn't want Cas anywhere near him, and as for me? He couldn't have put it any better. I'm not his type.

CHAPTER NINETEEN

Mace

Fuck it! I slam my hand on the bar top. Seems like I can't help doing wrong by trying to do right.

"Beer?"

"Whisky." I snarl my response at Dirt. A tumbler is in my hand double fast. I drain it in two gulps, then ask for another. The second goes down only fractionally slower, but I'm beginning to mellow at last. *That kid's face.* He knew he'd gone too far. But he wanted too much, too fast. Cas had assured Vanna, and also me, that he understood the situation, that Lizard couldn't remember wasn't his fault. But it must have been hard for him to stand there this morning and hear his father deny him and then say his mother wasn't someone he'd have gone for. All the pleasure had been wiped from Cas's face, and the boy I'd found myself taking to the shop must be the one Vanna had to deal with each day.

My reaction had been the right one, hadn't it? My loyalty is first and foremost to my brother. At first, I'd thought, maybe Lizard deserved to discover the family he'd lost, but it's obvious he and Cas didn't take to each other, and he's better off left in ignorance.

Vanna could push it, but as she hasn't tackled the issue, or come after what's rightfully hers, child support at the least, in the last ten years. I'm sure she isn't going to cause trouble now. Christ, it must have hurt when Lizard had so rudely dismissed her earlier today. Sure, he has his choice of younger pussy, but Vanna's not that old.

She'd taken care with her appearance today, and no one had told her how good she looked, and fuck me, but I feel guilty about that. I had been going to remark on it, but the time hadn't been right. Even with her new hairdo, stylish clothes which hugged her still good figure, Lizard hadn't given her a second glance. She wasn't, as he'd put it so succinctly, his type.

Still, I'd gotten up close and personal with the type of shit she has to deal with, with that kid. I doubt she's allowed him to run wild, but he's done that anyway. If ever a boy needed a father's guiding hand, that was Cas. But he's not going to get that from Lizard, and while I admire Vanna, I'm no more the settling down type than my brother.

Though, Liz had been a family man at one time, and according to Vanna, they'd been happy. It's clear though, that ship has sailed now.

"Are you feeling alright, Lizard?" I hear called from behind me and turn to spy what Vi is talking about. Liz is chasing down tablets with his beer.

"Another headache?" I sympathise as I walk over, hoping Cas's behaviour had nothing to do with it.

He nods, then puts his hand to his head, clearly regretting his action.

"You go to the optometrist like you were going to?"

Keeping his head still as he remembers not to move it again, he confirms, "My vision's twenty-twenty she said. No need for glasses."

So his headaches must be something else. "You go to your VA appointment?"

His lips press together, then he admits, "Not yet, but I think I will. Can't keep putting up with these pains, Mace."

"You have been getting them a lot. Advil work?"

"Eventually. Maybe they can prescribe something stronger."

The fact he's even thinking about it shows his pain must be bad. "If you want company when you go, I'll be with you, Brother."

He leans his head back against the couch and sighs. "At least it's back to normal now without the kids."

"Yeah." I grin. "Will save us a few bucks at least, but I'm going to miss Esme."

"She won't see that drawing of hers Ink's doing on your bike."

She might. I've already thought of taking a ride down to Flagstaff to show her once it's done, and to check she's doing alright.

"Oh fuck no." Sparky's voice sounds from the bar and his fist thumps the wood. "Not a-fuckin-gain."

Turning around, I groan.

"What's up, Brother?" Lizard asks without opening his eyes.

"Vi's just put another fuckin' swear jar on the bar."

Prez's old lady hears me and comes over with a big grin on her face. "When Theo's around, you watch your mouths. We'll have another one soon when Mel and Pyro's kid's born."

"Got to bring this up in church," Liz mumbles. "This is a fuckin' biker clubhouse, not a kindergarten." His fingers press into his temples again.

"I can't tell the difference sometimes." Vi laughs, then she frowns. "You sure you're okay, Liz?"

"Hunky dory." Lizard opens his eyes and winks. Looks like that Advil might be kicking in. He's certainly got a little more colour.

At that moment, the clubhouse door opens, and in walks Shayla. She'd been staying out of the way at Mo's. Jayden's with her.

Shayla's critical eyes scan the room, clearly noticing Esme's missing. I walk over to her and as soon as I'm close, she asks anxiously, "Everything go okay here?"

I notice the sadness in her face. "You're going to miss her, aren't you?"

"I am," she confirms. "I thought I'd be relieved, you know? But I've been looking out for her all these months, and it feels a bit like I've lost a limb. She's such a sweet kid, Mace."

"Her parents love her." Vi has appeared, overheard, and tries to put Shayla's mind at ease. "Esme ran straight to them with no hesitation. It destroyed her dad to learn what happened to her."

I'm glad to hear it went down well, not having been here myself. "I'm sure they'll get her the help she needs. Time for you to think about you, now, Shayla, and what you want. Time for you to heal." I give Vi a nod of thanks that she'd updated us, but signal with my eyes that I'll take it from here.

I lead Shayla to a free couch and hold up two fingers to Dirt. Almost before we've got our asses on the seat, two beers appear in front of us. Picking up one of the bottles, she takes a long swallow.

"Needed that." She wipes the back of her hand over her mouth. "This afternoon, with Mo, was… interesting."

I chuckle. I expect it was. Mo's quite a force to be reckoned with. She's Hellfire's wife, and when he was the prez, was the club's first lady, even if she steered clear of the clubhouse most of the time. Of course, her history isn't pretty. She was raped by Blackie, the prez before Hellfire, and Hellfire killed the man who was his father. While it's never been confirmed, rather than Hell being Demon's dad, we suspect he's his brother. But who needs to know the true fucking family lines? Blood, as I'd told Cas, counts for nothing. Hellfire had raised Demon like a son, whatever the truth of the matter. Still, Mo had never completely gotten over her unease with the club.

That thought makes me wonder whether Shayla will ever recover.

"You talk to Mo?" I wonder if it might have helped if she

had, though part of me worries. You can never tell which way Mo's going to jump. "Mo's been through some bad shit herself."

Shayla's head tilts. "No, she didn't say anything, and I didn't offer. She was pleasant enough but didn't seem receptive to confidences."

It could have been a missed chance. "I still think you should speak to someone."

Shayla understands what I'm saying. "I don't know, Mace. I don't see myself talking to a therapist, or not yet. I've been so focused on running, on keeping Esme out of Major's hands, that I haven't really thought about myself, apart from getting rid of this fucking tattoo, of course. Talking means dredging everything up again. I don't know if I'll ever be ready."

"You will, babe. You will. You'll move on."

She shakes her head. Her disbelief is the reason I think seeing a therapist will work. She'll only exist, not thrive, when she distrusts all men. As I watch her drink her beer again, her throat working so gracefully as she swallows, I admit I'd like her to at least trust me. I also admit I have fantasies about her being in my bed but have no idea whether I'd ever be able to get her into it.

When she goes to lean forward and replace the empty bottle on the table, I help out by taking it from her. As our fingers accidentally touch, she jumps as though scalded, then looks sheepish.

"Babe, why don't I look into making you an appointment?"

She frowns. "No point, Mace. Now that Esme's gone, I was thinking of moving on."

My brow creases. Now that she's put it out there, I know I don't want her to go, and not just because I don't think it's safe. I don't want her leaving for selfish reasons. "Sort of getting used to you being around. Why don't you stay? You've got to get the rest of your tat done for a start. You're safe here. You're not going to get any trouble from anyone, and Pyro's offered you a job starting Monday."

"The job sounded good when I had Esme to think of. Now

I'm alone..." her voice trails off. "I don't know what to do, Mace."

"What were your plans, your dreams? Before you were taken?" Suddenly a thought hits me. "Did you have a man? Were you married?" If so, wouldn't she have gone back to him? Asked for help at the least.

She blinks slowly. "I had a man. Well, I thought I had. When I escaped, I had no money. I managed to borrow a phone from someone at a shelter, and I called him. His voice... Hearing his voice made me hope everything would be alright. But I'd been gone a year, and he'd moved on. There was a woman talking in the background. I begged him for help, but he didn't believe my story. Said it had hurt him too much when I'd walked out and not bothered to contact him. I tried to say it wasn't my fault, but he refused to hear it. He'd assumed I'd left for another man. I told him I hadn't, tried to explain..." Her face distorts with remembered pain. "He called me a whore. When I asked just for a bit of money to tide me over—a loan, not a gift—he told me to earn it on my back."

"You want to give me his fuckin' name?"

"Why?"

"So I can kill him for you."

The fleeting grin breaking through her pain shows me she thinks I'm joking. I'm not.

She grows serious again. "His suggestion was not even an option. You know I can't stand a man touching me. I can't even stand a man being close. That time, when we first ran, and I needed a ride out of Vegas... I froze, I vomited after. I know I couldn't do that again."

I don't point out we're sitting opposite each other, so close our knees are no more than an inch apart. Leaned forward as we both are, our foreheads are all but touching. I can feel her exhaled breaths on my face. I don't mention any of that.

"I've tried a new recipe." Mel's standing beside me, a plate in her hand. "Want to test it out?"

We both accept her offer of a delicious looking cupcake without further persuasion. Shayla takes a mouthful and groans as the flavour hits her taste buds. "Mmm. So good."

"I've got another batch, I've just taken out of the oven." Mel's smiling broadly at Shayla's obvious appreciation. "Want to be my tester?"

Shayla almost leaps to her feet. "Sure," she says, stuffing the rest of the cake into her mouth. "Lead the way."

I smile after her as she walks off. The happier she is here, the longer, hopefully, she'll stay.

Her seat doesn't stay vacant for long, and soon Ink is sitting opposite me. "Beth's been roped in for taste testing."

"Shayla too," I tell him.

"What's between you and her?" Ink asks. "You looked quite cosy sitting there."

"Nothing," I reply, while admitting to myself I'm starting to wish that there was. "She's thinking of moving on, and I was trying to persuade her to stay."

"Why would you stop her leaving, Mace?" Ink queries, leaning back and stretching out his long legs, crossing them at the ankles. "If she stays, we'll need to watch our backs in case Major catches up with her."

"If she goes, and he does, she'll be facing that problem alone. That thought doesn't sit easy with me."

He gives me a long look. "With Beth and I it was sex," Ink starts. "Instant sexual attraction. I denied it was more than that, of course, but once I had her, I knew I didn't want anyone else."

My brow furrows as I wonder where he's going with this.

"You and Shayla? You're friends first, aren't you?"

"Whoa." I hold up my hands. "Yeah, I'm friendly with her. She needs someone in her corner." I think how she told me about the asshole of her ex. "You know me, Ink. I'm not a one-woman man. And one thing's for certain, Shayla needs someone to be there for her. She's not out for a fling, or anything for that matter.

The last thing she needs is a man who'll fuck her and leave her, and what more have I to offer than that?"

He laughs. "Not so long ago, I was saying exactly the same thing, Mace. And you know what? The more I protested, the harder I fought, the deeper I fell."

I'm not falling for Shayla. I'd like to fuck her, yes. Especially now her figure's getting more rounded as she's putting on weight—probably from taste testing everything Mel bakes. But to take her as my old lady? To take anyone as my partner? No. Simply not going to happen. No way.

I tell him precisely that.

Ink, the bastard leatherneck just laughs. "We'll see, fucker." He's looking over my shoulder.

I've served, I've learned how to stay alive, so I'm aware that someone is approaching behind me. A heady perfume meets my nostrils, so I don't jump when arms circle my neck, and the smooth soft skin of a female cheek settles close to my ear.

"Want some fun?"

I don't have to turn around to know who's there. I unwrap her arms, firmly pushing them down and away. "Not now, Tulia."

Ink raises his eyebrow and smirks.

CHAPTER TWENTY

Lizard

The Advil had finally kicked in and the headache had soon receded to a dull ache. I'd felt exhausted though, like I often do after one of the attacks hit. Although I hadn't seen the need to keep up with my scheduled appointments, now I'm beginning to accept I have to talk to someone about these sudden blasts of pain. Heaven forbid one should hit when I'm out on my bike.

I get checks because of the blow I'd received to my head. They always follow the same pattern, every appointment going the same way. Seems the doctors still want to prod me and probe, but I can't see the point.

Got any memories back?

No. I know there are a few things I don't remember, but as long as I don't forget the important shit, I'm no longer bothered.

Any problems?

No. As long as I can live, ride, fuck, and do my job, I'm happy and content.

See you next year.

That's why I stopped going.

Although I didn't think I had a problem with my sight, I had banked on being prescribed glasses which might stop these headaches. But no, my eyes are apparently better than fine. Although, like the vast majority of people, I'll probably need help to see well in time, but there are no signs of degradation now.

Having to acknowledge I'm getting more head pain than a woman PMSing, it's time, as I admitted to Mace, to get myself seen.

Especially as it's fucking with my life. It's Saturday night, and I've gone to bed early missing the party. This is not me.

Sleep comes easily.

But then I wake, dripping with sweat with the bedsheets twisted around me. I scramble for the details of the dream I just had, but as normal, they evade me.

Rolling onto my back, I reach out my hand to the left side of my bed. It's empty, not even warm to show someone had been there.

Why should there be? Placing my hands under my head, I give myself a mental shake. Christ, maybe the dream I can't remember is still fixed in my brain.

I close my eyes.

I'm Lizard, otherwise known as Norton James. I ride with the Satan's Devils MC and have done for the past ten years. I'm twenty-six years old, and my birthday is the tenth of January. I'm not looking forward to tomorrow. I'm leaving on another fucking tour, and I've got a bad feeling about it inside me.

What the fuck?

This time, I do shake my head. I'm thirty-eight for fuck's sake. I get out of bed and pull on my jeans, then stretch my hands over my head.

I'm Lizard, otherwise known as Norton James. I ride with the Satan's Devils MC and have done for the past ten years. I'm thirty-eight years old, and my birthday is the tenth of January. I'm a tattoo artist and I run Devil's Ink on behalf of my brothers. I've no ties, no family and intend to stay that way.

There. That's right. *I'm going on a tour…*

No, no. Again, I shake my head. *That's not right.*

Entering the bathroom, I stand in front of the toilet bowl. *Fuck. Left the seat up again. She's going to be mad at me.*

Who?

I feel a cold chill go through me, and again physically try to shake it off, while raising my eyes to look into the mirror. My lips curve. *Not my hair or eye colour, but my nose, my mouth. That's what my baby boy inherited from me. Christ, I'm going to miss them when I'm overseas...*

Baby? What the fuck? And I'm going fucking nowhere. I'm right where I belong. What fucking dream has gotten hold of me?

I finish my piss, automatically tug my dick back into my pants, but I can't drag my eyes away from the reflection of my face. But it's not my face that I see. It's younger, red hair and green eyes, but the features are mine.

The features are mine.

The features are mine.

I'm seeing red hair.

The features are mine.

The eyes are green.

My baby boy's eyes were green.

My head starts to pound.

The image in front of me shimmers. The hair colour morphs from dirty blond to red. Hazel eyes turn to green.

I close my eyes. Cas. *Castiel.*

No. No. No, no, no, no, no. I was twenty-six when I went on tour. My boy was two.

I've got no kids. No. No way.

I was twenty-four on my last tour.

Cas is not related to me.

And Vanna? *She's not my type...*

Vanna. *She's not my type. Not my type. Not my type...*

I hear a keening sound that seems to be coming from me. My head explodes with pain, agony so great I can barely see. I stagger back into my room, grab my cut and take out the bottle of Advil. It's fucking empty.

I launch myself toward the door, weaving like a drunk, slamming into the wood as though my limbs don't belong to me.

Mace. Mace will get me something for my head. He's in the next room. All I've got to do is open the door, take a few steps, and he'll get me some relief.

Fuck, but this is the worst one yet.

I open the door, take the first step, then crash into the wall, dropping to my knees, my hands cradling my head.

"Help," I cry weakly.

"Who the fuck's crashing around this time on a... Liz?"

For Christ's sake stop! Someone is banging on a door, each thump slamming into my head.

"Liz? For fuck's sake, what's wrong, Lizard?"

"Cas..."

CHAPTER TWENTY-ONE

Mace

Who *the fuck is crashing around this time of the morning?*

I smile as I hear Judge's voice. It's not just me they've woken up. Judge will sort it. I turn over, plump my pillow, and close my eyes. I'm going back to sleep.

But apparently, I'm not as a loud banging on my door sounds. "What the fuck now?" I grumble to myself, knowing the enforcer side of me is going to come out if I'm being disturbed just because someone's had too much to drink.

I open my door and immediately spy my brother on his knees.

"Liz? For fuck's sake, what's wrong, Lizard?"

"Cas…"

Then he's flat on the floor.

"Liz? Come on, Brother. Wake up. You lay one on last night?"

"He went to bed early, Mace." Sparky, also disturbed it seems, informs me as he comes up hastily buttoning his pants. "He could have had a bottle in his room, but I didn't see him drink."

Leaning down I smell his breath, I get the odour of body sweat, but no alcohol.

"Liz?" I give his shoulder a gentle shake. "Liz, Bro, you're worrying me. Wake the fuck up." Then I shout to no one in particular, "Get Rusty."

Only minutes later when Liz still hasn't stirred, Rusty appears, his fingers scratching at the ginger hairs covering his bare chest. "What's up with him?" he says through a wide yawn.

"Don't know. Just found him like this."

"Drunk?"

"Don't think so."

As Rusty folds to his knees, creaking sounds coming as he does so, I watch as he checks Lizard's pulse, then gently raises his eyelids.

"I don't like this, Mace," he admits, his worried eyes rising to meet mine. "Think we need to call a bus."

"Can we take him?"

Rusty shakes his head. "The faster the paramedics are here the better. Hell, if he's not passed out drunk, fuck knows what could have happened. His pulse is erratic, could be a heart attack or a stroke for all I can tell."

Sparky is already on his phone calling nine-one-one. He's relating what Rusty has just said.

"Brother, hang in there," I'm crouched down again. I take Lizard's hand, it seems cold. It's only then I remember what he had said. *Cas.* Or had he? Had he been trying to say something else? Perhaps he'd been trying to tell me he can't breathe or something. Maybe I just imagined he'd said his son's name. Wishful thinking perhaps.

Or had he remembered, and the shock had been so severe as to have such drastic results? Fuck, I hope not. It would have been my fault allowing Vanna to bring Cas here.

The sound of sirens is a welcome relief, especially when the sound is cut off as it means help is here.

Beaver ushers the paramedics up the stairs.

"Stand back," one speaks authoritatively.

Looking around, I spy all of the brothers who live here are now out of their rooms and gathered around. Getting up, I enforce the medic's instructions. "Give them some fuckin' space."

"Has he been drinking?"

"We don't think so," I answer the medic. "Could have, but I'd say no."

"He was on his knees, then just collapsed," says Judge.

"Pulse is weak and erratic," Rusty observes.

The medics check everything for themselves. It's no surprise when they decide to take him in. I remember just as they're putting Liz onto a stretcher.

"He's been getting severe headaches. They've increased in frequency lately. Oh, and he was invalided out of the Marines as he suffered a severe brain injury from being too close to an explosion. He lost parts of his memory which have never returned."

They're clearly wasting no time. Neither am I. As they take Lizard away, I'm back in my room pulling on a shirt and my cut then my boots and picking up keys, using my fingers to comb down my hair. I'm not the only one to have gotten hastily dressed and headed down the stairs and out through the main door. There's a lot of company with me as I run for my bike.

Lizard, you old fucker. You're going to be alright. He's got to be. He's still young, got a good life ahead of him. All he's got to do now is wake up and live it.

The waiting area becomes more and more crowded, and in the end the hospital personnel moves us all to a room where we can wait in private. Before an hour's gone by, even the brothers and old ladies who live off-compound have turned up.

Demon's pacing left to right. Frustrated that he's a man down and he doesn't know why. He comes to a halt in front of me, a fist slamming into his palm.

"If someone had taken a shot at him, I'd be after that fucker now. Feel so damn helpless, Mace. His body has turned against him."

Beef comes over to join us. "Should Vanna be here?" He

glances around presumably to check no one overheard his quietly spoken words.

"No," Demon answers him. "We've not been told anything. He might have already woken up and be chasing the nurses by now. Bring her here and we'd have to explain their relationship."

"Family of Norton James?" A male nurse has appeared by the door. When everyone stands, he scans all our faces. "The doctor would like to talk to someone about the headaches Mr James has been getting."

"I will." I step forward, liking to think I know my brother more than most.

"Is there any news?" Demon physically moves me to one side.

"I'm sorry, no. Mr James is still unconscious."

So much for chasing the nurses. I give Demon a nod, then slide around him and follow the nurse.

I'm shown into the emergency bay where they're treating Lizard. He's hooked up to machines and looks so damn pale. For a moment, I just stand staring, suppressing the impulse to shake the doctor and tell him to fucking wake him up. To do anything to get his eyes to open and his mouth to start working. But Lizard stays asleep, and the only sound is that fucking machine beeping.

"Thank you for coming back here Mr…"

"Grey," I supply. "Fox Grey. But I'm known as Mace."

"Mace you prefer, I take it?"

I don't care what he fucking calls me as long as he tells me Liz is going to be okay.

"Someone, you perhaps, told the paramedics that Mr James has been getting headaches. Were these unusual for him?"

"Yes. Oh, he'd occasionally lay one on and get a hangover like we all do, but then he started complaining of headaches at odd times during the day. They've been getting worse and increasing in frequency. He got his eyes tested as he's a tattoo artist and uses them a lot, but his sight is okay."

"When did the headaches start?"

I think back. "Five, six months ago? I can't really pinpoint it. Maybe before that, but I didn't notice. Oh, and he had a traumatic brain injury about twelve years back. When he served."

"Yes, I've got his medical and TBI records. Had anything happened to start the headaches off? Did he come off his bike? Knock his head at all? Get into a fight and receive a blow?"

"No." I don't even have to think about it. "He hasn't come off his bike, and he's not been fighting." If our gym had been up and running there could have been a chance, but as it is, we've nowhere to spar. "He might have had a friendly slap around the head, but nothing serious. Oh, but that injury he had. He lost his memory."

"That was also noted in his records. His short-term memory improved I see, but there's a big gap in his life. Has that started to come back at all?"

I'm unsure whether it's worthwhile mentioning, but I do anyway. Anything must be a help. So, I tell him about Vanna and Cas, and that for the past two weekends, they've visited the clubhouse. But as the doctor says, his headaches started long before that, and in his view, those are the symptoms he should be worrying about.

"MRI's free now, Doctor Hollister."

"Let's take him down. Can you find your way back to the waiting room?"

I say I can.

"Oh," he stops me as they're transferring the portable monitoring equipment to his gurney. "If this woman is his wife, perhaps she should be here?"

"They've lived apart for more than ten years, Doc. No divorce, but only a couple of my brothers know what she is to him. When Liz comes around, he'll think it's an invasion of his privacy if she was informed and his past that he can't remember comes out. It was his therapist's advice that they live separately."

His eyes widen at that. "His official next of kin is listed as one David Black."

I nod. It would be. "That's our Prez."

"He's here?"

Again, I nod, then step aside so they can take Lizard away. As I watch him being wheeled down the corridor, I wish I believed in some sort of deity so I could offer up a prayer. I don't. I just hope his time to meet Satan hasn't yet arrived.

"He's gone for an MRI." I update everyone as soon as I enter the room they're in. "Hopefully we'll know more after that."

"Why wasn't that the first thing they did?" Cad snaps.

I shrug. I don't know. But maybe he had to wait his turn or be stabilised or some such shit.

"Man, this is bad. Never thought anything could stop that man."

I nod at Wills. Lizard has always been active and healthy, his ability to shake off a cold is renowned. To see someone like him brought low affects us all. But now I know about the blow to the head and the severity of it, I'm wondering if my brother was a ticking time bomb, just waiting to explode.

Did any of us cause it? I'd told the doctor the truth about him not having any serious bangs to the head, though I'd cuffed him on the ear myself a couple of times. But hell, some of the things he comes out with, he deserves it. Could a jesting blow have caused him to collapse? Christ, I fucking hope not.

I swear the clock on the wall is ticking far too slowly. I seem to be counting off minutes which feel like hours. Some of the brothers go on a coffee run, and Mel, Vi and Beth go to raid the vending machines for candy.

When Beef stands to stretch his legs, I grab one of the few chairs, and sit with my legs splayed and my hands clasped between them, my head bowed. *Lizard. You have got to be okay. You can't fuckin' die now. Who am I going to share women with? Ink's got Beth, he's no fun anymore. You've got to recover with your cock in working order, and we'll share some pussy together.*

Not Shayla though. If I ever get near her with my cock, ain't gonna be sharing her. No, she's all mine—for the night anyway.

She's the only one of the women not here now. The prospects will have to keep her company. Karl, Beaver, Dirt and Nails are holding down the fort back home.

The door opens, but it's only those who went for coffee coming in and passing cups around. Next time, it's the girls returning and giving out sugary bars.

Finally, when the garbage bin is filled to overflowing with disposable cups, the door opens and at last it's the doctor.

"David Black."

"That's me," says Demon. "But we're all his family and want to know how he is, and what you've found."

"He's still the same as when he came in, but we've done an MRI scan. Mr James has got a meningioma, a tumour in his brain. It's fairly large, and I suspect it's been growing for some time having heard about these headaches he's been having."

"A tumour? Is… is it cancer?" Demon cautiously asks.

That dreaded fucking C word. I hold my breath waiting for the doctor's reply.

"We can't tell at the moment whether it's malignant or benign. I also can't tell you right now about the treatment, whether we'll be able to shrink it, or whether it needs surgery to be removed, but it can't be left as it is, as it's clearly interfering with his functions, hence the coma he is in. We've got the on-call neurologist coming to assess him."

"Will he recover?" Demon asks. Again, I hold my breath.

"I'm sorry, but I can't tell you that either. Hopefully, we'll know more when the neurologist has been able to examine him. He'll be transferred to the neurology ward shortly."

"Is he likely to wake up?" Ink asks.

My hands fist as I wait to hear the doctor say *I don't know* one more time. I'm not to be disappointed.

"I'm very sorry, but it's impossible to tell. It is possible, but I would say unlikely unless we can ease the pressure being caused by the meningioma."

I pipe up with a question of my own. "Is this likely to have been caused by his original brain injury?"

I wait for the answer I'm sure I'll hear once again, but this time the doctor surprises me. "The VA might disagree, or at least that would be their go-to response, but yes, I think that's quite possible. A lot of work has been done which links subsequent meningiomas with previous traumatic damage to the brain. Of course, as these take years to form, cause and effect are hard to prove, but research would suggest there are a disproportionate number of these tumours appearing in vets who've suffered a TBI."

Knowing doesn't help Lizard, but it helps me. If true, it would mean it wasn't down to me forcing Vanna and Cas onto him.

CHAPTER TWENTY-TWO

Mace

"What's the news, Prez?"

Demon and I have barely entered the clubroom when questions start to fly. With the unlikely prognosis that Lizard wouldn't be waking any time soon on his own, a few hours ago, men had started to return to the clubhouse. I'd stayed on with Demon and am now right behind him.

"The neurologist has seen him." He begins his update to the hushed room. "His view is that the tumour needs to be removed."

"Will they do a biopsy first? To find out whether it's cancer or not?" Sparky walks closer.

"No point as it needs to come out anyway. Apparently, it's causing intracranial pressure which is responsible for putting him into a coma. They're worried there may be a bleed that the tumour is masking."

"What are his chances?" Judge asks, his jaw clenched.

Demon shakes his head. "At the moment, they are being cautious and aren't prepared to say. Removing the tumour may bring him back to us, or it could go the other way."

I hear gasps from the couches where the women are sitting. Jayden's hand is covering her mouth, and Vi's dabbing tears from her eyes. Beth has her arm around Mel, and Steph has her face buried in Max's fur. Jeannie and Sindy looked equally shocked. As are we all, this has happened so fast.

Ever since we'd spoken to the experts, I've been trying to come to terms with what I heard. The thought of my brother having an operation on his fucking brain is shattering. The idea I might never laugh, joke, drink, or share women with him again is, well, I haven't words to describe what that would mean to me.

We're bikers and we know our lives could be cut short at any time. We could come off our bikes or be shot by members of a rival MC. That this life is full of danger is part of the attraction. Who wants to live a nine-to-five in a safe suburban house? Not me, that's for fucking certain. I just never suspected Liz could be betrayed by his own body.

"When?" Beef asks.

"Tomorrow, Monday. They want to make sure he's stabilised first."

"Could the tumour do more damage in that time?" Wills looks concerned.

I contribute to the discussion. "It's a slow growing one. Lizard must have been living with this for literally years. They're convinced they've got time."

Prez looks around, noting everyone seems to be here, then catches my eye and raises his chin. "Church in an hour," he announces.

I nod. Convinced he's doing the right thing as we'd discussed while sitting vigil, hoping Lizard would come around. We've got some decisions to make which is why Prez is calling everyone together.

Knowing I could do with a shower, having missed out on mine earlier this morning, I cross the room to the stairs and start to make my way up. On the top step sits Shayla. As she looks up at me, I see her eyes glistening.

"I heard," she admits in a whisper.

Christ. Of all the men here, she's most at her ease with me and Lizard, us being the ones she'd first told her sorry tale to. Of course she's going to feel sad for the man whose prognosis is uncertain.

"You could have come down. Liz's condition isn't a secret," I tell her.

"I didn't want to intrude," she replies. "It's bad, isn't it?"

It's been a long ass day, starting even before dawn had lightened the sky when Lizard collapsed outside my room. He'd been trying to get to me, I'm certain. He just didn't make it in time. I lean my head against the wall before I answer her. Then I just say, "It's bad, babe."

It's as though I've only just allowed myself to really acknowledge I might never see my brother again. I thought I'd been dealing, but know it's just a front I've been putting on. Now my heart aches as my possible loss cuts through me, as well as the guilt as to the part I might have played.

"I can't lose him," I spit out. "Fuck, Shayla. He's not just a club brother, we were fighting for our country at the same time. Might not have served alongside him, he was a Marine and I was Army, but the tie's there all the same, both up against the same enemy. We were so fuckin' close." I keep to myself the closeness that we shared fuckin' girls together, and settle for, "I had a bond with him that's hard to explain. Sure, he's an asshole, but aren't we all? If he goes—"

"He's a fighter," she insists. "Might not know him well, but I'm certain of that. If there's any chance, he'll come back to you."

"He might. But what if it fucks his brain up?" I draw my hands down my face. "I don't know what to do. Prez wants to meet in an hour. I've come up to get a quick shower, now I've not even the energy to do that. I'm the fuckin' enforcer, babe. How can I do my job when I can't even think straight?"

She stands, and one of her hands lands on my shoulder, then the other on the opposite side. Gently, she digs her fingers in, releases, then does it again.

Christ. That feels so fucking good. I roll my head as her touch eases some of my tension.

As her fingers continue to squeeze and relax, I let out a groan. "You've got a magic touch."

I hear her breathe in deeply, then she says in a decisive tone, "Come with me."

I take the hand she holds out but use my own weight to pull myself up. Then, intrigued, I follow her into the room she's using. A room with such bad connotations, no brother wants to move into it, so it's been used for a variety of other purposes. Connor, Beth's brother, was the last person to stay here when he was injured. No one else wants to go into the room which was Skull's. It's as if his stench still hangs over it. The odour of cop and betrayal.

Now it's filled with her and her perfume and already the place seems lighter.

I stand by the door, uncertain why she's invited me in here.

She indicates the end of the bed. "Sit on the edge there."

When I do, she climbs on the bed behind me. "You're too tall, Mace. I couldn't do this properly out there." She uses her fingers and palms to knead my taut neck and shoulder muscles. Whether it's her, or just the gentle touch that I need, more of my tension starts to ease.

She's left the door open, but that's okay. I may be in her bedroom, but I'm conscious of this massive step forward, and know I can't take advantage or frighten her away. I'm making sure my hands stay anchored on my knees, no hint of a threat or that I'm about to overpower her. Being totally honest, even Shayla's hands on me wouldn't have my cock sitting up, not after the day that I've had. My thoughts are all with my brother, fighting for his very existence. The neurologist had warned us brains are tricky, even if Liz recovers, he may never be the same.

My thoughts come out of my mouth. "What if he can never ride his bike again? Or talk?" Fuck, I'd miss his voice and those comments he makes. "What if he can't feed or look after himself?"

"Mace, don't think that way." Her voice, like her touch, is calming. "Lizard once told me, I shouldn't borrow trouble. He was right. You've just got to take it day by day. Doctors can work miracles these days, and even if he comes out the other side not the same as he was, you and your brothers will deal. One thing I've learned while I've been here is the love you all have for each other."

She's right. If he can't ride his bike, he can't be a member of the club, but that's just semantics. Not one of us would abandon a brother in need.

"He's a good man," she tells me, her hands never stop moving. "Another tattoo artist wouldn't have cared how Major had marked me."

"Property patches mean something to us, darlin'," I explain. "Part of his concern was blowback on the club."

I feel her shrug. "He cares for you, his brothers. But whatever you say or how you try to justify it, he's been good to me." Her hands lift away. "Why don't you lie down, on your front?"

That she's confident enough to suggest it warms me even though my thoughts are chilling. I do as she suggests, and feel her straddle me, her hands now massaging my shoulders and back, stopping just above my ass.

"You're good at this," I tell her, feeling myself relax.

"I work with heavy shit," she says. "Sometimes I overdo it or have to stretch in unfamiliar ways to get to part of an engine. I discovered this great massage parlour and often went there to get my aches soothed away. I'm just trying to do what they did to me."

"You're doing great."

For a moment we're quiet, me starting to feel like I could drift away and doze off.

"Has Lizard got any family?"

Now isn't that the million-dollar question? "His mom died,

his dad couldn't cope. Lost himself in the bottle. Lizard was taken away and entered the system. Went through various foster homes and then joined the Marines. I don't think his dad is still breathing, but Lizard wouldn't want anything to do with him anyway." I offer her what truth I can, keeping the rest to myself.

My mind goes to Cas. If that kid doesn't pull himself together, he could go the same way as his dad. Be taken away from his mom if social services think she's not a good enough mother. Fuck, and I just sent her away. *I'd been thinking of Liz.* If, heaven forbid, he never recovers, wouldn't he want someone to be there for his kid and his wife? I'd been trying to protect him, but what if I've made things worse?

"What's the time, babe?"

"It's okay, I've got an eye on the clock. You've still got twenty minutes before your meeting."

"I meant to have a shower."

"You want to go get one?"

"No." It's here I want to stay. Her touch, so soothing, so comforting, it's helping me to come to terms with what's happened today. I feel so fucking helpless. There's nothing to fight, no one to question. This problem is one I can't solve in any of my usual ways.

We're quiet as she continues to work my muscles. When at last she says I should be on my way, I realise some of my inner strength has returned. While her administrations have done nothing to take my troubles away, somehow, I feel better able to face them.

When she stands, I roll onto my back, then curl my abs and sit up. She's moved a few feet away.

I don't approach, I make no move to touch her. I just say a heartfelt, "Thank you, babe."

She offers a quick smile. "If there's anything I can do to help, Mace..."

"Stay," I tell her, then when she goes to protest, I tell her again, "Just stay here with us. Fuck knows how long Liz will be in the hospital, Shay. I don't need to have to worry about where you are as well."

"You'd worry about me?" She seems surprised.

"Every fuckin' day."

Her eyes widen, and her head tilts to one side. A whole minute passes before she speaks, as though she's working things through in her head. "Okay," she starts, slowly, the word coming as she breathes out. "I won't make plans to move on until Liz is back home."

CHAPTER TWENTY-THREE

Shayla

I'd been a normal woman until Major had taken me. My life was predictable, I'd go to work, come home and then cook a meal for my boyfriend and clean up after him. I wasn't sure I'd be staying with Rodger long-term, but the benefits of having someone there for company outweighed the disadvantages of being an unpaid servant. I wasn't anything particularly special, so hadn't set my hopes too high. In time I knew I wanted a family but wasn't sure I was with the right man.

In my previous life, I'd never have entertained the idea that I'd end up where I am, in the clubhouse of an outlaw MC. I would never mix with these kinds of men, would never even dream of going to a business owned by them if I wanted a tattoo —not that I'd probably have gotten one in the first place, far too daring for a girl like me. Under the circumstances I found myself in, I needed to go somewhere where people maybe wouldn't obey all the rules and would do the work on someone like Esme. Hence, I chose a tattoo parlour run by bikers.

I'd been wrong, they did run an honest business. But instead of turning me away, they'd offered me sanctuary, and I've ended up the one place I'd never imagined I'd be.

Of course, I never expected my life would be turned upside

down in the way it had been. That fateful day carried no indication that anything out of the ordinary was going to happen. I had no premonition, no warning. A simple request to deliver paperwork at the accountant's wasn't strange or unusual at all. I'd agreed, then placed a quick phone call to Rodger saying I'd be late. It met with the reaction I could have predicted, the normal grumpy response that his dinner wouldn't be on the table at the right time.

I'd driven into Vegas, wondering if perhaps it was now time for me and Rodger to part ways. I wasn't even certain I loved him anymore, and sex had become something of an obligation, rather than an act I looked forward to with anticipation. Pleasant enough when we got down to it, but too much of a bother at times.

Rodger's sex drive had also diminished over time, but I expect that's what happens to most couples.

When the accountant had asked me to go for a drink, I'd accepted. Not because I fancied the man, and there was no attraction on his side either, but it had been a break from the monotony of my routine and, if I was honest, a welcome delay in going home to see the man who'd be holding a grudge that I'd left him to fend for himself. Not that he'd be violent, or even shout at me. His treatment would be the opposite, moody silence would be his weapon of choice.

The couple of drinks, one wine, one soda for me, had turned out to be enjoyable as we shared jokes and had a laugh, him relating tales of some of his clients, and me sharing stories of some of mine. He'd treated me as an equal, not as a woman but a person in my own right, just as I'd grown to expect while doing my job. I worked in a male-dominated environment, and one in which I'd grown comfortable. Sure, at times, there would be the odd innuendo or joke, but I'd made sure I'd gotten my own back with an equal quip. I was respected by the work I did, not the shapeliness of my legs.

When I'd left the accountant, we'd shaken hands then I walked off into the night.

The smile that had been placed on my face had slowly slid off when I thought about Rodger and what I'd be returning to. He didn't see me as a partner, we had strict roles in life. He wore the trousers and I, well, I kept house. Even though I had a good job and brought in the same money as he did.

Many women would be happy with my lot in life. But to me, something was missing. I just didn't know what.

It was the musings filling my head which blocked out my awareness of my surroundings. Not that I'd done anything different were I thinking about something else instead, I can't blame Rodger for what happened. Of course I knew women shouldn't walk alone at night, but I never thought something would happen to me. Until it did.

I'd been completely oblivious that the luxury of wondering whether the man I chose to be with was the one with whom I wanted to stay, or anything I had any say over would be stripped away. That I could accept or turn down any man who wanted to fuck me was no longer an option. When I was taken, my preference counted for nothing. I had no say in anything. It was a hard lesson to learn, but learn it I did. I'd do what I was told, or I'd be beaten and tortured until I complied.

My comfortable, if boring, life had disappeared in a flash. My world became one of pain, fear and suffering instead. Until Esme appeared, I'd become resigned that my only release would end with my death.

Esme had given me something to fight for. My determination only grew as she became so scared, she wouldn't talk. Things that were done to me shouldn't be suffered by any woman, let alone a child. I knew I'd do anything to save her, even when I'd given up on saving myself.

At the time, I couldn't see how we could get out, just knew we either had to, or I'd die in the attempt. Major's belief that he'd fully broken me offered a chance. Desperation drove me to carry out the attempt which seemed to have little likelihood of success. But fortune had been with us that night, and we'd fled.

It was fear of her being recaptured that spurred me to do what I had done and allow that truck driver to have me, so he'd take us out of Nevada. He'd griped after that it had been far from the best fuck of his life, as all I could do was lie there shaking and unmoving, hating his hands on me, and as for his dick? I froze when that had touched me.

But he'd fulfilled his part of the bargain and hadn't pressed for a repeat.

It was at that point I knew I'd never willingly let a man near me again in my life.

I hated what I'd become. I was now a woman fearful of men. Far from regarding them as equals, I now knew how they could control me with their superior strength and their ability to inflict pain. I was terrified of darkness descending if I wasn't safe inside at night. I was a wreck but held it together for Esme. Esme had kept me as alive as much as I'd done her.

I hadn't told Mace when he'd persuaded me to give up my waitressing job that I'd already been in danger of being fired. Andy was losing patience and profit with me working there. I'd dropped too many plates to count, jumping when a man got too close, or had tried to grab my ass as I was bent over a table cleaning up. I hated not earning a living, but it hadn't taken much persuasion for me to stop going to the diner to work.

One moment in time. One shift in the universe and the planets aligned against me. Everything had changed, my life turned on its head.

I often think back to that final night, not the day when I last saw Rodger, but going out for a drink with the accountant. I'd been a confident woman, completely comfortable spending time with a man I knew via work. I didn't question I could hold my own in a masculine world.

My experiences have revealed my true self. Now, far from being a strong independent woman, I know I'm weak. Maybe I always was, seeing as how I'd allowed Rodger to take advantage for far too long.

Now I know the depravities men will stoop to. They don't even have to have brains, it's their brawn which counts. They can act on their desires when I can do nothing to stop them. Men, I've learned, don't understand 'no, stop, it hurts'. They don't care as long as they get what they're after.

I couldn't let myself be taken again; I wouldn't survive if Major found me. I can't say why, but something tells me Major doesn't mark someone as property and then let them go, not without doing everything he could to recover them, leaving no stone unturned in the process. He'll kill me for covering his tattoo.

I'd tried to dismiss that thought as soon as it went through my head, but the evidence was something I couldn't forget. One of the other women rubbed and rubbed her back against some brickwork in an effort to remove it herself. That her back was raw and bloody wasn't enough. He poured petrol on her, set her alight and forced the rest of us to watch her burning. The message had been clear. *We were his for the rest of our lives.*

I knew getting mine and Esme's tattoos removed were a risk, but given the options of staying free or him taking me back, it was one I was willing to take. I never wanted anyone to see my back and ask me who I belonged to, or heaven help me, try to find him so they can do the opposite of what the Satan's Devils were doing, and return me to Major.

When I'd first arrived at the compound, I was nervous, wondering what they wanted from me. But they raised no finger to hurt me, nor made any demands I'd be unable to fulfil. I saw the Devils were doing all they could to help me, even though I don't understand why, except it seems, their view of women is in direct contrast to Major's. They found Esme's parents and having checked they were a loving family, reunited her with them. Their actions couldn't be faulted. Me? They're allowing to stay while the work on my tattoo is completed. I've felt secure here, safe from Major.

But I'm no longer their focus, and nor should I be. The Devils are preoccupied with one of their own in the hospital. Just how safe is it to stay?

It's best to keep moving.

There's an uneasiness inside me about allowing myself to get too comfortable here. If I'm tempted to put down roots in one place, Major is certain to catch up with me. I'd promised myself when I'd escaped that I'd keep moving on. It worries me how I'm starting to relax with the men of the club around me. That's dangerous. I can't afford to let my guard down.

So why did I just have my hands on Mace?

Mace has been nothing but kind to me, careful and respectful, but still he's got a cock and balls which makes him no different to the rest. I had been determined to keep my distance from him and everyone else.

But tonight, he was hurting. His best friend could be dying, or if he comes around, who knows who he'll awake as. Mace might have lost the man he knows for good.

Something like this is draining, I know. I'd already lost my parents in a car accident when I was just a kid, and my Gramma had raised me. I'd sat by her hospital bed, hoping she'd wake one last time, but she never did. For her it was blissful, her suffering from the cancer which had ravaged her ended at last. I'd felt lost and helpless when she'd taken her last breath. Yes, I know the pain of that hoping, that eternal optimism that you'll speak to someone again, that it hadn't been the last time you'd heard their voice.

With Lizard there's more hope, or at least I pray there is. If it hadn't been for Lizard, I'd never have come to the club and Esme would still be with me, and not home with her family.

If Lizard had just covered my tattoo without delving deeper, Esme and I would be struggling simply to put food in our mouths. He knew there was something seriously wrong when I tried to pass her off as an adult. But while he could have, he didn't wash his hands of us and send us away. He was the reason we were given refuge, a place of safety, somewhere to catch my breath.

I owe Lizard.

When Mace had sat down beside me as if he had the weight of the world on his shoulders and seemed so worried and tense, I knew there was nothing I could do to help Lizard, but perhaps I could help his friend instead.

Mace's short hair allowed me to see his muscles were knotted and tight. Having received the benefit of many a massage, I knew what to do to ease his physical ache. Without stopping to question myself, I'd placed my hands on his shoulders.

The groan, not in the least sexual, but of relief, had encouraged me to keep kneading, to keep working out those kinks. Then, I'd found myself inviting him into my room.

I don't think he'd noticed me momentarily freeze, my sudden fear he'd take it as an offer for something else. But when he didn't mention the door staying open, and made no threatening move, I relaxed once again.

As did he. I could feel his muscles loosening as my hands worked and we talked. I spent more time than I expected alone with a man, but Mace didn't make a move or a pass, for which I was more than grateful. It was like how the men who I used to work with would treat me, as if I was one of them. Something to offer other than my female attributes.

Then out of the blue he asked me to promise I wouldn't leave. *Because he'd worry about me.*

I'm not used to anyone being concerned for me. Rodger hadn't given a damn about my account of what had actually happened. He'd made up a story in his head and preferred to believe that fiction instead, so he could get back to the woman who'd replaced me without having to carry any guilt.

Mace cares. For a woman who means nothing to him. For a woman who's damaged far beyond mending.

For a woman who can give nothing back.

But if staying a little longer makes his mind easier and allows him to concentrate on his friend, that's little enough to ask of me and something in my power to give.

As long as Major doesn't catch up with me.

CHAPTER TWENTY-FOUR

Mace

Shayla's promise to stick around and her confidence Liz will be returning right as rain bolsters me as I descend the stairs and enter the meeting room. Her massage leaving me feeling more energised than any shower in the world could.

As I walk toward my chair, I notice that the Prez and the VP are still missing, other than that, I'm the last one to arrive.

"Why are we here?" Judge asks to no one in particular.

"No fuckin' idea," Pal responds. "But obviously Prez has something to say."

"Probably setting up a rotation to be at the hospital," Thunder puts in.

"Not allowed in his room," I tell him.

"Think one of us should be there anyway. Need someone close for when he wakes up," Cad says.

If he wakes up. There's a feeling of dread inside me that Lizard may not survive the operation. If the tumour proves malignant, or even benign but has done serious damage, perhaps it's best if he never does. *Can't think that way.* But it's hard to stop. *Keep positive.* But I, *we*, need to prepare ourselves for the worst. If the worst wasn't possible, we wouldn't be sitting around this table today.

"Still having difficulty getting my head around it," Ink states, making me realise the conversation is continuing and I'd zoned out for a while. "Yesterday he was fine."

"Yesterday he was in agony. Went to bed early," Sparky corrects.

It reminds me I knew about his headaches, and I did fuck all about them. What if I'd marched him to the VA to get him looked at? *What if… what if…* I could drive myself crazy if I continue this torture about what I could have done and hadn't.

The door opens. Prez and Beef walk in and take their seats. All conversation stops as everyone waits for what Prez will say. Except for me. I already know.

Demon looks drained and tired as he starts to speak. "Called you all together as we've got to make some decisions for Liz."

"If you're going to talk about long-term care or funeral fuckin' arrangements—" Ink begins.

"And don't mention pulling the fuckin' plug," growls Thunder.

Prez slams his fist on the table. "No, I'm fuckin' not talking about any of that. Far too soon to know what we're dealing with, and that's the reason I'm bringing everyone up to speed. We don't know which way it's going to go for Liz, so whatever we decide has ramifications for him."

"Decide on what?" Thunder asks, looking confused.

"Mace, will you fill them in?"

I toss Demon a glare that he's leaving it up to me, then take a deep breath as I try to find the right place to start. "When Liz was on his last tour, he got fucked up and it messed with his brain. That, you all know."

"He's in a fuckin' hospital bed, as a result," Buzz observes. "Think that gives us the idea."

I ignore him. "What you don't know, is that it had lasting effects. He's lost a huge chunk of his memory, meaning he's got a wife and a kid who he doesn't know. He can't remember getting married, or his son being born. The gap in his head spans about five years or so."

Collectively, everyone sits forward, hanging onto my every word.

Ink is shaking his head. "No fuckin' way. There is no way Lizard's ever been married, as for a kid, he's got none, or none that he knows."

Prez takes over. "You're right Ink, none that he knows, and that's due to the fucking big hole in his memory. Point is, not knowing he was married, he never got divorced, well, who can blame him? How can you divorce a wife you don't know exists?"

"She walked out and fucking left him?" Hellfire is first to react.

"No," I refute fast. "He left her. See, they tried to make a go of it." I sigh, wondering how best to explain it. "At first, he could remember nothing at all. Nothing stuck from one day to the next. He was recovering, but slowly. Forcing him to face something he couldn't remember wasn't helping one bit. The advice she was given was to let him go. She loved, *loves* him, so acted on their advice, only expecting it to be temporary. But, as you now know, he never did get his memory back."

"But she exists," Rusty says. The thoughtful look on his, and mirrored on other faces, makes me wonder who's going to be the first to put two and two together.

"She does," agrees Beef. "We've got to decide whether she ought to know about Lizard. While Prez's name's written in the official records, she's actually his next of kin. Both her and her son. If anything is going to happen to Liz, perhaps she deserves to be told."

It's Thunder who puts two and two together first. He sits forward, palms flat to the table. "Vanna and Cas. Christ, no wonder the kid looks so much like him."

"What the fuck?" Like all the others, eyes come to me. "How long have you known, Mace?"

I hold up my hands. "Not long. Yeah, I may have misled you a bit. I know I'd implied I'd known her for years, but in truth it's not been long at all. That she is the wife of a good fuckin' friend was not a lie." *One of the best,* I add in my head.

"Did he know?" Judge snarls. "You brought her here, Mace. Did seeing her tip him over the edge?" He glares at me accusingly.

"Why did you bring her here?" asks Sparky.

"Christ, Mace. You thinking you made a fuckin' mistake?" Bomber looks distraught.

"He's got a fuckin' tumour," I remind them sharply, defending and controlling myself at the same time. "Whether or not seeing Vanna and Cas triggered something, it was going to get him at some point." *Wasn't it?* "And first, I didn't bring her, she came here herself. And second, you saw him," I respond defensively. "He had no fuckin' idea who she was. Told her she wasn't his type if you remember." But that's another of my 'what-ifs' coming back to haunt me. Is there a chance seeing Vanna and Cas had fucked with his mind, made things worse or accelerated them?

"Why the fuck has she turned up now?" Buzz asks quite reasonably. "Why, after all these years?"

"Money," Hellfire snaps. "Bitch needs money."

Shaking my head and frowning at Hell, I take a moment to explain the trouble she's having with the boy, how he could do with a guiding hand.

"Saw that my fuckin' self," Rusty says when I've finished my summary.

"It was Liz's ride he touched and started," Pyro begins, his hand cupping his chin. "That sounds like it could have been a cry for help. Kid wanted his father's attention any way he could get it."

"Didn't work," Judge remarks. "Got him sent off the compound instead."

"Why didn't you tell us, Prez?" Hell sends an accusing look my way, before frowning at his son.

Demon snarls at his father. "Yeah? I can just see us now, seated around the table with Lizard in attendance and discussing a wife and kid he didn't even know he had." His tone is the epitome of sarcasm. "Tell him his kid might go to juvie or into the system? Laid that on him nice and thick? How would that have gone down, Hellfire?"

"Lizard's not here," Thunder starts, looking like he's gathering his thoughts together, "and we sent her away from the club. Say the worst happens and the kid gets taken away and put into the system, or goes to juvie. What if Lizard gets his memory back and finds out we could have done something to prevent it? I couldn't look my brother in the face and say I did nothing. If that kid stays with his mom who's clearly at the end of her wits, unless someone steps up and helps out, that kid's going to go from bad to worse. We all know, we've fucking lived it."

"Juvie for me." Sparky raises his hand. "One stupid fuckin' mistake and I was sent down."

"Foster care." Cad raises his head. "Didn't even do anything to earn that punishment 'cept exist. Worked out in my case, but I was one of the lucky ones."

"Juvie then prison," admits Buzz. "But it wasn't all bad, learned my accounting skills while I was in there, as well as how to kill a man with my bare hands."

"Useful skills, both." Cad winks.

Prez glares. "Here are the two things to decide on. First, do we tell Vanna about Lizard and how ill he is, and second, do we help out with the kid?"

"She still loves him," I tell them, in case they need additional persuasion. "That ring on her finger was given to her by him, and she's been faithful since the day he left."

Hellfire stares at his son. "You don't think Lizard is coming home, do you?"

Demon looks at me, and I wince, then listen as he tells them, sadly, "There's a fuckin' lot that can go wrong. Reading between the lines of what the neurologist was telling us, it's hard to say this, but his chances are little better than fifty-fifty."

That pronouncement makes up Hell's mind. "Then you can't keep the wife out of this, especially if she's still carrying a torch for him. What if you were unconscious, possibly dying and facing a life-threatening operation? Vi would want to be there."

Demon gives his dad a sharp nod. "My thoughts exactly. She's never asked for support from Lizard. Never wanted him to pay up for something he believed wasn't his. If Lizard had his memory, he'd be devastated at abandoning her and his kid. My vote is that we step up and do for him what he can't."

The debate goes on. Wills asked what would happen if Lizard woke up and found out what we'd done and *still* denied his wife and kid. But despite that, on balance, there seemed to be only one thing to be done. The vote is unanimous as we agree to bring Vanna up to speed with what's happened to her man.

When an additional suggestion is made that I should be the one who breaks the news, I suspect it's part punishment for bringing her here and confronting Liz with a teenager who looks so much like him, it could have caused him to collapse and slip into a coma.

When the others leave, I hang back, wondering how the fuck I'm going to find the right words.

Prez puts his hand on my shoulder in passing. "You okay with this Mace?"

I shrug. I have to be.

"Want my advice? Sleep on it first. Give her one last night of peace. She'll still have time to get here before the operation, and you'll have time to decide exactly what you're going to say."

His counsel is good. I take it. I'm not anticipating destroying someone's world with any pleasure.

As I take myself off to bed, I avoid the sweet butts, knowing I'm too tired and drained to want to bring my cock out to play tonight. I pause outside Skull's old room, wishing I could enter and just hold Shayla. Not fuck her, I don't want to do that, but just have her company during the long hours ahead.

I'm exhausted, but know I'll probably not sleep.

It's the first time I've ever wanted a woman for anything other than sex, or, for as long as I can remember.

$$\overline{}$$

CHAPTER TWENTY-FIVE

$$\overline{}$$

Vanna

Getting a call at five in the morning is never one that's going to bring good news. Knowing it's too early for telemarketers, I gingerly pick up the phone and answer the call from an unknown number, hoping someone's dialled the wrong one.

"Hello?"

"Vanna, it's Mace."

"Has something happened?" I sit up in bed.

"Vanna, I need you and Cas to come to the compound." There's a difference to Mace's voice, a catch in it, as though he's finding it hard to speak.

"What's happened?" I ask again, my gut rolling, knowing the only reason he'd call me this early has to have something to do with Lizard. "Has Liz had an accident?" Or, perhaps, it's not bad news and hopefully I ask, "Has he remembered something? Does he want to see Cas?"

A second passes before Mace speaks again. When he tells me exactly what has happened, my head spins and I feel like I'm going to be sick, immediately guilty that I'd ever considered my life would be easier if my husband were dead. Mace wouldn't have gotten in contact if that wasn't a possibility I'm facing. My stomach churns as I realise this time, I might lose him forever. I've always taken some comfort in him being around, even if we're apart. I know I don't care if he never remembers, I just want him alive.

Mace has given me a moment to digest what he's told me, but I need much longer than that. I try to kick my brain into gear. "His operation's today?" I confirm, wondering if I heard right the first time.

"Yeah. Look, Vanna, I have to warn you. It's serious."

"I'm coming." Try to keep me away, even though it might cost me my job. Any operation is risky, and my husband's having a tumour removed from his brain. A growth they don't know whether it's harmless or cancerous. There are so many things that could go wrong, I need to be there. Cas will have to miss school, but surely this is a good excuse. "I'll be in Pueblo in a couple of hours. Where's the hospital again? We'll go straight there." After Cas's display on Saturday, the fact Mace is keeping me in the loop doesn't necessarily suggest we'd be welcome back on the compound.

"That works. I'll text you the address. And Vanna? We've told all the brothers who you are, by now they'll have told their old ladies... They all know your Lizard's old lady, and that Cas is his kid."

That, at least, brings me some relief. I've hated not being able to claim him as mine, even if it was in name only.

I put down my phone which immediately pings with the promised text and hesitate for a moment, wondering whether it might be better for me to leave Cas in Denver. But this could be the last time he'll see his father alive if Liz doesn't pull through the operation. He's fourteen, not a baby.

Cas is groggy when I wake him, but soon is alert and listening, his face falling as I tell him the news. By the time I've explained to him the little Mace had told me, I've got a serious and worried teenager on my hands. I give him the choice, but of course he wants to see his dad and be there for him. I almost broke when I explained it could be the last time. I couldn't give him false expectations.

I don't remember much of the journey. With Cas quiet beside me, I drive on autopilot. I get caught up in rush-hour traffic heading into Pueblo, but the GPS takes us directly to the hospital. It's still relatively early so I find a parking place, noticing there's a large number of Harleys taking over some of the best spots. It doesn't take a genius to work out who they belong to, and who they're here for.

Cas looks at the building in front of us, hesitant to get out of the car. "I was rude to him Saturday," he remembers. "I shouted at him. Did I upset him, Mom?"

"No, Cas," I say firmly. "It was nothing you said or did. A tumour doesn't grow overnight. Nothing tipped him over the top except for what was already in his head." I don't admit I'm worried sick it was just seeing me and Cas that caused this.

When he gets out, he comes around my side of the car and flies at me, hugging me tight. We hold each other for a moment, both of us taking comfort in each other, bolstering ourselves for what lies ahead. Then, with his arm still around me, we approach the front entrance. As I'm wondering what department I should be heading to, I see a familiar face. It's Mace, standing outside having a cigarette.

Lizard smokes. Maybe that made the tumour worse in his head. *Who knows?*

"Vanna. Cas." He lifts his chin toward us.

"Any news?"

Mace nods. "The op's going ahead later this morning. Demon explained you were coming in, and the doc said you could see him before he's prepped."

"Has there been any change?" I ask anxiously.

"No. Not for better, not for worse."

"I'll be able to see him?"

"Yeah, kid." Mace's eyes soften when they land on Cas, and

he quickly stubs out his cigarette on the sole of his boot and places the end in the container provided. "I'll take you in."

There are bikers in the waiting room, all of whom I recognise, and more in the corridor outside the department with the title Neurology over the door. As we pass, I'm given chin lifts, just like how Mace had greeted me outside. A couple give reassuring pats to Cas's shoulders.

Mace presses a button, the door opens, and we're ushered in.

When we reach Lizard's room, I'm taken back in time, and I feel a wave of dizziness pass over me. *For weeks I'd sat by his bed. I'd been there when he'd coded and had to be revived. There when it had happened again.*

Last time he recovered, I remind myself. But he'd woken a different man. A man who's first words had been, *Who the fuck are you?*

Has he been living on borrowed time all these years? Had his time really been then? Had he escaped death's clutches, only to have it come for him again?

As I stand back, Cas steps forward. He takes hold of his dad's hand, and while tears roll down his cheeks, he squeezes it. "I don't care if you don't know who I am," he tells the man lying motionless on the bed. "I just want you to live, Dad. I promise I won't shout at you again. I'm sorry if I upset you..."

"Kid." Mace is there. "It wasn't anything you did, okay? Your dad wouldn't want you to feel guilty."

"He's going to be alright, isn't he, Mace?" Cas turns his wet eyes onto the enforcer, seeking an assurance that no one can give.

Mace tries his best. "One thing's for certain, Lizard isn't going to give up. If there's a way to come back to you, he's going to take it. He's not done riding through life, okay, Cas? Have faith in him. Might not look like it, but I know he'll be fighting."

"I've been here before," I tell them. "I've sat by the bed of a man the doctors warned me might not live. But he did. He pulled through." My life might have become a living hell when he'd lost all his memory, but I couldn't resent Liz for carrying on and living his.

When the nurses usher us out to prepare him for his operation, I meet his neurosurgeon, who tries to put the complicated medical procedure into words I can understand.

"I'll be performing a craniotomy. That involves removing a small section of his skull to take out as much of the tumour as we can. I might not be able to get all of it, but enough to ease his symptoms at least."

"And he'll come out of the coma?" I ask, my voice breaking with the anxiety I'm feeling.

"That's what we hope," the surgeon says, but he offers no odds or promises.

"Will he have a hole in his head?" Cas asks.

"No. We'll glue back the piece of bone we take out." He looks from me to Cas. "I know it's worrying and scary, but I assure you, I, and my team, are very experienced in these operations. It's a common enough procedure for us. The unknown is whether the tumour is benign or malignant, and whether we'll be able to remove it all. Until I get inside his head, we won't know precisely what we're dealing with."

"How long will the operation take?" I ask.

"At least four, maybe six hours. I'll make sure you're updated as soon as we're done."

"Thank you."

Mace ushers us away.

The waiting room is crowded with bikers. Two, I recall as Paladin and Wills, get up and offer us seats. Cas and I sit down. My head drops into my hands as if worry makes it too heavy to hold up. *How can I go through this again?*

"He's fuckin' strong." Buzzard hunkers down in front of me and takes my hands. "He'll pull through." He squeezes my fingers, then stands back up.

I give him a wan smile. "I've been here before. Sat by his side willing him to wake up. In the end, he did." It was just that he wasn't my Lizard any longer.

"He didn't recognise you at all?" Thunder asks, as if I'd spoken aloud.

"No," I shake my head. "He had no idea who the stranger was crying in his room."

"Do you remember your dad before, Cas?" Jayden comes over. She glares at Judge sitting next to Cas, and the biker gets up and offers her his seat with an exaggerated flourish.

Cas looks at Jayden. "Not really. Mom's told me a lot about how he used to play with me, but I don't remember much. He didn't want anything to do with me when he came out of the hospital."

"At first he was away for months at a time on tours," I tell them. "He wasn't able to spend much time with Cas. He wasn't even there for the birth as this one decided to come early."

"You've had it hard, haven't you, darlin'?" The older biker with ginger hair states.

I shrug. "At least I knew Lizard was alive. So many people have it worse. I was grieving, but at least it wasn't for a dead body. I always had hope."

"Heard about you getting into trouble, Cas," a stern voice says. "You've got to knock that shit on the head."

Cas looks sheepish and looks down at his feet as Demon's father talks to him.

"When's the court case?" asks Demon.

"I don't know yet. He's had the preliminary one, but he hasn't had a court date as yet."

"I, er, I spoke to my dad." Mel nods at Ink sitting to my left. He nudges Beth, shifts along a seat, then repositions her on his lap. Mel takes the place he vacated, looking tiny sitting next to the two compared-to-her giants. "He'll represent you if you want. He's really good, Vanna. Has your current lawyer gone into character references for you?"

I shake my head. "No, she's been focusing on Cas."

"In Dad's view, proving you're a good mother might help keep Cas out of a custodial sentence."

But I'm not a good mother, am I? Else Cas wouldn't have gone off the rails.

"I had no dad growing up." Judge comes over and crouches in front of us. "Know how that makes you feel kid. But now your relationship with Lizard is out in the open, we'll step up." He waves his hand around him. "See all these men, Cas? We're your dad's brothers, which means we're your uncles."

"You know what Judge is saying?" Ink's eyes narrow as he peers around Beth. "You fuck up and you'll have a whole club of angry bikers making sure you learn a lesson you'll never forget." Cas goes still. When I go to speak, Ink holds up his hand. "You know why?" As my son shakes his head, Ink goes on to explain, "Because we care. You're one of ours now, we've adopted you. We care that you do the best with your life and don't fuck it up."

Cas looks from one to the other of the new 'uncles' he's found. Each give him chin lifts as his eyes fall on them.

I wanted a man to show Cas how he should behave. Now he's not got just one, he's got a whole club.

"Hey, Vanna," Vi calls out. "You've got sisters as well, you hear?"

That's the first thing I've heard today that melts a little of the ice inside.

"What happens when Dad wakes?" Cas asks Judge, who's remained crouched in front of him. "He still won't recognise me and Mom and will wonder what the hell you're doing."

Judge glances at Mace and then Demon. It's the prez who replies, "Can't promise Liz will play happy family, or even want to. But if he's half the man I know, then once he knows he has them, he'll step up to his responsibilities. If he's not well enough to have the truth dropped on him, well, we'll work it out. Whatever happens, you've got us now, and we'll be there for you whenever you need us."

Almost six hours has passed before the door opens, and a nurse steps in. "Mr Black and Mrs James?"

I stand, and so does Demon, who signals to Mace and has a quiet word in his ear. Mace signals something to Judge who stands and takes the seat by my son.

"Mom…?"

"Stay with us, Cas," Ink commands from his other side.

I'm shaking. When Mace puts his arm around me, I realise why Demon invited him along. He's here *as my support should I be about to hear the news I don't want. That something's gone wrong.*

The nurse takes us to see the neurosurgeon who doesn't delay telling us how Lizard is.

"I'm pleased to tell you Mr James is out of surgery now. He's still under anaesthesia and being closely monitored, but I was able to remove the entire tumour. There was a slight bleed behind it as I suspected, but that's tied off now."

Ignoring the good news, I ask for the worst. "Was it cancer?" If it is, that's not going to be the end of Lizard's problems. I don't dare breathe as I wait for the response and feel Mace tense beside me.

"The pathologist examined it. The shape, chromosomes and DNA of the cells all appear to be normal and are not secreting hormones. The tumour was self-contained without fingers spreading into other tissue."

"Which means?" The words are going right over my head.

"It was a benign tumour. Nothing to suggest any chemo or radiation therapy is required."

If Mace's arms weren't holding me up, I'd have fallen to the floor.

"Will he come around once the anaesthetic wears off?" Demon asks.

"I'd say it's very likely. I suspect, having gotten it all, that chances are good that in time, he'll make a good recovery barring any unforeseen complications. But I do warn you, this is a serious operation, and recovery won't happen overnight. His brain will be swollen which can have various consequences. He may not be able to talk, and it may affect his movement."

"But he will recover?" I should have expected poking around in someone's head would affect them, but stupidly, I hadn't.

"How far and how fast is impossible to predict."

"Can I sit with him?" I'm prepared to take up my vigil again.

The neurologist smiles. "We'll monitor him a little longer in recovery. You can wait for him in his room if you want. The nurse will show you where to go."

"You two go," says Demon. "When he's awake, come and get me. I'll go back to the waiting room and let everyone know." He pauses and looks down at me. "This is good news, Vanna. He's alive, he came through."

Once Lizard is wheeled into the room where Mace and I have been waiting, it's so similar to twelve years ago when Lizard was recovering from his initial head injury. Me sitting beside his bed waiting, hoping, praying that he'd open his eyes. Of course, back then, no one was waiting with me. My mother—at that time we were still talking—would take Cas and look after him for me, for that month I'd barely left Lizard alone.

Just as then, I stare at the machine that's recording his heart rate, my mind going back to those times the beep had become a continuous sound. Twice it had happened, twice they'd had to intervene to get his heart pumping blood around his body again. I'd all but died with him each time. Only the thought of Cas sustained me.

"He'll be fine, Vanna." Mace is staring at me, an intense expression on his face.

"Once he wakes, I'll go," I tell him, knowing I have to. "He won't recognise me, and it will confuse him as to why I'm here. We'll tell him I was keeping you company."

"No lies, Vanna. If Liz hears that, then finds out who you are to him, he'll murder me if in his head he's linked you and me."

There's truth in that I suppose.

It's a waiting game just like I remember from before. I like it no better.

Beep. Beep. Beep.

The incessant noise would drive me crazy if it weren't that it shows my man is alive. I eye the large white dressing on his head, and then my eyes drop to the features of the face. I still love as much as the day I said my vows. His hair is longer now, down past his shoulders, when then it was military short. Idly, I think he's probably had a patch shaved for his surgery, and wonder whether he'll have to shave off the rest to match it. I hope he grows it again, as it suits him long.

All these thoughts go through my head as Mace and I sit in silence as hour after hour goes past, the only interruptions being the nurse coming in to check on the man lying so still in the bed.

"Did you see that?" Mace asks sharply but quietly. "His eyelid twitched. Liz? Lizard, Brother? Can you hear me?"

"Lizard?" I prompt him myself.

The man in the bed groans. Then his eyes start to flutter, then they open. They scan the room and land on me.

He groans again, then his lips slowly curve, and he breathes out a word that's difficult to understand but sounds like my name. I draw in breath sharply as his eyes close, willing him to wake up and say it again. I hardly dare breathe, certain I imagined it.

Mace smiles at me, he'd heard it too.

Lizard sleeps on, I sit, hoping beyond hope I'd seen recognition in his face.

Next time he wakes, he seems more alert. He says something, but it's unintelligible. He makes an effort and tries again. "Vanna."

I'm still. *He knows me.* He. Knows. Me.

"You look different," he mumbles. His head must pain him, as he reaches up his left hand to touch it. As he encounters strands of his hair, his brow furrows in confusion. He tugs at his dirty blond locks, then grimaces. "What the fuck is this?"

"It's your hair, Brother," Mace tells him, his tone light, almost playful with the relief Lizard is talking again.

"It's not my fucking hair," Lizard growls. Then his eyes sharpen, and he blinks rapidly as if trying to bring Mace into focus. "Who the fuck are you?" he asks. "I ain't your brother. Haven't got one."

He recognises me, but not Mace? I see Mace's eyes widen in shock, but I've been here before. At least this time, he knows me, and selfishly, for me, that's enough.

"Lizard?" I ask slowly, bringing his attention back to me.

"What's happened to me, Vanna?" He frowns. "How did I get here? I was on tour… then… I can't remember. Am I stateside?"

This is everything I've wanted for twelve years. For my husband to recognise me. But something's wrong, it's as though the clock's been wound back again. I reach for his right hand and grasp it, noticing he doesn't squeeze back. "You had a brain tumour, Liz, but they've gotten it all out. It was benign, so nothing to worry about. Turns out that's why you were having headaches."

But my explanation isn't accepted. "What are you talking about? Headaches? Can't remember having any. Don't know how I got here." His eyes close in pain. "Where am I?"

I'm not sure what to answer, so settle for, "Home."

"Good," he breathes out. "Home until I ship out again. Where's our baby, Vanna? Where's little Cas? Has he grown since I've been gone?"

My eyes lock with Mace's.

The nurse Mace had summoned enters. "Oh, you're awake. Glad to have you back with us Mr James. How are you feeling?"

"My head hurts."

"It will, I'm afraid, you've had brain surgery. The doctor has prescribed painkillers, there's a morphine pump beside you."

She places it by his right hand, but Lizard makes no move to use it. "Don't want to feel sleepy."

I'm about to tell Lizard he doesn't need to stay conscious, rest is probably the best thing to help his recovery. Selfishly, I want to stay talking to him in case this memory recall is only temporary, but I stay quiet.

The nurse checks his eyes, then asks if he can move his fingers and toes.

After a moment, Lizard begins to get agitated when he realises he can't move his right arm or leg.

"Lizard, the doctor warned the swelling on your brain might cause temporary lack of movement." I try to calm him down.

"Temporary?"

"I'll get the doctor to come and explain," the nurse says calmly. "But you're talking, and that's a good sign Mr James. A lot of patients can't when they first awake." Then, she asks. "Do you know where you are?"

"I presume I was flown stateside after some incident or other. I'm in the hospital."

She purses her lips but doesn't contradict him. "And do you remember your name and personal details?"

He gives a slight grin. "I'm Norton James, otherwise known as Lizard. I'm twenty-six years old, I'm married to a wonderful woman called Vanna, and I've a two-year-old son named Castiel. And you," he turns to Mace, his expression hardening. "Don't know who the fuck you are and don't like you sniffing around my wife. You can get gone."

At that moment I know I'm going to lose it. I stand and run to the door and out into the hallway leaving Lizard with Mace and the nurse. My face is in my hands and my shoulders are shaking.

Mace has followed me out. "It's okay, Vanna. It's okay. Liz is going to be fine."

I raise my head so he can see I'm half crying and half laughing hysterically. "He remembers me, but not you. He's lost twelve years, Mace."

CHAPTER TWENTY-SIX

Vanna

"I'm sorry, Mace." I make an effort to pull myself together, knowing I do have a habit of laughing at inappropriate moments. My relief at Lizard coming around and then recognising me had morphed into morbid laughter when it had really sunk in what his brain had done. Wiped the last twelve years, while allowing him to remember he was married with a child. A child who's still two years old in his mind.

"Are you going back in?"

"Of course I am. That's my husband in there." I just needed to get myself back in control.

Mace stares at me, his gaze settling on me for a moment, and seconds tick by before he speaks. "This is a fuckin' mess, Vanna. What do you want to do about Cas?"

I have no idea. *Borrow a two-year-old so I don't upset him?*

"He needs to know, Vanna."

But I've been here before. Telling him facts when he didn't want to hear them.

"It's different this time," Mace insists, clearly reading my expression.

But what's changed? He didn't accept the truth back then. How can I explain to a dad that this teenager is his and he's no longer two years old? Would he be able to cope with the truth? That the reason I look different is that I'm twelve years older, and his hair is long as he now chooses to wear it that way.

"Talk to him, Vanna. Try and explain to him."

"What if I fuck everything up? What if he collapses again?" *What if he can't handle what he's being told?*

"He won't," Mace says with certainty. "The tumour is gone. Hopefully this memory loss is only temporary. The doctor said the op may have some effects until the swelling goes down."

"What if it's like last time, Mace? What if he never remembers again? I think I need to talk to the doctor or someone..."

Mace leans in. "A fuckin' therapist made you give up on him. Go with your gut instinct this time, Vanna. I'll stay out of the way as I'm agitating him, but I won't go far. We won't be giving up on him, and I won't listen to any fuckin' therapist who tells me to stay away from my brother."

I bite my lip. "You really think it's the right thing to do?"

"Vanna, he'll see you look older. The evidence is right in front of his eyes. You can't rewind the clock, even if you wanted to. How else would you explain Cas?"

The door opens and the nurse comes out.

Mace turns to her. "He seems very confused."

"It's not unusual after this kind of surgery. I'm pleased with him actually, his eyesight, hearing, and speech check out which can all be initial problems after surgery. We'll assess his mobility when he's a little stronger."

"Is it okay to talk to him? To bring him up-to-date with the years he's forgotten?" I'm worried sick about setting him back.

"He may start remembering as you talk to him. It's quite normal for someone to get muddled when they've undergone an operation like this and have difficulty placing names and faces. It's certainly not unusual."

I don't think the nurse is right. That's what I was told last time, *give him time and he'll remember.* But they'd been wrong.

"What else can you do, Vanna?" Mace stares after the

retreating nurse. His eyes appear to be on her ass. He turns back to me when she disappears around a corner. "Cas is going to want to see his dad." He wipes his hand over his face. "Christ, but that kid has been through a lot. It's going to hit him hard that his dad now remembers him, but only as a babe in arms."

"A toddler," I automatically correct. "Cas was eighteen months when Lizard went on his last tour. He'd all but completed six months when the bomb went off. Cas turned two while Lizard was still in the hospital." I'd been too focused on keeping my husband alive to celebrate my son's second birthday. Something I still feel guilty for.

"He'll want you." Mace gives me a prod to get me moving back into Lizard's room.

I'm torn. Half of me longs to go back and talk to him, knowing he knows who I am. The other half knows our problems are far from over and wishes I could get into my car and put miles between us, but I can't run from this. Pulling back my shoulders I step back inside.

"Vanna." Lizard gives me a weak smile. "Come sit beside me."

"How are you feeling?"

"The nurse gave me some shit instead of the morphine. The pain's already easing. She said the weakness on my right side was normal. But fuck that." His mouth twists. "What's happened to me, Vanna? And you, your hair… I can't get over it. How could it grow so long in six months?"

"You grew yours too. I like it." I don't know how to handle this.

His hand feels his straggly lengths, again pulling at it as if to prove it's his. Then he frowns and snarls, "Tell me what the fuck's gone on. How fuckin' long have I been here if my hair's grown out?"

"Shouldn't you rest?" He's only just come around from brain surgery, surely, he should rest for a bit? But in typical male fashion he dismisses my concern.

"I'm not waiting any longer. Tell me, Evangeline."

When he uses my full name, I know he's serious. I take his right hand and hold it tight, a liberty I never dreamed I'd be taking again and a feeling of rightness wars with the unease I'm feeling.

"You were hurt overseas."

"Sort of guessed that." He touches the bandage on his head with his left hand. "How bad, Vanna? Did it cause the tumour, or was that already in my head?"

"You were hurt badly. You sustained a traumatic brain injury. For a while it was touch and go, and we didn't think you'd survive."

"Christ." He leans his head back and closes his eyes. "But I'm going to be okay, now? I feel so fuckin' weak, Vanna." His fingers twitch in my hand, but don't tighten.

"You're going to be fine, Lizard." I put as much strength in my voice as I can.

"Worrying about me was how you got those lines on your face?" Now his fingers trace the etchings left by time. Again, with his left hand.

"Lizard. I don't know how to tell you this."

"Spit it out, babe. Get whatever it is off your chest. You said I was fine, but what the fuck is it? Am I going to die?"

I take a deep breath. "You're not dying. But this, this isn't the first time you've been in the hospital. It's the second. This time you had a brain tumour, and they had to cut it out. It was benign, and they got it all. No need for more treatment, you've just got to recover, okay?"

His brow creases. "The second time?" When I nod, he continues, "I don't remember being in the hospital before."

"It was twelve years ago." I tell him the worst.

He inhales sharply, and his brow creases in confusion. "No."

"Yes." I don't know what to say. How to explain.

His eyes examine me again, his brow creasing. "What's the fuckin' date?" he rasps.

I take out my phone and show him.

Again, his head rests back, and he closes his eyes. "How the fuck did I lose twelve years? Have I been in a coma and just woken up?"

"No," I choke. "You've been living a good and full life. You're the manager of a tattoo parlour—"

"I got my dream job?" That seems to brighten him up. "It pays the bills then?"

Instead of replying, I carry on, "You live and ride with a motorcycle club. The Satan's Devils MC."

His eyes are looking at me sharply. "You're kidding, right?"

"I'm telling the truth, Lizard."

For a moment he just regards me as though trying to judge whether I'm joking or not. Then, he sighs, and once more touches that bandage. "Christ, my head must be fucked up. I thought I heard you say I ride with a motorcycle club."

"I did, Lizard. You do."

"I'm dreaming, aren't I? Having a fuckin' nightmare. Pinch me, Vanna. I want to wake up."

He's in such distress, I sob, wishing I could. I try to drop the conversation, but he won't let up, asking me to repeat what I'm telling him again and again.

Eventually, he touches his hair again. "I can't compute it Vanna. Twelve years have gone past when I've been a fully functioning human being with a good job. Manager, huh?" He moves his head side to side very slowly. "Can almost accept that part. But riding with a motorcycle club? Living with them? Fuck babe, how the hell did I get mixed up in that shit?" He frowns. "They legit?"

I shrug. "They say they are, but they wear the one-percenter patch."

His face tightens. "I got you mixed up in it too? You, and little Cas?"

"They're good men, Liz." I find myself defending them and then tell him the truth. "I don't know how you joined them.

Look, Liz. I really don't know how to tell you this." His intense stare makes me carry on. "After the first time in the hospital, Lizard, you lost your memory. You didn't recognise me or Cas."

His jaw drops. He's quiet for a moment. "There's more, isn't there, Vanna. Tell me."

"You were suffering." I try to explain to him. "Living with us wasn't helping you. I was your wife, but to you, both Cas and I were strangers. It was fucking with your head. You left, and your therapist said that was the best for you."

"I couldn't remember you? What the fuck are you saying, Evangeline?" His eyes are going wild.

"Liz, I think you should get some rest." I'm worried I'm telling him too much, too soon.

"Evangeline," he growls. "Tell me what the fuck you're talking about. Now."

It's breaking my heart to tell him this. "You lost about five years. You couldn't remember us meeting, marrying, or Cas being born."

"Jesus H Christ. When did I recover? When did we get back together? How long did I forget you for? For fuck's sake, Vanna. How could I forget *you*? Tell me, for the love of God. How long was it before I recognised you again?"

He's getting agitated which can't be good for him.

"Tell me. Fuckin' tell me."

Do I tell him or run away, as that's the only way this conversation will stop? He's not going to give up.

"Evangeline," he snarls. "When did I remember you?"

The word comes out on a sob, though I try to swallow it. "Today." My voice breaks. "Today, Lizard. This is the first time you've recognised me in twelve years."

As the tears start flowing, he reaches over with his left arm and pulls me down against his chest, holding me as tight as a man who's only just come out of surgery can, as if he's never going to let me go.

We lie like that for a few minutes, my cheek against his heart, feeling it beating strongly. Me taking this chance in case I lose him again, hoping this time he'll hold tight to the memory.

"Twelve years." I hear his voice and feel it rumble against my skin. "Twelve fucking years we've been apart."

"Ten," I correct. "We tried for two years but couldn't reconnect. It's then you left me."

"And went off to join a fuckin' biker club." Suddenly he tenses. "That shit stops now. Not getting you involved in something like that. The only good thing about us being apart is that I apparently didn't drag you down with me."

"Liz…" I want to defend his club, but he's not finished.

"What have I missed, apart from Cas growing up? Have you moved on? Found a new man, Vanna? Tell me. Vanna. Fuck. It feels to me like I only left to go on tour six months ago, but we've…" His voice breaks, and then he continues, "We tried to make it work for two years, so ten I've been gone? I suppose I couldn't blame you if you're another man's now. Is it that fucker who was in here before?"

"No." I free myself from his hold so I can stare intently into his eyes. "No, Lizard. I still wear your ring." I show my hand to him. "I've remained faithful. I never gave up hope."

"What about me?" he says gruffly. "If I didn't know I had a wife… Christ." He huffs a mirthless laugh. "Don't tell me there's another woman I've laid claim to." He raises his left hand and stares at it. "I don't wear my ring?"

"They had to cut it off the first time, your hand swelled." It had broken my heart, but it was necessary. "You didn't find anyone else, Liz," I reassure him fast, not telling him that, unlike me, he hadn't remained celibate.

He hugs me again, again with just that left arm. I watch the right, but it doesn't twitch. That worries me. Almost as much as this conversation does.

"If I remained faithful, I must have known you were out there, and I was just waiting for the right time to come back."

He'll find out as soon as he goes back to the club. *If* he does, I correct. But as soon as they see him, Titsy, Sheila and the others will be all over him. I decide to leave it, I'm laying far too much on him now.

But he's remembered too well. Seems I couldn't control the expression on my face.

"There's more, isn't there? Tell me. Tell me now." He waits.

"Lizard, you didn't have a special someone, but you didn't go wanting if you know what I mean."

"Babe?"

"The MC has club girls…"

"Oh fuck." He looks and sounds horrified. "Babe…"

I decide to be honest. "Liz, I didn't like seeing it, but you didn't know you were married. You can't be blamed for something you didn't know you'd done." Am I being truthful letting him believe I accept it? It hurts. A lot.

But he sees the pain in my eyes. "I'll never hurt you again, Vanna. I promise."

"I only found out about ten days ago, Liz. I came to find you. Why doesn't matter for now." I don't want to heap more problems on him.

"I want to see Cas." He says after a moment, "How old is he again?"

"He's fourteen. And he's here. Do you want me to get him?"

"Yeah," the word's breathed out. "So much to get my head around. My baby's a teenager, almost a grown man."

"Is it too much? Do you want to rest before you see him?"

"Rest?" he huffs. "I'm fuckin' terrified I'll forget everything if I close my eyes and sleep. Twelve years, babe. Twelve years have gone by and I don't fuckin' remember. And before that? Another period I blanked out apparently." He grimaces. "What if I forget everything again? What if I forget who I fuckin' am? What if I end up a vegetable, unable to remember anything at all?"

Seeing my big strong man scared out of his wits is horrifying. I wonder if I've made a mistake, but Mace was right. I couldn't have done otherwise. I couldn't have hidden how I've aged and the resultant body changes, and soon Liz will notice his. I couldn't have paraded Cas in front of him, when he last remembers him as two years old. What else could I have done?

"You won't forget," I tell him firmly. "The doctor said there's probably a link between the tumour and the original brain injury. Now that's gone, there's no reason to think your faculties will decline again."

"I want to see Cas," he repeats.

"I'll go and get him." I start to stand, but Liz holds me back. His eyes examining my face, this time, as if memorising it.

"Don't take long," he says quickly. "For fuck's sake, Vanna, come back."

"Lizard," I tell him firmly, knowing what he's worrying about, "you won't forget me again. I promise." Hopefully he can't see my fingers crossed behind my back.

As I go to the door, I hear him say to himself in disbelief, "Twelve fucking years."

Cas stands as soon as I enter the waiting room. "He remembers? Can I see him, Mom?"

"He remembers, but only up to the start of his last tour. I've explained to him Cas, but..."

"He expects a two-year-old." Cas looks tense. "Mace told me."

"I've told him, Cas. He knows to expect a teenager, but he is struggling with the idea."

"Does he remember the club at all?" asks Demon, tersely.

I give him a sad look. "I'm sorry, no. Or not yet. But he's just had a major brain operation, so who knows what to expect?"

"How's he physically?" asks Beef.

"I'm really not sure," I tell expectant faces. "Weak. He should be sleeping but he's afraid to give in. He doesn't seem able to move his right-hand side, but he's ignoring that for now. He's too worried about what's going on with his head."

CHAPTER TWENTY-SEVEN

Lizard

Vanna's gone to get my son. The boy I'd forgotten about for twelve years. How the fuck could I do that? Twelve years!

I'm a biker? A member of an outlaw gang? Jeez. If she'd told me I'd flown to the moon, I could just as well believe that.

"You feeling okay, Mr James?" A nurse comes in and checks the readings of the machine beeping beside me. "It looks like you're becoming stressed. You really should try to get some rest."

"I've forgotten twelve years," I tell her. "I remember my wife as a twenty-two-year-old, she's now thirty-four. And I'm apparently nearing my forties. How the fuck do you think I'm feeling? I'm scared I'll forget even more."

"Calm down, Mr James."

"Calm down? How can I fuckin' keep calm when I don't understand what's going on in my head?"

She looks at me for a moment. "I'll get someone to talk to you, okay?"

"I don't need fuckin' therapy. I need to know what's wrong with my head."

"I can help you with that," a deep voice says. "Mr James. I'm the consulting neurologist. I performed your operation."

"I've woken up remembering my wife who I've apparently forgotten I had for twelve years, Doc, as well as everything that happened over that time. Am I going to forget again?"

He pulls up a chair and regards me seriously. "I work on brains every day, and things never cease to surprise me. You originally suffered a TBI, a traumatic brain injury. It's not unusual that triggers a loss of memory. Sometimes it's physical damage to part of your brain, sometimes it's PTSD, or simply that you want to forget. For example, if your marriage wasn't happy, you could have hidden it from yourself."

"No fuckin' way," I tell him. "I love Vanna, and she loves me. We've got a son..." my voice trails off. I have a son who I've apparently neglected for a very long time because I didn't know he existed.

"You know we only use a fraction of our brains?"

I recall hearing that somewhere. I raise my chin.

"You're an interesting case, Mr James. Sometimes memories are still there, but locked away, unable to be accessed. There have been cases of people who've forgotten who they are, then get flashbacks and finally remember years on. You suffered a traumatic event and injury to your temporal lobes. If I was a betting man, I'd place money on that being the cause of your initial loss of memory, particularly as I understand that after your original injury your short-term memory was affected as well. That you started to be able to lay down new memories suggests the brain healing itself over time."

"If I was healing myself, why didn't I remember my wife and kid before now?"

"Because of the tumour. One the size of yours would have been growing for quite a while. That you remember now suggests its removal, or maybe the surgery I did to correct a small bleed, was the trigger for your memories coming back."

"So why can't I remember what I've done for the past few years?"

"You've just undergone a serious operation on your head.

There will be some swelling which will gradually go down. Common side effects include loss of concentration and trouble remembering things. There are definitely physical reasons. I wouldn't have expected you to wake and be cured immediately. PTSD could be playing a part. You've moved on, made a new life, left the old one behind. You feel guilty, so instead of trying to assimilate your fresh memories of your life before, you're believing you're back twelve years ago. Sometimes our thoughts take the easiest path."

"My brain's fucked." I take it he's suggesting that my way of coping is pretending it never happened, instead of admitting what an asshole I've been to Vanna and Cas by denying them all these years.

He chuckles. "That's not a medical term I'd use. Don't push yourself too hard. I'll set you up with a therapist, and we'll work on getting your memories back. You'll also need to have some physical therapy to help you recover your strength on your right-hand side."

After giving me a bit of medical jargon about the operation itself, and what I can expect during my recovery, he gets up to leave.

"How soon can I get out of here, Doc?"

"I would hope by the weekend. It depends on how you do." He opens the door. "Ah, Mrs James. Your husband needs rest. Please don't stay too long."

Vanna comes in. "You sure you're up to this, Lizard?"

"Is he here?" I ask fast. At her nod, I swallow a couple of times. "I want to see my son."

A boy, no, a young man enters. Well I'll be fucked. He's as tall as me. Last time I saw him, he'd barely come up to my knee.

"You've grown," I squeak, then cough to clear my throat, having to ignore the blast of pain which goes through me. Still, I refuse to use the morphine pump that's beside me.

"You're hurting," Vanna accuses. "Liz, this is too much for you, too soon."

I hold out my hand, curling my finger toward Cas. "Come closer. Let me get a good look at you."

I'm meeting a stranger. Someone who carries my blood, someone who even looks like me, despite the colouring he got from his mom. I have no fucking idea what to say to him.

"How are you feeling, Dad?"

"Like a mule kicked me in the head," I reply, startling at the word he called me. How can I equate this with the child who last called me 'Daddy'?

Vanna looks from me to Cas, then back to me again. "What did the doctor say?"

I know she's asked to distract us from this awkward moment, when neither of her men seem to know what to do or find words to come out of their mouths.

"He said my retrograde amnesia over the past twelve years could have been caused by physical damage to the brain, compounded by the growth of the tumour."

"Why have you forgotten again, Dad?" Cas asks. "Why don't you remember the club or your friends?"

I stare at him, then at Vanna. "Could be the swelling that's yet to go down, could be PTSD, my brain shutting out the pain of how I've mistreated you both."

"You coming home, Dad?"

What a fucking question to ask. I have no idea of the answer. I swallow back the yes as I realise, I don't even know where home is now. I presume we're still in San Diego? Does Vanna live in the same house? Will she want me back after all this time? When I glance at my wife, I notice a strained expression on her face. I'd married a young girl and did my best to look after her. Even when I was overseas, I'd checked in regularly with her, paid all the bills and provided for them both. For twelve years now she'd been on her own, raising a son with no one beside her. Already I can see changes, and not just the physical signs of a woman who's grown older. There's a new maturity about her. A confidence in the way she holds herself. She might still love me, but does she want me back in her life? Does she want a man who hadn't been there for her?

How much have the years changed me? I'm apparently a biker, for fuck's sake. I'd been in the Marines, and that's all I can remember. What made me enter the outlaw lifestyle, I've no fucking idea. I can't remember myself ever thinking of bikers as anything other than adrenaline junkies with scant regard for anyone else, or even as criminals. If I really joined that type of gang, am I still the man I was? Has my thinking and outlook been altered forever?

I could answer Cas's question with a simple yes, as that's what he's obviously expecting, but it's far more complicated than that. I'll have to learn who Vanna is all over again and reprove I'm the man for her. As for Cas himself, how's he going to react with me stepping into the role of being a father?

Then there's the little fact that I've apparently been with whores. *That* doesn't bear thinking about. I just hope I gloved up and didn't catch anything.

"You don't want to come back." Cas supplies the answer when I take too long to reply.

"Cas, Son. No, it's not that." I try to put my thoughts into words. "You've been without me for twelve years. I'd love to say I'll step back in and pick up where we left off, but I'll be stuck in the past, and you've moved on. Gonna take a moment to get used to that. Your mom might not want me back, or not straight-away." The last sentence was hard to get out of my mouth. *Vanna not want me?* I can't bear to think about that. She's my wife for fuck's sake. Or was, twelve years back.

"At least you won't need to change diapers." Vanna smiles. "Of course you can come home with us, you'll need to conva-lesce somewhere."

I'd hate to be a burden on anyone. Perhaps I should go to my own place. If I have one, that is. *Do I even have a home? Own, rent?* Or had Vanna said something about living at a motorcycle club? Surely not, I like my own space. "Where do I live?"

"You live here, in Pueblo. At the club. We live in Denver."

I moved? "Why are we not still in California?"

"I don't know." Vanna's biting her lip. "You moved first. When I found where you'd gone, I followed you. I, I thought if I still saw you occasionally, you might remember."

"You stalked me?" But fuck, I'm glad that she had. "Babe, I'm so grateful you didn't give up on me."

Then I catch sight of my son, and I almost feel him wishing that she had. If I'd died, she'd have mourned, moved on, maybe married a good man to be his father. But I'm still alive, not even sure who I am now, or whether I can be the man I once was.

What if I can no longer be the man she remembers, or, would even that be enough for her now?

My head hurts like a bitch. I know I'm overdoing it. My eyes close.

"I've had enough of this," I hear Vanna say. Snapping my eyes open, I see her pressing the button that will send morphine into my veins. "You're in pain, you need rest."

The old Vanna wouldn't have been so presumptuous, but I find I'm admiring the new version.

Already my eyelids feel heavy.

"Cas and I will leave you now. Get some rest, we'll be back tomorrow."

My eyes snap open. "Promise?" I ask, sounding like a needy child.

"I promise."

She leans down, and I feel the brush of her lips against mine.

"Night, Dad."

"Night, Son."

Crazy dreams come at me. The loud sound of guns firing, the sharp cracks of sniper rifles, the boom of an explosion. Faces I don't recognise appearing and melting into faces of men I served with. *Hatch. I'll catch up with Hatch when I get home.*

Struggling up through the mire of sleep, I wake. For a moment I have difficulty separating reality from the morphine-induced dreams of the night. Had I dreamed everything? Have twelve years really passed?

What's real and what's not?

Hatch? If so much time has gone by, he may not remember me. Or hate that I hadn't been in touch. How could I have forgotten him? He's my best bud. He'd been by my side… Fuck. I can't remember any more.

"Good morning, Mr James." A too bright male nurse enters my room.

"What year is it?"

When he tells me, despite my initial optimism, my talk with Vanna yesterday hadn't been a dream.

Lost in my thoughts, I ignore what he's doing as he takes my blood pressure. He then asks me to move my limbs.

"Do you think you can stand?" When I growl yes, he encourages me. "Slowly does it," he warns when I sit up too fast.

"Christ, I feel weak," I complain. My head is spinning and for a moment I don't think I can stand.

"It's quite normal to feel worse immediately after an operation like you've had. You need to give yourself time."

"I'm alright." I wave off his help. When I get to my feet, I stumble as my right leg folds and would have fallen had the nurse not helped me to sit back down.

"You might need crutches for a while," he offers. "Were you weak in that leg before?"

How the fuck should I know?

"He wasn't," a stranger's voice sounds. "He was fit and strong."

I may not know him, but it would appear, he knows me. "Who are you?" Still struggling to stand, I eye the man who's walked into my room as though he's got every right to be there. He's dark-haired and has brown eyes which seem to flare. He looks around my age.

"I'm Demon. Your prez."

Whatever I've been doing for the last twelve years, I'm a

changed man now. My Vanna would never want a biker as a father for Cas, or a husband associated with criminals. No. If I'm going to regain my wife and son, I'm going to have to alter my life.

"You're not my anything," I tell him fast. "I want nothing to do with you or your fuckin' club. Now get out of my room and don't bother coming back."

CHAPTER TWENTY-EIGHT

Mace

"Are you alright?"

I glance up at Shayla who's standing in the entrance to my room and give a quick shake of my head.

"Want to talk about it?"

I examine her face and think how to answer her question. It appears her company is just what I need. "Yes."

"The women have been talking," she says as she walks in. She indicates the bed, when I nod, she sits beside me, keeping a safe distance between us. "I'm not sure I understand. Vanna is Lizard's wife, and Cas is his kid? Am I right, Mace? How does that work? He's never acknowledged them."

I know what she's thinking, so I knock her ill thoughts of my brother on the head. "Lizard wasn't being a dick, Shay. He'd truthfully forgotten his life before he joined us, or a big fuckin' part of it." I put it as simply as I can. "Now he's remembered his wife and kid, but the joke's on us. He's now forgotten all his time with the club. Worse, he told Demon to get lost."

"Isn't that good, for him? And obviously for Vanna and Cas? She's got her man back, and he's got his kid."

I fall back, one foot still on the floor, one knee bent so my other sole rests on the edge of the bed. My arm is over my eyes.

"I don't know," I tell her, letting her into my thoughts. "It might be good now, but Liz lived for his job, loved his bike. What if he goes back to Vanna, settles into a nice suburban life, then remembers what he's lost? The man I knew would have given his life for the club."

"The man you knew didn't want a wife or a child." Seeing the expression on my face, she adds, "Women talk."

I expect they have been trying to make sense of the little they know. But they'll only have heard snippets of the story as the men will keep the main details to themselves. Vanna and Cas had gone straight to their room last night. I know she's trying to work it through for herself.

It's strangely comforting sitting here with Shayla. If I wanted to talk, Ink or any one of my brothers would give me their time, as I'd spare mine for anyone else, but it's different with Shayla. She's concerned for me more than any of the others, she's something that I look on as mine. Oh, not in the forever sense or even sexually.

"You know," she starts after a couple of minutes, "I'm wondering if the man you thought you knew didn't exist. What if he didn't want an old lady or family as deep down, he knew he had one waiting for him to find himself again? What if he's both parts of a whole? What if he's Vanna's Lizard as well as yours? But just didn't know it at the time."

"He went with whores." I roll my eyes at her. "Doesn't seem much like a family man."

"Would you?" she asks, her eyes creasing. "If you had someone, would you be faithful?"

I don't tell her the situation would never arise, but I give it some thought and provide a truthful response. "If I was with someone, I'd never stray." A safe answer as the whole of this is moot.

"How's the boy handling it?"

"It's hard for the kid, he's confused. He doesn't know his dad at all, only from what Vanna had told him over the years. He's just about accepted there's a club full of uncles for him to lean on, and he was as pleased as fuck to know he had our support. Now Lizard's saying he wants nothing to do with the club or our life, and the kid's likely to be ripped away from us. Cas doesn't know what to think."

"Perhaps that will change. It's still early in his recovery. Don't write him off just yet, Mace."

It is still early. At least Prez has been able to get updates as he's still next of kin on Liz's records, though I'm sure Vanna wouldn't keep his condition from us. "I thought his op would be the end of it, you know? But apparently messing with the brain is a dangerous thing. He's weak on his right-hand side, almost as though he's had a stroke, and he can't walk too well which is frustrating him. His right hand doesn't work properly either."

"Is that his dominant one?"

"Yes."

"Oh."

Oh. There is the other problem. The consultant wasn't able to give Prez a prognosis. They expect improvement once the swelling goes down, but he could be left with permanent damage. As he is now, he can neither do his job nor ride a bike.

"He'll be getting occupational therapy," I tell her. "We can only hope it works."

"It's early days," she reminds me again.

"Next problem," I speak half to myself, "is where he goes when he's released. Prez is concerned if he goes back with Vanna."

"Why? Surely that would be for the best?" She draws up her knees and wraps her arms around them.

I stare at her while I give her the reasons. "Vanna needs to work, and Cas is at school. Liz would be on his own most of the time. If he falls or needs help, no one would be there. Whereas here, someone's always around."

"That makes sense." She looks thoughtful. "But what about the tattoo parlour? Can you manage without him?"

That's the other problem we have. Even if he came back to the club, he's not fit enough to work. "Vi's stepping up to do the admin side, Jonah and Whale seem to be coping with the trade. But we're down an artist, and a good one at that. It's a big fuckin' mess, Shay. I keep thinking it's all my fault. Did I do wrong bringing Vanna onto the compound? Maybe if I hadn't…"

"Can you hear yourself, Mace? Liz had a *tumour*." She rolls her eyes. "I think you should be thankful instead of blaming yourself. What would have happened if he'd blacked out when he'd been riding his bike?"

I stare at her, realising she's right. If he'd been riding in a group, he might have taken a few of us down with him. If he'd been on his own, fuck, it doesn't bear thinking about. He could have died alone by the side of the road. I wipe my hand over my eyes. He had a tumour which was going to affect him at some time, all my actions could have done was bring it on slightly earlier. At least when he collapsed, he was here with help around.

"I miss him, Shay."

"I wish there was something I could do to help."

"Letting me talk to you helps," I tell her. "And that you're staying around. It's one less thing for me to worry about."

"I still don't know why you'd worry about me, Mace."

She's bemused not fishing. I don't answer, I'm actually not sure myself. There's just something about her that I like. I like talking to her, she's easy company. I just wish there was more I could do to take that pain out of her eyes. Once I know more about Lizard, I promise myself I'll look into therapy for her.

"Well I'm not going anywhere, at least for now." She offers a smile. "Pyro said he's grateful I'm around. They needed an extra pair of hands with you lot at the hospital."

I know that. Pyro's also told me he's been impressed with how she's willing to get stuck into any manner of things which need to be done. Apparently, she'd educated one of the newer mechanics when he'd accidentally topped off a tank with gas instead of diesel. Tore him a new one and made him empty the shit out and replace it. Pyro had been impressed that she'd noticed, and luckily before any damage was done. "Ro's pleased with your work."

She dismisses the compliment, instead telling me, "I worry about Esme."

"Vi rang to ask about her. Her mom said she's doing okay. Still not talking much but settling back into her home. They've seen their doctor and are arranging for a child therapist. I don't think you need to worry, she'll be fine."

Her lips press together. "I miss her, Mace. Kind of got used to having her around."

"She's back where she belongs, with her folks." I think for a moment. "Hey, when Ink's finished my bike, I was thinking of riding down to Flagstaff to show it to her. Why don't you come along?"

"On your bike?" Her yelp of surprise makes me snort.

Yeah. I've surprised myself. Never thought of taking a bitch on the back, but if the whole purpose of going is to take it to show the painted tank to Esme, then I'll be riding. I'm hardly going to trailer it there. It doesn't cause me to break out in hives thinking of Shayla riding behind me. In fact, I might well enjoy it.

"It's a long way," she muses, not immediately dismissing the idea.

"Nine, ten hours. We could make a stop in Albuquerque, that's about halfway."

"I'd love to see Esme again, it's just, I've never been on a motorcycle, Mace."

"How about I take you for a ride soon, see what you think of it?" I can't imagine how anyone could not like riding, but hey, some don't.

She looks at me shyly. "I think I'd like that. Just to try. It's been so long since I've done anything fun."

My heart breaks for her. I'm sure it must be. Everyone needs to cut loose and let free at some time, and in my book, riding is the best way to do it.

"As soon as we're clearer on what's happening with Lizard, we'll sort something out, Shay. Just a short ride, see how you like it. Maybe head out to the mountains, get some fresh air in our lungs. What?"

She's shaking her head, but when she speaks it seems it's not with dismissal. "I'd like that," she tells me, shyly.

I wonder if she's realised yet just how close she'll be to me when she gets up behind me on my big two-wheeler. It's the intimacy which makes taking a female behind them something special to many men, breasts pushed up against my back, her mound pressed against my ass, and her arms around my waist. Fuck, now I'm getting hard just thinking about it, and the last thing I need to do is frighten her off before we start.

I force myself to think of something else. I stand, then look down at her. "Thanks for coming in, Shay."

She shrugs. "Talking sometimes helps."

I can think of something that would help more, but it's far too soon to approach that. I'm going to have to leave her, otherwise an unruly part of me will make my thoughts known. "I'm going to get a drink."

"I'll be down soon."

She will be too. She's been getting braver since working at the shop, as if giving her mind something else to focus on and her hands something to do has settled her in some way. Or maybe it's just because she's getting to know us and is no longer so afraid.

I walk down the stairs, standing aside to let Vanna pass. I place my hand on her arm to halt her as I see tears in her eyes.

"You okay, Vanna? Is Liz alright?"

"Liz is improving every day, but he's gone for a scan. They said that will take it out of him, so I've come back to grab a shower and a change of clothes."

"You look upset."

She shrugs. "After the week I've had, I thought it couldn't get worse. But it has. My boss just rang to tell me I'm fired."

She hasn't a job any longer? Well I suppose that's an obstacle removed to her looking after Lizard.

She continues, "And as if that wasn't enough, when I was with Lizard, I missed a call from the police back in Denver."

Ah. "Did you call them back?"

"Not yet," she breathes. "I'm trying to pluck up the courage. I'm dreading what they might say."

Placing my hand on her shoulder, I give her advice. "Call them. Whatever it is, you can deal with it once you know. Worrying about talking to the cops on top of everything else won't help."

"You're right." She gives a small smile, then disappears in the direction of Demon's room which she and Cas are still using.

I continue downward and see Cas at the pool table. He's knocking balls around with the cue but not playing with anyone. I grab the beer I came down for, then cross the room to him.

"How's it going?"

"Oh, hey, Mace. Cool, I suppose."

"You suppose?" I take a cue from the rack on the wall. "Want to set them up?"

He does so. I toss a coin, he calls it and breaks. Kid's not bad, but I'm better. He starts frowning when I sink ball after ball, sighing with relief when I miss one.

"You happy having your dad back?"

"It's hard…" He pauses to take a shot and then walks around the table to line up the next one. "I don't know him, and he doesn't know me. He's like a stranger."

"It will take time. Hey, what about that one? That's the shot I'd go for."

"Good point." He takes a breath, holds it, and pots the next ball. "It's been just me and Mom for so long, it will take time getting used to him being there." He grins and looks across the table at me. "He's no idea how to treat a teenager."

"Cas!"

"Over here, Mom. What's up?" Cas swings around looking concerned.

"The police have dropped the charges."

"What the f…hell? Really? Well hot damn." Cas fist pumps the air.

I turn away to hide my grin. *It worked.* Yes, a bit of money changing hands had the man who owned the car Cas had stolen suddenly having a problem with his memory. He'd been persuaded to change his story and say he could have been mistaken when he'd so firmly identified Cas. With no witness, the police couldn't prove anything. Thank fuck the kid had at least had the sense to wear gloves. I'll have to tell Judge his ride out to Denver had paid off.

"I can't believe it," breathes Vanna. "It's too good to be true."

"I won't be going to juvie," Cas rasps out, as though he's having difficulty believing it.

"You've been given a fresh start, Cas," I tell him, "Make good use of it and don't fuck it up. Because next time, we might not step in and save you."

"You did this?" Vanna's eyes come to mine fast.

I tell them because Cas needs to know that it wasn't the luck of the Devil that saved him, it was the intervention of Devils instead. "Yeah." I focus on the kid. "Luckily the car was returned undamaged to the owner. A bit of money changed hands, and suddenly his memory became faulty. It might not have worked if Cas had crashed the car rather than sliding it into the ditch. If so, it would have been harder to persuade him."

"How much?" Vanna asks tightly. "How much, so I can pay you back?"

"Didn't do it for you, Vanna. We did it for Liz. Didn't want him to reconnect with his son only to lose him. But Cas? Yeah, he owes us, it's not down to anyone else. Man fucks up, he should suffer the consequences."

My growling tone takes the smirk off the kid's face.

CHAPTER TWENTY-NINE

Vanna

MRI scans after a brain operation are routine I'd been assured, just confirmation that everything was proceeding as expected. Having his head mucked around with could be painful for Lizard though and will take it out of him. He'll need to rest afterward. Hence, I'd taken the opportunity to come back to the compound for a while. But I'm anxious to return just in case they'd found something that was cause for worry.

Before I return, there's something I need to do.

Leaving a jubilant Cas with Mace, I go and knock on Demon's office door. He's inside as I'd hoped and looks up concerned as I enter.

"Lizard okay?"

"Getting there. He's got crutches now to help him get around and is coping better with using them." My face twists.

"Doubt he's a patient, patient." Demon grins.

"No, he's definitely not. Look, I've had a call from the police that Cas is off the hook, and hear that's down to you bribing the man he stole the car from. While I don't want you to think I'm not grateful, it's not the way I want my son brought up. He should learn he has to pay for his mistakes."

Demon regards me thoughtfully. "Lizard hasn't found his son only to lose him again. We stepped in because we saw that there might be something we could do. We weren't going to threaten or hurt the man, but offer to put some dollars in his pocket? Wouldn't harm anyone but would make my brother's mind and recovery easier."

Lizard's still adjusting to having an almost-man in his life, I haven't yet broached the trouble Cas had gotten into. Having the slate clean does make it that less difficult at least. But I don't want any misunderstanding or things being done under false pretences. "Lizard doesn't want anything to do with you, Demon. That hasn't changed."

"He made that clear. I've been keeping my distance to give him a chance to regain his strength. Whether or not he wants to acknowledge the relationship, he's still one of us. We look after our own, Vanna. Not going to stop watching out for him just because his memory is fucked."

"Are you saying I did?" My hackles start to rise. "I stuck it out for two years, Demon, until I watched him walk out. I kept tabs on him, followed him a thousand miles just in the hope that eventually he'd come back."

"Whoa!" He holds up his hands. "I know you did, Vanna. You put your life on hold for him and your kid. No one's saying there was any more you could have done. We just feel the same about him that you do. He might not remember who we are, but we're not going to forget him."

If I kept him alive in my memory, I suppose it's understandable they'd do the same. But there's still one problem as I hate owing anyone anything. "Cas needs to pay you back. I don't know how, but—"

"Yes he does," Demon interrupts. "I'm sure we can find work for him. Don't want his cash, but his muscles will do instead."

"There's a problem with that, Demon. Lizard is looking at being discharged this weekend, and I'll be taking him back to Denver. There's no saying when, or if, we'll ever return." At this moment, I'd have to say it's highly unlikely. Lizard is adamant he wants nothing to do with the club.

"About that," Demon starts, and leans forward, clasping his hands together on his desk. "I want you to stay here—"

"Apart from what Lizard feels about it, I can't do that," I interrupt. "I've got my…" *No, I haven't, I've just been fired.* I start again, "Cas has got school."

"What will Liz do while you're out working all day? What if he falls? Or has a convulsion? Have you thought about that?"

"I won't be working immediately. I've just been told I've lost my job. But I'll need to find a new one, the bills won't pay themselves."

"Fuck, woman. You've got Liz now. Let him carry the load. He left you to do it alone for long enough." Again, those eyes fix on me while I realise, I hadn't thought of that. But if Liz can't work, he won't be able to bring in much money. His military pension probably isn't going to be enough.

"I'll be home with Liz until I can find another job," I say firmly.

"What do you do?"

"I'm an admin assistant."

He looks thoughtful, and his fingers pinch the bridge of his nose. "Liz being out of commission is causing us a problem at his shop. Vi's taken on the admin stuff that he used to do, but her doing that means we're down another tattooist. We took Weston on because there was more work than they could handle. How about you take that job? Help us out and keep things ticking over until Liz is fit again."

"Liz has a problem with his hand and might never be able to tattoo again." Again, I don't want anyone to live with false hope.

"And it might be temporary and sort itself as his body heals." Demon's not letting me get away with that.

Liz had been pleased he'd gotten his dream job, as he'd called it. But we haven't discussed he might not be able to do it again. With him, I've been concentrating on the positives, but out of his sight, I've been forcing myself to be realistic.

"But I live in Denver," I object. "And Cas's school—"

"We've got schools in Pueblo. Did you know that?"

I roll my eyes. "Cas won't want to leave his friends."

"Seems his friends aren't good ones if he gets into the shit he's done. Do the kid good to make new ones."

Demon may well have a point. But, "Lizard won't want to come to the club. He hates bikers and everything they stand for. He'd have a fit if he knew I was working for you."

"Hell, woman. Have you even met us? Have you not accepted our hospitality? Are you not happy to have us help out with Cas? Fuck." Demon looks angry. "Liz's view's from before he met us, he changed once, and he can change again. You know how he came to us?"

I shake my head, admitting no. Lizard can't remember and no one else told me his story.

"He was invited to stay with a friend of his in Denver, a man called Hatch." I nod, I knew that much.

"They'd been in basic together," I confirm.

"Yeah. Well, Hatch had a motorcycle, and encouraged Liz to get one. They were out riding one day, and some idiot in a truck was texting or something, swerved over their side of the road. They were riding two up, Hatch on the outside. He got the brunt of it, head-on collision, died immediately. Liz laid his bike down but escaped with scratches."

I gasp.

"It happened close to Pueblo. Liz's bike needed to be fixed, it was trailered into our shop. Liz needed someone. Mace was at the shop at the time. Saw he was in shock and brought him back to the club. Well, Hatch's place was rented, and he was dead, so Liz had nowhere to go. We offered him a room, and apart from collecting his clothes and attending Hatch's funeral, he never returned to Denver. He found his place here. As you know, he'd always been interested in tattooing, so we set him to work in our shop, let him do his apprenticeship which he came through with flying colours. The civilian who managed it was looking to retire, so once Liz proved himself, we gave him the job and never had reason to regret it."

Demon stops talking and cocks a brow at me.

"You think he'll do that again? Stay here and see something he likes and change his mind about the club?"

"Lizard is a biker, Vanna. He's one of us. So yeah, I think there's a pretty good chance. Even if he never remembers, he could start all over again. Repeat the process and again take the journey from strangers to friends." He sighs deeply. "If you're considering you, personally, would prefer to slot Lizard into your nice civilian life, think about this. Ink, Mace, Pyro and Liz are tight, and you know why?" It's a rhetorical question as he waits for no answer. "They've all served. They've all got the same need, to be part of a team. To know there are others around them who'll all have their six. The man he was then, and the man he is now, will more than want that. It's as crucial to him as air, food and water."

I frown. "Are you saying Cas and I won't be enough for him?"

"Yes." He gives it to me direct. "Was Lizard ever a nine-to-five man? Was he happy being a civilian?"

His question pulls me up. "I don't know," I respond honestly. "I met him when he was a Marine. After he got out, well, that's when he couldn't remember. He was unsettled, but I thought that was because of the injury to his head."

"I suspect it was because he was missing the camaraderie that comes with having his team around him. That's why he headed for Hatch, and that's why he stayed when he arrived here."

Maybe he's right. Maybe not.

"And," Demon continues, "think about the benefits of him being here while he convalesces. If you're at the clubhouse, you'll have support. Looking after any invalid is challenging. Liz is going to get frustrated when he can't do things for himself. Being here, you'll have people to share the burden, to help him if he needs it, and for you to go to and vent with when it gets too much. He and Cas can ease into a relationship without being thrown immediately into being a son and a dad."

I hadn't really thought what it would be like after I took Lizard home. Like so many things thrown at us in life, it was something I'd have to deal with as best I could. I have a small two-bedroom rented house and have to admit to doubt in my mind about Liz and I slipping back into sharing a room, or more precisely, a bed. I haven't been intimate with him in a very long time, and while I still find him attractive, he's expecting a much younger woman to undress and slide between the sheets. Ideally, we need time before we pick up where we left off, if that's even going to be possible.

But here, would I equally be expected to share his room? "What would be the sleeping arrangements?"

"There are two bedrooms you can use. Lizard's own, of course, and mine and Vi's where you are now. Who goes where is up to you to decide. No need to change where you are at the moment, you can continue sharing with Cas."

Has he got answers to everything? "You're missing one important thing. How the hell do I get him to come here?"

"Can he drive?" There's a glint in Demon's eyes.

I shake my head and narrow my eyes. Of course, he can't.

He chuckles. "Then I don't think he's got much choice."

He's suggesting I kidnap my husband. The thought actually makes me smile. But he's right, there's little Lizard could do about it. Obviously bringing him here against his will is not the answer, though how I can persuade him I don't know. I'll have to give it a try. I stand. "I've got to get back. I'll think about what you've said, Demon. I have to do what's right, for him and for Cas."

"And for you." Those intense dark eyes stare into mine. "Tell him we're thinking of him, okay?"

"I can't even do that, Demon. He hasn't a clue we're here. I think he thinks we're staying in a hotel or something." I haven't lied, just haven't corrected his misassumptions.

A jerk of his chin shows me I don't need to explain.

I have a quick word with Cas on my way out. As expected, he wants to hear any news if things haven't gone as expected with the scan but would prefer to stay here rather than come with me. I understand. Firstly, it's boring sitting around a hospital bed for any length of time, and secondly, conversations are stilted between Lizard and his son. I know both are trying, but one doesn't know how to assimilate a strange man into his life, and Lizard resents a child being close to having grown into a man. They both need learn who each other is now, and I suspect their relationship won't settle until they've both had some time.

On the drive back to the hospital, I think about the job Demon offered me, a temporary one only until Liz can either take back the reins or decide to move on from this life he can't remember. I'm sure it can't be too hard, it's not a big shop after all. And I might appreciate being able to get out from under Liz's feet all the time. I'm not the woman I was ten years ago, I've spent too long being independent. Like Cas, I've got to forge a different type of relationship with Liz now. He might think he can step back in and pick up where he left off, but he can't.

When I walk into his room, Liz is sitting up, awkwardly forking some food into his mouth with his left hand.

"Hi. How was the scan?"

"Fuckin' uncomfortable," he grumbles. "Made my head hurt."

"Did you get some rest afterwards?"

He nods.

"Did they say how it was looking?" Typical man. Looks like I'll have to drag every answer out of him.

"There's still a lot of swelling that needs to go down, but it's going in the right direction, apparently. They're going to do another scan on Friday, then if that's okay, I can go home on Saturday."

"That's great." Getting him out of here will hopefully be a major step toward his recovery.

"They want to know who my doctor will be in Denver, so they can get my notes sent down."

"I'll deal with that," I say promptly, while in the back of my mind I come up with another good reason for staying local. He'd be close if he needs to see the consultant again. Consistency is often good in any treatment.

Liz seems comfortable with my offer to sort things out on his behalf. He places the empty plate on the table and changes the subject. "Tell me about Cas. What does he like to do? How's he getting on at school?"

I spend some time giving him a rundown of our son's likes, dislikes and achievements, with Lizard querying stuff he doesn't know, such as the latest Xbox games when I say Cas is a fan. He shakes his head when he realises how much has moved on in the twelve years he's forgotten. Then when he's caught up with the present, he asks me what it was like bringing Cas up on my own. I try to make light of it, but I can see him appreciate at times it was hard.

At one point he reaches over and takes hold of my hand, squeezing it. "I'm sorry."

"It's not your fault Liz. You couldn't have done anything to prevent it."

Talking has tired him out. I pick up a magazine I'd brought in with me and read as he dozes, not really concentrating on the words on the page, as recollections of the conversation I'd had with Demon go through my head.

I'd accepted my new reality would be taking my husband home to Denver and trying to make the best of things once we got there. But Liz has been gone more years than we were actually married. I still love him, else I'd have removed the wedding band from my finger, wouldn't I? But much of this man lying sleeping on the hospital bed is a stranger. I'll have to find out if I can live with the man he is now, and he'll have to do the same with me.

As Liz isn't in danger of dying, mid-evening I cease my vigil by the side of his bed and drive back to the compound. Of course, I barely get in the door before I get questions thrown at me.

"How is he, Vanna?"

"Improving," I inform the two men who asked, Rusty and Hellfire. "He's had a scan and they're pleased with the progress he's made. He'll have another on Friday, and then should be able to come out at the weekend."

I notice all the men are around and remember it's Wednesday, and they held their meeting called church earlier. My eyes narrow as I see the whores coming out to play, and I walk over to Cas who's immersed in a game of pool with Pyro.

Waiting discreetly until Pyro wins, I step in only after the last ball is sunk. "Cas, time to get upstairs."

Glancing anxiously behind me, I see Pyro catching my silent plea for help and he gives me a quick grin. "Time for me to get Mel home."

Cas starts to object, but I toss him my best mom glare. "Wills has set an Xbox up for you in our room. You can play on that for a while."

"Don't see why I can't stay down here," he complains.

Pyro's passing, having collected Mel from the kitchen and overhears. "Kids and old ladies aren't welcome after a certain time. You know this, Cas."

"I know what goes on." My son looks stubborn.

"You want to outstay your welcome?" Pyro sternly replies. "Men want to be men, Cas. That means no one underage in the clubroom."

Cas tosses his pool cue onto the table and stomps across the room to the stairs. I give a weak smile toward Pyro, then follow my son. Live porn, or any porn is not something I want my son subjected to or not just yet, nor the drunken and rowdy behaviour when the men let down their hair.

I want to make myself scarce too. I know this was Lizard's life when he lived apart from me. It's hard to accept he knows all these club girls intimately and I hate that they've had more years with him than he had with me.

I climb the stairs slowly. All I've wanted for twelve years is for my husband to come back. Now it seems he intends to, I realise what a stranger he'll be, and how difficult it will be just to pick up where we left off. Add Cas and his teenage behaviour into the mix, and I know it could be explosive. Instead of a male figure being a positive influence in his life, it might be a disaster and send Cas further off the rails. Liz has no idea how to be a dad to someone his age.

He thinks he can control him like a two-year-old. He can't, he needs completely different handling. One thing I've learned is, it's best to give way on things that don't really matter in order to have wins where they count.

I suppose the best news is that the charges against Cas have been dropped. But is that a good thing or bad? Will it just teach him he can get away with that shit? That's not the lesson he should be learning.

I huff a laugh. I always thought if my husband ever recovered his memory all my problems would disappear. In reality, it appears they're only just starting.

CHAPTER THIRTY

Lizard

I apparently recovered from a traumatic brain injury I got in Afghanistan. Well, if you can call it a recovery. I forgot my wife, didn't acknowledge my kid, and even accused her of stepping out on me as I couldn't remember him being born. Fuck, I probably accused her of faking the marriage certificate.

Now I've forgotten that I ever forgot, though my memory is still playing tricks on me. I remember Hatch—must make time to contact him as soon as I'm well enough—and of course remember Vanna, but not as she is now. And Cas? Well, it seems I've got a teenager and not a little kid. That's fucking hard to wrap my head around.

As I can last envisage her, Vanna hadn't lost all her baby weight. I recall her worrying about it though that hadn't mattered a damn to me. Those stretch marks and slightly rounded belly were just evidence she'd grown my baby inside her for nine months. Now? Well, in my head I'm more than a decade younger, and I'd never thought I'd go for an older woman. While I'd never admit it, that's what she seems to me. Why can't I look at her and feel horny, just as I used to?

She's my wife. She's stayed faithful. I owe it to her to stay with her, pick up where we left off, and step into my role as Cas's father.

Can we make this work?

There's been changes to me, changes I don't remember. My body is covered in tats and I don't even know why I got some of them, or what the images signify. I've got a full back patch with the Satan's Devils' insignia. I'd been horrified to spot that. It was proof they hadn't been lying when I was told I was a member of an outlaw motorcycle gang, the sort my real friends had always warned me about. That's not who I am. The loss of my memory must have caused an aberration in my brain, as who I was, and who I've woken up as, would never ride with such men.

They're criminals, we all know that. MCs run drugs, women and guns. They live with constant danger, fighting rival MCs and hiding what they do from the cops. Maybe a deeply hidden desire to end myself attracted me into their life?

I hope they're leaving my woman and kid alone. I'm thankful Vanna and Cas are at a hotel, and not at the club. I'll have to see what money I've got and help Vanna out to pay for that. Hopefully I'll be out Saturday and we can return to her home. Her home, not mine. I've never seen it. All I can remember is living with her in San Diego.

We'll be in the same bedroom.

Will we fuck? I'm not sure I'll be able to, not having yet felt the slightest twitch in my cock, but my recent surgery will be a good excuse that will work at least for the immediate future.

I'm feeling cheated. The mirror in the bathroom shows nobody is lying when they say twelve years has passed by. It's undeniable that I've grown older. My face is lined, even more so than Vanna's, my skin leathery presumably from riding in all weathers and my hair long in a style I immediately hated. I even found a couple of grey pubic hairs when I'd had a close look.

In truth though, I feel about seventy. I hate the weakness on my right side. I've been told I'm a tattoo artist and a good one at that, though it's hard to believe that seeing the state I'm currently in. My hand isn't strong enough to hold a gun, and it shakes so much when I just try to lift it. How can I work when I can't even hold a fork? For the time being, I'll have to rely on Vanna and whatever military pension I get. Another thing stacked against us; I've never leaned so heavily on a woman before.

Whether or not my movement comes back, I'll have to leave my current job. For one thing, it's here, not Denver, and the other, I want nothing to do with the owners, the Satan's Devils motorcycle club. It's probably a front to launder money. I must have been lucky not to have been arrested and serve time in the intervening years. Or, if I have, no one's yet told me.

The doctors have said it's unpredictable whether I'll get my memory back. Something tells me I'm suppressing it, as there's no way I want to return to who I was. Who'd want to remember they were a biker for fuck's sake? Not me, that's for sure. Instead, I'll move forward, I'll step up and be a husband and father.

Am I? Can I?

"How are you feeling, Dad?"

"Hi, Cas. Come in. Where's your mother?"

"She's talking to the nurse." Cad frowns as he comes over, giving me a critical look. "You're going to look odd when they remove that bandage."

I am indeed. Too anxious to deal with anything but removing the tumour, they'd shaved the part of my head where they'd operated and removed a piece of my skull before, apparently, gluing it back in again, but left my hair long everywhere else. I prefer the military haircut, always have. "I'll shave it all off," I tell him. I won't mind doing that. Who lets their hair grow long anyway? Only rockers and greasy riders with a motorcycle club.

"That's a shame, but perhaps you can grow it again."

"Isn't it time you cut your hair, Cas?" I'd prefer him clean-cut with a short back and sides.

He gives me a look I don't think a son should give his father.

It's certainly not one of respect. "My hair, my choice. I'll do what I want, *Dad*."

"Cas," I growl, warningly.

"Dad?" he challenges back.

"You're doing well, the nurses say." Vanna's cheerful voice cuts through the growing animosity in the room. "The plan is you're still coming home tomorrow."

I realise she's always been there as a buffer between us, and this is the first time I've been alone with my kid. It hadn't been a good experience. Kid seems to need a strong hand, Vanna's clearly let him run wild. He's got to learn how to respect his elders.

What was I like at his age? Grateful for everything I got as I recall. Left to go hungry and neglected too often. I'd learned to be quiet and invisible in most of the foster homes I'd been in. Kept my head down for my own safety and never rocked the boat.

It was how I'd coped when I went into the Marines, appreciating the structure and routine, and obeying orders without question. Perhaps it would do Cas good to join up when he's eighteen?

And be like me? Invalided out and no good to anyone at the age of twenty-four? Is that really what I want for him?

I was unlucky.

I was lucky not to end up dead.

Maybe Vanna would have preferred that? After a period of mourning, she could have found someone else. That thought makes me growl. I might not be certain I want her, but I wouldn't want her to be with anyone else.

Vanna's eyes snap to mine. "You okay, Liz? Your head hurting?"

"When isn't it?" I bite back, but without bitterness. It's the cost of me living through what I had, and the doctors say the headaches should improve as the swelling goes down in my head.

"You ever play *Assassin's Creed*, Dad?"

I take it as the olive branch it probably is. Cas trying to forge some connection with me. "That's the new game, not long been out."

"Oh, yeah. I've got latest version. I bought it with my Christmas money. I love the free roaming."

Free roaming? What crap is this? Another sign the world has moved on, leaving me in its wake. Fucking hell, I can't even connect with my son over a game, we don't speak the same language.

I glare at Vanna. "Isn't that for over eighteen?"

Cas rolls his eyes. "Everyone plays it, Dad."

"He's right," Vanna says, her eyes meeting mine.

"He should be playing Super Mario." The first game I can think of comes into my mind.

Cas's look of disdain makes me annoyed.

"Cas, can you go get me a coffee?" Vanna reaches into her purse and extracts some bills from her wallet.

"Sure. You want anything, Dad?"

I want an obedient kid, and a mom who buys suitable games for him, but all I answer is, "No."

When he leaves the room, I turn on Vanna. "There's a reason for age limits on those games. They're too violent."

"I'd rather he was playing that then out on the streets," she snaps back. "I manage the time he's playing, try to make sure he gets his homework done. It's a compromise bringing up a teenager, Liz. Look, I won't say I've not made mistakes," a look of pain comes over her face, "but I've tried to bring him up right."

I've hurt her by my accusations. When I reach out my hand, she takes it. "You'll have me with you to share the load from now on, Evangeline. You won't be alone any longer."

I'd hoped, expected, to see a look of relief, but instead, the lines on her forehead increase.

Her expression pulls me up. She's built a life revolving

around her and the kid. I start worrying there's no room for me in it. Maybe too much water has gone under the bridge? Maybe we're too different to pick up where we left off?

Her face softens at my frown. "Lizard, Cas could really do with a father in his life, but it's been the two of us for so long, it's not going to be easy. Don't be too hard on him, he'll just rebel. Get to know him before you start laying the law down, okay?"

I appreciate what she's saying, and it hits me that there's stuff I've not been told. From what I've seen though, the kid needs to learn respect, and who better to show him how to behave than the man who gave him life?

Cas comes back with Vanna's coffee, but she barely has time to drink it before the physio appears to take me through my torture regime. Not wanting her to see what a failure of a husband she has now, I send both of them away so I can be put through hell in private.

By the time he's finished with me, I'm a wreck. *Squeeze the ball with your hand, he said.* Sounded quite simple, but the effort to get my muscles to send the right signals to my fingers made my arm and head hurt. As for walking on crutches, that wasn't too bad, but I wasn't going to be released until I proved I could manage stairs.

I was determined to do it. *Bad foot down, good foot up.* Or, as he'd put it, down to hell and up to heaven so I wouldn't forget. But that shit was hard. It wasn't going to beat me, though, I want out of this place.

There I was wondering whether Vanna as she is now is the woman I really want as my wife when it looks like I could be getting the better part of the bargain. What's she getting? A thirty-eight-year-old man who can't walk unaided.

The last thing I want is a wife who has to be my nurse.

The physio eventually takes pity on me. "Enough for today."

"Again," I tell him, determined to make this work. What kind of husband and father would I be if I didn't make strides in my recovery?

At last, back in my room, I ask him to be honest. I swallow, hoping to hear the right answer.

"Will I ever be able to use my hand and leg properly, eventually?"

He pauses, checks my notes, then looks at me. "I know this isn't what you want to hear, but it's simply impossible to tell. You've still got swelling on the brain which is the reason you're having difficulty with certain things. It could be worse, sometimes after the removal of a tumour, speech is affected, and it's also fairly common for people to have to learn how to swallow again. It all depends on the area where the tumour was, and how the brain was affected when it was removed. As the swelling goes down, you'll recover gradually. There's already a lot of progress you've made. You might make a full recovery, or you could be left with some residual weakness on that side."

"You're not much comfort." I try to keep the whine out of my voice, but it's hard.

"You asked me for honesty. I can't give guarantees either way. But staying positive, keeping up with your exercises will help."

"I need my records transferred so I can continue therapy."

He nods. "I understand your wife has been talking about how to continue your treatment." He holds out his hand to me, I take it, trying to clasp my fingers around his. "This is our last session," he says as he shakes it. "I'll sign you off as fit to be discharged as far as your physical abilities go. Good luck, Mr James."

CHAPTER THIRTY-ONE

Vanna

The next day I'm descending the staircase with my small suitcase in my hand, a sullen Cas following behind me, still muttering under his breath.

"I don't see why we have to leave."

Praying God grants me patience, I don't bother explaining again. Liz is so adamant he wants nothing to do with the Satan's Devils MC, there's no way I can bring him here. Even though I'm turning down a job offer in order to take him back to the town where I'm very much unemployed. After I've spent what's left of my last paycheck, I don't even know how I'll be able to make rent.

I've been through many options in my head. I've even tried to look for a place here in Pueblo but there's nothing available in my budget. No, the only answer is to do as Liz expects, and that's for Cas and me to return to Denver and take him with us, and hope for the best.

But Cas doesn't want to leave. Part of it, I suspect, is that he's scared of no longer being the man of the house. That worries me too. I've seen glimpses of conflict between my son and his father and know it's not going to be easy to have Lizard transition back into our lives.

I pause on the bottom step, as three people are blocking my way.

"So, what are the main differences, Shayla?" Mace asks.

The woman shrugs. "Tractors produce torque as their purpose is pulling. Cars, bikes and trucks carry shit. They've got suspension, tractors haven't. Oh, and they're not tuned for speed."

"You're doing okay, though," Pyro butts in. "Sure, suspension is something you're overly familiar with, but we can work on that."

"So cars are built for comfort?" Mace chuckles.

"Sort of," Shayla replies.

"Excuse us." Deep in discussion, they haven't noticed me or Cas. Now I've attracted attention, I notice Mace's sharp eyes on my suitcase.

"Thought you were collecting Lizard and bringing him back here?"

Cas says in a low tone, "I fucking wish we were."

I silence him with one practiced mom look, then turn back to the man who'd asked. "I wish I could, Mace. But he's not the man you knew, he's the man he was before he joined the club. He gets agitated whenever I try to speak of you. He thinks he hates what you stand for."

"And what the fuck does he think we're about?" Pyro snarls.

"He thinks you're a gang—into criminal stuff."

"You didn't think of telling him the truth at all?" Mel's husband snaps.

"What do you think?" It's my turn to spit the words out. I've tried and tried, being convinced it would be the best solution all around to stay at the club. But Liz was equally adamant he wasn't going to consider it for a moment. Nothing I could say could defend them adequately, as I haven't known them long, and Liz thought they'd hidden their bad side from me—because they wanted their foot soldier back.

"Demon's not going to like it," Mace warns.

"It's for the best," I tell him, going back over the similar arguments I'd had with Cas and had used to convince myself Lizard might be right. "His brain's still healing. Maybe in time he'll remember the club and want to come back. I wouldn't get in his way or stop him—"

"You sure about that?" Mace growls. "From where I'm standing, you're probably glad to get your man to yourself, but don't forget Vanna. He's ours too. He's our fuckin' brother."

"I've told her that," Cas barks out. "She won't listen."

I throw up my hands. "It's not me you have to convince, but him. Come on, Cas. Your dad will be waiting for us."

I walk off, expecting, *hoping*, my son will follow. To my relief, he does.

It's what I've always wanted isn't it? For my husband to come home, and then all will be right with the world. So why, I think, as I get into my car, automatically checking Cas is fastening his seat belt, do I feel I'm leaving the best support I could have had behind? Help I might well come to need.

You're on your own, Vanna. Just as you always have been. Yeah. That sounds about right.

When we get to the hospital, Cas is sullen and Liz impatient. Sorting his discharge papers out takes a while, particularly as he can't hold a pen and has to sign left-handed. At last a wheelchair and volunteer appears, and with his crutches balanced over his legs, he's wheeled through the hospital and outside.

As soon as he's able to, he stands, and after placing the crutches under his arms, balances on his own two feet.

"Where are you parked?"

"There." I point out the modest model car which is all I can afford. It's good enough, getting me from A to B.

He looks at it and shakes his head. "Fuck, this must have been a new model when Cas was two, Vanna. You had it all that time?"

"No, I had our old Honda, you remember that? Well, it died, and this was cheap. It runs okay, so it suits us."

"My friend's dad's car's amazing. Does everything automatically," Cas excitedly tells him, getting onto one of his favourite subjects. "Automatic wipers, lights which dip themselves. All-around parking sensors and blind spot warnings."

"Sounds like a load of useless crap to me," Liz complains. "All a car needs is an engine, gearbox and steering. Long as it starts and stops that's all that matters."

As I pull out of the parking lot and onto the main road, Cas sits back in his seat again, his arms folded. Guess all that sounds like science fiction to Liz, and Cas's attempt at conversation had failed.

"Can we have the radio on, Mom?"

Well, listening to music would be better than trying to make small talk with a son in a bad mood and a husband who doesn't seem much better. I'm just reaching for the knob when I hear a motorcycle engine. No, more than one. Then at least a dozen appear in the mirror. A couple overtake us, I wait for the rest to go past, but they don't. They arrange themselves all around us, in front, to my rear, and one in the lane outside of me.

"What the fuck is going on?" Liz sits forward, his head moving in all directions as he takes in the threat that surrounds us.

Damn it. I indicate right, and one of the bikes blocks my turnoff lane. Glancing to my side, I see Beef, and he's pointing ahead. It doesn't take a genius to understand what they want of me.

"That sign said Denver," Liz says tersely. "Knock that asshole off his fuckin' bike."

"Don't you dare, Mom. That's Judge!"

"How the fuck do you know who they are?" Liz snarls over his shoulder at Cas, but just as quickly looks back to me. "Where's your phone, Vanna? I'll call the police."

Quickly I reach down, pick up my purse and throw it in the back seat. Cas picks it up and holds it tight in his hands.

"No police." The last thing I want to do is summon the law on our friends.

"Vanna," Liz growls. "Unless you mow those fuckers down, they're going to direct us where they want us to go. That's fuckin' kidnapping."

"There's another turnoff up here," I tell him calmly.

But no, the bikers are ahead of me, and again foil my attempt to get on the right road.

"They're not letting us go, Mom." Cas's voice sounds full of glee, and a glance in the rearview mirror shows him grinning.

If I didn't sense it would annoy my husband, I'd be grinning as well. But I keep my face impassive. "Guess we're going to the compound."

"Cas. Give me your mom's phone. Now, boy. Fuckin' obey me."

But Cas doesn't, and I give up trying to get back on the correct route. Well, we're almost there now, let's see how this is going to play out.

I don't know what Demon has in mind, or whether he's prepared for just how angry the man at my side is going to be.

The gates slide open. Surrounded by bikes, I drive through. Knowing what to do, I continue driving around the back, and park next to the club's SUVs and trucks. When I turn off the engine, silence descends.

"Don't fuckin' park, Vanna. Turn around and drive out. Ram the gates if they've closed them."

I sigh deeply. "Lizard. This is your home, your family. Give them a chance."

"They're a criminal gang," he hisses. "What's this all about Vanna? You like the biker lifestyle? You been fuckin' around on me?"

Tears come into my eyes. This wasn't where I planned to end up today, but in God's honest truth, I don't know the man sitting beside me.

"I don't care what relation you are to me," comes an irate voice from the back seat, "but you don't make my mom cry."

For an answer, Liz opens the door and gets out. His attempt to storm off fails when his right leg gives way, and he ends up sprawled on the ground.

"Way to make an entrance, Brother," Demon's voice booms, then he reaches down to lend him a hand up.

"Get off me. Give me my crutches," Liz demands, his eyes spitting hatred at the man trying to help him to his feet.

But in the end, he has to reluctantly accept assistance. When he's upright, he balances on his wooden supports. "Told you before, I don't know who the fuck you are, and I don't want anything to do with you. Now if you'll get out of our way, Vanna can take me and Cas to Denver."

Beef has come to my door and opened it. When I get out, he wipes a tear from my eye, and pulls me in for a brotherly hug. Until his arms surround me, I hadn't realised how much I needed it.

Whether Cas expected Liz to magically get his memory back as soon as we arrived in Liz's old home, or whether his dad being this way had simply upset him, he gets out of the car, looking lost.

"Come here, lil' Bro." Mace waves him over, and pulls him in, then lets him go with a back slap.

Liz's eyes go from me in Beef's arms to Cas standing next to Mace, then his shoulders slump. "So that's the way of it, is it? Well there's no fuckin' way I'm staying here. Vanna." His focus comes back to me. "Too much has obviously happened. It was a fucking dream I could step back into your life." He pauses, then looks at Demon. "Look, I've got no argument with you man, as long as you let me go. Just give me a phone and I'll call Hatch. He'll come and collect me."

His president doesn't attempt to sugarcoat what I've kept from my man. "Hatch is dead, Liz. He died ten years back. His death is what brought you to us."

Lizard is stunned. Flummoxed, he doesn't seem to know what to do with that piece of information. After his mouth opens and shuts a few times, he queries, "Dead? Hatch is gone? He can't be."

"Come inside," Demon suggests, his tone softened. "If you want to know how it happened, I'll tell you about it. We came to the funeral with you."

"He's dead?" Lizard repeats. He looks at me. I don't have to say anything, he can see the truth on my face.

It seems Lizard's sorrow over the death of his friend at least temporarily trumps his distaste at being here. When Demon steps back and indicates the back entrance to the club, the one that leads in through the kitchen, Liz follows him as though in a daze.

"Who's Hatch?" Cas asks, quietly.

"Your dad's friend. Another Marine."

We're right behind him as he steps inside. It's Saturday and from the delicious aroma Mel's here and baking.

"Well you're a sight for sore eyes, Liz." Steph makes a beeline for him. "Will you break if I hug you?"

Her eyes aren't quite looking at him. "You blind?" he says bluntly. "If you are, how the fuck do you know it's me?"

"Your smell, of course. Mind you, it's all disinfectant and hospital aromas. Not your normal sweaty armpits for once." Her lips quirk.

Liz clearly doesn't know what to make of her, and just suffers her attentions when her arms go around him.

"Unhand my woman," says Beef, stepping forward and claiming her, his arms wrapping around her tightly, and pulling her back.

"Want a cinnamon bun, Liz? I baked them 'specially for you." Mel's holding out a tub. "They're your favourites." Liz steadies himself on one crutch, takes it automatically, then puts it down unopened on the counter.

"Liz, you don't know how good it is to see you back," Vi steps in, carrying Theo.

Lizard's eyes open wide. "What are you lot? Whores for the club?"

"They're our old ladies," Demon tells him sharply, his tone full of warning. "And I don't care if your brain is fucked up, Brother. You'll treat them with some fuckin' respect. Now come with me. We've got some talking to do."

CHAPTER THIRTY-TWO

Mace

We took a risk today. If Vanna had been serious about taking Lizard back to Denver, or Lizard being determined to go, that steering wheel could have been wrenched to the side and one of us could have ended up dirty side down. Deep down Vanna must have wanted to come back to the club, she hadn't taken much persuasion to bring Lizard. Had that been relief I'd seen in her eyes once she'd arrived?

If it was, I can see why. I'm having difficulty reconciling the man I've known as my brother for the past ten years with the angry person in front of me. If it wasn't that I hoped the man I knew was still inside, and that I could blame the swelling in his head for the way he is now, he'd already have had my fist in his face.

I'm not sure what I expected. Him to walk in and magically become our Lizard again? Well, fuck that. He doesn't know us at all, and nothing in the club seems familiar. It's easier now to understand why Vanna had let him go after two years of trying to live with a man who didn't know her. Already, after a few minutes, I'm thinking of doing just that.

As I follow Demon toward his office, I know we've got to try, even though all our efforts might fail. Christ, I just hope the man I loved as my brother is still in there, somewhere.

Demon goes to sit behind his desk and waves Liz to a seat. I refrain from offering assistance even though Liz has difficulty manoeuvring the crutches and getting himself seated. Beef sits to one side, Thunder pulls up the other chair. I stand in my normal position, leaning with my back against the door. Liz doesn't know it, but he's being given an audience with the senior officers of the club.

Lizard rubs his hand over his face, and doesn't waste time asking, "Hatch?"

Prez explains what happened ten years ago, and how Lizard came to the club, Liz's face going through a variety of emotions as he does so. "You were cut up, Liz. We gave you a place to stay. You liked it, liked us. After the funeral, you became a prospect. Got patched in a year later." As Liz looks dumbfounded, Prez leans forward. "You gave us a chance then, just asking that now you give us another."

"I remember nothing," Liz states, after taking a moment to digest this information. "Hatch, darn it. Should be able to remember his death. Seems disrespectful to the man not to recall it." I want to say it's not his fault, but he's continuing, "I fucking hate this, I don't know who I am. Seems I was first one man, Vanna's husband and a Marine. But he went overseas, came back with a brain injury, and turned into someone else, a biker if you are to be believed. Now I've had a fuckin' tumour removed, and I'm a different man all over again. If what you say is true, and I really was a part of this, I appreciate what you're trying to do. But maybe it's wrong for me to be here, I might not now see the club the way you say I did. Everyone here is a stranger."

Demon sits back in his chair and folds his arms. "And so we were once before. We invited you into the fold, and were no longer strangers, but friends and brothers. Nothing to say we can't do that again. I'm Demon, we've already met. Sitting to your right is Beef, the VP, and Thunder, sergeant-at-arms is on your left. Behind you is Mace, he's the enforcer."

"Names tell me nothing." The news of his friend's death seems to make Lizard less combative. "Hatch's death, well that's as raw to me now as it probably was then. I can't remember him moving to Denver, but I can see myself leaning on him when I split from Vanna. His death would have hit me hard. Probably hoped to find my own at the hands of the club, or of your enemies. Or hell, by just the life that you lead."

"What life do we lead, Liz?" Demon's deceptively calm.

Liz shrugs and tells us what he believes, "A criminal one."

"Wrong," says the VP. "You've met my wife. You think she'd be involved in a criminal lifestyle? And Mel, Pyro's woman, bakes muffins for fuck's sake, she doesn't cook up meth."

"We run clean businesses. Wouldn't touch drugs with a ten-foot pole and don't deal in guns. Sure, we run a strip club, but the dancers are there voluntarily, and no one is forced. It's a job for them, like any other." I'm angry he's given us such a label. "We've got a bowling alley as well."

"You run our tattoo parlour," Thunder puts in. "A fuckin' good one with a good rep."

With his left hand, Lizard lifts his right. "Won't be any fuckin' good to you there now."

"You not going to recover?" Beef asks sharply.

"I could do or could not. Doctors know fuck all."

Prez eyes Lizard for a moment. "See, here's the thing, Lizard. You've lived here at the compound for ten years. All your shit is here, your clothes, your bike. You've got a room, maybe not much, but it's your home."

"I don't remember," Lizard says tersely.

Prez ignores him. "You've never been to Vanna's house. You've got nothing of yours there, not even a change of under-wear. You don't know her situation. *I* know she's lost her job, and I've offered her a new one. Temporarily, at least."

"What job?" Lizard asks fast. "She's not going to be working in your strip club—"

"For fuck's sake." The words are startled out of my mouth. "She wouldn't do that, and we wouldn't ask her."

"She's going to be doing the admin and management shit at the tattoo parlour. Until you're able to take it up again." Demon takes back over.

"She didn't tell me she lost her job. Why did she?" There's a spark of the old Lizard there, with an unspoken promise of retribution should it be needed.

"Because her boss is an asshole and thought she was taking too much time off."

Lizard's shoulders drop. "Because of me?"

Demon doesn't lie. "Partly. And partly because of Cas."

"Why Cas?" Lizard puts in sharply. "What's up with the boy?"

"It's time you learned everything, Liz. So, I'm going to tell you. That kid of yours, well, he got into trouble with the law, which was why she came to find you. Thought the kid could use a man's hand in changing the direction he was taking in life."

"What did he do?" Lizard asks, his face reddening.

"Hotwired a car."

"She's off her fuckin' head if she came to criminals for help."

Demon growls but doesn't bother refuting the label Lizard's used for the second time. "She hoped you'd step up and help your son. It was serious, Liz. Kid was looking at juvie or even being taken away from his mom."

Liz takes a second to digest the words, his face tightens. "Is he still?"

"No. We sorted it. That's what family does, Lizard."

"Kid gets one pass, Liz." I tell him. "He gets into trouble again, we won't lift a finger to help. He knows this." He does. I'd made it clear to him.

"I'll speak to him."

My head starts to shake at the same moment Demon asks him, "Lizard, what experience do you have with teenagers?"

As Liz's shoulders make an up and down motion, Demon adds, "We don't either, apart from all once having been one. I do know, you need to concentrate on getting a relationship with him as he is now. It's a thin line you'll be walking and could easily alienate him. Lean on us, let us do the hard part. If you go it alone with Vanna in Denver, you're likely to make some big mistakes, maybe even end up leaving Vanna no choice but to choose between you and him."

Lizard at least seems to be listening to Prez's words. "What are you suggesting, Demon?"

Prez's face relaxes a little. "You need time to recover, heal as best you're able to. You and Vanna, you and Cas, need to establish your relationships. Give us a month, that's all I'm asking. Use the clubhouse as a place to convalesce. Get to know Vanna without her slipping back into routines with no place for you in them. Learn about Cas with what support you need from brothers around you. Let us help you recover."

"I don't want Cas involved in anything criminal."

"For fuck's sake brother, if you weren't already hurting, I'd slap you around the fuckin' head myself," I tell him, sharply. "We are not involved in anything outside the law." Well, not currently.

His mouth purses and he's quiet for a moment. When he speaks, it sounds like he's coming around to the idea. "I give you a month. What then?"

"No. We're giving you a month, Brother. A month when you can relearn us, and we can see if you're still the man we want riding with us. A month when you can reconnect with your wife, see if she's still it for you, and if you're her one. A month when you can learn how to cope with a teenager—although in that case, a lifetime probably wouldn't be long enough." Demon chuckles. "You'll be able to learn his likes, dislikes, and whether you can live together. We're giving you time, Brother. Use it wisely."

"And if I want to leave after the month, you won't stop me going to Denver?"

Demon stares at him intently. "You have my word, Brother." After letting that sink in for a few seconds, he nods toward me. "Why don't you go with Mace and see your room? It might trigger your memory."

Lizard looks hopeful for a second, then sadness covers his face. Nothing so far has brought any memories back. Stepping forward without a word, I hold out my arm, and he braces against it, using me as a support to get to his feet. Beef passes him his crutches, and I let him go once he finds his balance. When he turns to thank me, I get a glimpse of the man I've known for so many years before his look becomes shuttered again. Nevertheless, he turns to Demon.

"I'm not saying my fears about the club and what you stand for are wrong. But for the life of me, I can see no benefit to you in letting me stay. So, I'll take your offer at face value. I feel I should thank you."

"No need for thanks, Lizard. We're just having your six as you would have done for any of us were the positions reversed."

"Come, Brother," I hold the door open, not unsurprised to see Vanna hovering outside. "I'll show you where you live."

"Everything okay?" she asks, her brow furrowed.

Lizard regards her for a moment. "I'm staying here for a month, Vanna. Hopefully I'll have more strength then." He nods down at his crutches. "I need help, and it's not fair on you to be my sole support. I'm persuaded of that."

I don't miss the look of relief that crosses her face. I jerk my chin indicating she should follow us up the stairs.

Liz tackles the staircase carefully. I offer my arm, he shakes his head. "Up to heaven," he says rather strangely, as he moves his left leg, waits until he gets his balance, then pulls up the right. I allow him the time he needs to get to the top.

Demon's given me the spare key, so I open Lizard's door, standing back to let him inside. This is the first time Vanna's had an insight into Lizard's home where he's lived since he was patched in. Interestingly she hangs by the door, as if waiting for an invitation. Lizard swings himself in with the aid of both crutches, then lowers one to the bed, and balancing on the other, looks around him. He hops to the closet and opens it, spying his clothes hanging up neatly, then opens drawers which, if he's like me, hold underwear and socks. He eyes his motorcycle boots waiting for his feet by the bed.

"Do you recognise anything, Lizard?" Though it's in vain, I'm hoping he'll remember something.

He shakes his head. "Nothing. Looks like someone else lives here." He picks up a photo on the bedside table, his head tilting as he sees himself, me, Ink, and Cad holding up a fish. Yeah, we had a day out and made a lucky catch. We all look relaxed, happy and smiling. Thunder had taken the photo as I recall.

He replaces the photo, face down, then he continues to explore and opens the drawer by the side of the bed. I wince on Vanna's behalf as he brings out sealed and open cartons of condoms. He takes them out, hobbles to the waste bin and drops them all in, then turns to his wife and catches her eye.

"I won't need these." When Vanna gasps audibly, he continues, "Well, I won't, will I?"

"If you don't want to fuck," she answers crudely, her voices staccato, "then no."

His eyes widen. "I didn't mean that. You're…"

"I was on the pill years ago. I don't take it now. Why should I, when I haven't had a man in my life?"

"Er, I think I'll back out of this conversation."

Both partner's eyes snap to mine, then lose interest in me. I turn to leave, asking Vanna if I can pass. Lizard's voice stops me.

"Mace. Take that with you."

Turning I see it's Lizard's cut which he's viewing with disgust.

"Liz—" I start.

But Vanna gets there before me. "You were so proud to wear that Liz. Over the past couple of weekends, I didn't see you without it. You earned the right to wear those patches. Leave it where it is. It might eventually remind you of who you were."

"What if I remember them and in doing that, forget *you* again?" Liz roars. "What if I wake up and have forgotten completely who I am and am nothing but a blank slate? I can't trust my fuckin' brain, can I? Why should a vest made of leather remind me who I am, when I lived with you for two years and didn't fuckin' remember?" His anger, his indifference to the club seem to disappear and he has tears rolling down his face. "I've fucked up your life, Vanna. Obviously I mean something to Mace, Demon and the others, and I'm fucking them up now. I fuck everything up. All because—"

"All because of the explosion that wasn't your fault, Brother," I snap. "You were doing your duty, serving your country. No, you didn't fuckin' deserve what you got. But you're alive, others aren't. Vanna's strong, she dealt with you being gone. Give us some credit, too, Brother. You decide you want to ride with us again? Well, your fitness permitting, that's what you can do. You take each day as it comes. You don't have to decide right now what you're going to do with the rest of your life."

Vanna tells him fast, "You've got time, Liz. We've got time."

"What if I forget everything?" he asks again, his eyes haunted.

"Then we'll fuckin' remind you," I promise. "Day after day if you'll listen to us. Our stories, Vanna's too, will become your new memories. No pressure, no fuss."

"We'll get you through," Vanna vows.

Now I do step around Vanna and leave them to it, closing the door so husband and wife can have some privacy.

Out in the hallway I pause and draw in a deep shuddering breath.

"Are you alright?"

Seems she always appears at the right time, when I don't know until that point, she's precisely what I was needing.

"No." I indicate my room, and Shayla walks inside. It's only when I've thrown myself on the chair and she's perched on the bed that I resume, letting my remorse and sorrow flood out, speaking to her like I could to no other, even one of my brothers.

"Liz hadn't recognised me at the hospital, so I knew what to expect. I thought I was prepared for it. But seeing him here and him not recognising a thing? Not even his cut, or any of us…" I pause, clearing my throat as my voice is breaking. "Shay, it's a fuckin' disaster. He's angry, he's upset. I can't even imagine what it's like for him to know he's lived years which he loses in a flash, only knowing the truth of it because of a date on a fucking calendar. And Vanna? Christ." I seem to be on a roll and can't stop. "Now I realise the half of what she went through. If it's bad for me, what was it like for her? And for that poor kid Cas? Now it's happening all over again." Vanna's so strong, but she's had to be.

"It's a nightmare come true," Shayla says softly. Rising, she crosses the room to me, and leaning over, pulls my head against her chest. I take comfort from her eagerly. My cheek, cushioned against her breast, can hear her heart beating.

I'm the enforcer. I'm meant to be strong. But at this moment, I'm done with fighting.

A stray tear rolls from my eye as I wonder whether there's any way back from this for Lizard, or for any of us.

CHAPTER THIRTY-THREE

Lizard

I'm Lizard, otherwise known as Norton James. I'm… thirty-eight years old or so I'm told, and my birthday is the tenth of January. I'm married to Vanna and have a little boy—no, that's wrong—a teenage son called Cas.

I wake alone in a bed I'm told is mine. It's comfortable for sure, the pillow is just right, but it's unfamiliar. The clothes hanging in the closet fit, as do the shoes and boots, but I can't for the life of me remember purchasing or wearing them.

Vanna and I had a long discussion yesterday, triggered by my discovery of a drawer stuffed full of condoms in what I was told was my room. While she'd already told me about the club girls, I'd been devastated to find out my wife had actually witnessed me going off with them. That I'd flaunted my infidelity in her face. *What kind of man had I been?* Clearly, Demon wants me to become that man again, but even if I could, do I want to?

I'd had my own thoughts which I hadn't shared. What if my memory returns, and I'm drawn to them rather than Vanna? Has the damage already been done and I'm going to lose her? I can tell she has reservations about me. Is it that she doesn't like the man I'm supposed to have been for ten years? Is she worried what I'll make of the older her, or can she not forgive me being unfaithful, even though I must have thought at the time I'd been totally free? *I can't believe it was me who did that.*

I wasn't surprised when she suggested we sleep apart and not rush into anything, by which she meant a physical relationship, or, while I'm not fit enough yet, even the closeness of sharing a bed.

She said we've got time, but I'm not sure of that. What if I don't recover but get worse? What if my mind gives out on me completely? What if the universe hasn't yet stopped toying with me?

When I'd woken in the hospital bed and Vanna had been there, it had seemed so simple. When I got out, I'd go home with her and pick up from where we left off. Even learning the ten-year gap, I hadn't initially considered the ramifications. Perhaps it would be easier if it was just her and me. But it's not, there's Cas to consider.

I can look at Evangeline and know she's my wife. Matured, yes, but still the girl I met and thought enough of to marry. I still love her, she still comes first in my world. Cas, though? He's like a stranger. He doesn't even look like my little boy. *He looks like me.* There's no denying our relationship, and I wouldn't want to do that, but I don't *know* him at all. He's got some of my traits, some of Vanna's, and some which are his uniquely.

Reaching out, I pick up the stress ball I'd left by the side of my bed and religiously start doing the exercises I'd been shown. Fuck it, but if I can't do anything about my head, I'll work on my body instead. What kind of husband or a father would I make, disabled and on crutches for the rest of my life?

As I squeeze, then relax that ball with my right hand, I think about yesterday afternoon and the words Mace had said. I might have been prejudiced against coming to the club for what I thought had been valid reasons, but nothing and no one here had so far lived up to my most dire expectations. Demon had suggested I could rediscover my place here, even if I'd never remembered being here before. Could get to know the men who regard themselves as my family all over again. *Do I want that? What would it mean for me and Vanna?*

Hatch was the only man who I remember being close to. Members of my unit of course, we'd all trusted each other to have our backs. But Hatch, he was special. If Mace and Demon are to be believed, I've now a club full of brothers who used to mean as much to me as my brother-in-arms. Could I ever regain that? Should I give them a chance?

Yet another reason for me to regain my strength.

I contribute by being a tattoo artist. *What if I can never hold a tat gun again?*

What if I'm washed up and useless, at thirty-eight years old?

I'm going to get well.

That starts with me getting out of this bed. That starts with me moving forward, not looking back. Meet the men downstairs and have an open mind. With my fucked-up brain, my preconceptions about them need to be knocked on the head. If they were once my friends, and… I pick up the photo by the side of my bed, seeing my face there with Mace, and others I don't remember or recognise. If I once smiled with them like that, who says I can't do that again?

To hell with the past, it's the future which I should be setting my sights on.

When there's a knock on the door, I'm unsurprised to see Vanna there, concern written over her face. At my slight chin rise, she comes over to me. *Is she wondering whether I'll recognise her? Fearing during the night I'll have forgotten again?*

"How are you feeling today? Did you have a good night?" Her question is asked almost tentatively.

"Surprisingly, yes." I was going to add I don't normally sleep well in a strange bed, then realise while my head has no idea where I am, my body must have recognised and remembered.

Her eyes examine me critically. "Have you taken your meds? Do you need help with your dressing? Can I get anything for you? Do you want some breakfast in bed? Do—"

"Vanna," I bark a little snappily. "I'm fine, okay? I'll get up in a moment and come downstairs."

"Do you need help? Showering, getting dressed?"

"I'm not a fuckin' baby," I growl, not wanting her to nurse me.

Her eyes harden slightly. "If I'm not there when you come down, it's because I'm going with Vi to the tattoo parlour. She's going to go through the work with me, to check I'm happy taking it on."

"You're not going to be here for my first day on the compound?" *What kind of wife is she?*

Then I answer my own question. *A wife who's been independent for ten years, because she's had to be.* More than that, I was next to useless for the two years before that.

"I need to work, Lizard. I need money."

I hate the fact she'll be working and I won't be.

I take a deep breath. I know my emotions swing this way and that, she deserves my admiration, not anger. "What do you do? What jobs have you had?" My right hand twitches, as if wanting to reach out, but I'm not sure for what. It's a peculiar sensation, and one, which like so many things I don't understand, I ignore.

"I'm an admin assistant. I've had a couple of different jobs. I was a receptionist for a short time, and I've found I'm good with numbers, so I took a bookkeeping course. Basically, I do what anyone needs to keep a business running smoothly."

"Sounds like you'll be exactly what they want." While I'm useless and washed up. It's hard for me to reconcile the girl who I remembered as a stay-at-home wife and mother. Sounds like she's gained some skills since I've been gone, as well as a new confidence. I think I like this new Vanna. A worrying thought comes to me. *Am I good enough for her?*

"Okay, I'll leave you to it. I'll see you later on. Oh, and Cas has gone to the shop with Mace, there's an engine he wants to work on, so offered to take Cas along."

So I'll be going down into a clubhouse full of strangers. Great. My expression must show my distaste.

"I won't be out long." She reads my reluctance. "Vi's only going to show me the ropes, make sure it's within my skillset. A couple of hours tops. You could stay here and rest while I'm gone. But I have to do this, Lizard. I can't stay here without giving something back."

"Like I am?"

"Oh, Liz." She comes closer. "From what I hear, you've done a lot for the club. No one's worried about you not being able to work as yet. They just want you to get strong and back to your old self."

"What if I can't, Vanna? What if what you see now is all you're going to get? Is that going to be enough for you?" *Christ, I sound needy.*

She shrugs. "It is what it is, Lizard. We'll cope, whether your disability is permanent or not."

But will she be there with me? At this point, I'm not sure. She's changed, she's independent, and me? Well, I'm not even the man I once was.

When the door closes behind her, I get out of bed. Showering and dressing is exhausting. I have to do everything one-handed, and that's not even my dominant one, but my stubborn side doesn't regret refusing Vanna's offer of help. If I'm going to improve, I've got to do things for myself.

Though the effort has taken it out of me, and my head is pounding, I refuse to do what my body suggests and lay down on the bed once again. I've had enough time doing nothing over the past few days. Instead, I just sit on the bed for a moment, waiting for the wave of dizziness to pass. When I feel sufficiently recovered, I eye the motorcycle boots and pull them toward me.

The leather looks scuffed as though I've worn them a million times, and there's wear on the left on the inside, a mark as though it's been rubbing against something. I realise it's come from operating the gears on the bike. *What model have I got?*

Seems strange that I own and ride something I didn't know existed.

I pull on the boots and find they are incredibly comfortable. Supportive too. Deciding to keep them on, I pull my crutches toward me. Time to make my entry into the clubhouse.

There's a ball of nervousness inside me. Vanna's probably left by now, and Cas has chosen to spend time with another biker and not his old man. Can I blame them for deserting me? Probably not. I'm an invalid and impatient with it. I'm tense as hell trying to deal with a fucked-up mind and probably not pleasant to be around.

In their view, they haven't left me alone, they've left me with family. I need to find out if I want to claim it as my own.

It takes me an age to descend the stairs, *bad leg first, down into hell.* The physio's description amuses me, and that's where I feel I'm heading now. Half expecting to find a den of iniquity, men snorting drugs, cleaning guns or fucking the whores, I at last take the final step and enter the clubroom.

There's a man behind the bar cleaning the surface. After a moment he comes around it, carrying a black bag, and proceeds to pick up the rubbish left lying around. There's a cloth hanging from his back pocket which he uses where necessary to wipe tables down.

His eyes catch sight of me. "Hi, Lizard." He waits, but when I give no sign of recognition, he enlightens me. "I'm Nails. One of the prospects. Dirt's my friend, and he's currently outside manning the gate. Beaver and Karl are the other two, they'll be around later."

"Prospect?" Even the word sounds unfamiliar.

"Like a recruit?"

That he's put it into words I can understand makes me wonder. "You served?"

"Me and Dirt, yeah. Same unit." His face falls. "We were being transported back to camp. Ran over a fucking IED. Dirt and I were lucky, all the rest of the unit were killed. Except for

Bagel here." He points to a dog I hadn't noticed before. It had been sleeping. Hearing its name, it stands and wanders across. I notice one of its hind legs is missing.

"That how he lost his limb?"

Nails grimaces. "Yes. Bringing him back stateside and keeping him seemed fitting. Though he's not got much call for his expertise nowadays. He's a sniffer dog. Bombs."

"No explosives in the clubhouse?"

Nails laughs, thinking I've made a joke, then sees my face and says scornfully, "Of course not. Anyway, Liz, Jeannie's got breakfast on in the kitchen if you're hungry. Oh, and, anything you want, me or one of the other prospects will do or get it for you."

Well, I think to myself as I make my way in the direction he's pointing, *Nails seems to be okay.* As for the dog, Bagel's either taken a liking to me or can smell the bacon, as he seems to be following me.

The kitchen is where the action is. There are four men seated around a table, another standing with his back against one of the counters. An older woman moves him so she can open a cupboard, tut-tutting as she shoos him away.

It's her that turns as my crutches clack over the wooden floor.

"Lizard!" Her eyes brighten. "Oh my God, Lizard. I heard you were back. I'm so pleased to see you."

My brow rises. I don't know her from Adam.

She gives a little shake of her head. "I'm sorry, I forgot what Demon warned me. I'm Jeannie." Coming closer, she stares up into my face, then pokes me gently in the chest. "Don't tell anyone, but you were one of my favourites."

"We're all your favourites," grumbles one of the men. "Liz ain't anything special." He looks up at me and winks. "I'm Bomber. Jeannie here is my old lady. We've been married darn near forty years."

That surprises me. I thought any arrangement between these men and women would be temporary, the women used, discarded and passed on. But forty years? Not many people can last that long.

Jeannie looks at her man and rolls her eyes. "I'd have done less time if I murdered someone."

"Thought you'd have killed Bomber before now," observes the man leaning against the counter. "I don't know how you stand him. Hey, Liz. You remember me, Brother?"

"No." I make no apology for it, but I do notice the crestfallen look that crosses his face.

"I'm Ink. I'm another leatherneck."

My brow creases. "We served together?"

Ink makes a negative gesture. "Nah, met here in the club." He indicates a chair, and gratefully I sit. "I've got a woman, Beth. She'll be around later today."

"Can't fuckin' miss her," puts in the man sitting opposite me. "She's a fuckin' giant of a bitch."

He gets a slap around the head. "Watch your mouth, Judge."

"Fuckin' youngsters today. No darn respect." But Bomber's got a twinkle in his eye as he says it.

"I'm Buzzard," the man sitting to my right starts. "I'm the treasurer of the club."

"And he's here," Jeannie swipes him with a dish towel, "as his wife Sindy can't cook."

"Hey, I object to that." A middle-aged woman walks in, leans over and snags a piece of bacon that Jeannie's just taken out of the oven. "Not that I'm any good in the kitchen, but not everyone needs to know that."

"Think that ship has sailed sweetheart." Buzz stands, takes her hand, and pulls her over. Retaking his seat, she ignores the empty chair beside him, and plonks herself on his lap. "After twenty years, I think everyone's figured out why I eat so many meals in the club." He turns to me, chuckling. "She can burn water."

"I cannot," she mumbles around her mouthful of bacon. "I wouldn't know how to turn the stove on."

There's a round of good-natured chuckles at that.

"Buzz actually is a good cook." Jeannie points a spatula at the treasurer. "He's just lazy as fuck."

"Who are you?" I query the fourth man at the table.

He scratches the top of his head before telling me, "I'm Wills. I part-manage the strip club."

"The new girl work out okay?" Bomber asks. "Last night was her first Saturday, wasn't it?"

"She did good," Wills responds. "Couple of assholes tried to get their hands on her, but we shut 'em down. Kicked them out."

"Hey, Liz, why that frown?" Ink's staring at me.

It's not my place to say anything. I may not have seen evidence yet of drugs or guns, but they're admitting they do profit off girls.

"Wills," Ink may be talking to the other man, but his eyes are focused on me, "tell Liz about Lia. I don't think he understands."

"Lia?" Wills' hand covers his mouth to stifle a large yawn. "She needed money so went out to earn it on the street. She was on a corner waiting for the next John to stop, when he did, he was one of those do-gooders wanting to get girls like her off the street. Problem was, his way of providing education was with his fists. Scared the fuck out of her. When the bruises healed, she had no way of earning a living. Lia doesn't object to taking off her clothes, so when she came to us for help, we paid for her to have some pole dancing classes, then gave her a job as a dancer. She's now safe and protected. Off the streets and not living in fear of having her life beaten out of her. And before you ask, no, sex isn't one of the club's services."

Ink's still staring at me. "Still think we exploit women? I could run through the rest of the girls. They've all got similar stories. We," he points to himself and the others, "never touch the girls. Some are only there because it's the only job they can do for sure. Others enjoy the power they feel when men are watching them dance. They work for us as we pay well, and they are protected. In return, they give their all, and we run a popular, clean and successful club."

I return his gaze, then give a sharp nod. The way he's put it, it doesn't sound as bad as what I had been thinking.

A plate piled high with bacon, eggs, sausage links and hash browns appears in front of me. As Jeannie hands more around, conversation halts as everyone digs into their food.

Fuck. I take a deep breath then wonder how I'm going to tackle this, surprised as fuck when Ink leans over, picks up the knife and fork and slices my food into bite-sized chunks, before sitting down and starting on his own plate.

He'd not said a word, just did what needed to be done without me having to suffer the embarrassment of asking, and without waiting for me to express gratitude when he was done. No one comments at all.

The practicality of it takes away the shame I was feeling and allows me to dig into the best plate of food I can remember.

"Not in here, Ink. People are eating." Jeannie admonishes Ink when he gets out a pack of cigarettes.

He stands and waves the pack at me. "Want to come outside and have a smoke, Liz?"

I frown, trying to remember. "Do I smoke?"

"You did." Jeannie's standing, looking thoughtful. "But maybe that's not what you need right now, Liz."

I wave Ink off, she's probably right. If I don't need nicotine, don't feel a desire to fill my lungs with smoke, maybe it's for the best. I doubt medics would recommend it. If I've given them up, it's something good to come out of my predicament.

CHAPTER THIRTY-FOUR

Shayla

It was like one of those movies yesterday which are comedic and tragic at the same time. The bikers had exited en masse, kidnapped a man for all the right reasons and brought back a stranger who ended up in the last place he wanted to be, the club.

Mace had been devastated, as broken as I'd ever seen him. On one hand, he's pleased his friend is alive and looks like he'll be staying that way, on the other, he's not his friend anymore. He's not the man he rode with or shared drinks and, I've heard rumours, women with—not that I've witnessed that myself. Since I've been here, he's obviously being very discreet about where he gets his needs served or who with.

I knew Mace would need a friend and thought I had something to offer him. However much I want to hold my own in a man's world, women and men tend to think differently. Men are about action, wanting to rush and take down their enemies brandishing their swords, while women, not having the superior strength, tend to use their heads and bring a different perspective to things. It's why the vast majority of murderers are masculine, often crimes in the heat of the moment. Women tend to think twice.

Men are supposed to keep their emotions locked down. I could tell Mace was upset and needed someone who'd listen while he let his sadness out. I hadn't missed the moisture in his eyes which betrayed him.

Mace will be confused and must find it difficult to comprehend the change in his brother and friend. Of course, all his brothers will be feeling the same to some degree. Only Vanna would fully understand how they're feeling. But each will be suffering in different ways, their primary response being what action they should take, while they all should take a moment to process.

Ink, I think, will be the next most affected, but he's got Beth to help him through. Mace, though, who's he got? No one, except for the club girls and I'm not particularly impressed by them, from what little encounters I've had. My gut feel is that if you're able to live in the physical world not needing any lasting connection with the man you're fucking, you're probably lacking on the emotional front yourself, maybe having a lower self-esteem either gained through nature or nurture.

While I certainly can't provide to Mace the comfort someone like Tulia or Breezy could, I have something to offer. Just being there, listening, and giving him a safe place to be as sad and down as he wants. Sometimes you have to let the sorrow out, to hit rock bottom before you can climb up and allow grief to overwhelm you as it's going to do at some point.

I'd sat with him, listened to him, let him talk it out. Commiserated, but never suggested there was anything wrong with the way he felt.

That he trusted me to see him at his lowest point hadn't escaped me.

And, it was me giving him something back, when all this time I'd been mainly taking.

Mace is a good man. He's asked me for nothing.

Would he want more if I was able to offer it?

What if I wasn't damaged beyond repair? What if there is

some way out for me, a way back to something akin to the person I was?

My job at the auto-shop has given me purpose. It has given me a reason to get up every day and feel I'm contributing. When I first started working, I was scared, not so much of Mace, Ink or Pyro, but of the civilians they have working there. But wearing my overalls, with no makeup and my hair pulled up in a messy bun, I'm not so much female as asexual.

Whether Pyro had had a talk with them or not, no one had made so much as a suggestive comment in my hearing, and as I proved my skills could match theirs, I began to be treated just as a co-worker. It triggered memories that I'd forgotten were there, and soon I found myself as comfortable working at the shop as I had in the job I'd been forced to abandon over a year ago.

I don't deal with customers as I'm wary of strangers. I stay in the service area working on the cars and bikes. I jump at loud voices, when someone drops a tool suddenly, or when a door bangs or an engine misfires. But I'm not the only one who has problems. Sid, a mechanic, had gone white one day when thunder boomed right overhead. It didn't surprise me to learn he'd served overseas, and his reaction was a result of PTSD. It explained why no one had regarded me as an oddity.

I like my job, like the men I work with. I'm feeling a little more confident each day. Do I still want to move on? No, I don't. I want to stay here, but should I? That's the question. At times, I get a tingling sensation as if not all's right with the world, as if someone's watching me. As if Major is closing in. He could be casting his net to catch me even now.

I've stayed too long.

I don't want to leave.

I helped carry the load during the past week when Lizard was in the hospital, comfortable enough to continue to go to the auto-shop even without the brothers there. Sid and the other civilians had said nothing, but little gestures, the odd word, told me they had my back. I'd become more convinced than ever that Pyro had spoken to them.

Between the civilians and I, we kept on top of the urgent jobs, but with three men out, the work was piling up which is why today, Sunday, I've come into the shop with Mace to catch up on the backlog.

"You mind Cas being here with us?"

"Of course not, Mace. You needn't ask."

"Demon suggested it. He's sending Vanna to the tattoo parlour for a couple of hours with Vi and wants Cas out of the way too. He thinks if Lizard's forced to mingle with his brothers, he might get more comfortable around the club. Sure has got some weird thoughts about what we stand for," Mace explains, but then his lips press together. "I don't know if it will work. He might retreat without his family as a buffer or never appear in the first place."

I don't respond having no idea how it will go either.

It's an hour or so when I hit a snag.

"This is so darn fussy!" I complain.

Mace leans over to see what the problem is. "Hey, let me." Though his fingers are much fatter than mine, he's still able to reach under the engine and tighten the bolt.

Swallowing the blow to my pride, I quip at him, "I'm used to working with things you can actually see and get hold of."

He smirks and winks. "I can see how large things you can get hold of are better."

My mouth drops open, but instead of wanting to put distance between us, I bat his arm at his comment delivered in a suggestive tone and admonish sternly, "Mace."

Instead of pushing it, he looks around, calling Cas over. "Want to see how this is done?"

Cas is turning out to be a quick learner, and Mace a good teacher. I've been impressed with how much Cas has picked up. Mace has been showing him how to tune a motorbike engine this morning. It's involved a lot of joking around, and I've enjoyed both their company. I especially enjoyed that of Mace who's in much better spirits today, and I like to think I was partly responsible for putting that smile back on his face.

I was a bit taken aback when Mace couldn't resist showing him how to hotwire the variety of cars that are waiting to be fixed or serviced, not actually doing it, but pointing out where the ignition wires are in each of the different vehicles. My concerns were eased as I also heard him giving Cas a strict lecture that the kid is never to act on the new knowledge he's gained.

By the end of the morning, we've just about cleared the backlog of work that piled up when they were keeping vigil while Liz was in the hospital, or distracted when he woke up and dismissed them. I'm glad I volunteered to come in and help. I've really enjoyed myself and it's been good spending time with Mace.

Particularly as there are signs Mace isn't immune to me.

Out of the corner of my eye, there have been a couple of times when I've noticed Mace pausing whatever he was doing to stare at my ass as I leaned over an engine. It's weird, but I don't feel freaked out. Maybe it's because Cas is here and Mace can't act inappropriately, or maybe it's down to Mace himself. Something inside made me feel powerful that I could have such an effect on him.

My old boyfriend Rodger would be way down the scale, maybe a two or three, but as I'd no illusions I'd be more than that myself, I was happy to think we suited each other. Mace, now, he's more than a ten. He's off the top end of the scale. His short hair and beard frame a nicely shaped head, his features aren't delicate or pretty, rugged I suppose, but in my eyes so damn handsome. His arms are muscular, his t-shirt clings to well defined pecs, and his arms are a canvass of colourful tattoos.

That such a man, who women would probably die to get him just to glance their way, is staring at my ass, and, if I'm not mistaken, has to adjust himself after, is astonishing. Not that he let me get more than a glimpse of that, he'd turned fast and discreetly, his face reddening as though embarrassed. It probably matched the shade of my own cheeks.

I should be scared.

It's Mace. He'd never hurt me.

As I'm trying to work out if I'm the stupidest woman in the world not to be running a mile at the thought Mace might be attracted to me, and acknowledging I may not be totally immune to him, a phone rings interrupting my thoughts.

It's Cas's. He answers.

"Yeah, Mom… Okay… Sure, no problem."

"You don't need me anymore, do you Mace?" he asks as he replaces his phone in his pocket. "Mom's on her way back to the compound, and said she's going to swing by and pick me up."

"No, that's fine. We're about done anyway, aren't we, Shay?"

I love how he shortens my name. He's the only one who does. I nod to show my agreement. Cas has been a great help. Apart from Mace teaching him some of the basics, he's been sweeping and tidying up. Liz should be proud of his son, he needs someone to keep him the right side of the line is all. If he's pointed in the right direction, I reckon he'll turn out okay.

Mace leans against the workbench and folds his arms, his eyes on Cas. "Are you getting on any better with your Dad?"

Instead of brushing him off, Cas impresses me, as he clearly ponders how to answer his question. His brow furrows, and his lips press together, then he gives a little shrug. "I'd hated that he'd walked out and left when I was a little kid. I couldn't understand. When Mom had told us he'd forgotten us, I didn't believe it. How do you forget your damn son? Then I met him and realised it was true."

"It must have been so hard." I take no shame eavesdropping on the conversation, interested to hear the situation from Cas's side.

"You, Mace. You and the rest of my uncles," he gives Mace a quick grin, "well, I may not have had a dad, but I had you. Then

Dad came back, but again, he's a changed man, and wants to take me away from the club and my newfound family. He doesn't know what to do with a grown-up kid, and he still treats me as though I'm a baby."

"It must be difficult for him too," I observe. "He's probably trying too hard and overcompensating, getting it wrong when he thinks he's doing it right. Any dad wants to have a hand in bringing up their kid, but with you, it's been left too late. You need guidance, not a heavy hand. It's a bit like Mace, or one of the others, meeting a woman he likes, and she comes along with a teenage son. It's a big commitment, in many ways more challenging than taking on a baby."

Mace gives me a look I can't interpret, but my attention is quickly back on Cas again.

He sounds glum. "I'm worried we'll just butt heads all the time."

I chuckle. Sounds like a normal boy of fourteen to me. "Isn't that always the way at your age, Cas? See, I used to work with a man who had a teenage kid. He used to tell me the usual words out of his son's mouth were 'I hate you, Dad'."

"She's right," Mace tells Cas. "You're still a kid, but you're growing into a man. At your age, everyone bucks the rules: screen time when playing games, homework, curfews. Grownups still set the rules for reasons you can't understand."

Cas replies sagely, "I've found him at the wrong time, haven't I? If I was younger, I'd want to do things with my dad, now I'd rather spend time with my friends."

"You'll find things to do with Liz that you both enjoy," Mace predicts.

I hope, in time, they'll find a common interest. Bikes for a start. That's if, of course, Liz stays with the club.

"Cas? You here?"

"Hi Vanna," Mace calls loudly. "We're out back."

She appears. "Hi Mace. Shayla. Is it okay if I take him now?"

"Yeah. He's been a great help. See you later, Cas." Mace winks at him, then we both watch as they leave.

"You're good with him," I tell him honestly as the sound of the car fades into the distance. "You got any kids of your own?"

"Fuck no," he says fast. "I've always made fuckin' sure of that." He looks around. "Hey, we're about done here now. Want to go get some lunch? Be a good time to see if you like riding on my bike."

I glance down at the latex gloves I wear to protect my fingers from the oil and grime. "I don't know," I say, hesitantly, my voice quieter and less certain now Cas has gone.

"Come on," he encourages me gently. "I'll keep you safe, Shay. You might find you love it. We won't go too far as it's your first time."

It's that use of my shortened name again, sounding almost like a caress from his lips. Heaven help me, but it just does something to me. Suddenly I grin and meet his eyes, feeling a mischief I haven't felt in so long as I tease him. "Not all the way, then?"

He barks a strangled laugh, showing how much my bravado has shocked him.

Is this where he tells me I've read him wrong? That he's not interested in me that way?

I'm holding my breath, not actually knowing whether I want him to slap me back down or encourage me.

I'm not ready.

I'll never be.

Then, with a cocky slant to his head as if knowing he's trying his luck he suggests, "Maybe first base?"

First base.

If he'd indicated more, I'd have fled screaming. But those words suggesting he knows anything would need to start slow make me give consideration to starting this journey. With him. Only with him. A kiss.

Lips meeting lips. Maybe arms trapping me. *What if I run screaming?*

Mace is the type of man I'd have zeroed right in on if I'd met him *before.*

Just. A. Kiss.

A week, a day, an hour ago, I'd never have believed I do anything other than back away.

What's changed? Maybe it's the realisation I'm not totally weak. Not when I have the power to affect this devastatingly handsome man standing in front of me.

The question is, is he strong where it counts? Does he have command over his desires?

I could let Major continue to ruin my future, or, I could go for what deep down I want.

I could trust Mace.

CHAPTER THIRTY-FIVE

Mace

First base, I'd suggested.

Too much, too soon?

I'd got a chubby earlier from just staring at her ass. I think she noticed, yet she's still here. Maybe she's not offended, or worse, scared.

What is she going to say? I wonder, as she looks away, and then toward me again. I read her face carefully. At the first sign of unease, I'll back away fast.

She licks her lips. Hardly daring to breathe, I take a step toward her, then another, slowly, like a cat stalking prey, not wanting to scare her away. Placing my fingers under her chin, I use the soft touch to turn her face up. "I like you Shay," I finally admit. "Not asking for more, but I'd really like to kiss you. That's if you want that to."

"Can I say no?"

"Of course." I'm shocked, disappointed. I'd thought I'd been making headway.

"You wouldn't push me for more? I don't want to mislead you, Mace. I'm not sure if I'll ever be ready for that."

Perhaps it's not a no she doesn't want to kiss me at all, but she's just testing the waters out?

"Shay, darlin'. I know what you've been through. I know you've still got that asshole's name on your back. I'm so fuckin' conscious that you never want to feel trapped again." Seeing I've got her attention, I smooth my hand over my beard, while struggling to find the right words to say. "Getting a girl to fuck has never been hard for me. I don't just mean the club girls who are there for that anyway, but my bike, this cut... Before then, my uniform and people knowing I served." My shoulders rise, then I let them fall. "Whatever, but I could get a girl who just wanted to experience a bad boy in their bed whenever I wanted it."

She bristles. "You're telling me you expect me to drop my panties for you?"

"No," I refute fast, seeing she's looking like taking a step back. "I'm explaining I've never had to work for sex in my life. I know you're not going to be easy. I know because of everything you've been through, I've got to go slower than I've ever gone before. I accept I might not even get to my destination. Whether I do or not, that's down to you, babe."

"Stop, Mace." Her head moves side to side. "I don't know what I want." Her arms go around her body as she hugs herself. "When I first got out, I never wanted a man to touch me ever again in my whole life, let alone talk about me in possessive tones. I never wanted him to refer to me as 'mine', never wanted to be someone's again."

"Shay…"

"Hear me out?" she pleads. When I nod, she resumes. "For the last few months all I was doing was existing. Trying to keep Esme and myself safe, moving around. Trying to get cash without selling my body. I had no chance to think about me, what I wanted or what my future would look like. Not a good track record is it? Staying with a man who it turns out was an ass, then being stolen by Major."

"Not your fault, Shayla."

"Isn't it?"

Oh, fuck me. She's got tears in her eyes.

"Babe," I start, but again she stops me.

"You brought me to the compound. Made me see there was a different life. Sure, there are the club girls, but even I can see they're here because they want to be, and the men are never cruel or hurt them."

I may get a twinge of guilt as the thought of ginger enters my mind. But even then, we made sure the girls enjoyed it.

"Then there are the old ladies. They wear property patches, but they're not owned. They're happy, loved and seem to have the kind of relationship I dreamed of growing up."

I'm glad we've made a good impression on her. But I've got to come clean. "I'm not in the market for an old lady, Shay. Got to be upfront about that. But I'm prepared to work hard to help you learn to trust again. No idea where this will take us. If we ever get to that point, we might be together one night and hate each other. It might last a week, a month, hell, even a year. I can't promise more, I don't see myself as a forever man." Neither did Ink, I remember quickly, and look at him now. No one could doubt his commitment to Beth. Lizard though, Liz had always vowed he'd be happy living out his days as a single man, but now he seems over the moon he's got a family. I consider myself lucky I don't have a wife and kid waiting in the wings.

"You're honest," she tells me.

"Could you say anything different, Shay? Do you really think you could look at a man and want him to be yours forever? Hell, I suppose I should ask whether you could ever consider having a man like me in your bed with what you've been through."

She huffs a laugh. "I doubt you need me or anyone to tell you what a handsome man you are. Add on that bad boy image," she winks, "and I'd be crazy not to want to jump your bones."

"Do you?" I ask, optimistically.

Her head tilts to one side as she stares at me. "Right now? No." Her voice drops and becomes husky. "I never thought I'd be saying this, but out of anyone I could meet, in time, I think maybe you'd be the one who'd have a chance to persuade me."

I know the gift she's giving me with those words. She's giving me hope. Shayla in my bed? It would be a fucking dream come true.

It's more than her glorious ass and tits. There's just something about this woman. Her inner strength which I doubt she recognises, the way she put the needs of a child who wasn't hers in front of her own, the job she does so competently in a masculine world, and the way she's come through what she has, suggests I don't fucking deserve her. But if I get my chance, I'll keep her for myself until whatever I'm feeling burns out.

"So, that ride out? Lunch?" I prompt her.

She grins. "I could eat."

So could I. But I doubt we're discussing the same items I'd like to see on a menu.

The only person I've taken on the back of my bike has been Cas. Seems I'm about to start making a habit of it now. I find the spare helmet he'd used, make sure it's a comfortable fit, then lead her to where I'd parked my bike. Most of the paintwork is done now, and that stallion rearing is an incredible sight. Ink's just got some final touching up to do.

"Esme's going to love that." Shayla's eyes open wide. I hope the kid does. Ink has done amazing work, and I'm fucking pleased with it.

"She going to remember drawing it?" I frown, wondering if Esme will realise the significance.

After thinking for a bit, Shayla's head dips up and down. "I think so. But if you've still got her sketch, take it along, it could jog her memory if she's forgotten."

After pressing the button that makes the door rise, I wheel the bike out into the sunshine. Behind me I hear shuffling and know Shayla's slipping out of her overalls. Dragging up the gentleman from deep down inside me, I don't turn around to watch.

When she comes alongside, my lips curve up rather than down. She's wearing jeans, and heavy-duty boots. What's suitable for working on autos will certainly do for a bike. Her denim jacket will work as well.

She sets the alarm without me reminding her, closes the door and locks it, then looks at me dubiously after I throw my leg over the bike.

"Get on behind me, babe. Put your hand on my shoulder if you like."

A moment of indecision before she finally takes the plunge. The bike's suspension dips with her weight behind me. It's not that she's heavier than Cas, in fact she's lighter, but she feels different.

"What do I do?" she asks, her tone full of concern. "Apart from trying not to fall off?"

"You won't fall off," I chuckle. "Babe, just put your arms around my waist and hold tight. Then do what I do, lean with me and the bike. Oh, and mind the pipes, they'll get hot."

I can feel her trembling. Whether it's fear of the bike ride ahead or of being so close to me, I'm not certain. Hopefully she'll become comfortable with both in a short while. I've got a small mom and pop place in mind as our destination. It's far enough for her to have a good riding experience, but if she's not enjoying it, we won't have too long a ride back. If she really hates it, I can summon a prospect with a cage.

Kicking down into first gear, I gently ease off the clutch, starting off gradually. My foot returns to neutral then kicks up through the gears as I pick up speed. Her hands feel like they've got a death grip on my waste.

It's still a novelty having a passenger behind me, and I have to get used to the different handling of the bike. I take it easy, cornering slightly slower than normal, and only speeding up on the straights. Without any form of communication, I haven't a clue how she's taking to this, but I'm hoping she's enjoying it as much as I am.

Riding a bike can be lonely unless you're with a pack. With her warmth behind me, I don't feel alone. While there's no way we can discuss it, she's seeing and experiencing everything as I am. The exhilarating curves, the bumps in the slightly uneven parts of the road, and the straights where I twist the throttle and the breeze in our faces picks up.

The wind therapy, as always, seems to heal my soul. By the time I arrive at our destination, I feel fully relaxed. I cut the engine and pat her leg, instructing her to get off, then back the bike into a parking spot. When I look forward again, I get a look at her face and frown.

Is she traumatised?

"Shayla?" I start, cautiously, hoping to fuck I haven't put her off bikes for life. *I rode carefully.* In my head, I go back over the short journey, I couldn't remember anything that might have scared her, but then, some people are simply worried about the vulnerability of being on a bike.

Her mouth looks tight, her eyes are wide open. Her breath is coming a little too fast. There's a flush to her cheeks which wasn't there earlier.

"Shayla?" I repeat, this time more concerned. Thinking I will have to summon that prospect with a truck to take her back, I reach for her hand, it's trembling.

She stares down at our joined fingers and then through long eyelashes up at my face. "Mace," she begins, then stops, licks her lips and tries again. "Mace, do you think we could try first base before we go in and eat?"

Well I'll be fucked. The muscles in my cheeks begin to tighten as my mouth forms a crescent. Seems either the vibration of the bike or being so close to me has had an effect. One that I very much like.

"I think," I bend my head so we're less than a few inches apart, "that's a fuckin' excellent idea." Slowly, so fucking slowly, I close the distance.

One of my hands still holds hers. Using only that to anchor her to me, I gently brush my lips over her soft ones, a sweet innocent kiss I haven't deployed since I was younger than Cas.

It's her who wants more. She curls her free hand around my neck, trying to prevent my escape and increasing the pressure where our lips meet. I let her lead as her tongue demands entry into my mouth, then imitate her actions.

Even though it's become more sensual, it's still an innocent kiss. Perfectly acceptable in a place where there are families and children close by. Nevertheless, it's sexually charged and full of promise. I can't get enough of her taste, my appetite for food has fled, it's her I want instead. I get a waft of the shampoo she uses, and my free hand brushes against the soft smooth skin of her face, brushing aside the silky strands of her hair. While from the restaurant behind us there's a clattering of plates, the sound is drowned out by the little moan that escapes from her.

My cock thickens and I know it's time to pull back, before my wrong head takes over and demands I take her to a more discreet place, and fuck this second and third base lark, take her straight to fourth.

"Mace...?" Her eyes are wide, and her fingers touch her lips.

"Perfect, babe." And it was. I can't find other words to describe it. Simply kissing a girl is not who I am. Club whores don't need such foreplay, and would far rather have my mouth somewhere else. If a citizen girl demands it, I'll oblige, but only to get her into the mood. With Shayla? The kiss was an end in itself. Of course it left me wanting more, but also with a feeling of satisfaction. I know I'll want to do that again. Heck, I can barely stop myself reaching for her now.

I jerk my chin toward the restaurant, and no words need to be said. Still holding her hand tightly, I lead her inside.

As we eat, I listen to her glowing recount of how much she enjoyed riding my bike as if I needed words to prove it. Her enthusiasm makes me hope it will be sooner, rather than later, we'll be making that trip to Flagstaff.

If one short journey makes her want to kiss me like she's just done, I have to wonder what effect a longer one will have.

CHAPTER THIRTY-SIX

Lizard

While there's still an underlying current of unease deep inside me, I have to admit the biker compound is completely different to anything I expected. I may not recognise the people that live here, but they all treat me like a friend, without any uneasiness or distrust that they'd show toward a stranger.

My stomach replete with an excellent breakfast that was particularly tasty after hospital food, I take another coffee out into the surprisingly clean and comfortable clubroom, seating myself on a couch which I'd expected to find old and worn, but still looks relatively new. I ease myself back and rest my head. It wouldn't take much for me to doze off, but I try and fight the wave of tiredness that floods over me.

I consider the people I've met. Demon and his wife Vi, the president and first lady. Thunder who's the sergeant-at-arms, and Mace the enforcer, whatever that means. Beef who's the VP and Steph, his old lady who's blind. Then Buzzard and Sindy, Bomber and Jeannie who I haven't quite got the measure of yet. One minute she's all smiles and laughter, and the next, well, let's just say she runs a tight ship. Sparky who introduced himself as the road captain, and Cad who apparently spends most of his life with his computers—a man so pale I half expect him to admit he sleeps in a coffin.

Then there's Ink, who seems to believe himself a close friend as well as a fellow Marine. I've also met Rusty, an older man, who's particularly interested in my health. Pyro seems solid, and Mel, his wife, is expecting their first kid. Paladin had appeared right at the end of breakfast with Jayden who barely looks legal, but I'm assured she definitely is. Wills and Judge, two younger men who haven't long been members.

Nails and Dirt are two of the prospects. Bagel's their dog, and Max is Beef's wife's guide dog. The other prospects, *what are their names?* Oh yeah, Karl and Beaver, I've not yet met.

I give a small smile, my brain having successfully passed my simple test of remembering everyone I've come across. Wait, wasn't there also a man called Hellfire? Demon's dad I was told?

When I'd first suffered my brain injury, my short-term memory had been fucked, or so Vanna had told me. That I can put faces to names is a sure sign that's not happening again. At least I can remember something I heard five minutes ago.

"Dad?"

"Shush. He's resting."

"What?" I jerk awake, knowing I had indeed drifted off. "What time is it?" When they tell me, it appears I've been asleep for two hours. Jeez. I'm like an old man. I know I've aged years which I can't remember, but I'm not as old as all that.

"You're going to be tired." Vanna sits down beside me. "The doctors explained it will take up to six weeks for your brain to get back to normal."

"Normal? Our Liz?" Ink walks past, pausing to wink at me. "Can't wait to see that. Will be a fuckin' first for him, that's for certain."

I don't know why, but something about him pulling my leg seems right.

I ignore the childish urge to show him my finger. "How did you get on at the shop, Cas?"

I notice my son's eyes brighten. "Mace showed me how to tune up an engine."

"You like mucking around with bikes?"

"Bikes, cars." He shrugs. "Sure. I like them. Can't wait until I can legally drive."

I notice Vanna stiffen at the word legally and remember the trouble Cas had been in. I quirk a brow at her.

Vanna nods at me, and speaks to him, "Cas, you've got to wait. You've got to promise me—"

"Too fuckin' right he does," a voice bellows.

We all look up to see the VP has overheard. He addresses my son sternly. "You've had one pass, kid. Next time, we won't save your ass. You fuck up again and you're on your own."

Cas nods seriously as if this has already been explained to him. Should have been my job, but I still don't know how to talk to him. Beef eyes him for a moment, seems to read sincerity in his face, then jerks his chin and strides off to do whatever he'd been on his way to get done.

"Lizard, this morning I've been doing some thinking. I, *we*, need to talk to you."

I raise my eyebrow again. I might have lost my memory, but people starting conversations with the need to talk often signals the topic isn't going to be what I want to hear.

"Talk then," I invite her. *Is this where she's going to tell me she doesn't like the man I've become?*

"Your memory loss, we don't know whether it's permanent, whether it's going to come back. Even if it does, whether you'll want to be part of the club, or whether…"

"Whether my body is too fucked up."

If the flicker of pain crossing her face is anything to go by, I'd indeed put into words what she had more delicately been trying to say. Her look of compassion is too intense to be one that should be shown to a husband by his wife. I should be the strength in this relationship, not her. When her hand covers mine, I almost snatch it away. But she's got hold of my right, and the darn thing will barely work.

"Liz. Until the swelling goes down, we won't have any idea about your memory or what you'll be capable of doing."

I nod, wondering where she's going with this.

"Things happened so fast yesterday. I've been so tied up with you and your needs, that I'd forgotten one important thing until Vi asked what I was going to do about it." A look crosses her face as though she can't believe what she'd done. "Cas needs to go to school. He's already had a week off. Either he goes back to Denver, or he'll have to transfer here. I don't even know what will be involved."

"Summer break is coming up in a few weeks," Cas puts in. "It will be best if I continue at my current school until then."

"What about the friends who got you into trouble last time?" Or was it that he got them into the mess? I wonder whether I'll ever have the relationship with him where he'll tell me everything.

I notice Vanna's face has hardened. "You heard what Beef said. No second chances. Cas keeps his nose out of trouble, or all bets are off."

"I like Beef and Mace. I like the club," says Cas. "I don't want to mess anything up or disappoint them."

That he hasn't mentioned disappointing me, doesn't pass me by. But this is not the time to address it, and if I'm honest, I don't even know how. But Cas continuing at his current school until summer break makes sense. "So, are we going back to Denver tonight?" *Changes. So many changes.* I realise I'm comfortable enough to feel relaxed here now, and at least I'm sleeping in my own bed, though I don't remember it. In Denver, I'll be in a house I hadn't had a chance to put into my memory banks either then or now. And unless Vanna doubles up with Cas again, I'll be sleeping with my wife. Unable to meet any physical expectations, or it's possible that I'm unwilling.

"We're going, you're staying here," Vanna says fast, like

ripping a Band-Aid off. "There's so many reasons. But we'll be back at the weekend."

"No," I tell her, simply, staring her straight in the eye. I cover her hand with my left one, aware it's shaking slightly. "Vanna, I can't lose you now. What if my brain flips again, and it's you I can't remember?"

My honesty, my fear, has her throwing herself at me, holding me tight. My left arm clasps her to me.

"You won't forget me again, Lizard. Weekends will give us a chance to get to know the people we are now. It's only for six weeks." She hugs me tightly, then puts distance between us again.

Six weeks, only seeing her two days out of seven? She's mentioned the length of time I need for my recovery, not just the month I promised to the club. *Too long.* What if I start to remember myself as a biker? What if I start being tempted by the younger girls? I'll have to ask her to trust me when I'm not sure whether I'd be able to trust myself. Right now, I'd never dream of being unfaithful, couldn't believe I'd even think about going with a woman who wasn't my wife, but for ten years it seems I had no such reservations.

"Vanna, please take me with you, or you and the boy both stay. We'll sort out his schooling somehow or other."

Cas is looking from me to Vanna, then he gets up and walks away. His face is unreadable. Guess he doesn't care what happens between his mom and his dad if he gets his way. Isn't that the case with teenagers? Aren't they selfish? Or that's what I've heard.

As my eyes go back to my wife, I realise she's oblivious to our son leaving us. Perhaps she's used to his short attention span. Anyway, she's listing all the reasons why I should stay here. Close to the doctors who treated me, people around all the time. In Denver, she'd need to be out job hunting. Which reminds me, I presume Buzzard, the treasurer would be the one to help me sort out how I'm financially sorted. Technically, I'm away from my job on medical leave, but I doubt I've got insurance or will continue to be paid. My bosses are an outlaw MC after all's said and done.

Which reminds me. "If you stay here, Vanna, you don't have to look for work. Or didn't you like the tattoo parlour?"

"That's not the point, Liz. It's Cas who's most important."

"What about your husband?" I snap.

She throws up her hands. "Don't make me choose between you," she warns. "If I could clone myself, I would. You're recovering from a major surgery, of course I want to be by your side, but you've got friends here to care for you."

"Then move the kid's school."

As our discussion has become more heated, I'm staring at her, she's glaring at me, and neither of us register Cas's return until he drops into the chair opposite.

There's a satisfied grin on his face as he announces, "All sorted."

"What?" we ask simultaneously as our heads swing around.

He shrugs. "Mom stays here with you, Dad, and I go back to Denver and finish the school year. Then we've got the summer to decide where we'll be living."

"You're not staying with Jordan," Vanna starts.

"No," Cas agrees, smirking. "I've just rung Lindy, explained the situation and I'll be staying with her." He grimaces slightly. "I think it might be harder than living with you, Mom. She's already talking about a curfew, going straight home from school, and doing my homework. She made me promise to live by her rules. I'll be staying there Monday to Friday and come back here at weekends."

"Who's Lindy?" I query.

Vanna has pulled her shoulders straight, and the smile on her face is genuine. "She's my friend, a *good* friend from Denver. Cas is right, she will be strict with him, so I've got no worries there. I didn't think of asking her."

"You've been doing everything on your own too long, Mom,"

Cas puts in rather objectively for a boy of his age. "You never lean on anyone. Lindy was more than happy to help, and pleased Dad's out of hospital and recovering."

"She expecting you there today?"

"Yup. Said she's going to get a roast on later. You can take me whenever you want to. I'll go repack my bag, again."

He must have unpacked after we were escorted back to the compound yesterday.

I want to offer to drive him. Fuck, I want to get off this couch without having to work through the logistics of getting my crutches under me. The least I can do is offer to keep my wife company.

"I'll come with you."

"No, Liz. I don't want to take the risk. What if we hit a bump in the road and it hurts your head? You're tired and should be resting. It's not just there, it's back again too, remember. That's at least four hours driving—"

"Sorted," Cas says in a singsong voice from right beside me. He looks proud of himself.

I'd seen him headed to the stairs, but it seems he hadn't made it up them. Beef's standing next to him with a hand on his shoulder.

It's the VP who enlightens us as to what they've been talking about. "Lizard, whether you remember or not, you're a member. Cas is your kid. Prospects are there for whatever you want them for. If you need help taking your boots on and off, just ask them, hell got a problem taking your pants off for a shit, they'll be pulling them down for you. They'll do whatever you ask. So fuckin' ask one of them to drive Cas to Denver."

"Will they mind?" I ask, seeing a solution there. Vanna won't have to do four hours of driving, and while I don't like admitting it, staying here resting will be better for me.

"Will they mind taking your pants off so you can crap?" Beef's grinning widely.

"I meant, fuckin' taking my kid to Denver," I growl. "I'm perfectly capable of handling my own shit."

Beef snorts. "Fuckin' sure you are, Brother." He nudges me not so gently on the shoulder. "As for the prospects? If they want their patch bad enough, they won't say one fuckin' word of complaint."

CHAPTER THIRTY-SEVEN

Vanna

"Are you sure you don't mind, Lindy?" I say into the phone. It's a lot to ask of her.

"Of course I don't. I mind more you didn't already think to ask me. This is your chance to see if you can get back together with Lizard. There's only been one person for you, Vanna, you've stayed faithful to him all this time. This gives you a chance to get to know him again without simultaneously having to manage a relationship between him and his son."

I don't tell her he's not been faithful to me. I'm still not totally comfortable with that. Telling myself he didn't know he had commitments at the time only goes partway to accepting other women have had what I thought was mine alone.

"I'm wondering if I'm doing the right thing," I admit. "He needs to get to know Cas…"

"He'll have his chance at the weekends," she says fast. "Vanna, Cas is a teenager, no more difficult than others his age, but his hormones are running riot right now, you know that. You and Lizard need to see whether you can work things out together. If you can, you can put on a united front. Won't do Cas any good to have one parent saying he can, and the other he can't. The way I see it is if Lizard feels pressured to step up and take the parental role, he might take the wrong one as he's suddenly had an unruly son dumped on him out of the blue. He could be overindulgent, or too strict and push him away. I think you and Lizard concentrating on yourselves for now is better than adding Cas into the mix from the get-go."

She's right I suppose. Though I still feel I'm abandoning my son.

"Cas wants this, you know?" Lindy impresses on me. "When he called, he sounded mixed up. He wanted a dad, but he's got a man he doesn't know. Worse than that, someone who doesn't know himself. While Cas is here during the week, it will stabilise him. Apart from not being with you at home, he'll have his normal routine. At weekends he'll come to visit you, but he'll know he's got an escape route if it gets too much. Don't worry about him, I won't go easy on him. He's agreed to abide by what I say."

"He's told me that before too," I grumble.

She laughs. "You're his mom, you're supposed to knock your heads together. I'm his friend, his proxy aunt. He'll be on his best behaviour with me. I know despite what I say you're going to be concerned, you're his mom. But you're only two hours away. If there are any problems, I'll give you a call."

She's right. It isn't like I'm at the other side of the world if I needed to get back to Denver. "I can't tell you how grateful I am."

"You can pay me back by introducing me to a hot biker."

I bark a laugh. "You never know."

We end the call after exchanging a few more pleasantries. As soon as I say my goodbyes, Cas enters the room.

"You called her?" At my I nod, he adds, "I told you she was okay with it."

"Are you alright, Cas? Please tell me you don't think I'm putting Lizard's needs in front of yours."

"Mom." His tone is serious as he walks over to me. "I've been your top priority since I was born. Sure, though I don't always admit it, I still need my mom. Can't see a day when I won't. But at the moment, Dad needs you more, and you're right to put him first. Maybe we'll end up moving here, maybe we won't. Maybe Dad will make his home with us, or perhaps you won't be able to make it work. But right now, he's hurting, Mom."

"He could have come back with us to Denver." Should I feel guilty I don't want him there? Not this stranger in a place I made for Cas and me.

"Mom. I don't know anything about relationships, but this one is so hard. You've got to get to know each other all over again, and that's best done in a place you've both got space. Our house is cramped. Crowded together, we could just get on each other's nerves."

"Where did you learn to be so sensible?"

He grins. "Well, I didn't get my sense from my mom." He ducks to miss my playful swipe.

Half an hour later, he's getting into an SUV with Dirt driving, with instructions to text me as soon as he arrives which make him and the prospect exchange glances which are heavily based on the rolling of eyes. Then I'm waving him off as Nails opens the gate. I stand, watching the car as they drive out of sight.

"You're going to miss him." Liz tells me what I already know.

I don't reply, just think to myself that I'll feel like I'm missing a limb. I trust Lindy, though. He's fourteen, not a baby, but I still have tears in my eyes.

The old Lizard would have held me, comforted me. That he makes no move to do so shows how far apart we are. Perhaps Lindy was right. Taking away the necessity to keep one eye on my son gives me the chance to know whether the feelings I've maintained for Liz all these years, apply to the man beside me.

Over the next week, we settle into a routine. Lindy gives me daily updates and Cas seems to be behaving himself. My son checks in by text, letting me know he's doing alright, and asking whether Liz is making any improvements.

He is, but slowly, almost imperceptibly, but that's to be

expected as recovery is bound to take time. He's still plagued by headaches, and takes a lot of naps, often needing persuasion to rest as the doctor's had told him. But when I can't convince him to go and lie down, one of his brothers does so for me. I can see why they elected Mace to enforce the rules, having hidden a smile more than once at the way he barks for Liz to *go get his head the fuck down.*

Knowing there'll be people watching out for Lizard, I don't need to worry about him as I settle into my new job, finding it's not demanding at all and enjoying it. Jonah's a laugh, and while Weston is quiet, he's pleasant and good at his work. Vi's relieved to be able to concentrate on what she loves, sketching designs and working a tattoo gun.

The first week I concentrate on getting the books up-to-date, and by Wednesday afternoon have presented the accounts to Buzzard, who scrutinises them carefully while I shift from foot to foot, feeling like I've been summoned in front of the principal. When at last he turns with a smile and a sharp nod, I'm relieved. Seems I've done it right after all.

Friday afternoon it's Beaver this time who drives up to Denver to collect Cas and bring him back while I'm still at work. The last couple of hours go slowly, and I'm out that door fast when six o'clock comes around.

Jeannie nods as I enter via the kitchen, having parked around the back. "Cas is in there with Lizard." She jerks her head toward the clubroom.

"Mom." Cas stands as I approach, and soon his arms come around me for a quick hug. Not too long, as it's not cool to show too much affection for his mom in public.

"I've missed you," I tell him, holding him at arm's length and examining him head to toe, just to check he hasn't lost weight or has visible injuries. *Is it my imagination or has he grown taller?*

"I've only been gone five days," he retorts, but he's grinning.

Hearing someone clearing their throat, I glance down at Liz.

It's such a hassle getting to his feet, he doesn't bother to stand, but there's a big smile on his face.

"Dad's hand is better, isn't it?" Cas tells me.

Again I look toward Liz, and then at his right hand as he flexes and closes it. *Has it improved?* If so, it's a minimal improvement, but possibly more noticeable to Cas who hasn't seen him all week.

"You know, I think the boy's right." Lizard sounds pleased.

"It has, Dad," Cad insists. "See if you can hold this." He picks up an empty bottle that's been left on the adjacent table and hands it to him.

Very, very carefully, Liz tries to hold it in his right hand, and then tries to lift it up. His eyes meet mine and they're beaming. He couldn't do that last week. Baby steps, but in the right direction.

When Cas takes his bag upstairs, I follow him up. His week's been fine, he tells me, his schoolwork is all good. He got a B on a math test, which is excellent for him. But before I can fully interrogate him, he turns the tables on me.

"How have you and Dad been, Mom?"

I can't tell him any more than we're much about the same as when he left. I walk to the bed and sit on it. The bed, luckily a large king-size, that tonight I'll share with my son, and not the man I'm supposed to love. Do I love him? Or am I clinging on to the man I knew before? Is he really the same as he was then? Are the differences because I've moved on? Or is he not so much stuck in the past as he thinks? Have his experiences shaped him, even though he can't remember actual facts or events?

"Mom." Cas comes to sit beside me. "To be honest, I'd hoped, but didn't expect to return to find everything resolved. Of course I want Dad in my life, but I want you happy." He picks up my left hand, and as he'd done when he was small, turns my wedding ring on my finger. "If Dad had stayed, if he hadn't been hurt in that explosion, then it could be that you'd have grown apart and gotten divorced. You may not still be together."

"I've never wanted anyone else, Cas."

"Because you always knew he was out there. I wouldn't have minded, Mom, if you had found someone. As long as I got on with him, of course."

"What if Dad and I do get back together? Would you be okay with that?"

He shrugs. "This is what these weekends are for, aren't they, Mom? They're for all of us."

Saturday I work, but Sunday the shop is closed, so I'm free to spend the day with Lizard and Cas.

It's actually Lizard who comes up with the idea. He approaches it a little awkwardly.

"Do you want to do something different today?" When I question him with my eyes, he continues, "I'm fed up with these walls around me, and I'm sure you are too. I've been talking to Mace. The San Isabel National Forest isn't too far away, and it's a lovely day. Of course I won't be able to walk far, but I thought we could take a picnic. Just get out and get some fresh air."

It sounds good to me. "Cas?"

"Yeah, Dad. I'm up for that."

Biting my tongue, I try not to comment. *Is this my son?* Or has Lindy sent someone else back in his place? Outdoors and picnics are certainly not at the top of the list of things I'd have said he likes to do most.

Having gotten into this idea that prospects are there to be used, Liz has a quick word with Beef, and only an hour later, Dirt is driving us out in the SUV. His invite I take because Liz has a lack of confidence in himself and he doesn't want to be alone with just me and Cas, in case he topples off his crutches or something.

When we arrive, Liz is the last one out of the vehicle, taking his time to get his crutches into place and under him. While he's become more practiced with them in the intervening week, now Cas has pointed it out to me, I see there are small improvements. His movements are stronger, and he's putting a little weight on his right leg. He's also more confident as he swings himself along, with Dirt hovering close and making himself useful by carrying the picnic basket which Jeannie had prepared.

It had been a good suggestion to get away from the club. Once Liz has himself settled on a blanket, Dirt makes himself scarce, leaving us alone. The sun shines in a cloudless sky, and a gentle breeze blows the scent of wildflowers and pine our way. The highest peaks of the mountains are still covered with snow. It's beautiful and peaceful.

Jeannie's done us proud, and the food is consumed fast. Cas walks off to explore, and reaching out, I take Liz's hand.

"I needed this," I tell him.

"How's work? You getting on okay?"

"I'm enjoying it." I wink at him. "Now I've sorted out the mess you made of the books."

For a moment I wonder whether I should have teased him as there's a strange look on his face. Then he shakes his head. "You've changed so much, Evangeline, but in a good way. So much more confident, so much new knowledge in that head. Back then you were my wife and I loved you, but I never thought you were my equal. Sounds bad, I know. But it was my job to provide and care for you. Now that's been turned on its head."

"Do you mind?" I query, softly. Knowing if we've got out of lockstep, there'll be no pretending we can pick up where we left off. I won't go back to the woman who simply tends house.

"You know? I don't think I do. I admire you, Vanna. Admire who've you've become. But now I wonder whether I'm good enough for you."

CHAPTER THIRTY-EIGHT

Lizard

Watching Vanna's face as she has to wave Cas off again after the enjoyable outing we had today, it's impossible to read what's in her mind.

I hadn't been certain a picnic would be a good idea, or one that would have gone down well with a boy his age, but it turned out to be enjoyable for all of us. A chance to unwind, relax, and be a family unit for a few hours.

Now Vanna's being parted from her son again. She's sad, that's easy to see, and clearly hates to be apart from him. That she needs to be is down to me. Does she resent it? Resent me? I don't know.

Something holds me back from stepping in and offering her comfort. It's not just the crutches I still need as support that prevent me taking her into my arms.

I don't know my place anymore.

It would have been a mistake to try to pick up from where I'd believed I'd left off, before my career in the Marines had ended so abruptly with that blow to my head. Vanna is not the same woman she was then. Am I still the same man?

Problem with having a darn swollen brain is that I'm not sure who I am, who I was, or what I've the potential to become. Whether I could ever be worthy of being a husband for her.

So when the car disappears out of the gate, I catch her eye, jerk my chin, then my crutches clatter across the pavement as I make my way back inside. Alone.

The doctors had told me rest was my friend, and even I have to admit I'm tired after the outing today. An evening doze turned into an early night. When I wake, it's morning again. I shower, dress, then descend to the clubroom and take up my normal seat on the couch where I've taken to spending most of my days.

I hate being an invalid lying in bed. I've got into a routine of getting up, then coming down and taking up residence here. That way I'm involved in what's going on. That first day I admit it was so I could check nothing nefarious was going on, which would make me insist on leaving with my wife and son. But now it's habit, and I've grown to enjoy the steady stream of interruptions and visits from the women and men.

Fuck. There's a pain, a throbbing in my hopefully starting to heal brain. I lean back my head, digging my fingertips into my temples, trying to massage the ache away.

"You okay, Liz?"

I glance up at the man who's standing close. "Yeah. Nothing out of the ordinary. Just the pain that's always hovering there."

"Can I get you something? Glass of water? Beer?"

"Nah, Mace. I'm okay." I close my eyes again, but don't sense him moving away. I've had enough of soft drinks and am loath to touch beer in case the alcohol makes my head worse. A question floats into my head, and I let it out of my mouth. "Why do you call Ink 'Leatherneck', but not me?"

There's a pause before he replies. "Apart from mentioning your first tour a couple of times, you never spoke about your other tours or the time you served. It seemed more something you wanted to forget, rather than be reminded of."

Or, as it turns out, I didn't need any help not to remember. I'm becoming more comfortable, the pain's easing away, but I don't want to open my eyes in case it returns.

"How many tours did you do, Brother?" Mace asks in a casual tone. I appreciate him sitting down and staying talking to me.

I think back. "Three where I came back whole. The fourth? Don't recall how I got home."

I hear him draw in a breath. "What else do you remember, Liz?"

Lightbulbs are flashing in my head, things closer than they've been before, but nothing I can grab hold of. Images swirl but disappear before they can fully form.

"It doesn't matter, Liz," he says fast, sounding concerned.

I open my eyes.

"You sure you're alright?"

"Tired, but that's nothing new."

"Okay then." He stands but leans in and pats my shoulder. "Ink wants to talk to you later."

Idly I wonder what about.

I'm not alone long. Vanna's my next visitor.

"How was your day?"

She flops down on the seat. "Slow, but I managed to get some semblance of order in the files. There were handfuls of scribbled notes in a drawer and I transferred the important stuff onto the computer. Your handwriting's awful, Liz."

I give her a sheepish look. "Yeah, sorry about that."

She brushes her hand over her face, and I notice she's tired. My gut clenches when I realise she's used to working herself to the bone to support her and Cas, and now she's also taken responsibility for me. Not that I need her help financially, or not yet. I'd had that chat with Buzzard, and he told me I was good while I was still a member.

But I've also discovered that if I can't ride, I won't be a Satan's Devil whether I want to stay one or not. The choice will be taken away from me. Picking up the stress ball that's always close to me, I squeeze it in my hand. Cas had noticed an improvement, and perhaps there was. But I'm coming along too slow for my liking.

"Mind if I join you?" Ink sits down taking our permission for granted and places his beer on the table between us. "I know you won't remember, but Mace came up with the idea of converting one of the old factory buildings into a gym."

I'm actually aware of that. Escorted by a prospect in case I tripped, I'd gone outside to take some exercise and explore my surroundings, noticing construction work going on, and had asked what it was. I raise my chin.

"Mace," he continues, "having come up with the idea, dropped it like a hot potato and passed it on to me to get it up and running." He leans in and says conspiratorially, "Fact is, I hate Beth working out in the gym in town, want her close by instead. Anyway, I may have jumped the gun a bit, got some equipment arriving next week."

I frown. "I didn't think it was that far along."

"It's not," he grins. "So I'm having to make space in the basement."

"And you're telling me this, why?"

"One piece is an elliptical. A cross-trainer. Thought if you started off gentle, it could build strength in your arms and legs."

"He's not ready for that," puts in Vanna, her brow creased.

"I might be," I reply to them both. "I'm seeing the physical therapist in a couple of days, I'll ask him what he thinks."

"Good plan." Ink nods, taking the beer he hasn't touched and rising. He pats me on the shoulder. "Need to get you riding again, Brother."

Wind in my hair, pavement under my wheels and me seated on my Harley fitted out with Screamin' Eagle parts. I can't fucking wait. My eyes crease, and I shake my head, pain hurting me again.

"Liz?"

"I'm okay, Vanna." Or I will be in a little bit. These pains don't last long now.

Two days later both the doctor and the therapist clear me for gentle exercise, another scan shows the swelling's going down at the rate expected. They're pleased with my progress even if I think it should be going faster. Neither will make promises about how far I'll get, and that I may have to be prepared to have some form of lasting disability, and can offer no chances of how much, if anything, I'll ever remember. Well, fuck that. Their view that being alive should be enough is not one I share. My head might be fucked, but I'll do what I can with my body.

The headaches are a consequence of the operation I'd had and should go in time, it's just the brain healing itself.

My dressing is finally removed, and I realise it's time to do something about my hair, as I've a bald patch on my scalp. It's a shame, as while I can't remember growing my hair, I've become used to seeing myself with longer locks. Now it's all got to come off if I'm going to resemble a human being and not a freak.

Mace keeps his hair military short and has offered to clip mine. When I return from the hospital, I give him the go ahead, and follow him into his room and then to his bathroom.

"Christ, I look like an FNG," I tell him, as I see myself in the mirror for the first time after he finishes. "You've taken it a bit short."

"Shorter is best," he tells me. "The site where you had your operation won't show so much. I'm amazed there's so little scarring. Did they really cut part of your skull out?"

"Yeah. Frightening, isn't it?" I shudder, thinking of having a surgeon's hands inside my head. I'm glad I'd been unaware of it, knowing some people are conscious during brain operations.

Mace finishes brushing hair off my neck and shoulders. "There, all done. It will be easier as you can just shower and go now. Cas coming tomorrow?"

"Yes."

"How are you getting along with him?"

"Alright, I think. It's so fuckin' strange having a son near grown up."

Mace comes around in front of me. "The Liz I knew never wanted a wife and kids. You ever think it's because in the depths of your mind, you knew you already had a family and didn't want to replace them?"

I inhale, then sigh the breath out. "I don't remember that I didn't remember. And if that's not fucked up, I don't know what is."

"How you getting on with Vanna? Things moving in the right direction?"

"Truth man?" He nods, so I give it to him. "We can't move past being friends. Nowhere near approaching lovers. Sometimes I wonder whether going back to her house, being forced to live together would have made a difference. We'd have to share the same bed for a start."

"Or one of you would have ended up sleeping on the couch."

Quite possibly, and knowing my luck, it would have been Vanna. She wouldn't have let me as I'm still recovering.

"She's an attractive woman, Liz. Hey." He holds up his hands as I stiffen. "Just calling it for what it is. You must have noticed."

Taking another deep breath, I wave down at my groin. "I'm not interested in her that way."

His eyes widen. "You're telling me she doesn't give you a fuckin' chubby?"

I jerk my head up and down sadly.

"You get hard when you see the club girls?"

"Fuck no," I reply aghast. Apparently I once did, but they don't get me horny now.

He prods me in the shoulder. "You're a dick, you know that?" I do, unfortunately, that's the point. "What is it about 'you've just had a brain op' that you don't understand? I know you probably think it has a mind of its own, but for your information, your dick's under control of the head on your shoulders."

I gaze at him. *Is he right? Am I not getting horny because I can't anymore?* I don't know what's more horrifying. That I can no longer get it up for my wife, or that I can't for anyone at all.

He reads my mind. "Christ, Liz. I'm not saying Viagra is in your future. I'm saying you need to give yourself time. If nothing's getting your dick to stand to attention, it's probably just your brain still sorting shit out."

I hope he's right. "Thing is Mace, there's a brick wall between me and Vanna, and I'm not talking about the one between my room and the next. We talk, politely, but as strangers. I just can't think how to start breaking that darn wall down."

"Hey," he continues, "think about this. Say if you'd parted from Vanna twelve years ago, got divorced or something. If you'd lived separate lives all that time, then met her again and wanted to get back with her, would you have invited her straight back into your bed?"

"Of course I fuckin' wouldn't. That would be awkward. We'd have to…" I pause and look at him thoughtfully. "I'd have to court her again. You're fuckin' right, Mace. I need to take her on a date."

He claps his hands as if I'd performed a trick. "Well that would be a good place to start in my humble opinion."

I decide to turn the tables. "You seem pretty friendly with the woman, Shayla."

One side of his mouth turns up. "If I'm honest, I don't know what I want, Liz. Never saw myself with an old lady, but she doesn't deserve a man who'd fuck her and run. We're friends, like you and Vanna, but the difference is, she turns me the fuck on. If I was going to settle down, it would be with a woman like Shayla. For now, I'm just going with the flow and seeing where it leads us."

"And if it leads to your bed?"

"I hope it does, Brother. Just not sure of what happens after."

I pull my crutches toward me, far more practiced now, it only takes seconds before I'm standing. "Thanks, man, for the haircut and the advice."

He waves off my gratitude. "Anytime. Now get out of here."

I grin and walk to the door. With my hand on the doorknob I half turn and say over my shoulder, "Why the fuck am I thinking of ginger?" Then, certain my brain's now playing olfactory tricks on me, I shake my head and make my exit.

Instead of descending the stairs, I go to the room where Vanna is staying. When I knock, she opens the door wearing a robe which she pulls around her tightly. A towel twisted into a turban covers her hair, and the red glow of her skin tells me she's just gotten out of the shower.

She doesn't invite me in, and I don't ask to enter, her clothing, or lack off, a step of intimacy neither of us are ready for yet. But I do lean in closer and inhale. Whatever shampoo or shower gel she's just used is enticing, melding beautifully with the perfume that's hers.

"Liz. Your hair!" Her eyes widen.

"Had to be done, Vanna."

"It's so short." One hand holds the robe together, the other reaches out and I bend so she can run it across my scalp. "Stubbly," she informs me.

"You like it?"

"I used to, but now it reminds me of when you were in the Marines."

I can tell by her face it had been a worrying time for her, her concern not unfounded considering the way my service had ended. "I'll grow it again."

"Just do what you're most comfortable with."

Should it worry me that she doesn't have an opinion? Or does she feel unable to voice it? I set that aside for now, and tell her, "Tomorrow night, you, me and Cas are going for a family meal. Away from the club. Then, on Monday, I'm taking you out."

One side of her mouth curves. "Are you telling or asking?"

I smile. "Which would work?"

"In this case, either. I think that both are a good idea."

I give her the full intense weight of my stare. "Let's just make this clear. Monday is date night. We're going to start over."

I try to read her expression but can't tell whether she thinks if that's a good or bad thing.

CHAPTER THIRTY-NINE

Mace

Shayla working at the shop is playing havoc with my libido. That I'm smoking more hasn't gone unnoticed by Pyro. Seems every time she leans over—to get to something on an engine or a spare part off the workbench, it doesn't matter the fuck what for—I get sight of her perfect ass, or the curve of her tits, and I have to take five to bring myself under control.

The club girls hold no interest for me, seems my dick has decided it only wants her.

I'm taking things slowly, making sure not to rush her, just trying to make her more comfortable around me. Ignoring the effect she has on my dick, I enjoy being around her. Since our lunch date we haven't progressed further, but I've maintained the ground I'd gained, sneaking kisses when there's no one around us, and my hand often brushes against hers when I reach for a tool, or step too close when passing her. She's good company, and we often share jokes as we work, her often mocking me I wouldn't know what to do with a real engine.

My evenings had been tied up lately. Wills had had to head out of town for a few days, which meant I'd stepped up and taken his role temporarily at the strip club. But he's on his way back now, which leaves me free to ask Shayla out again.

I take the opportunity when Pyro steps out to deliver a car, and Ink is fuck knows where. Beckoning to her, I open the door to the storeroom, checking first that none of the civilian workers are inside.

"What are you doing, Mace?" she asks, suspiciously.

"Just getting some privacy to ask you out, darlin'. This way you can turn me down without any asshole being any the wiser." I wink.

She chuckles softly. "Another date? Was lunch the first one then? Is this your way of asking if we can progress to second base?"

It might well be. I grin. "Is that where I can put my hands on your delicious backside?"

"As long as I can get mine on yours." My eyes open wide at her reply. She stuns me more when she adds, "Might have to move quickly through the bases, I don't want to be responsible for you getting cancer." She starts to laugh at the expression on my face, and my eyebrows rise higher. "You…" she starts, stops, then tries again, "All I need to do is wiggle my ass, and you're running outside."

"You do that on purpose?" I growl. I'd thought it was just something she did unconsciously. "You been fuckin' taunting me woman? Fuck. I thought I was hiding what a pervert I was, ogling your ass all the time."

"You think I don't stare at yours?"

What? I hesitate to ask but want to know the answer. "Do I, er… Do I have the same effect on you?" *Please say yes.*

"Well I may have thought of taking up smoking a few times." She winks. "But I don't have something to hide."

"True," I lean in closer, "but please tell me you have to bring spare panties to work."

She knocks against my arm. "Mace. I'm so not telling you that."

I was right not to rush things. Seems taking it slow, getting her used to me being around, has worked. "So, tomorrow. You want to come out with me?"

"Not tonight?"

I wish I could. "Church tonight, darlin'. But tomorrow I'm all yours."

When she raises her face, I know she wants me to kiss her, but she tells me first, her voice breathy, "Mace, you taunt me as much as I taunt you. But I don't know if..."

"I won't push if you're not ready. First base will do for now, Shay." I can't imagine ever saying that to another woman, but with her it's true.

"What are your waiting for?" As she speaks, she's rising on tiptoe, one of her hands going behind my neck, pulling my mouth down to meet hers.

I give her this, let her control the pace, and this time it's a groan that passes through my lips. Not of frustration, but of sheer pleasure at her taste. The only problem with kissing her in the storeroom is that I'm certain to need yet another cigarette after. But hell, it's worth it.

That's where I am now, outside, willing my cock to calm the fuck down which isn't easy as I've the tang of her on my tongue and her perfume in my nostrils. The thought of spending one-on-one time with her tomorrow night is going through my head as I take a draw of smoke down into my lungs and blow it out.

Of course, Pyro has to return at that moment. "Christ, man. Again? You bought shares in a fuckin' tobacco company?"

I ignore him and take another drag.

He raises his eyes to the sky, then looking back down, asks, "You got anything you can't leave until the morning?" When I consider my workload inside, then shake my head, he explains why he asked, "Demon called asking if I could spare you. He wants a meet with you and the other officers before church."

"Now?"

"Yeah."

"No worries, I can leave the Mustang, there's no rush on it. I'll just get my shit and go." I take a second to explain to Shayla why I'm leaving early.

It's not unusual for us to have pre-church meetings, so I don't expect anything of any importance to come up. I've been working my butt off all day, when I've not been gawking at Shayla's attributes, and am hot and sweaty, so head for the bar to grab a cold beer. Then put my head around the door of Demon's office.

"Can you give me five to take a shower?"

"Nah, we're waiting on you, Mace."

His loss not mine, I've gotten used to the odour of sweat.

"Should have given him the time," Thunder complains, pretending to hold his nose as I take the chair next to him.

"Asshole." I elbow him in the ribs, then raise the bottle to my lips and take a long swig.

Demon glares at his sergeant-at-arms. When Thunder smirks, but raises his hands, he proceeds to enlighten us as to the reason he's got us assembled. "This is gonna have to be raised in church. Wanted to give you the heads-up and get your initial thoughts on it first."

Again, this isn't unusual. If it's something the club needs to know about it, officers who know about it first can best lead discussions toward where we think they ought to be heading.

Sitting back in his seat, Demon rubs the side of his nose. "Red's found Major. Well, found out something about him."

"Took him long enough," Beef remarks.

"Yeah, well, this isn't a pimp who leaves his cards in phone booths."

"They hand out leaflets on the strip in Vegas," Thunder remarks. "No need for any fuckin' secrecy there."

"As I was saying," Thunder's once again treated to a glare, "Major is high-end, expensive and exclusive. His clients are well vetted and know what he's offering so there's no risk in any of the girls complaining they don't want to be there—in fact that's part of their attraction. What those motherfuckin' clients pay for is someone considered disposable. How they use them and how far they go is up to them. The only provision being, if they're permanently scarred or killed, there's a premium to be paid."

I just stare as my blood runs cold. *Just what did Shayla go through before she managed to get free?* To be sold for the hour, the night, or whatever, knowing the men could do anything they had a deviant desire for? Even go so far as to kill her? My fingers curl into my palms, nails digging into the skin hard enough to leave half-moon marks.

She'd told me enough for me to know she was taken unwilling, but by people like that? I don't know if I could bear to hear the half of what she might have suffered.

"Hard hearing, Brother." Beef's words get my eyes going his way.

"Tell me we're going to take him down." That's all I want.

Prez shakes his head. "Mace, I know you've got a soft spot for Shayla, and we all fuckin' hate Esme was involved, but Major's swimming in dollars. His money keeps him out of sight and can also buy him protection. His clients are tight-lipped to the extent it took Red this long to find someone who'd talk to him. That they themselves are fucked-up bastards with money to burn only goes without saying. Red only got the info after planting Twister in the right circles and got him moaning about bitches setting boundaries. Dude approached him but was wary until they'd met a few times. When he eventually let him in, it was with a promise he knew where to secure girls where nothing was off-limits. He also told Twister he'd be tracked down and killed were he to say anything."

"Rope and Cuff had heard rumours there was such a man operating in Vegas." Beef's mouth twists. "Some of the motherfuckers with those appetites tried to join the BDSM club they go to but were soon shown the door as they were too sadistic."

"So, he's got money and protection," I observe through gritted teeth. "What exactly did Red say?"

"That he's not comfortable with stirring up shit when it doesn't directly concern the club. In his view, it's not only taking Major out, it's dealing with the disappointment of his clients. The blowback would be enormous."

My mouth drops open. Shayla escaped, but what exactly had happened to her previously? We can't let this man stay breathing.

"We're not taking revenge?" Thunder questions at the same time I say, "We're not rescuing the other girls?"

Thunder glances at me then shakes his head. "They're all someone's sister or daughter, and we're leaving them to end up dead? Not happy with that, Prez."

"I want him wiped out of existence." I stare at Demon, but his face is set.

"As it stands, he's not a threat to the club either to us here or Red's crew in Vegas. Hate to say it, Mace, but he's just one player in these types of games. You reckon we should step in and deal with all the fucking traffickers and pimps?"

"Prez, I know we can't take them all on, but Major, fuckin' right I do. He fuckin' had Shayla. He marked her. Only Shayla's quick thinking saved Esme from a fate she'd probably wish to escape from by death. He marked that kid, Demon. Fuckin' marked her. I want revenge. Even a slow death is less than he deserves."

"Mace," Prez snaps. "Esme's back with her parents, and Brett Waterman has taken actions to make sure she's safe. Shayla is here under our protection. What if making a move against Major goes wrong, and all it does is bring them to his attention? Yeah, just the thought of what he fuckin' does makes me want to throw up, but I've got everyone's safety under consideration. I'm proposing we make no move unless we know Shayla or Esme are in direct danger."

For once, I hate my prez's decision. I sit shaking my head,

unable to comprehend he's even suggested it. As an outsider, I appreciate how he's thinking, that his priority is keeping everyone here safe, and that means not attracting the attention of a powerful enemy in Vegas. But he's not seeing it from where I'm standing. It's my woman who suffered at this fucker's hands. Suffered in ways I don't want to imagine. *My woman?* I realise I don't dislike the sound of it.

"Have you spoken to Esme's parents?" Thunder asks.

"Updated them, yes. They've passed an 'anonymous' tip-off onto the cops. Hopefully the heat will come down on Major from that direction, and I'm quite content under the circumstances to let the feds do their job. Had enough bother when we got involved in cop business last time." I know he's referring to Ink being arrested. A wrong time, wrong place matter, but he could have gone away for three decades, so albeit reluctantly, I understand Demon's thinking.

"Will you be keeping Shayla close, Mace? Thinking of claiming her?" Beef asks.

"Yeah to the first, nah, to the second." How can I fuckin' claim a woman who never wants to be property again? But I am starting to think I might want to keep her.

"Look, let's cut to the chase so Mace can have his shower before sitting down with the rest of the brothers." I take it that's Demon's way of letting me know I do indeed stink. "We'll update everyone but head off any suggestion of tackling Major head-on. Red's got eyes on him, Mace, so if he looks like he's heading our way, we'll revisit the subject again. Shayla's safe here, as long as she doesn't leave." He stares at me.

To me, what he's said, is unacceptable. If the club's not going to do anything, I'll go to Vegas, take out the fucker myself. Knowing they'll try to stop me, I keep my thoughts quiet.

"No going it alone, Mace." The VP glares at me. I startle, not having known mind reading was one of his skills. "Yeah, I know what you're thinking as I'd do the same in your place. I was in on the call with Red, okay? None of us like this but going head-to-head with a man like Major wouldn't work. He's so well fuckin' protected no one knows anything about him. Rope and Cuff are going to try to get on the inside, well," he grins, but it quickly fades, "while they've got peculiar tastes, they can exaggerate the lengths they will go to, and Twister's already got an in. Any retribution will have to be worked on carefully. Us rolling in hot and heavy won't help for now. The important thing is keeping your woman safe."

"We're not letting him get away with this." I glare at Demon. "Let me go to Vegas and help smoke him out."

"And leave Shayla here? Or take her with you?"

At Prez's challenge, I realise neither option is attractive. My shoulders slump as I realise, I'm defeated.

"Second thing before you go get that shower, Mace. Lizard."

"What about him, Prez?"

"He asked Thunder whether he knew if his FXDR was at the shop or here at the club."

I sit up fast. "He asked about his *bike*?"

Thunder grins. "Yup. I let it go by and just said no idea. Didn't make a big thing of it. You know the funny thing? He wouldn't have been able to afford a brand-new model Harley when it first came out if he'd been paying support for his wife and kid. Strange how things work out."

I shake my head, not certain where Thunder's going with that and getting back to the point in hand. "He's remembered more about the time when he served. He asked why I called Ink 'Leatherneck' but not him. I wasn't conscious I'd done so in his hearing, but wasn't sure, and like you, ignored it." I raise my chin at Thunder. "Didn't push as I couldn't be certain I hadn't either. And…" I break off.

"And?" prompts Beef.

"Nothing." My cheeks feel hot.

"And?" Beef's not letting up.

I sigh. "When I'd cut his hair and he left my room, he

wondered why it made him think of ginger." I glare, but it does no good.

"There's a fuckin' story there." Thunder leans back, crossing one ankle over the other and linking his fingers behind his head and chuckling loudly. "Want to share, Brother?"

"I'd bet sharing is at the root of it, isn't it, Mace?" Beef cottons on fast and laughs loudly. "Ginger root at least." He snorts. "Can I assume it was on a female victim and not Lizard himself? Scrub that. If it is, please don't tell me. I don't need that visual."

"It was Titsy and Breezy," I say fast. I don't want that picture in my head either. Much as I like my brother, I don't want to get anywhere near his ass.

"So things are starting to come back," Demon starts slowly. He seems to have a silent conversation with the VP, ending with a nod. "What we've been discussing is bringing him into church, seeing if the discussions will prompt more of his memory."

I raise my hand. "Wearing my enforcer hat, I'm worried about that."

Thunder copies my action, flashing his fingers briefly. "As sergeant-at-arms, I am too."

Raising my chin toward him, I take over, "He seems to be settling in, but hasn't mentioned staying after the month has passed. He talks about going back to Denver with Vanna if they can make it work. What if he walks away carrying our information in his head?"

"We get people to prospect so we can find out if we can trust them to bury a body and keep its location locked down. I don't know this man, Lizard now purports to be. Mace is right. It's dangerous." Thunder nods my way.

"So we keep talks of bodies and burying to a minimum." Beef looks far less worried than me.

"What's he going to hear? Our finances and how our businesses are doing? Not exactly trade secrets. Buzz does submit everything to the taxman."

"Not quite everything, Prez." Beef grins.

I sit forward, clasping my hands and lowering my head while I think. I address my next words to the floor. "If he comes to church, he has to wear his cut." I look up to see their reaction.

"Too fuckin' right," says Beef.

CHAPTER FORTY

Lizard

"Church?" I stare up at Demon. "Isn't that your secret meeting, no non-members allowed?"

He glares down at me. "You're a fuckin' member. This here is proof of it." He pushes the leather vest I'd hidden at the back of my closet at me, but the last thing I'm going to protest is how he got hold of it. I'm more concerned with why he wants me to wear it, and whether or not I do myself.

I'm surrounded daily by these men wearing their leather so can't escape the smell. But there's something about the scent of the vest now in my lap that triggers a flash of light behind my eyes. My eyes squeeze shut.

"Brother?"

I wave my hand. "It will pass in a sec." It does. I open my eyes again to see Demon looking concerned.

"Perhaps it's too soon."

Maybe I'm more like my son than I think, or probably that should be the other way around as now he's suggesting I don't go, I stubbornly want to do the opposite. I struggle to my feet, balancing on just one crutch, and realise I should have put my cut on sitting down.

Demon's huffs good-naturedly as he sees my predicament

and helps me get myself organised and my arms though the right holes. As the weight settles on my shoulders, I realise it doesn't feel alien in the slightest. It feels… right.

Hating my right arm's still wasted and weak, and my right leg isn't much help to my left, I limp behind Demon, pausing as he does in front of the prospect holding a box full of phones. Realising what's being asked of me, I take out my own and place it in with the rest. Then, I step inside the hallowed area where only members are allowed. Mace, Thunder, and Beef are already sitting down, but the other members haven't arrived as yet.

There's a tingling sensation within my skull, not pain, sort of as if ice is melting. Used to odd feelings now my brain's been fucked with, I ignore it, and walking around to the opposite side of the table, head for a seat halfway down.

I notice Mace cocking an eyebrow at Thunder, and the sergeant-at-arms answering grin. When they don't say a word, I speak.

"What? Should I sit somewhere else?" I hadn't thought to ask.

"Nope," Mace pops the 'p'. "You're fine right where you are, Brother."

The door opens to reveal Judge who comes in and sits down. Seconds later, Wills walks in. Now the door is constantly opening as one by one, everyone else arrives. Each spares me a surprised glance, then a grin or a chin lift.

"Fuckin' good to see you there, Brother." Ink sits his ass opposite me. "Been too fuckin' long."

As soon as everyone's seated, Demon kicks off by banging the gavel. "Right. How we doing, Buzz?"

I listen as Buzzard runs through the financial health of the club, talking about the strip club takings increasing on nights when guest dancers make appearances and suggesting to Sparky and Wills, they should try to get more in as they're a good draw. He comments, with a wink in my direction, that the accounts for Devil's Ink are better produced than they've ever been before. I should think they are with Vanna having put my handwritten notes on the computer now.

I touch my hand to my head as I hear a noise like the buzzing of a saw, but as no one else notices, I realise again, it's only in my head like some form of tinnitus.

The auto-shop is good—Shayla's providing much-needed assistance—and Devil's Pins is still getting sufficient customers in through the door.

Ink gives his update when asked. "Dirt's nearly finished with plumbing in the showers and heads. Drywalls are up. Just the decorating, and the purchase and installation of equipment to complete now. Then the final inspections and we're good to go."

"Give us some warning so we can get publicity done. Have you talked with Buzzard about membership fees yet?"

"Yeah." Ink nods toward the treasurer. "If we can get enough people signed up, then it should pay for itself."

"Staff?"

"Got a couple of hopefuls lined up for interviews."

"That sounds great." Demon looks impressed.

"You'll get more uptake in memberships after Christmas," Mace observes. "People will join up as part of their New Year's resolutions and then won't turn up more than a couple of times."

"But keep up with their membership just to say they've joined a gym," Judge chuckles.

"Shame Christmas is six months off," Bomber puts in.

Ink stares across at me. "Tomorrow, Brother. I want you downstairs trying that elliptical out."

I give him a nod. Not sure how much I'll be able to do, or whether I can get the thing moving at all, but if I don't try, I won't get anywhere.

"Moving on." Demon sighs, pinches the bridge of his nose for a moment, then continues onto the topic that looks like it's one he doesn't want to broach. "Red's found Major."

Major. Why does that name have significance? Something akin to an itch I can't scratch is twinging in my head, but I can't quite catch hold of it.

I content myself with doing what everyone else does and look toward the head of the table for more information.

"Prez?" Thunder starts, leaning forward so he can jerk his head in my direction, then back to Demon.

Demon stares at me for a moment, then shakes his head, leaving me to wonder what the silent conversation was about. *Something to do with me.*

Whatever it was, Demon moves on. "Major runs a tight and lucrative business. If you want a girl you can do with what you like, you go to Major. If you want to choke a girl until she expires, if you've the money, Major will supply her and deal with the remains when you've finished." There are gasps from around me as I watch the members reactions. From what I've learned about them, their expressions of disgust are what I expect and genuine. Far from my previous thoughts, Satan's Devils don't mistreat women.

"That makes me feel sick." Judge glances down the table at Mace.

"Brother…" Hellfire starts, but his voice trails off. He too is looking at the enforcer.

Mace answers as if he'd completed a question. "I don't know, Hell. She hasn't gone into any detail at all."

"How does he get his business? Man providing services like that can't advertise on the street," Sparky asks.

"People with particular appetites will know where to go to," Ink observes through gritted teeth.

"And that's how Red eventually found him," Demon confirms.

"Satan's Devils going after him? Shut that crap down?"

Beef jerks his head toward Demon and takes over answering Bomber. "Take him out, someone will step in and take his place. Where there's an appetite there will always be someone offering what people want to take. Important thing is to make sure he's not heading our, or the girls', way. Red's got people going in undercover, we'll wait to hear what they find out."

Wills' hand slams onto the table. "Not good enough. I want to deal with Major personally for what he's done and what he planned to do with that kid."

"I second that," says Bomber. "Don't want that fucker to live."

"Major's something you grind into the dirt," Rusty adds in.

"Major's a piece of shit," Hell states. "But Demon's right. He'll have money and backers behind him. The services he supplies don't come cheap. And Red's in his town. If Satan's Devils aren't in his sights, then why risk all our lives just to take one motherfucker out, when Beef's right, someone else will step up and do the same as him."

I notice they're talking openly in front of me. But I'm not uncomfortable with this conversation at all. They're not talking about killing an innocent man. I realise I'm just as bloodthirsty as them.

"Doesn't sit right with me, either," observes Cad, but in a more measured tone. "But Red's got boots on the ground. I'd like to know what info he has. If it's okay with you, Prez, I'll talk to Keys. Might be more that he can give me about Major to explain the stand Red's taking."

"I agree," Demon responds to the too-pale man. "Presumably a lot of his business is run on the dark web. See what you can dig up. The situation doesn't sit easy with Red either, but we're not dealing with a two-bit pimp. Major's a powerful man."

Major. Major. Major. Major.

"Vi get Shayla's fuckin' property tat sorted?" I ask, when at last I remember the words which are worse now I know the implication. *Property of Major.* Not a patch inked by a loving man, but the worst kind of ownership, signifying he can do anything he likes.

The table falls completely silent.

"Liz?" Mace starts, speaking slowly as though to a child. "What the fuck did you just say?"

My brow creases, and I run back over my words. Can't see anything wrong with them, I just asked a simple question. "Has Shayla gotten her tat covered?" I realise I should check in at the shop. I might not be able to use my hand to lay down ink, but I can check whether shit's running okay.

"What do you remember, Lizard?" Demon signals for silence from everyone else.

My eyes widen as an explosion ignites in my head, every bit as powerful as the one I can't remember but fucked up my brain at the start. I stand, stagger as my right leg crumbles, and crash to the ground, cradling my hands around my skull which feels simultaneously like ice water flooding it, followed by red hot lava.

"Liz? Liz?"

"Rusty, help him!"

"Call a fuckin' ambulance. We need medics here."

"Christ, this was too much for him, too soon. Shouldn't have invited him in."

Synapses are firing, neurotransmitters going wild. *I'm Lizard, otherwise known as Norton James. I ride with the Satan's Devils MC and have done for the past ten years. I'm thirty-eight years old, and my birthday is the tenth of January. I'm a tattoo artist and I run Devil's Ink on behalf of my brothers. I've got a wife and child.*

I flail my hands, blindly seeking contact with someone, anyone, grabbing hold when I feel someone's hand. "No doc, no medic." I gasp as though I've run a marathon. "I'm okay. I'm okay," I repeat it again. "I'm *okay.*"

"Liz." It's Mace's voice dripping concern. "Liz, Brother. You need to get checked out."

"No," I say, this time more firmly. Bracing my left arm beneath me, I push up into a sitting position. My right arm and leg have needles and pins, a pricking sensation like blood returning to dead limbs.

"Yes," Demon says in a voice that brooks no argument. "You're going to the hospital."

I look up into the eyes of my president. "I can remember. Everything." The pressure in my skull is receding, leaving behind a new clarity of mind, and bringing with it a whole new level of pain. "Tell me. Someone please tell me, I did not forget my wife and kid for twelve fuckin' years." Of course that's what everyone has been telling me. But remembering the dick I've been in the intervening time makes me want to believe that's a figment of my imagination.

But the silence tells me I'm not hallucinating, and that perhaps for the first time since I returned from that final tour, I remember everything.

I wish I could forget all over again.

Is remembering just temporary? What if my brain implodes and I lose it all? What if this is a final reprieve before a massive brain bleed or stroke takes me out? Maybe they're right, and I should see a doctor.

"I'll go to the hospital," I tell them. "But please, don't tell Vanna. Not until I know what the fuck's going on." How can I face her, knowing what I do now? Being told you left your wife and kid and were happy living a new life while they were struggling is one thing, remembering it, totally different. Accepting that albeit unknowingly, I was an asshole for ten years. Remembering Hatch dying, being there when he did, seeing that truck take him out far worse than just hearing that he was gone. Seeing everything in full technicolour. And, oh shit, fucking the whores… with Mace of all people. Being unfaithful to my wife. Right now I wish blackness would flood over me again. Coming to terms with who I really am and living with what I did, well, that seems like too high a mountain to climb.

"Judge," Demon instructs, "go into the clubroom. If Vanna's there, distract her. Mace can take Liz out the back way through the kitchen and get him to the emergency room. Let's see what he's dealing with before worrying her."

CHAPTER FORTY-ONE

Mace

Once again I'm at the hospital, and once again I'm with my brother. I don't know what to think. Liz getting his memory back should be a cause for celebration, but he'd collapsed the first time right outside my door, and nearly fuckin' died. To see him fall yet again in church, well, the worst of thoughts had gone through my mind.

The emergency room obviously takes a man with a possible brain bleed seriously, and he was immediately taken out back.

"Mr Grey? Fox Grey?"

"Yeah?" I stand, putting the magazine I'd been mindlessly perusing on the seat I'm vacating. "That's me."

"Mr James would like you to come through if you will?"

I'm taken through the maze of corridors until I get to the neurology wing and find Liz sitting on a bed in a room.

"How are you, Liz? Are they going to admit you?"

"No," he puts his hand to his head, "I don't think so. I'm waiting on the doctor coming to explain the results of the scan to me. I just wanted someone here, you know?"

"In case it's bad news?"

His tired eyes meet mine. "In case I forget what he says."

Christ, it must be awful not to trust your brain anymore. I

watch him, he's now focused on his hand which he's opening and shutting. Making a proper fist for the first time in weeks. A physical as well as mental improvement? Surely that's a good sign.

We're not waiting too long until the door opens, and a man in a white coat comes in. He nods at me, but then his eyes land on Lizard.

"Mr James." The way he announces his name gives nothing away. I notice after viewing Liz, he turns his attention to the tablet in his hands. "I've got the results of your scan here, and everything looks good to me. The swelling has gone down considerably."

"I can remember, Doc. *Everything*."

"That's good. Retrograde amnesia is often temporary caused by the swelling after the operation."

"Doc," Liz repeats. "I can remember *everything*. My memory of my final tours—not how I got the initial injury or the recovery period after, but I do know that I was married and had a wife and son." He purses his lips and scrunches up his brow. "I can remember coming to Pueblo and joining the MC."

"You had a tumour, Mr James, which we removed. Look, I know we like to think of ourselves as experts, and science is advancing every day, but we still don't emphatically know how memories are laid down in the brain, or where they are stored. Every injury we treat, every patient's recovery, helps build a picture. But just when we're certain we can point to something and say, ah, that's it, something else contradicts it. I couldn't have predicted your memory would have been restored as it has, but I couldn't have said it wouldn't either."

"Is it going to last, Doc? Will I forget again?"

He taps at the screen. "There's no reason to believe so. You're recovering physically as well as can be hoped. There's no reason to believe you won't continue to improve. You may still have residual weakness in your right side, or you could get back to near or complete normal. Of course, no one can rule out a stroke in the future, but while the chances of that might be slightly increased in your case, you shouldn't worry unnecessarily."

Well, that sounds like good news to me. Something can come up and blindside any of us at any time, looks like Lizard has no greater reason to be concerned than any of us. No point ruining your life wondering if the next time you ride, you'll end dirty side up. There are so many unknowns like cancer or heart attacks. All of us want to live our full allotted years, but many won't make it that far. Appears Lizard's got as much chance as anyone else.

"We'll keep up with your check-ups, and please continue to see your psychotherapist, but apart from that, enjoy your life, Mr James."

With a final nod in my direction, he leaves.

Back in the truck, Lizard is silent.

"You ready to speak to Vanna?"

He huffs a mirthless laugh. "Not sure I'll ever be ready for that."

"Liz, she knows everything." I can't understand.

"But now I know as well," he tries to explain. "I went with whores, Mace. I was unfaithful to my wife. How the fuck could I do that?"

"You love her?"

The answer comes fast. "Always have. Always will."

"You want a wife and kid?"

"With everything that I am."

I try to explain what I think. "The Lizard I knew never did. For ten years, Liz, you've only wanted to be a single man. I'm convinced you knew you were already taken."

"But I went with whores," he repeats, torturing himself.

"And Vanna used her vibrator. I sort of told her that's all they meant to you."

His head turns sharply toward me. "Should I be worried you discussed my wife's use of a sex toy with her?"

I chuckle, quickly raising both hands off the steering wheel before putting them back. "I've seen you're able to form a fist now, Brother. So no, I assure you, you do not need to worry about that."

"I do need to speak to Vanna, but I'm not looking forward to the conversation ahead."

We arrive at the compound and Karl slides open the gate.

After I park, I pass Liz's one crutch to him, it was the only one we brought, and notice he's putting more weight on his right leg now. As I walk behind, watching him carefully, ready to help if he becomes unsteady, I wonder how that talk with Vanna will go, mentally agreeing it won't be an easy one. What does Lizard want to do now he knows he's a true Satan's Devil? Will he stay with us? Or continue with his plan to go live with his family in Denver?

Inside, I leave him to go find his wife.

It doesn't surprise me that Prez is impatiently striding toward me. "Liz okay?"

I update him, then several of my brothers, agreeing, yes, this is great news, then finally am free to take myself up to my room, wondering how Vanna is taking Liz's revelation.

What must it be like to have someone who's cared enough to remain faithful to you for twelve years? I suspect it might have been different if she hadn't had a son to raise which had occupied her time, but still, she cared for Lizard and wore his ring. She still cares. I'm certain she'll forgive him for things he'd done when he'd literally lost his mind. A love like that, so strong and enduring, won't splinter now.

I fuck the club girls, but don't talk to them. On the plus side, I never have to explain myself or come up with justifications for my actions. The other side of the coin is that I've no one to care, no one to share my triumphs or problems with. I've got brothers, of course, but it's not like having a woman's point of view that can be so different to a man's, or someone to lean on, or to lean on you. Men tend to suck things up, women see through our bullshit.

Sure, Liz will have a long journey ahead to get to the relationship that he wants with his wife, but I've no doubt they'll make it. Even though it will be a rocky road at times, I find myself envying him. Vanna will make a great old lady, anyone can see that.

Is that what I'm missing even though I don't' know it? I've told my brothers Shayla is going to be mine. So why am I waiting?

Exiting my room, I go to hers, knocking softly in case she's already sleeping.

"Who is it?"

"Mace."

I hear the key turning in the lock and the door opens. She finds me leaning against the doorframe, a hand stifling a yawn coming from my mouth.

"You look done in," she tells me, her brow creasing. "Has anything happened?"

"It's been a fucker of a day," I tell her, placing my arm on the top of the frame and resting my cheek against it.

"Want to talk about it?" I do. That's why I came.

When I nod, she steps aside and I walk in, going across to the chair and sitting there, resisting taking the liberty of sitting beside her on the bed.

She curls her legs under her as she perches on the mattress. "What's happened?"

"Lizard's got his memory back. I've just been at the hospital with him. Seems the swelling has really started to go down. He's got more movement too."

Clapping her hands together once, she looks delighted. "That sounds like a massive step forward."

I lean forward, clasping my hands. "It is." The smile slides from my face. "I learned something else today." My lips press together and I look down, before looking up. "We know who Major is, and just what kind of services he was supplying, which means the kind of things you had to do. Fuck, Shayla," I snarl, again bowing my head.

I hear a strangled sound and glance up to see her with her hand covering her mouth. Then, twin spots of red come to her cheeks. I don't know what I expected her reaction to be, but when she smartly crosses the room, comes to a halt in front of me, I can see her body trembling, but it's not with fear. It's with rage.

"So it was alright when you thought men were just fucking me? You can cope with knowing I'm a whore who warms a stranger's bed, but you don't like the thought of me being strangled until I gasp for any air that I can take into my lungs. You don't want to think of me being chained, beaten, tortured… urinated on. That I feared for my life every time I was sent out to perform. That each time I knew it could be my last. That's not alright? *That* disgusts you?"

"Fuck, Shayla." I stand fast, my fingers curling around her arms, biting into them making sure she can't pull away. "Fuck, if you think that, you don't know the type of man I am. What disgusts me is the thought of you being that scared, that hurt, that alone. I can't bear the thought of the abuse you went through. I hate that any man took you without consent, that they were able to act out their depravities on you. That, I fucking hate. I hate that as much as I fuckin' love you."

The final words hang in the air. They've shocked me as much as they shock her.

I knew I wanted her, knew she was going to be in my bed. But love? It's not a word I thought would ever come from my lips but as soon as I said it, I knew it was true.

Her eyes turn up to mine. "Take it back, Mace."

"No."

"You can't love me. Not now you know how damaged I am," she cries.

"Do you think I fuckin' care? It's you I want, Shayla. What

you've been through is so horrific, it makes me sick to my stomach. I hate that it's left its mark on you. But it's this you I love. The girl who's come through and emerged the other side like a butterfly from a cocoon. A girl who's brave, resourceful, and so fuckin' strong. Can't think of another woman I want by my side."

"I told you I wanted you. You don't have to…"

"I can fuck any number of girls, Shay. It wouldn't just be fuckin' with you." Releasing my grip, I take one of her hands, placing it over my heart. "You've wormed your way inside here, without me noticing what you were doing. So, yeah, I love you." I capture her gaze with my own, staring so intently as I will her to believe me.

She breaks the lock I have on her eyes as she turns her face away. "I'm not strong, I'm weak. He's still out there, Mace. All I've been is scared of him coming after me, I haven't given a thought to the women who are still there. Who are still being pimped out, who may be sold and never return. Should I have gone to the cops?"

"Babe, you were trying to stay out of his hands. You did right. Major runs an expensive service, his clients have money. Fuck knows what his reach is. You were literally running for your life and Esme's. I don't see you could have done anything else. You go to the cops? They may not even give a shit about it. You only had a name, no address, and I doubt you knew who his clients were."

"I should have done, should *do* more."

"Shayla." I'm right in her face, and again my hands grip her arms. "Esme's parents have reported him. She's a sweet kid, they're a respectable family. They'll have the cops onside and looking into him. The cops know about Major, you can't add anything else. The only thing you'd do by reporting him too is risk putting yourself on his radar."

"It could have been me, Mace. Me, dead, all because of the whims of some sick man."

Thank fuck it wasn't. Now I wish I hadn't told her. My hands are still on her biceps, and I notice while her anger has dissipated, she's still shaking.

"You're safe," I tell her. "I'm not going to let anything happen to you, okay? No one can get onto the compound, not even Major. At the shop you've got me, Ink and Pyro there as well. He won't get to you."

Her lip is trembling, and her eyes are wild and scared. I can't help myself, I pull her into my arms, and she melts into me. "Shayla, darlin', I promise I won't let anything ever hurt you again. It's just, having heard who Major is, I can't bear to think of what you went through."

"You don't want to know."

"I probably don't, and you don't have to tell me, but I'm here if you ever want to talk. I'm not going anywhere, sweetheart. If you need to tell me for you, then do. None of the details will affect how I feel about you."

"I don't believe you love me. I can't."

She's been let down before, by a man who she should have been able to rely on, who didn't even send her a few dollars to get her back on her feet. She's seen the very worst from men. I can see how she'd have a hard job believing me. Fuck, it's hard to get my own head around the fact that I actually feel this depth of emotion for her.

I sit on the bed and pull her down beside me. "Before I met you, I went with the club girls. Mutual fun, darlin', I'd never leave a girl wanting. Since I met you, babe, I haven't been able to think about them, nothing about them appeals to me. Casual sex isn't something I want anymore. I used to laugh at my brothers when they settled down, I couldn't see myself as a one-woman man, until I met you."

"I don't understand."

I huff a laugh. "I'm not explaining it well as I can't comprehend it myself. But that first kiss we shared? More satisfying than a whole night of sex with one of the club girls."

Her eyes are wide as she turns them on me. "I know you

want sex with me, Mace. You know I know that. Think we made that pretty clear yesterday. You don't need to dress it up as something it's not."

"I'm not," I promise her. "I'm sure I can oblige if it's only my body you want, but I want so much more with you."

"This doesn't sound like something you'd say, Mace."

I chuckle. "It's not. All new to me, babe."

Her hand gently strokes down my face as she stares at me intently. Then she whispers reverently, "You're serious, aren't you?" When I raise and dip my chin, she surprises the hell out of me when she says, "Stay with me, Mace. Stay tonight."

I've got a strong will, but with her? "Babe, if I stay the night, if I sleep in your bed, I'm not going to be able to keep my hands to myself."

"Then, don't." Her words look like they surprise her.

I brush my fingers through her hair, brushing it back from her face. "I worry I'll trigger you. Now I understand what those assholes did…"

"They did nothing I wanted them too." She looks down to my groin. I'd been trying to ignore it, but the fucker's rising with just the invitation she's offered. Her eyes widen, but with interest and not fear. Then she looks back and meets my eyes. "A few weeks ago, I'd have run from the hills at the thought of ever being close to any man again. But slowly I've learned, you're a man of your word. I know, here." She places her hand over my heart. "I know you respect me, respect my feelings, and I know I can trust you. Please, Mace. I want to try."

I cradle my hands either side of her face and lower my lips, but before I let them meet hers, I have to elicit a promise. "Anything, Shay, any-fuckin'-thing I do you don't like, you tell me. Okay?"

Her head dips up and down once. It's enough. I lower my lips and lose myself in her taste. Our mouths meet, meld, tongues chase tongues, moans escape and hands clutch. I know we're wearing too many clothes. I want nothing more than to have my skin against hers.

Knowing I'm the first man she's allowed into her bed since she was snatched off the street and forced into sex work is a heavy responsibility. I'm determined to make this special for her, to take every memory of each touch taken without permission away. To sear myself on her body and brain so there's no room for her to think of anything else.

I reach for her t-shirt, she holds up her arms as if I've done this all my life and allows me to slide it over her head, our lips parting only as long as it's necessary to do so. Then she's tugging at mine. I grab the back of the neck and help her take it off, again, our kiss only pausing momentarily. I crush her body against mine, not even perving at her bra covered tits, too eager to feel the warmth of her skin against my chest.

As I slide my hands up and down her back, I encounter a dressing toward the base of her spine. "Sore?" I'm instantly thinking of positions where it won't rub.

"No," she replies. "The dressing can come off now, but I'm too nervous to look. Vi tried to show me in the mirror, but I looked away. I'm such a coward."

I instantly know she means she thinks his name will still show. It might, I know she'll need more sessions to complete the work, but in the end, it will be as if it was never there at all. I've seen and been a recipient of some of Vi's handiwork. Not a coverup, but she did amazingly well when she gave me a new piece.

My hands move up, pausing at the clasp on her bra. "Tell me yes," I all but beg, my words vibrating against her cheek.

"Yes," she replies huskily.

I don't hesitate, with a practiced move I push inwards so the hooks come free of the eyes, then let the bra fall open and push the straps down her arms.

"Let me see you," I plead.

With a final peck to my lips, she pulls away and sits back. Her arms, still tangled in the bra, remain at her sides.

"Fuckin' perfect," I tell her, not lying at all. If I could have summoned up the ultimate pair of breasts in my mind, they'd have been topped by hers.

I can't wait to sample them. Lowering my head, I suck a nipple into my mouth, sucking on it gently, and registering her sharp intake of breath. Then I apply the same treatment to the other.

"Lie down," I instruct. "I want to see all of you now."

With no hesitation at all, she shrugs free of her bra and discarding it by the side of the bed, she lets me ease her back until her head is on the pillow.

I don't waste time. With my eyes on her face, checking she's right here with me, I ease my thumbs into the elastic of her pyjama bottoms she'd obviously worn ready for bed, and take her panties down with it.

She's bare, just how I like my women. I tell her so.

"I hate it." She stuffs her hand against her mouth. "I had no choice, it was lasered."

"Fuck." There's nothing else to be said. I try to make her see the bright side. "But it does mean you can feel my beard." It's not much more than stubble, but she hisses slightly as I rub her, giving her sensations I'm sure she'll enjoy.

"Maccceeee." She draws out my name. Then tries it again, "Mace."

"What do you want, darlin'?" From the way her legs are rubbing together, it doesn't take much for me to hazard a guess. "Want me to eat you out?"

"Oh, God, yes."

I chuckle, making sure she can feel the vibration. "Not God, but a devil instead."

I part her legs gently and settle between them. It doesn't take much to encourage her clit out of its protective hood, and I alternate between licking her clit and sucking and tonguing that bundle of nerves, my hand and fingers making up for where my tongue is not.

She's writhing, as I wanted, thinking about nothing but how good I'm making her feel.

Under my free hand I can feel ripples of her stomach muscles, then she goes taut and screams. I become gentler with my administrations as I bring her back down. It's been a long time since a man has made sex about her.

"Fuck, Mace. That was good."

"Good? Feel like I'm damned with faint praise, sweetheart. Seems I'm going to have to up my game."

She notices the grin on my face. "Very good?" she offers as a substitute.

"Better." Growing serious I study her carefully. "Ready for more?"

"God, yes."

I laugh again. Okay, so I don't mind being a god with her. I turn so I can sit on the bed and get my boots off my feet, then stand so I can take off my jeans and underwear. Turning toward her, I see her eyes fixed to my cock. I taunt her by tugging on it.

"Mace, I want that."

I grin. "I kind of hoped you would."

"I like your tats."

"I'll let you study them later, but first things first, babe." My cock is throbbing almost painfully in anticipation of the event ahead. I slide on the condom I'd extracted from my back pocket before the jeans fell to the ground.

Her eyes have dilated, and she can't take her eyes off my dick. "You ready for me, darlin'?"

"So ready," she breathes.

I have never felt like this in my life before. Never expected to, never dreamed I'd find a woman I wanted to keep in my life. I fuck and don't give a damn about it, it's just another part of being alive, as insignificant as riding my bike, enjoyable yes, but not momentous. At this moment, the thought of making love—not fucking, this won't be that—for the first time to Shayla has made me nervous. I don't want to fuck it up. I already know I want to claim her, though I won't name it that. What if we don't fit? If she doesn't like it? If I'm mediocre at best?

Fuck. I've never questioned my performance, but it's never been as important as this.

"Mace? What's wrong?"

Christ, I'm taking too long, staring like a lunatic at her perfect cunt. I decide to go for honesty.

"I don't want to fuck this up. I want this to be perfect."

"It's you, Mace. It will be."

Her reassurance is all I need. I move onto the bed and leaning my body over hers, take her lips in another of our earth-scorching kisses. Then I pull back to watch her face as I start to push my cock into her. She's wet, but tight and it's a fight to get inside.

She's lying passive beneath me. *Passive.*

A light bulb suddenly goes off in my head. *I'm an asshole.* She's been used, abused for months. Holding the condom, I pull out and throw myself on my back.

"Mace?" she asks, tentatively. Beside me I feel her body stiffen.

"You drive." I turn my head to the side, grinning into her face. "Use me, babe. Take what you need. You don't want this? You just say the word."

"I want this," she wails. "Mace, don't you want me?"

"Take me." My cock's throbbing, at full mast, bobbing as blood pulses through the veins. "Ride me, baby. You're in charge."

Not always, that man isn't me. But right now, something tells me this is what she needs. Those assholes took and didn't give, now it's time for her to chase her own pleasure and use me.

Pulling herself to her knees, carefully she straddles my thighs. Her eyes lock with mine as she rises. When her hands touch my cock, I hiss. Just the feeling of her fingers on that so-ready-for-her part of me is driving me crazy.

"Don't mind your hands on me, babe, but keep that up and I won't last long." I open eyes which have fallen shut by themselves, and I wink. "I don't care, I'll come either way. But if you want me—"

"I should move this along?" As she completes my sentence, I notice the stress lines which had appeared on her forehead have smoothed out again.

Now she positions my cock at her entrance, and deliberately, tortuously slow, lowers herself onto my dick. She rises and falls, her teeth biting her lips as air whistles out through my teeth. When she's finally worked me fully inside, her hands land on my chest. Using my body to brace against, she begins to fuck me.

I let my hands gently rest on her hips, not trapping, just for support. I get to watch her head thrown back, as she uses my body to bring herself close.

My cock thickens, my spine tingles, but still I hold myself back.

"Mace," she cries out, her brow drawn down.

"What do you need? Need me to work that pretty clit, babe?"

"Mace. Please."

I do, rubbing as best I can, and at last I feel her muscles clamping down on me.

"Mace I'm gonna..."

"Me too..." I shout.

We come together. Two sweaty bodies pulsating in time, two foreheads meeting as she brings her head down.

After our breathing has slowed, she lifts up, and I hold that condom steady, then curl my abs to sit up. "Gotta..."

"Yeah, go get rid of the evidence." She grins.

I do. When I return from the bathroom, I pause a moment, my eyes feasting on the sight of this woman in the bed. The only thing wrong is that it's hers and not mine. Half closing my eyes, I imagine her in my room.

"Come," I say fast. When her head tilts, I tell her again, "Come to my bed. Cause that's where I want you sleeping from now on."

"That sounds permanent."

"It's what I want." I know as I utter them, truer words I've never said.

She's quiet for a moment. Then she stands, wrapping the sheet around her. When she bends to pick up her clothes, I reach out my hand to stop her. "I'll come back for your shit, later."

One hand holds the covering to her, the other reaches for mine. It takes less than a minute to change rooms, and less again before it's my bed she's lying on, my comforter under her perfect ass.

I catch my breath. She looks right, as if it's her place, an adornment to my room I hadn't realised I was missing.

Crossing the room to her, I slide behind her, pulling her back to my front. Out of my mouth come words I never expected to say in my life. "Stay with me, Shayla. Stay. Here in my bed, here at the compound, or a new home we'll get together instead. Stay, Shayla. Stay with me."

She's quiet for a moment, then says, "If I stay, I may never leave."

"Didn't say anything about you leaving, babe."

I swallow back the words I'd love to say. I don't tell her she's mine, I don't tell her I'd like it to be my property patch on her back.

She'll be my ol' lady. But some of the meaning we put to that will probably never be spoken between us.

Her breathing starts to even out, and I think she's dropped off to sleep, but then she murmurs, "Rodger told me he loved me, Mace. But he lied. He wanted someone to keep house, and I was convenient. Look how easily he replaced me, while Vanna waited for Lizard more than a decade."

Rodger. Hell, there are probably hundreds of men with that name in Vegas, but maybe if I'm sneaky I can get a last name someday. Then I'll go pay him a visit.

"If you disappeared, Shay, I'd move heaven and earth to find you. I might not have expected to feel this way, but I do love you. I've never said that to a woman before."

"I can't say it back," she tells me, honestly. "Not yet. Loving a man gives them power over me."

I'm going to show her although she may have said the words to someone else, she's never truly been in love before. Somehow, one day, I'm going to hear her say she loves me.

How can I be so confident? Because I'm going to do everything to be the man she can give her heart to, knowing it will never be broken again.

CHAPTER FORTY-TWO

Vanna

The *rap-rap* wakes me. It's dark outside. A hollow feeling settles inside me as I reach for my phone. It's four-thirty a.m. Being woken at this hour means only one thing. *Trouble.* It's almost exactly the same time as I was woken with the call telling me Lizard had been injured and was going to be medevac'd out and flown home. The time indelibly written on my brain. *That* had been a Thursday too.

Does history repeat itself?

Only one way to find out. I jerk up and out of bed, slipping into my robe and go to the door.

"What's happened?" I ask Lizard fast when I open it. If he's okay, it must be my other male I worry about. "Is it Cas?"

"Nah, Castiel's fine, babe. I needed to talk to you."

"It's barely dawn," I observe, my worry not dissipating at all. "What's so important it couldn't wait?"

There's a difference about him, a confidence that's been missing since I found him again, or at least, since he'd been able to recognise me. He raises his hand, lays it flat against my robe covered chest and pushes me into the room, steps inside, and closes the door behind him.

"I grabbed a couple hours of downtime after I came back

from the emergency room, but I could wait no longer, Vanna. I need to talk to you."

He's been to the hospital? "What is it, Liz? Oh God, what happened to you? Are you worse?"

But I notice he's only using one crutch, and while he's still using it to help, he's putting even more weight on the leg that hadn't been much use to him before.

"What's happened?" I repeat. My life's been blow after blow, I'm conditioned to expect the worse now.

"Let's sit and talk."

Again he pushes until the backs of my knees hit the bed, then with a hand on my shoulder he encourages me down, and sits beside me.

"Vanna, don't worry. It's good, not bad." He rubs at his head. "Things came back so fast they blindsided me. Pain, flashes." He chuckles softly. "Literally my life flashing before my eyes. Brothers were worried and got me checked out. Swelling's gone down, babe. Things have shifted in my head. My memory is back. Almost *all* my memory."

"You still remember me?" I ask, fast. My breath stalling as fear rushes through me.

"Fuck, yes." His eyes are full of concern as they turn toward me. "I remember everything about you, babe. Only things missing are how I got home from that tour and the aftermath, and exactly what happened before I left."

I turn, my hand fluttering in the air before resting on his cheek. Pulling it away, he brings it to his mouth and places a tender kiss to my palm. "I remember you. Remember getting the call telling me Cas had been born. Remember coming home on leave to see him, my gorgeous baby boy. Don't remember much about me being an ass, or how we split up. But I do remember coming to Colorado."

"Which means, you remember the club?"

A faint rise and dip of his head. "Yeah. I remember Hatch, remember visiting him in Denver." Now there's a flicker of pain.

"Remember how the club offered me a home, a place to belong. I remember the last ten years. As I said, not much about the two before that. Can't remember being at home. Remember I left but know fuck all why."

"You were badly banged up, Lizard." It makes sense to me. "You couldn't remember who you were one moment to the next. Your short-term memory gradually resolved itself, but it was hard." My eyes glaze as I think back. "Every day you had to relearn who Cas and I were, and the next you'd forget all over again. When you did remember, you thought our marriage was a lie, and that Cas was fathered by someone else."

"I was fucked up," he agrees, shaking his head. "I can't see how you can ever forgive me, Van."

"It wasn't you, Lizard."

He takes a breath and tells me what's on his mind. "I need to know why you're here. I need to know whether you're here out of duty as you still wear my ring on your finger, or whether you want to try again as man and wife." I open my mouth, he gives another little shake of his head. "I fucked whores, Vanna. Let's get that out in the open now. I didn't know I was taken. You might have worn yours, but I had no ring on my finger. Nothing to tell me I wasn't a free man."

"They had to cut it off," I remind him. "Seemed insignificant compared with keeping you alive." Such a small thing, but would that token have helped him remember? I never thought about it at the time.

He's thoughtful for a moment. "There's nothing I want more than to win you back. But I want to get shit straight right now. No point either of us hoping for things which aren't going to happen. I know you wanted me to have a hand in bringing up Cas, and whatever happens between us, I'll be there as his father. But you and me? Got to lay it on the line here, I want everything. I want a wife by my side *and* in my bed at night. Can you put the past behind you and come back to me, Vanna? As a true partner?"

"I'm older, Liz."

"So am I." He wipes his hand over his hair now shorn short. "I might have been imagining myself twelve years younger, but I'm not. I'm older, more wrinkled, and greyer. I've got miles under my belt too, darlin'."

He's not grey on his head. Oh, but… I force myself not to consider his groin area.

"The girls," I start. "They're all young and pretty."

"Fuck, woman. Don't compare yourself to them." There's now heat in the eyes he turns on me. "This feel like I don't want you?" I might have avoided looking at it, but when he places my hand over his thickened cock, I can't avoid feeling it. "This is for you, Vanna. Seems something else now works. Doesn't even twitch when I think of the girls, but it's hard as steel for you."

He smiles at me, that megawatt panty-dropping grin that I remember as he repeats, "I want you. Question is, do you want your husband?"

I raise my hand away, too tempted to explore and see if it's the same as I remember. It would be easy to say yes. Simple to accept the fairy tale he's offering, my prince re-awoken. Turn back the clock, or wind it on to where it should have been all the time.

"Liz, there's never been another man for me." It's my turn to stop him. "But for twelve years it's been me who's had to be the provider, the decision maker. I'm not the empty-headed girl you left."

"Appreciate that, Vanna. I've watched you these past few weeks, remember?" He chuckles. "Know what you mean now about sorting out the mess I left. I'm not much of a manager."

"You are," I disagree, bumping his shoulder with mine. "I just needed to sort out those handwritten notes you left all over the place." Then I reiterate again, "You left a homemaker, a housewife. I'm not able to pick up where we left it before."

"You'd have grown into yourself, whether I was there or not. Maybe not quite as you are now, but you'd have changed. Fuck,

I was away more than half the time as it was, that streak of independence would have developed anyway. I'd have matured along with it. The fact that you go head-to-head with me now? I fuckin' love it. I want a partner, not a meek woman who looks to me to make every decision." He looks away from me, growing serious. "I just hope I can become your equal."

"You will, Liz, I'm sure of that. The progress you've already made shows that."

Sincerity drips from his voice. "Since I came back from the hospital last night, I've been trying to think, trying to sort everything out in my head. I know what I want first up, I want you and Cas, babe." I go to speak, but he stops me with a little shake of his head. "I was beginning to like the men in this club, even before I regained my memory. In my perfect world, I'd have brothers at my back. If that's what you want too, it would mean you moving your life here from Denver. I don't mean live at the club, we'll find a house together. But if that doesn't appeal to you, we'll make life work, however you want to live it."

I remember what Demon had said about Lizard needing the club and know I couldn't take him away from it. Honestly, I'd miss everything about it as well. The support and company of Vi, Jayden, Steph, Mel and Beth, the older women too while I figured out what I was dealing with had been invaluable. The loss of their friendship would cause a hole in my life if we tried to start over in Denver. What have I there to keep me? Just one good friend who I can visit or who could come here. I've no job to return to. A fresh start could help Cas straighten himself out, and Lizard's inevitable parenting mistakes—mine too—could be tempered by my son's new uncles.

He's rubbing at his right wrist with his left hand, then flexing fingers which seem to have more movement than before. I know him too well, he's agitated, impatiently waiting for me to respond, but giving me space for my thoughts. I put him out of his misery.

"Cas could do moving away," I begin, my tone as serious as

his, showing my words have been thought through. "Lindy's said he's doing everything she's asked, but that his old crowd is trying to pull him back into their circle. Transferring here, making new friends, might be the best for him."

"He's a good kid. I need to step carefully with him though. Now," he taps his skull, "things are straighter in here, I can think of him as a teenager and not as a toddler. It's been hard when my brain couldn't accept time had moved on. With the void in my head, I could be told, but I couldn't understand."

"Boys his age are tough to handle, Liz. They want to push at boundaries and think they know more than they do." Resting my fingers on his thigh, I squeeze it. "It would be good to have someone to share the burden with me. If only to listen to my complaints."

"All I know about being a teenager was that I was one once. But hell, Vanna, I want Cas to have a better life than the one I had."

I think it's that that makes me realise he'd been thinking with a brain of a man aged twenty-six. Now those extra twelve years' experience are bringing more to his table. A patience and understanding which had been absent before.

He purses his lips. "You're saying you'll move here and let me be a father to our son. But what about as a husband?" He's picked up on what I haven't said. "Vanna, if you can't tell me now, just understand there's nothing more I want than to be by your side, to be a husband for you." His hand rises to my chin, and he turns me so I'm looking him in the eye. "I want you, Vanna. Or at least, I want us to give it a fuckin' good try."

"What would you do?" I ask out of interest. "If you met me on the street as I am now? Would you give me a second look, or would you walk on by?"

"A second look? You were a stunner, babe, and still are. I'd give you a third and fourth look, but no more. 'Cause by then, I'd have marched you back to my cave." He allows me a moment to snort, then asks, "Same question back at ya?"

"You? Hot as you are on that bike of yours?" I pretend to fan myself.

His turn to nudge me. "You think I'm hot?" He waggles his eyebrows.

"Hell yeah," I admit. "When you're not waking me at god-awful hours."

He has the grace to look sheepish. "Sorry about that. You were the first one I wanted to talk to about the memory I've gotten back. I just needed to have some time to come to terms with it myself, then it was you I came to."

"Should have told me, Liz. I would have gone to the hospital with you."

"I know. But Van, I didn't know what was going on. I didn't want to worry you." A muscle ticks in his cheek. "I was, *am*, scared. My memory went, my memory came back. I feel like a walking time bomb, you know? I'm almost frightened to go to sleep in case I don't remember shit when I wake up. I always knew there was something wrong. Every fuckin' day I'd wake up testing my memory out, not even thinking that wasn't what normal people did. I'm terrified I won't have long with you, I want to make the most of it."

Is this him voicing his fears, or a real risk? "What did the doctor say?"

He shrugs. "Doctors seem to think I'll be okay. But I know what tricks the brain can play."

I'd come to Pueblo and met Lizard when he was a member of the club but hadn't known who I was. I'd been with him when he'd gotten his old memories back and remembered me as his wife of twelve years ago. Neither man had been the Lizard I'd known, neither man had been one I was comfortable with. This man though… There are traces there of who he was before, but also a maturity gained over the years. This is the man I could see as the man by my side, and a dad to our boy.

"We'll cope, Lizard. Whatever happens. I've been waiting for you for twelve years, and I'm not going to run away now. We're a team. We always have been, even during those times you never consciously knew."

I stand, turn, and put my knees on the bed either side of his thighs, clasping his face in my hands. "The chances are good that you will stay as you are now with the bulk of your memory intact. I'm no doctor, but you had a TBI, which started a tumour growing. The tumour is now out, and unless it grows back, I'm sure there's nothing to be overly worried about. We could all have these bombs you're talking about ticking in our heads. Who can read the future? I could have dementia heading my way, who knows? All we can do is grab what we've got and hang onto it with both hands. Live for the now, Liz. Not the future which is unknown."

He stares at me. "How did you get so wise?" Then, without waiting for an answer, slides his hand around the back of my head and takes advantage of the position I put myself in.

As his lips move over mine, I close my eyes, feeling emotional tears prick. *I'm home.*

Half an hour ago, I'd have said I'd needed more time. Five minutes ago, I'd have said it was too soon. But now, as his tongue sweeps into my mouth, I respond just as if twelve years hadn't passed. My hands grip his shoulders, fingers digging in, holding him tight, never wanting him to leave me again.

His familiar taste that I haven't forgotten sends shivers down my spine. When his hands part my robe and slip under my t-shirt, the familiar touch fondling my breasts makes me sigh into his mouth and grind my pelvis against his thickened dick.

When he removes his mouth from mine, it's only to rasp against my ear, "If you don't want this to end up with my cock in your pussy, tell me to stop now."

His words, filthier than he's used with me before, heighten my arousal.

I shake my head. It's obvious he misunderstands when he tries to lift me off him.

"I want you, Liz. Right here, right now."

He tries to raise me. Though his hand now seems able to open and shut, he's still got residual weakness on his right side, that, together with the fact I've put on weight, I know I need to help.

I clamber off and fall to my back on the bed.

"Take off your robe."

The heat in his eyes makes my insecurities fade, worries about the toll the years have taken on my body disappear. I scramble out of my robe and pull my top over my head. I've just one thought, I want him inside me now.

"Fuck, it's been too long, Vanna." His nostrils flare as he tugs at my sleep shorts. I help get rid of the offending object by toeing them down my legs, uncaring they catch around one ankle.

I'm suddenly shy, but his eyes blaze as they fall onto my body. I watch as he takes in the silvery stretch marks which had faded but not gone, my childbearing stomach even rounder now, but it's as if he doesn't care at all.

"You're fucking beautiful," he rasps as he lowers his face to my mound, breathing in deep, his eyes closing briefly. "Damn you smell good."

I can barely think anymore as he lowers his head, his tongue circling my clit, before sucking it into his mouth. His touch, so familiar yet so different as it's been years since anything's been this close to me except for my vibrator.

Tears leak from my eyes due to emotional overload as time slips away, my body responding to him as if it was only yesterday when he last touched me like this.

"Jesus, you're tight, babe." He works one finger inside me, then another. "So fuckin' tight. So fuckin' responsive, just like I remember." His voice catches as though this carries as much significance for him as it does for me. Then he adds a second finger and curls them around. *Christ. This is new.*

My toes curl and I arch my back as twin sensations hit as he assaults my G-spot and my clit.

"You gonna come for me, Evangeline?" he growls against my

mound, elongating my name in that sexy way he does.

Heaven help me, I don't have a chance against his talented fingers, tongue and vibration from that gravelly voice. My muscles ripple, tense, then I'm bowing my back off the bed. Jesus, I think I see stars. My vibrator doesn't come close to what this man can do with his mouth.

"Lizard," I get out once I'm able to breathe again. Raising my head, I swallow what I was going to tell him when I see him gazing at me. He's got tears in his eyes.

Unashamedly brushing one away that's leaked onto his cheek, Liz speaks instead. "Nothing, fuckin' nothing is better than watching you come. I don't know how I ever could forget."

"I think you've learned some new skills."

"Vanna, I…" he chokes.

"I'm not complaining," I tell him fast. "As long as it's only me who gets the benefit from now on."

"On that, you can fuckin' bet." He worms his way up the bed, then swears, twists and sits up, using his left hand to open the drawer by the right-hand side of the bed. He takes out a condom.

"Give it to me," I offer. "I'll put that on."

"Take care, woman. I'm close."

He sucks in air as I slide the latex down his cock. Heeding his warning, I restrain from fondling any more than I have to, then I lie back down. He sits back on his knees, pulling my ass up onto his thighs, and then he's working his way in. I gasp, it's been a long time, and he's bigger than my BOB.

He's in and starting to move. That twist, that swivel is new. Better. Wow. Then my ability to think is gone as the air is filled with the scent of sex and grunts, groans, and sighs of appreciation on both our parts.

I come again, and take him with me, his completion accompanied by a roar.

"Vanna, Vanna. Mine."

I take air into my depleted lungs and respond, "Yours."

CHAPTER FORTY-THREE

Lizard

I hadn't expected my conversation with Vanna to go quite the way it had, but I'm definitely not complaining. Something between us had just clicked, and actions which had been familiar twelve years back, before I suffered the damage to my head, had returned as if we slipped into a dance we'd never stopped.

It was different, she was tighter than I remembered, but maybe I was comparing her to the women I'd been with since I patched in. While I hate that I'd been with a variety of girls, it had left me with new techniques which had worked on her. I promised and meant it from the bottom of my heart that I'd never stray again.

I'd never have looked elsewhere had I remembered. I hadn't been me then, I'd been someone else. If I hadn't had had that blow to my head, I'd never have stepped out on her.

We'd cuddled, dozed, then made another attempt to make up for lost time. Quite successfully, I'd had her shouting my name, and hers might have escaped my mouth.

When we'd woken again, the sun was streaming in through the gaps in the blind, and she'd reached for her phone.

"Time?"

"Eleven. Christ. I've got to be at work in an hour."

"I'm the manager. I'll give you the day off."

"No," she contradicts, batting my arm. "*I'm* the manager, and I'm going in. You still need rest, Liz. Especially as you didn't get much sleep last night."

Hmm. For the first time in weeks I don't feel tired, and Demon would give me my old job back in a flash were I to ask. I may not be able to lay down ink, but I can probably stab at the keys on a keyboard well enough. But I'm not going to do that to her.

"You've got time to grab something to eat before you leave." I stand, stretch and yawn, and scratch under my armpits before leaning down and pulling on yesterday's jeans. My t-shirt I just carry. "I'll go shower in my room while you get ready and meet you downstairs. Oh, and Vanna. I want you in my bed tonight."

"Isn't it too soon?"

Fuck no. Years too late. "Will you at least think about it? I'm taking nothing back I said yesterday."

She agrees with a serious nod. I stare at her for a moment, drinking my fill, seeing how the years have not only matured but improved her. I realise I'm imprinting her on my mind, so terrified I'll again forget her.

"I want to renew our vows," I say fast. "I want a new ring." Something concrete to wear that will remind me forever.

Her expression shows me she knows exactly why. "You're okay, Liz."

"For now." All I can do is hope nothing changes.

As if she knows more words won't convince me, she sits up and waves her hand dismissively. "Scat. I need to get dressed. And if you stay…"

My serious mood fades and I grin, knowing exactly what will happen as I wouldn't be able to resist if I saw her naked again. I go.

Down in the clubroom, I wait for her, knowing Vanna's not a woman who takes too much time getting ready. As I hear her at the top of the stairs, I go stand at the bottom, balancing on the one crutch I'm still using. I've decided to use that elliptical while she's at work. Ink won't be here, he'll be at the auto-shop, but someone will be around who can spot me in case I fall off and knock my head. Heaven forbid. If that happens, I don't know who the fuck I'll be when I wake up.

We walk into the kitchen. With my eyes solely on her, I don't take much notice of who else is here. Using my right hand, I pull out a chair for her, then when she sits, take her mouth with mine.

"Oh for fuck's sake. That's it. What are you putting in the coffee, Jeannie? Or are you slipping something in the food?"

Jeannie bats Judge with the towel she's holding, then looks at me as I sit next to my wife. She stares for a moment, then her face widens into a grin.

"What the fuck you talking about, Judge?" I ask, then look around the table. There, at the opposite end is Mace, with Shayla planted on his lap.

As he sees me watching, he shrugs.

"Christ. It's in the air, isn't it? Is it catching?" Judge looks concerned. "'Cause I'm not ready for a bitch, no way."

"No one would have you, Brother. You're safe," Mace tells him, chuckling.

"You not working, Mace?" I ask him, wondering why he's here.

But he just kisses Shayla in the same way I'd just done to my wife. "Pyro's given us the day off. I had a late night last night." He sends a slightly accusing look my way.

"What's your excuse, sweetheart?" I direct my light-hearted query toward the woman on his lap.

"I had a late night too," she explains, with a wink at Mace.

"Jesus." Prez walks in. He looks at me, then at Mace, then shakes his head. "Love makes the fuckin' world go around, but it doesn't make bank from our businesses." His brown eyes are twinkling. He's got Vi, he can relate.

Jeannie hands me and Vanna each a plate, we start eating. I try my knife and successfully cut my own sausage.

"You getting your movement back?" Demon asks, eyeing me thoughtfully.

"Some," I admit. "Got to work on it. But it's certainly coming."

"Good. Would like to see you get back to work."

I hear a deep breath and glancing to my side see Vanna's face drop in disappointment. Demon notices as well.

"Vanna, that doesn't mean you stop working."

"Certainly doesn't." Vi walks in and puts her arms around her man. He smiles lovingly at her and gives a nod. "In a few months, I'll be stopping work."

"What?" I ask, incredulously, knowing she loves her job.

With a woman's intuition, Vanna asks, "Are congratulations in order?"

Vi nods. Vanna squeals, as does Jeannie who asks, "When?"

"Six months' time. Gives you, Liz, a chance to get your hand working again. And with Liz tattooing, we'll need a manager."

Vanna beams for a moment, then her face falls again, and she turns to me. "But that's your job."

"Honestly, sweetheart, I'd rather ink, that's what I'm good at. Took on everything at the shop as it was just myself and a part-timer when we started out. Moved into new premises, and sort of continued. The admin work started to take over. You'd be doing me a favour, doll."

"And us," Demon grins. "Buzz says you're a better bookkeeper."

I glare at him, but I don't really mind. Anything to keep Vanna close and happy.

She cleans her plate, drinks her coffee then stands. "As the boss is here," she nods at Demon, "I better run and not be late."

I tell her to have a good day, then as she goes to leave, I ask, "Haven't you forgotten something?" and tap my lips.

She redeems herself by bending her head and allowing me a non-PG kiss which makes me want to take her straight back to bed.

"Oh fuck. I'm outta here." Judge gets up and makes his way out of the kitchen to peals of laughter from Mace and Shayla.

"You're just jealous!" Mace calls out.

Judge gives him the finger.

"Give me a minute," I tell her, reaching for my crutch. "I'll see you out to your car."

We go out via the kitchen door as it's closer to where her car is parked.

"You think Cas is going to be alright with us getting back together?" I ask, opening the driver's door for her.

She hesitates before getting in, taking my question seriously. "He'll have to get used to sharing me, but I think he'll be good. He'll be pleased for me, and for himself. As long as you don't come down too hard on him."

My mind goes back to my prez's and Vi's happy news. "You used to want a big family, Van. Well, we did. We planned on three."

"Didn't happen, though, did it?" She shrugs.

"It's not too late. You're still young."

She turns to me, her eyes wide. "You want a baby with me?"

My lips press together. Seems no reason why not, and I'm not going to rob her of anything else. "Nothing I'd want more, Vanna. Just, I suppose you'll have to think about it carefully." I tap my head. "If my brain goes again…"

"Not going to borrow trouble before it comes, Liz. Isn't that what you used to say? If we have another child, if the worst happens, then I've done it once on my own and I'll do it again."

"If anything ever happens to me," I check she's listening carefully as this is important, "you belong to me, and I belong to the club. Club protects women, even if their man is long gone. You hear what I'm saying? You're part of us now, Vanna. You and Cas. You'll never have to do anything on your own again."

She looks like I've given her food for thought. She slides into the car with a wave of her hand.

"See you tonight, babe." I step back, rapping on the roof twice, then watch her leave.

Mace said I'd never wanted a woman and kids. I hadn't. To me, the reason is clear, because somewhere in the depths of my mind, I knew I'd already met my one. I was just waiting to find my way back to her.

I'd completely missed Cas growing up. Missed seeing him go to school, learning to read… I'd missed so fucking much. Hell, I wasn't there for his birth, only seeing him when I was on leave, then going again for half a year at a time. Hearing Vi mentioning she and Demon were expecting, it had hit me how I'd like the chance to experience everything about preparing for a baby, childbirth and raising a child for myself, with a new son or daughter. Would Cas like a brother or sister? Or is he too used to being an only child?

I hear the sound of footsteps and look up to see Dirt and Nails walking back from the direction of the gym we're building. "Hey, Prospect." Of course, both of them look up, smartening their steps and stopping in front of me all but standing to attention. If one saluted, it wouldn't surprise me.

"What you need, Liz?"

"Someone to spot me while I work out in the basement."

"Sure, man." Nail's raises his chin toward Dirt. "You okay…"

"Yeah, I'll do what needs to be done." Dirt turns to continue his way into the clubhouse but turns and nods in my direction. "Heard you got your memory back. Welcome home, Brother."

"Ain't your brother yet," I growl.

Dirt chuckles. "Yeah, as I said. Fuckin' good to have you back."

But I don't make it straight down to the basement.

"Liz!" Prez calls me over. "Check Vanna got to work okay. I'm sending Dirt out to Devil's Ink."

My senses are immediately on high alert, making me snap, "Why?"

"Cad's caught some whispers on the web."

"Whisper of what?"

"I don't know, just our name and chapter being mentioned. He's tracking it down. I just want everyone to keep sharp. Maybe nothing at all."

"He think's something's about to hit us?" Fuck. I've just got Vanna back, my second chance at happiness though the doubts deep down say I don't deserve it. Karma couldn't turn around and take her away from me now, could it? Would it be so cruel?

"I'll go to the shop." I'm not leaving her alone.

Demon raises an eyebrow. "She's safe enough there, the security is top notch. You think I'd let Vi work at Devil's Ink if I thought risk was more than a whisper? Dirt's going there as a precaution, nothing else. Just check she's arrived but don't worry her."

"I—"

"You're in no fuckin' shape, Brother." Trust Prez to give it to me straight. "You can't hold a gun, can't walk without help. You need to trust us to look after your woman while you work on getting your strength back. If something is coming for us, the best thing you can do is to get yourself fit and ready for it."

Shit. He's right. I'm no fuckin' good to anyone. Not at the present. But I will be. On that I'm determined.

What should I do about Vanna? If I tell her to keep an eye out, give her the slightest suspicion there's danger, I may be doing the last thing I want to. I'm trying to bring her into this life, not chase her away from it. Cad's heard something, but nothing definite. Demon's right, if the prez trusts his woman to be safe there, then I needn't worry much. But hell, that doesn't stop me. Not with my thoughts about life stabbing me in the back.

"I want Dirt escorting the women home."

Prez nods. "Going to have a brother there as well. Might even go myself."

I stand, noticing Nails off to one side waiting patiently. Sighing heavily, I realise I'm no fucking help at all now. Not when I can't ride my bike, and I can't shoot well left-handed. Not for the first time, I wish I was ambidextrous and not so damn right-side dominant.

"I'll be downstairs," I tell Demon, flexing my right hand and drawing his attention to it.

"Liz," he catches my eye and holds it. "We're at DEFCON four right now. May rise to a three later. If there's any change, I'll call everyone in, immediately."

I give a sharp nod understanding the language. We often borrow military terms and make them our own. Right now, we're strengthening security acting on available intelligence. It's rare for us to reach level one which from our point of view is all-out war.

I jerk my chin toward Nails, and taking my leave of Demon, pausing, I send a quick text.

Liz: Get to work okay?

Vanna: Checking up on me already? ☺

Liz: Missing you already

The three dots appear, disappear, then reappear again.

Vanna: I'll move into your room tonight.

I breathe out, realising how much that simple statement means to me. Vanna really does want to make it work. A smile curves my lips as I type my response.

Liz: Fucking love you, woman

Vanna: Love you too xx

There's more of a spring in my step as I carefully make my way down the narrow stairway leading to the basement. A corner has always been kept aside with weights and mats, but not much in the way of equipment. Now, in pride of place in the area we keep clear for Mace to conduct any interrogations, stands a brand-new elliptical.

Gingerly, I go to it. Without being asked, Nails steadies me, setting my crutch to one side. I step on first with my good leg, then follow with my bad, my left hand holding on with a death grip.

I start to push and pull, taking it slowly at first, then, trying to stretch myself, increase the resistance slowly. It's not long before sweat is pouring off me, my heart is beating fast, and I'm breathing evenly but quickly. It's a great feeling as endorphins flood through my body, helping to clear my mind as I work out.

I haven't done anything physical since I collapsed a few weeks back, so I'm relishing both the challenge and the feeling.

"You doing okay?" Nails checks.

"Yeah." I increase the resistance again, but it's hard to maintain the same speed at this level, so drop it back down.

"Ink's got some more equipment arriving next week. He's going to be setting it up in the gym."

"Yeah?"

"He's got a leg press, leg extension shit, and calf raises. Shoulder press too."

Sounds like he's gone to town, but again I can only get out one word. "Yeah?"

Nails chuckles. "Think he's got you covered man, you'll soon be back to yourself."

All I want to do is to ride my bike. And fuck my wife of course, but it seems I'm already able to do that. There, right at the top of my reasons to get fit is the desire to be able to protect my family.

I don't know how long I work out, but only cease when I'm beyond fatigued. I stop the movement and Nails helps me off. He hands me the crutch and while I'd prefer to try without it, my overworked muscles feel weak.

The late night, exertion of this morning and exercise just now has taken it out of me. Accepting I'm still recovering, I don't feel guilty at all when I take myself back to my room to sleep, knowing tonight Vanna will be sharing my bed with me.

Life settles into a pattern. Demon shakes his head each time I ask, but Cad's picked up nothing more on the spidery web he spends his time searching. Our status of alertness is still heightened, brothers don't ride alone, and women are protected wherever they go, but the sense of danger being imminent recedes.

While my wife works, I concentrate on becoming the husband she deserves, one strong enough to take some of the load off of her. Day by day, I notice changes about her and love every single one.

We're still using condoms, for now. But I've a feeling we'll be ditching those sooner rather than later.

After the first week of exercise, I dispense with the crutches, but still use a stick as I don't fully trust my right leg yet. As for my hand, I can hold shit now, and soon want to try handling a gun.

I've not yet thought about riding my bike, but at least have confidence I will get there.

As for Cas. Well, at the weekends when he's visiting, I've found he's an unruly little shit who I love unconditionally. He can go from being helpful and a delight to be with to a disrespectful and disobedient brat in a heartbeat. But being there, witnessing it, discussing with Vanna how best to handle him is one of the most amazing feelings in the world. I'm a dad, and I'm loving it. The good news is that while he acts up with us, he's at least behaving for Lindy and not getting up to mischief.

In just another week, summer break will be upon us, and he'll move here full-time. We've delayed hunting for a house until we can look together, wanting Cas to have his input, to choose a new home as a family unit.

Our plans are already in place as both Vanna and I had made them excitedly. We'll both go to Denver, and with the help of a prospect or two, pack up my wife and son's shit, sorting out stuff to bring back now, and what to put into storage for when we eventually find our own place. According to Mace though, we'll probably need to end up buying new furniture for the whole house. I'd hated to learn how Vanna had had to make do with mostly purchased second-hand items, but was glad he had warned me, otherwise I'd have walked in blind and have been presented with more evidence of her struggles when I should have been there to support her.

"You with us, Liz?"

What could have been a reprimand, is expressed as concern as Prez sees I've not been paying attention. I give a weak apologetic grin acknowledging I'd missed shit while I'd been daydreaming. Well, Buzzard's dry finance reports can get boring.

"Buzz is going over the tattoo parlour's books. Vanna's already given me the breakdown," I give back, hazarding a guess we've reached the part of church where they need my input.

Prez glares but doesn't say anything else. *Phew. Got away with it.*

"Pyro?" Demon's attention is now on another man. "You and Mace have any problems when you went to San Francisco?"

"None." Pyro grins widely. "Got that part without problem and came back. Everything went like clockwork."

Mace too is grinning like a loon. As I am too. Sure, that was the official story, in truth Pyro and Mace had been somewhere else.

Prez turns to me. "Now Shayla's moved out of it, your boy going to be staying in that spare room?"

"Sure is, Prez. Just until we can get a house organised."

Yes. It's the spare room now. It's connotations with the motherfucker who last laid name to it forever gone. The feds are down one undercover agent.

Agent Jordan has been retired.

"I want to check up on how the prospects are getting on," Prez speaks when the fist bumps and exclamations of pleasure die down. "Seems I'm always tripping over one now. Shall we talk about bringing Karl and Beaver to the table?"

"I vote yes," says Beef. "With everything going on with Lizard, they've been left on the back burner. They've both served their time."

"Yeah, blame me, why don't you?" I growl, but with a twinkle in my eye.

Beef clears his throat. "If you need me to make it formal, Prez, I'll put it on the table. I propose we agree to bring Beaver and—"

"Muffin!" yells Pyro. "Beaver and Muff."

All eyes go to Pyro. "Muffin?" I query aloud what everyone else is thinking; why poor Karl should end up with that moniker?

Pyro grins broadly. "Mel's always complaining he steals them."

"Weak, Brother." Thunder shakes his head. "Fuckin' weak logic there, but I like your thinking."

Prez's eyes roll to the ceiling and back down. "Anyone got any other suggestions?"

I notice Wills prods Judge. "I had a fuckin' lucky escape," he mumbles, but not quietly enough.

Beef's eyes narrow as he points at him. "Never too late to get a road name."

Wills holds up his hands. "I don't even like fuckin' muffins."

"You gay?" I ask fast, my eyes creasing. As brothers crack up around me, I realise how lucky I am to be living this life. For a moment there, I'd thought it was the last thing I wanted. Now I've regained my wife, my son, and my club. Was there ever a luckier bastard?

A gavel bang later and it's agreed Beaver and Muffin will be patched in.

"If there's nothing else…?" Prez looks like he's going to end the meeting.

Just as I'm thinking of dragging Vanna back to our bedroom, I notice Mace is fidgeting, and inwardly sigh when he raises his hand.

"Prez. You gave permission to Pyro, Prez. Skull's not a threat now. *That's* how we should be dealing with our enemies. In the same way Pyro needed closure, I can't relax while Major's still breathing. Even if he's not coming after us, he deserves retribution for what he did to Shayla. What he's still doing to other girls."

Prez sighs and pinches the bridge of his nose. "I hear you, Mace, and I appreciate how you're feeling. I'll get onto Red, see if he's come up with anything. Must admit I had hoped he'd come up with something before now. Last update I had was that Major appears untouchable."

"Not going to let this rest, Prez," Mace snarls.

"I understand that, Mace. But I have to look out for the good of the club, and that includes Red and his boys in Vegas. Any move we make can't bring heat down on the club, and he's got powerful clients who might want revenge for the loss of what he provides. Don't want to make more enemies unless there's no other way out."

"We've turned into a bunch of pussies," Mace all but shouts. "Major hurt my woman, he deserves to go down."

"Not saying he doesn't." Prez keeps his voice calm, the complete opposite to the enforcer.

"I had to wait over half a year," Pyro reminds Mace. "I'll tell you this, Brother," his face contorts into an evil grin, "revenge loses none of its taste when it's served cold."

I can understand why Mace is impatient to see Major six feet under. I hate the man myself for the way he marked Shayla and Esme. I try to put myself in my brother's shoes. How would I feel knowing Vanna had suffered like his woman? Every bit what he's feeling now.

I decide to keep a close eye on my brother, knowing it's only Shayla being at the club that's keeping him here and not seeing him set out for Vegas to take Major down by himself.

I hope his desire to stay close to her will be enough. Any action we take must be properly planned out, just like the revenge Pyro had served up for Mel.

CHAPTER FORTY-FOUR

Vanna

"That's your next session booked in." I smile at the customer as I hand him an appointment card showing the date and time of his next appointment.

Jonah comes over and turns the screen so he can see what he's got listed. "Nothing more today?"

"There was a tentative enquiry about a consult," I remind him, "but nothing concrete was booked."

"Give me a shout if anyone comes in. I'm going out back to make a coffee. Want one?"

I shake my head. I've had all the caffeine I need today, drinking more often as it's been fairly quiet.

Vi's gone home already as she was feeling tired and didn't have any clients. Weston's here as well as Jonah, but the afternoon's been slow up to now. Nothing to worry about, most walk-ins come toward the end of the week.

When Demon had first offered me the position, I'd thought it might have been a charitable gesture, something to make me feel useful. Since I've been here though, I've found I'm really answering a need. I can free Vi up to concentrate on tattooing or piercing, and at times we're so busy, we have to turn people away. I'm doing a lot of the social media stuff too, and that's something I enjoy. The books are looking good as well, and Buzzard is pleased when I update him each Wednesday.

I've just uploaded one of Weston's tattoos onto our Instagram page when my phone vibrates. As there are no customers around, I don't feel guilty answering the call. I check the display and a smile crosses my face.

"Hey, Lindy. How's it going? Is Cas—"

The shrill tone of her voice immediately has my senses on high alert. "I told him to come straight home, Vanna. Every day for the past five weeks, he's done exactly that. But he hasn't turned up and he's a couple of hours late now. I've tried his phone, but there's no answer."

"What?" I get to my feet. *Oh Cas, why couldn't you just do what you're told? Why, when you're so close to being able to leave Denver?*

I try to keep my voice calm while inside I'm seething. "I'm sure it's nothing to worry about, Lindy. Maybe he got chatting and lost track of the time. I'll ring around his friends and try and track him down."

"He's been so good, Vanna. That's why I called, him not letting me know anything is out of the usual. Will you let me know immediately if you find anything out? Or whether I have to get bail money ready?"

She might laugh, but she's a bit too close to what I'm worried about. Grrr. He was doing so well, he can't fuck it up now. Not when Lizard and I are settling into a makeover of our marriage. It's been working out great, Liz and I having time together, Cas visiting at weekends, father and son getting to know each other slowly. Cas seemed to be happy with Lindy and looking forward to moving to Pueblo. Why has he gone and fucked it up now? Damn him. My greatest fear is he's done something stupid. If he has, the cops aren't going to let him off a second time.

"I'll call as soon as I have anything to tell you," I tell her tightly, already thinking of Cas's friends whose parents are in my contacts. Hopefully, I'll quickly track him down and get him sent back to Lindy with his tail between his legs. "Let me know immediately if he turns up."

With a promise she will, she ends the call.

Damn it, Cas, why now? I'd been looking forward to getting his room ready, having him move here and us becoming a proper family unit. Getting a new home, building a new life. Liz and I are making a real go of it and successfully too. Now my son's put a spoke in my wheel of happiness. Huh. I suppose it throws Liz straight into the deep end of parenting a teenager.

I'm wasting no time, already scrolling through my contacts as I mentally berate Cas.

"Hi. It's Cas's mom, have you seen him? Is he with Jordan?"

The answer is no, and Jordan's at home playing on his Xbox, he's definitely not there. I get a negative response from Ryan's mom and Davy's. Scott's a bust as well. I ask them to check with their sons whether they saw him go off with anyone, or whether he has recently made a new friend who I'm not aware of, or if he's met a girl, he's taking a liking to. The answers are all negative. Cas got on the school bus as normal, left at his stop, and that's the last anyone saw of him.

I'd expected finding him would be easy, having assumed one of his friends would know where he'd gone. I hadn't expected all replies to be negative. What do I do now?

Has he run off? But why should he? Have I been reading him wrong, and he doesn't want to leave Denver? When I spoke to him yesterday, he was still full of the weekend at the compound and telling me how much he was looking forward to moving here permanently. He'd given me no inkling he was thinking of running away.

I start to grow very worried. *What could have happened to him?*

Other moms might have immediately informed their husbands, in my case, Liz is the person I hesitate to call. Other moms don't have men who are recovering from traumatic brain injuries, a tumour or recent surgery. Although his progress is coming along in leaps and bounds, I hate that I'm going to worry him now. My first thought was I could resolve it alone, as that's what I've been doing for twelve years. But now I've exhausted all the possibilities I can think of, I know I must involve him.

"Whoa. Trouble?" Jonah walks back carrying a cup of coffee, stopping dead when he sees the worry lines on my face.

"Could be," I agree, my teeth worrying my lip. "I'll go into the office and make a call."

"Anything I can do," he calls after me, "just let me know."

I close the door behind me, then take a deep breath and dial Lizard's number.

"Hey, babe. You okay?"

"No Liz, I'm not." I think some of my anger must go down the phone line, as I hear an intake of breath as though he's readying himself. "Cas is missing."

At his sharp intake of breath and demand to know what's happened, I run through what I already know. Yes, I've called his friends, no, nothing seemed odd. He's just disappeared into thin air.

"Come back to the compound."

"I was going to go straight to Denver." I need to be where Cas is to search myself.

"Babe, you've got me now, and the brothers. By the time you get here, I'll have briefed everyone. If we need to go to Denver, then we'll both go. Together." There's a pause, then he sighs and adds, "Teenagers are thoughtless assholes, Van. He probably got distracted and forgot the time. Could have seen a bit of tail and started chasing it."

I'm not alone anymore, I've got people who can help me. That's hard to get used to. Liz must be right. There has to be a simple explanation and Cas has neither been in an accident nor up to something he shouldn't. Moms always think the worst first, we're programmed to worry.

Outside, I'm not surprised to see Dirt's waiting by his bike and I give him a wave. It must be as boring as anything, but for the last few weeks all the old ladies have had escorts wherever we go. I'm unaware there's any threat to the club but seeing how they go out of their way to protect us women, even if there is, I feel no sense of danger, just amazed at the level of precaution they take.

Liz is waiting for me when I park the car. "Any news?"

"Lindy's not called, so he's not gone home. She'd not leave me hanging."

"Come inside." He stands back to let me precede him and I hear the confident click of his stick as he follows behind, easily keeping up with me. He waves me on through the kitchen and into the main room.

Mace stands as I approach, Pyro's with him as well as Ink and Judge. They've pulled a couple of tables together. Cad's there as well with a laptop in front of him.

The computer guy doesn't even let me sit down before he starts with his questions. "What's your friend's address? You say he was seen getting off the bus, but didn't arrive at her house?"

When I rattle off where Lindy lives, he quickly calls up a map. "Give me the location of where the bus would have dropped him."

I tell him. It stops near Davy's house and he just has to walk a block to Lindy's. While I'm still anxious, that I'm no longer dealing with this alone and not just Lizard, but his brothers are there for me gives me confidence we *will* find him, and there'll be a simple explanation for him disappearing. At least they have more ideas where to start than me.

Intrigued, I watch as Cad's fingers fly across the screen, but then he shakes his head. "No fuckin' CCTV cameras in the area. It's all residential."

"Any private feeds you can hack into?" Mace quickly asks.

"Not easily. Not without researching who's got them and who lives where."

"Just as fuckin' fast to go ask them," Pyro remarks.

"Should I call the police?" I ask.

"Won't do anything, sweetheart. A teenager's not where he's

supposed to be? They won't put out an alert on him until he's been gone a few more hours. Waste of manpower if he simply turns up home."

"Home!" I scramble for my phone. "Lindy, my house... Oh. Okay. Thanks."

At Liz's quizzical gaze I enlighten him. "Lindy had the same thought as me, that he might have gone back to our home to get something. But she's got my neighbour looking out for him, and there's no sign, nor has been any of him."

"What's up?"

I glance up at the deep voice to see Beef.

"My son's disappeared," Liz tells him, his lips firming. "Fuckin' kid may have gotten himself into trouble again."

Beef looks at me carefully. "Is that what you think, Vanna?"

"I don't know," I wail. "He's not answering his phone. I've rung all his friends that I've got numbers for. He never said who was with him when he took that car as he didn't want to drop anyone in it, so he could have arranged to meet someone I've not met."

"He's been behaving himself though, hasn't he?"

I nod at the VP. "He has." I turn to Liz and pick up my purse which I'd laid down when I arrived. "I need to get to Denver, see what's happening."

"Yeah, we'll get ready to roll." Mace nods.

My eyes widen. I expected Lizard to come with me, but it seems like others are coming as well.

"Lizard! Mace! Beef! Cad! My office now."

"Prez, we were just..."

"You need to hear this, Lizard." Demon's standing in the hallway, his face set and grim. "Before you go anywhere."

"My son..."

"My office now." It's not a request, it's a demand.

"Wait for me," Liz pleads. "I won't be long. Just got to sort out some club business."

"I've got to go find him, Lizard. Before he gets into trouble again." Nothing takes precedence over this. I'm angry at any delay. I start to stand, pulling my purse and car keys to me.

"Vanna. Wait for Lizard before you go. Dirt. Don't let her leave." My anger rises at Demon's abrupt instructions, but he's gone before I can protest.

Liz holds up one hand. "Give me five, please, Vanna. He's my son, too."

He, Beef and Mace disappear in the direction of Demon's office.

I'm torn, half just wanting to run out of there, half believing it's best to wait for Lizard to come with me. A mother's instinct tells me there's something wrong, that if I'm too late, Cas will have done something stupid, maybe put himself into the sights of the law. Or maybe he's been in an accident and is lying uncon-scious in the hospital… I take a step toward Dirt, preparing to push him out of the way.

"Vanna, wait for Lizard," Pyro calls out. "You go down there, what are you going to do? Where will you start?"

His direct question pulls me up. Go to Denver, and…? "I don't know," I wail. "I just need to be close by in case he needs me." My hand covers my mouth. "Anything could have happened to him."

"Cad's already run traces in the local hospitals' databases, no one of his name has been brought in. And so far, no one called Castiel James has been charged with anything."

I don't ask how Cad can work such magic, just hope that he's right.

"He'll be fine," Pyro tries to reassure me. "Christ, when I think back to how I was at that age, it's likely he's gone some-where on a whim without giving one thought to people worrying about him."

"You'll have one of your own soon enough," Judge points out.

Pyro grins. "Yeah, but I'll be able to enjoy them being a baby first. Got years until it gets to the teenager phase."

It was easier when Cas was a babe in arms. I didn't have to worry about him disappearing then.

As conversation falters, I tap my fingers impatiently against the side of my chair I've dropped down into again, anxious to get where I want to go, but what I'll do once I get there, Pyro's right. I really don't know. At least these men seem to know what they're doing, whereas I don't have a clue.

Cas, where are you? What have you gone and done now?

CHAPTER FORTY-FIVE

Lizard

"Prez, Vanna and I need to go to Denver…"

"Because Cas is missing." The tirade I had planned dies on my lips and my eyes widen as Demon fiddles with his phone, then holds it up so the screen is facing my way.

Squinting, I lean forward, forgetting to breathe when I see it's a picture of my son. It looks like he's handcuffed and tied to a chair. *What the fuck?* I hastily revise my initial thoughts that old as he is, I was planning on tanning my son's backside for worrying his parents. Seems it's not his fault now.

"Any message?" I snap, unable to believe what I'm seeing.

Demon swipes the screen and hands the phone over.

Unknown number: You missing something? Well so am I. I'll send you instructions on where and when we'll make the exchange. Major.

The sound of blood roars through my head as I fill with rage. My hands clench.

Mace makes a grab for the phone. "Fuckin' hell!" he shouts. "No fuckin' way is he getting his hands on Shayla." He slams the phone down on the desk and turns to the wall, his hands raking through his hair.

"Send it to me," Cad says tersely, his own phone pings, then he rushes out of the room.

"He's got Cas," I say, unnecessarily, then my voice rises. "Fuck, Prez. He's *got* Cas!"

Beef's looking between me and the enforcer. "So," he says gruffly. "We get Cas back and we're not making any fuckin' exchange. What have you told him, Prez? I suspect you've responded."

"I told him we have no fuckin' idea what he's talking about," Demon responds. "I demanded he give the boy back without harming a hair on his fuckin' head."

"You didn't think to say he wasn't ours?" Mace asks. "Kid lives in Denver, could have denied any connection. He might have thought there was no value holding him and let him go."

Prez gnashes his teeth. "Thought of it, dismissed it. Major's stable might include boys. Thought it best to let him know he was under our protection."

Jesus Christ! I feel the blood drain from my face as I process what he's suggesting. *Not Cas. No!*

Demon stares straight at me. "We'll get him back, Lizard. I fuckin' swear to you. We'll get him back."

"Ball's in Major's fuckin' court at the moment though, isn't it?" I hit the desk with my left fist, vibrating with anger and fear. *That's my boy out there.* Alone, unprotected, and in the hands of a man who doesn't give a fuck about people ending up dead. *How the fuck am I going to tell Vanna?*

The door opens. Before Cad's fully inside, he's shaking his head. "Can't get a fix on that phone, fucker's using some kind of blocker."

I ask the question no one has asked yet. "How did he know, Prez? How did he fuckin' know Shayla is even here? How did he know to take one of ours to get her back? How did he know about Cas?"

"Questions are a distraction right now, Liz. Fact is, he knows, and we've got to deal with it. Could have been anything, she's got his fucking tat on her back. Maybe one of the civilians saw it when she was working on a car, maybe Whale or Jonah said something. We'll find out if we've got a leak once we've got him back, okay?"

"He's had eyes on us. Had to have," Cad says tightly. "We've kept our women safe in Pueblo, and there's been no chance of him getting his hands on Theo. He must have been watching for a while. Must have noticed Cas visiting, followed him back to Denver."

Why, why the fuck did I not think of that? I'd worried about Vanna, made sure she never went anywhere alone, while I'd left my kid alone and unprotected. Abruptly, I stand.

"Where are you going, Liz?"

"Denver." I snap out the obvious.

"Sit," Demon barks. "Use your fuckin' head, Liz. How's running off blind going to help? He might be far away from Denver by now."

I retake the seat. Never in all of my life have I felt so totally useless. My body vibrates with a rise in adrenaline which has nowhere to go.

"How we going to play this, Prez?" Mace sounds broken. "I don't want Shayla anywhere near that fucker. I don't even want her to fuckin' know that Major's made contact or that he's got Cas. Fuck, the way she protected Esme, she'll be all over this, offering to give herself up for Liz's kid."

Demon eyes him. "That's the way I read her as well."

I look from one to the other. "Shayla's a grown woman, Cas is just a kid."

Mace's eyes go cold. "You saying you want to make the exchange, Lizard?"

"I don't know," comes out of my mouth as a wail. "Cas is just a kid. He'll be scared. He doesn't deserve this. He won't know what the fuck's going on, or why he's caught up in something that's got fuck all to do with him. His only crime being he's my fuckin' son. What the fuck am I going to tell Vanna?"

There'll be no drawing her into the club after this, not when it's put her child in danger. *I* don't want to be in the club if these are the ramifications for Cas. "I've got to go find him, Prez. Denver's got to be the place to start. I can't sit here doing nothing."

"We've no fuckin' idea that's where he is," Beef growls. "Fuck, Major could already have him on a plane heading to Vegas."

"Not if he wants to make the exchange. He could be close," Cad sensibly notes.

Prez's forefinger and thumb press the top of his nose. "That's if he's even going ahead with this. Major might decide he wants both Shayla and Cas. I'll call Red. See if he's come up with any of Major's bases. Get him on board with pulling apart his town. I'll also call Drummer. Get him to put feelers out. That Devil chap he knows who owns Grade A Security might have heard of Major."

The VP's brow creases. "What about Snatcher and Lost? Want to alert them?"

"Lost's too far south to help in a hurry, but I'll give him a heads-up. Snatcher? Yeah. If we need bodies to help search or men to protect the compound."

Snatcher, Prez of the Utah Chapter helped us out once before when the mafia knocked at our door, rode back to Utah a man down. Lost, I don't know much about, as he's prez down in San Diego and as Demon noted, there are too many miles between our chapters.

"What about RIP?" Beef asks. "Want me to have a word?"

"Good idea." Prez nods at him. "Be good to have the Wretched Soulz on board. They might help when it's one of our kids who's in danger." He pauses and looks at me and then Mace. "Can't do much more until Major gets back into contact."

"He's fuckin' toying with us," I cry. "Why didn't he give the instructions with the first message?"

"Because he wants us to suffer. He wants us to hurt, to

worry." Prez rubs at his nose. "He's giving himself time to set everything up in his favour."

Cad raises his chin at me. "He'll give us a while to digest the implications, then hit us with where to take her."

Mace slams his fist into the wall again. "Not taking her anywhere except away from here. Prez, I'll take Shayla to one of the other chapters. Tucson would be best if Drummer gives the okay—"

"Listen to yourself Mace and fuckin' think for a minute," Beef roars. "Major has to have eyes on us. What d'you think he'll be fuckin' looking out for?"

Mace slumps into a chair, and his eyes meet those of the VP. "He'll snatch her as soon as we try to move her."

Demon nods. "That could well be what he expects us to do. Then he'll end up with both her and Cas."

"If that's what he's planning, keeping her here might risk a direct hit on us," Cad says.

"He wants Shayla back, not dead," Beef reminds him. "I doubt he'll come at us with a frontal attack."

"You want to stake your woman's life on that, Beef?" Demon asks.

Cad stands. "I'll get Dirt and Nails keeping a real-time eye on the feeds from the cameras. I'll ask Pal to get the drone up to check whether anyone appears to be hanging around."

As conversations go on around me, I'm finding it hard to concentrate. It's my son that's in Major's hands. Even in the depths of my heartache, I realise my brothers are right. Going off half-cocked isn't the answer. Major doesn't just want Shayla, he'll want to punish us, especially when he finds we've covered her property tat. It's more than likely he'll not give up Cas, even if we'd consider for one fucking moment exchanging one for the other.

I force myself back to what's going on in time to hear Prez's next words.

"I want everyone here on lockdown." As Demon brushes his

hand over his face, I wonder if he's worrying whether Major will up his game and take someone else. It's bad enough my teenage son disappearing, but if Major got his hands on Theo, fuck knows what twisted plans he'd have for a young child. "Need to get the rest of the brothers in on this. Leave the businesses in civilian hands. I want every man, woman and Theo here under our protection. I'll risk no one else falling into his hands."

"What can I do?" My head drops into my hands. "What can I fuckin' do? Cas…"

"We can't do anything," Demon says. "I know it's fuckin' killing you brother, but all we can do is wait until Major gets back in touch."

"The man's sick," I scream at them. "Who knows what he's doing to my son."

"He won't touch him." Beef tries to sound reassuring. "If he wants Shayla back, he won't harm him."

Yet. The unspoken word hangs in the air.

"Liz is right, he's sick. And this time Demon, you won't stop me. He's fuckin' going in the ground."

The look I send Mace shows I'll be right there beside him.

"Not going to argue with you there, Brother. Now Major's attacked us directly, this is war. Mace? Will you go get everyone on standby, soon as we get the next message from Major and know his proposal for making an exchange, I want everyone in church. We're not fuckin' giving him Shayla. We'll get the kid back and take him down. Cad, make sure our security is sewn up tighter than a virgin's ass. Beef and I will make some calls, try to drum up some support. Liz…" Prez doesn't seem to know what to say to me.

A shuddering sigh wracks my body. How I don't know, but, "I'll try to get Vanna locked down. She can't leave the compound."

Mace offers me his hand, but I get up by myself, adrenaline fuelling my body to get moving.

Once in the corridor, I rest my head against the wall. Mace's hand lands on my shoulder.

"Brother…"

"I don't know what's going to happen," I tell him quietly, so my voice doesn't carry into the clubroom. "If he harms Cas, it'll destroy Vanna." It will destroy me too. The thought of not seeing my boy growing into a man. Not even knowing what was happening to him. No. That's never going to happen. I'll move heaven and earth to find him.

"He won't harm him, not while he's a bargaining chip."

"But he's not getting Shayla back," I remind him, adding quickly, "Not that I think we should make the trade. Not for a fuckin' second, Brother."

"And you know, beyond me sacrificing my ol' lady, there's *nothing* I won't do to get your son back."

"Liz?" Vanna's tearful voice reaches me. Of course she's hovering, waiting for me to emerge. "Lindy called. There's still no sign of Cas. It's as though he's disappeared into thin air. I'm so worried about him." She sobs, but there's strength in her voice when she adds, "I'm not waiting any longer, I'm going back to Denver right now, with or without you."

I exchange a quick look with Mace. She's obviously been thinking I've been dealing with club business, which I have. She just doesn't yet know it's about the boy everyone's out seeking.

Mace's lips thin and his eyes signal he's not envying me this conversation. I raise my chin, knowing it's equally difficult for him, and then take Vanna's arm.

"Where we going?" I notice then her car keys are in her hand.

"Upstairs, we need to talk."

Her eyes narrow. "Talk? We can talk on the way, Liz. Or if you can't be bothered to come, I'll go by myself. I've done enough talking, now I need to do something."

"What the fuck do you think you can do? He's not a dog trained to come at a certain whistle." Harsh, I know, but she's got to see sense. I'm worried sick about Cas, but Vanna's going to be destroyed when she hears even half of what I now know.

We might have been parted for years, but it appears she can still read me. Her body stills. "You know something," she accuses, her gaze settling on my face. "You *know* something about my son. Tell me, Liz."

"Vanna, come upstairs now." I can hold her with one hand, but not also hold onto the stick and pull her where I want her to go.

She shrugs off my hold easily and so fast, I take a moment to regain my balance. "You tell me now, Norton James."

The use of my legal name tells me she'll take no nonsense from me. "Vanna, please. I need to speak to you in private."

"You tell me this moment, or I'll go to Denver by myself. Cas is everything to me, Liz."

"And to me, Vanna. Look, babe—"

"Use my office," Cad, walking past suggests. "Steph's not there so it's empty."

I jerk my chin in thanks, and point to the door he's just come out of. "Please, Vanna. There's something you should know."

"Two minutes. That's all you've got," she warns, following me into Cad's office. There are two desks and three times that in the number of monitor screens. One desk is neat with everything in its place, the other a total mess. All wires traversing the floor are carefully taped. Even if I hadn't had prior knowledge, it's easy to tell which station is Steph's.

I wave my hand toward the doorway that Vanna's only just cleared. She turns, shuts the door, and stands with her back against it.

"A minute and a half," she informs me.

Christ. I have to think fast. I can't have her running off on a wild goose chase, not with the slightest risk Major might be waiting for her to do just that and scoop her up too. Instead of a well thought out argument which stops her running off while keeping her out of club business, the way she's starting to reach for the door handle has me blurting out, "Cas isn't in Denver. Well, he might be, but he's not anywhere where you're going to be able to find him."

"What the hell are you talking about? What do you know about this?" With each word, she moves closer. When she's right in front of me, her finger starts poking my chest, punctuating every word. "What do you know about Cas?"

"I'll tell you as much as I can—"

"You'll tell me every fucking thing, Liz. He's my son," she screeches. "I've a right to know where he is."

"I don't know where he is," I shout back. "Don't you think I'm as fuckin' cut up about him being missing as you are. I'm his father."

"You didn't know he existed for ten years. Denied he was yours for two before that." Her hand covers her heart. "You have no idea how I feel, don't pretend you do. You tell me *everything,* you hear me? Leave nothing out. Or I'm going back to Denver, going to the cops and I won't be coming back!"

How do you deal with a rightfully distraught woman? Fuck if I know. I rake my hands through hair no longer there, and grimacing, knowing I'm about to betray my brothers to put my true family first, I take a deep breath. "You know Shayla?"

"Mace's woman, of course."

"You know anything about her background?"

She's impatient to hear my explanation but her face grimaces. "I can guess her past isn't pretty, from the little she's said, but she hasn't told us any of the details, and none of us old ladies have pushed it. I know Vi's working to cover a tat up, but not what it is or why. An abusive boyfriend perhaps." She goes still. "That can't be it, that her old boyfriend wants her back? Has he taken Cas? If so, why? Why would he go after Cas? He's nothing to do with the club."

Should I let her go on believing it's one of Shayla's old flames? Tempting, but what if she goes straight to Mace's woman and demands to know who it is? That's what I'd do in her place, and with the independence that's grown in her, she's not going to sit back and let me drive at my pace.

"It's not an ex of Shayla's. Sit, Vanna, please." My leg, after the exercise and tension in my body, is beginning to shake. I wait until she does what I ask, though she's perched as if still in flight mode on the edge of the seat. I pull up the other chair, the one Cad uses. "Vanna, please… Darlin', look the club's going on lockdown, everyone is being called in. All Shayla can know is that the club's on general alert. She can't know this has anything to do with her."

"Why not?" Vanna looks unimpressed. "If someone's taken my son because of her, surely she'd want to help sort the mess out? Maybe she could talk to him—"

"It's not an ex," I interrupt. "He's an abusive pimp who branded her with his tat and who forced her into the sex trade. For nine months, she worked on her back for him." If only it was just that, it's so much worse. "He sells women to men to do anything, any-fuckin'-thing to them, Vanna. He took Esme for the same reason."

Vanna's mouth drops open. She'll have read about such things happening on the news, feel sorry for the people involved, but something like this will never have touched her life. Her face goes completely white before she breaks down in front of me.

"He's the one who's got Cas? This evil motherfucker's got my son?" She launches herself at me, her fingernails drawing blood from my cheeks, and screams, "Because if that's what you're telling me, you better get out there and find him, Liz. I want my son back! I. Want. My. Son. Back."

CHAPTER FORTY-SIX

Mace

Jesus. Everything's going to hell in a handbasket.

I brought Vanna onto the compound and invited Cas. If I hadn't done so, he'd never have been in Major's sights.

I confronted Lizard with his wife and child and possibly caused his tumour to make its effects known. Although he's making a good recovery, he's still physically not the brother he was.

I convinced Shayla to stay. If I hadn't, had I given her money and helped set her up someplace else, Major would have had no reason to take any of us.

Me. Me. Me. Me. Every mistake can be laid at my door.

Except for one. *I* didn't want Shayla to know, but Lizard had told Vanna, and like any woman told her son was in the hands of a dangerous man, she'd become distraught and vocally so, running out into the clubroom and shouting for Shayla.

It was clear she didn't blame her, just wanted to know all about the man who's kidnapped her son. But as soon as Shayla heard about it, she'd done exactly as I'd predicted and without a second thought, had offered herself up. I'd had to physically restrain her from running out of the clubhouse though fuck knows where she thought she would go. Her only thought was to save Lizard's son.

Now she's shaking, trembling in my arms as I try to reason with her.

"We don't know, Shay, baby. You running off with no direction isn't going to help. Even if I had the slightest intention of giving Major what he wants, we don't know where he's proposing to make the exchange. If he's watching the compound, you might run straight into his arms, and then he'll have both of you. There's no guarantee Major would keep to his bargain and let Cas go. Major might have clients who like boys…" My voice trails off, and unintentionally my arms tighten around her.

"W-w-w-hen, w-w-hen is he going to call back?" she asks, her voice stuttering.

"I don't know, babe." It's been a few hours now. "Guess he's keeping us dangling." He must be pretty confident that we won't be able to find him and ramping up our anxiety about bringing the boy back home. "He's probably thinking a mother's worry will persuade us to make the trade he wants. But nothing could do that, Shay, I promise you. Even Vanna wouldn't want that."

"Yes she w-w-ould. If she truly understood what M-M-Major could do with him. That sweet b-boy, Mace. I can't believe he's taken Cas."

Neither can I. It's hard for any of us to wrap our heads around. I know Lizard's berating himself for not watching out for him or moving him to Pueblo before his school year was up, education be damned. But it hadn't crossed any of our minds. We'd been concentrating on protecting Shayla and all the women, not thinking Major would come at us via the back door and take something so precious to us, a brother's kid.

As she sobs into my chest, I think over the events of the past few hours since we heard the news. After an hour and we still hadn't heard back from Major, Demon had called all the brothers in. Church consisted mainly of ranting and raging, making me think if there had been a swear jar in the room it would have been overflowing. Brothers have all taken a liking to Cas, and of course, there wasn't any suggestion we should give in to Major's demands. Shayla was mine, and by extension, one of theirs.

The meeting had come to an abrupt close when there'd been screaming from the clubroom, and it had been then I'd had to restrain Shayla and stop her from leaving.

Now it's a waiting game. Major is making us sweat.

Christ, how I feel for Lizard and Vanna, they must be at their fucking wits' end. They've no idea where their son is, or how he's being treated and must be thinking the worst.

Lurking at the back of my mind is the fear that Major's torturing or abusing him, and the next picture we're sent will be constructed to make sure he's got our attention. But I don't even whisper this, not allowing myself to dwell on what Cas could be suffering.

I knew we should have hit back at Major before this, fucking knew it. But also knew without any leads—the man doesn't seem to exist as no one can find him—there wasn't a target to put in my sights.

But we should have been doing something, anything more than we have been, to smoke him out before he got a hand on one of our kids.

A gentle tapping at the door has me standing. Shayla tenses as I stand, walk over, and open it.

"Demon wants to talk to you, Mace. I'll stay with Shayla."

I nod at Vi, noticing Nails standing in the hallway behind her. He raises his chin. *Good.* Looks like he'll be on guard too. I'm not the only one anticipating Shayla attempting to run for it, to attempt to make the exchange, her life for Cas's. Sometimes, I wish my old lady didn't have the strength she does possess. She was prepared to sacrifice everything for Esme and would do it again.

"Stay here, Shay," I instruct her. "I'll be back as soon as I can."

"If there's any news…"

"You'll be the first after me to hear it."

Stepping aside to let Vi in, I close the door behind me.

"I can't take this." I hear Liz screaming as I descend the stairs, and the sound of a chair being kicked over. "What the fuck is Major doing, leaving us hanging like this?"

"Calm the fuck down, Lizard."

"Prez…"

"Yeah, Liz. I expected him to call before this, but hey, I'm not in his head. You're no good to Cas if you get yourself riled."

"I'm no fuckin' good to him sitting on my ass doing nothing," Lizard shouts back.

"Brother…" I step toward him, but he pushes my arm away before I can get close enough to put it comfortingly on his shoulder.

He swings around to me. "I've been thinking. Let Cad put a tracker on Shayla. Let her go back to him. We get Cas back then go after her."

"Not going to happen, Lizard," I growl menacingly. "We don't use women to fight our battles. We've covered her tat, he could kill her for it." Shayla's already told me he'd done that before, set a woman on fire as an example to others. "She's my woman, Liz. She's not going back."

"Cas is my *son*," he screams.

Vanna's sitting with glazed eyes, tears streaming from them. Every couple of moments she dabs at them with a tissue, but she seems out of it. "She okay?" I ask no one in particular.

"I gave her a sedative," Rusty explains. "Had to fuckin' force it on her, but she wouldn't calm down."

"Can't you do the same for him?" I jerk my chin toward Liz.

"He's not fuckin' drugging me. You hear that? Soon as we know where we're heading, I'm riding out."

I bite my tongue to say he can't ride yet, as something tells me he'll give it a damn good try, and probably succeed. Nothing will keep him away from his kid. I don't blame him. Cas, who I like as much as I would a blood nephew, is innocent in all of this, and if we can't save him could be facing a short lifetime of misery.

"What's the fuckin' time now?" Liz cries out.

"Almost midnight."

"If he's waited this long, he might not make contact until the morning," Judge remarks.

"I'm not fuckin' waiting for morning." Liz spins around on his new target. "Cad, why the fuck can't you trace him?"

Cad's fingers are flying over the keyboard of his laptop and my guess is that he's doing everything he can. Soon as he has something to go on, he'll tell us. Trouble is, Liz can't see straight right now, and no one here blames him one bit.

"What?" Prez barks into his phone, then asks tersely, "Is it Major?"

A car horn sounds from the front of the clubhouse, then sounds again and again. Now it blares continuously as if someone's leaning on it.

My gun, like everyone else's is in our hands, chambers have already been checked and we're cocked and loaded and ready for whatever's coming at us. Lizard is already moving, but I've got my eyes on the Prez.

"There's a fuckin' older, but expensive, model Cadillac outside the gates. Engine running, fucker won't turn it off. Dirt's refusing to open up."

Correctly too, until we all get out there.

"Where d'you want us?"

"Thunder, Judge, go after Lizard. Fuckin' tackle him if you have to. If that's Major, then this will be some kind of trick and there'll be others with him. Mace, Beef, you're with me. Sparky, Muff, and Beaver, stay in here and shoot out the fucking windows if you have to. No one is getting in. Rest of you pan out and make sure we're fully covered."

Only seconds have passed, it sounds like much longer and still that horn sounds and the engine's making a throaty roar. The headlights are blazing at us, and we can't see the driver or how many are in the car.

"Dirt?" Prez calls once we're outside and away from the light beams. "Open the gate on my signal. Soon as he comes in, close it and we'll surround him. Shoot first, ask fuckin' questions later, but if the kid's there, make fuckin' sure he's not hit."

"Don't fire at the trunk," Beef says quickly.

Yes, quite possible Cas is in there.

"Can't see anyone else in the vicinity." Cad's joined us. "Checked all the camera feeds. None seem to have been fucked with, all reporting in real-time."

"I got the drone up but it's feeding back nothing but an empty road." Paladin's staring at his phone.

"Out back?"

"Nothing there," Paladin confirms.

"Okay, Dirt." Prez's hastily issued instruction gives the signal.

Dirt operates the remote control. All of us prepared without being asked for the car to stop midway jamming the entry open so more people can come in, but that sounds unlikely from what Cad and Pal have found.

The car comes in, a little too quickly, then the brakes are jammed on. Now we've a clearer view, there doesn't appear to be anyone in it, just the driver.

At Prez's nod, I approach the door cautiously. Gun pointing forward, fully prepared to fire and remove the risk immediately.

The car door opens slowly.

"Hands up where I can see them," I snarl.

"Mace?" a high-pitched voice asks me warily. "Mace, it's me. Cas."

Cas? "Cas!" Incredulously I rip the door fully open and pull him into my arms. "Cas?" I look down questioningly, hardly daring to believe I'm actually holding Liz's son in my arms. I notice there's blood on him. Lots of it.

"Where are you hurt?" I rasp, now pushing him slightly away, checking for injuries.

"I'm okay, It's not mine." His voice sounds shaky.

At Cas's statement, I can breathe again and then see Beef's doing what I should have been, checking the rest of the car, but Cas is alone.

"Mace? Can you turn off the engine? I got it started but…"

"You hotwired it?" I breathe, then snort.

"Give my fuckin' son to me. Cas. Cas. Are you okay? Let me look at you. You hurt?" Lizard doesn't seem to know whether to hug him or hold him at arm's length.

As I willingly let Cas got to his father, I reach in and pull apart the wires Cas had twisted together. Silence descends.

Prez steps up and barks in Cas's ear, "Are you in danger? Anyone follow you here?"

Cas turns around, but Liz retains one arm around his shoulder. Intelligently, he replies, "No one following me, but they'll guess where I've come."

"Dirt? Ditch the car somewhere no one will find it."

The prospect grins and tosses Prez a salute, then runs to the car and looks at the ignition, then shrugs. I'm impressed he hotwires it quickly. Someone opens the gates, and he disappears fast.

"Church now. You too, Cas."

Of course the kid needs to be there. He's the fucking star of the show. He escaped by himself. Christ, this kid has got balls.

Inside the clubroom, Vanna shakily stands, her eyes widening in disbelief, her hands reaching forward as she yells, "Cas!"

Pulling free of his dad, a split second later, he's in his sobbing mom's arms.

"You're hurt!" Vanna exclaims, like I'd done, seeing the blood covering her son.

"The blood isn't mine, Mom," the kid explains again.

"Sorry to break up the reunion, but we need to speak to him now," Prez tells her firmly. "Come Cas."

"Not leaving me out of this," Vanna throws at him, Cas's reappearance seemingly the antidote to whatever Rusty had given to her. "I've got my son back and I'm not letting him out of my sight." As Demon opens his mouth, her finger pokes him in his chest. "For the last few hours I've been thinking I might never see him again. You're not taking him away from me now, not even for a moment."

Prez bows his head, then gives a quick nod. "Okay, Liz. Bring your wife."

"Shayla deserves to know he's here, Prez. She might have some light to shine on shit once we learn how Cas escaped."

Demon looks up to the ceiling and then back down. "She can come too."

I take the stairs two at a time to get to her fast, barely taking the time to explain. Ignoring her startled gasp and the question I can't yet answer, I grab one of my clean t-shirts, then take her hand and lead her back down.

Someone's dragged in a couple of spare chairs which Liz has appropriated and squeezed in next to his. He motions Cas to one and Vanna sits to her son's right, both parents holding one of Cas's hands, his dad with a challenging glare on his face as though ready to ward off any objections to the seating arrangements. I just lead Shayla along to my seat next to Thunder, slide the clean shirt down the table and pull her down on my lap.

Prez bangs the gavel loudly, stopping the individual queries of 'how the fuck did you get here' to Cas.

"Can't tell you how fuckin' glad I am to see you, kid," Prez starts. "But I'd like to know how."

I think we all need an explanation of why he's covered in blood, but I hold my tongue for now.

Cas seems a little unnerved that all eyes are upon him, and

with obvious pleasure he reaches for my t-shirt, grimacing as he pulls the soaked one over his head, and putting the clean one on.

I raise my chin to Lizard, pleased to see the happy reunion, but trying to signal we need to move this on. If something's coming in our direction, I'd rather know sooner rather than later. Lizard's eyes catch mine, he nods, then turns to his son.

"Just start from the beginning Cas," Lizard gently encourages him. "We know a man called Major took you. What we don't know is how it went down. We lost track of you after you got off the school bus."

Cas pulls his hands out of those of his parents and clasps them together on the table in front of him. I notice they're shaking. "Yeah, well. I caught the bus as normal. Got off. I wasn't sure whether I had all the shit I needed to do my homework, so I was checking to see if I'd put my notes in my bag. I was only vaguely aware that a van had pulled up alongside me, but I didn't take any notice. Thought it was making a delivery to one of the houses around there." He breaks off and grimaces. "They took me so quickly, I was in the back before I knew what was happening, school bag alongside me. It was a panel van, I was in the back, no handle on the inside and a partition between me and the people in the front. I shouted and kicked."

He looks around and sees we're all staring at him.

"They pulled up somewhere isolated. Tied my hands and feet and put a gag on me. Then carried on driving again." Now he rubs at his elbows. "I kept rolling around in the back, I'll probably have bruises. I don't know how far, it seemed like forever. When we stopped, I was dragged out, and brought in front of a man who introduced himself as Major."

Shayla leans forward to look down the table at him. "Middle-aged, greying hair, with a paunch, not too much height on him?"

"Yeah." Cas too moves so he can catch her eye. "Short and fat."

There's a ripple of laughter as Cas sums him up.

"Anyway," Cas resumes, "I asked him why he'd taken me,

and he said it was because the Satan's Devils had something he wanted. I played ignorant, said I didn't know what he was talking about, that I didn't know anything about any Devils, Satan's or not." Cas looks down and grimaces. "He said I better hope that wasn't true, as you were the only hope I had, and that he hadn't yet decided whether or not to keep me. He said something about being a new toy." Cas shudders. "I didn't like him at all."

I see Lizard tensing.

"Go on, Cas," encourages Beef.

"He took my photo, then put me in a room. He untied my hands, but there was no way to escape. There were bars on the window and a lock on the door which I didn't have a clue how to pick."

"Sounds like there are some gaps in your education, kid." I look down at him and wink. "Guess I better teach you."

"Knowing how would have been useful." Cas grins weakly. "But they had thrown my school bag in with me and hadn't searched it or me, except for taking my phone."

"What d'you have in there, kid?" I prompt.

Cas looks shiftily toward his mother. "It doesn't matter if I tell you now, but Davie was the one who dared me to steal that car. He said I could join his gang if I proved myself. Well, after the trouble that caused, and after coming here, I told him I didn't want to anymore. But he wouldn't leave me alone, he kept threatening me..."

"Should have told me," says Liz.

Kid could have told any of us, we'd have had his back. But he was in Denver and us two hours away. He's grown up with a mom who's always fought her battles by herself.

"I've seen what he can do to someone who crosses him, so wanted to be able to defend myself. I got a switchblade—"

"They're illegal, aren't they?" Vanna's eyes have widened.

"Not in Colorado at the state level," Cad replies. "But some cities have ordinances banning them, and I'm pretty certain Denver is one."

"Still…"

"Moot point," Beef stares Vanna down, "if it saved your kid."

"You used it?" Again, it's me who encourages him to continue.

Cas looks down again. "I wasn't going to, but I listened at the door. Heard a couple of men talking about Major planning a trade which he wasn't going to carry through. Heard them joking about what Major could do with me. Went into some details that I don't want to repeat, not in front of my parents. Scared the fuck out of me."

No one's going to admonish him for swearing, nor ask him to expand. Not when we already have a pretty good idea what he'd be saying.

"Go on," urges Prez.

"So, I knew I was going to have to escape if I could. It was either going to be them or me, and they weren't good men. I started banging on the door. One man came in. I was ready for him." Cas's hands are trembling again, and he's gone pale. "I knew I was in a bind. I told myself I had to do anything to get out of there." He turns to his mom. "What they'd been saying was evil, Mom. They'd been laughing—"

"You'd have done what you had to," Liz states, his voice getting Cas to meet his eyes.

Father and son exchange glances, it seems to give Cas the strength to start again. "I had one chance. I lunged, up. I hadn't known his height or anything but wanted to incapacitate him. Instead… I hit his jugular. He dropped, gasping. The next man came in, not noticing immediately, so I stabbed into his stomach and upward, then while he was shocked, I got out the door and locked it with them inside."

His whole body is now shaking like a leaf and no fucking wonder. He's killed at least one, if not two men. That explains the blood.

"It was them or me," Cas cries out.

"No one's criticising you, boy," Hellfire booms. "We're in awe of you. You did what had to be done."

"Fuckin' proud of you, Son," Liz thunders. "Those men weren't human, they were fuckin' scum. Animals who deserved what they got. Fuckin' proud, you hear me?"

Lizard's words are echoed around the table.

Shayla leans forward on my lap. "Cas? Those men, well, they were probably ones who hurt me." *She means raped.* "I'm glad you hurt them."

I squeeze my fingers into her slightly.

"What then?" Prez asks.

Cas shrugs as if it was nothing. "I crept through the house, managed to get out. I didn't see anyone else, but there were cars parked and I tried them all until I found one that was unlocked and that I could start, one which Mace had talked me through hotwiring. Got it started and headed out. Didn't know where the hell I was for a while, just drove around. Then I saw a sign for Pueblo and headed this way."

"You can't drive," remarks Vanna.

"I can now," says Cas with a grin, followed by a frown. "Though it was a bit scary, and I didn't want to end up in a ditch again. I knew I had one chance, and that was to get here."

Cas's eyes close briefly.

"Fuckin' proud of you, Son." Liz says firmly. His eyes are glistening.

CHAPTER FORTY-SEVEN

Lizard

I told Cas I was fucking proud of him, but words weren't adequate to express just how impressed I was. Was I pleased he carried a switchblade? No, because whatever weapon you carry, someone's probably got one bigger, and that's a lesson Cas needs teaching. But if you do carry, you should be prepared to use it, and Cas has certainly shown that.

I hate he heard what Major intended for him, hate that he had to, from the sounds of it, kill or at least cause serious injury to escape, but he'd only done what was necessary. As I'd told him, men who talk about kids like that deserve to be put down like the scum they are.

Having told his story, the bravado he called on to make his escape seems to leave Cas, and he's now leaning into Vanna and her arms are around him.

Prez speaks gently, "Cas, I think your dad's spoken for us all. A man has to do what has to be done to get out of a tricky situation. You did good, little Brother." Words from the prez which Cas should take to heart. Especially when they're echoed from around the table. Grown men would have hesitated to do what my kid had done. "Now," Demon continues, "you need to get a shower and give your mom some loving as she's been worried out of her mind. So, Cas, Vanna, and Shayla, gonna ask that you leave us now."

I notice Shayla stand immediately, but she looks shaky on her feet, and sitting close to the couple, hear Mace reassure her he'll be with her as soon as he can.

"Cas, look after your mom." I nod pointedly at Vanna who looks like she's about to drop, a combination of relief, and of running on adrenaline all evening before Rusty at last persuaded her to take that chill pill.

When the three leave us, I fold my arms on the table and let my head drop onto them, breath leaves me in a shudder.

"Fuckin' amazing kid you've got there, Liz."

"Major thought he was dealing with a scared kid who didn't know which way was up. Couldn't have had any idea he'd be resourceful enough to escape. He didn't know he was dealing with one of our boys." Muff sums it up. My kid's a chip off his Satan's Devils' Dad's block.

No one needs to tell me how incredible he is, I already know. He'd done what he had to do to escape, but when it catches up with him, he'll go down hard. My mind's still swirling around what he'd done, and it takes a moment to remember there are other things at stake. Things the enforcer is about to remind me. We've won round one, but not the war.

"Major knows where Shayla is," Mace says tersely. "Now he's lost his bargaining chip, he'll be coming to take her back."

"The man clearly doesn't take kindly to losing his property," Hellfire remarks.

Demon's rapping the table. "Major's two men down, question is, is he ready to come at us straight away?" His fingers knock against the table again. "He's out of his hometown, was prepared to kidnap and trade, is he geared up for a full-on attack, or does he have to prepare for it?"

Cad's hands are flying over his keyboard. I watch his face. He types, waits with eyes scrunched, then types again. The tap-tapping hasn't just caught mine, but everyone's attention.

"Cad?" Prez asks.

When Cad holds up his hand obviously to ask us to wait, we do. Cad wouldn't be casually replying to a friend in church, so whatever he's doing will have something to do with the matter in hand.

"Damn," Cad swears, thumping his hand on the table. "He's fuckin' gone."

"Who?" Demon asks fast. "Who were you talking to, Cad?"

"Fuck knows," he replies. Which doesn't seem helpful, until he explains, "Got a contact on the dark web who seems to have eyes on Major."

"Who, Cad?" Demon asks again.

Cad shakes his head. "That's the problem, I don't know. We could take the info as kosher or dismiss it as someone wanting to lead us down the wrong track."

"Major himself? Trying to mislead us?" Bomber asks.

Cad stares at his screen as if willing it to give him answers. "I don't know who this is, but the IP address is in Utah. Apart from that, I can't track it down to anything else." He stares at Prez. "This dude has details about us, and I don't like it. He's mentioned Shayla and us, and that Major's lost Cas."

"Not that he's back with us?" Rusty queries fast.

"No, I don't think he knows that."

"Fucker knows too much about our business," Wills growls.

"Hang on, Cad. Who do we know in Utah?"

"Snatcher?" Beef suggests, mentioning the name of the prez there. "Could it be the Satan's Devils Utah chapter?"

"Uh-uh." Cad rejects the suggestion. "Utah's the one chapter who doesn't have a me or Mouse in it. They're about as computer illiterate as it's possible to get."

"Cad's right," Demon agrees. "Snatcher would offer us manpower but has never been able to help on the info side. Leaving the who aside for the moment, what's the intel, Cad? Is he just telling us what we already know, or offering something else?"

"Something else, Prez. Major has men who protect his business, but not ones trained to take out a compound like ours. He's looking for guns to hire."

"Mercenaries?"

Cad nods. "Looks that way. He must have made his move after Cas got away and put an ad up on the dark web. Apparently, he's getting ready for a hit in a few days' time."

"You can do that?" asks Beaver. "Just put up a wanted ad for mercenaries?"

"Sure, but not in the normal places, somewhere where only men of that ilk would go looking," Cad explains. "Buried deep on the dark web where no one else would find it. Which," he looks at Prez, "let's me know whoever this contact is, he's got skills way beyond mine."

I'm not the only one worried. An irate man lashing out and hitting us in the heat of his anger that he's lost Cas is one thing. A man planning, bringing in people who're presumably trained and know how to use the arms they're carrying is something else.

"What about sending the women and Theo away?" I suggest. "I know we dismissed it before, but I'd prefer Vanna and Cas to be far away when any shit goes down."

Demon looks tired. "Personally speaking, I'd like Vi and Theo removed from any harm, but there's a risk Major's still watching everything we're doing. He learned enough to take Cas, who the fuck knows what other information he has?"

Ink's shaking his head. "We'd have to go with them to prevent an ambush on the road. What if Major's looking for revenge as well as Mace's woman? He could come at us when we've only half the brothers here to protect the compound."

"We stay on lockdown," Demon decides, having weighed the risks up. "We sew this place up tight. Cad? Your contact able to tell us when to expect the hit?"

"From what he's said, it will take a couple of days for Major to set up what he needs to."

"You sure it's not a message from Major himself, trying to mislead us?"

Cad looks thoughtful. "It's always a chance. But something tells me, it's worth taking this info as legit."

Prez pinches the bridge of his nose. "We'll work toward that while staying prepared for Major to come to us before the deadline."

"I don't like it, Prez," Pyro throws in, looking pale. I know he'll be terrified of anything happening to his pregnant wife. While having someone else to protect is new to me, I have to remember, there are other men with the same feelings. "But if I've got a couple of days, I've got some ideas."

Demon nods. "Ideas are what we want, Brothers. We're going to have everything that means something to us here. Ro, what are you thinking?"

"Well, Prez. They could hit us from the front, or the sides, or the rear. If it was me, I'd be looking at multiple entry points to hit us hard. So, I'm thinking I'll get my hands on some trip wires and mines, put a ring around our perimeter. If a fucker gets too close to one of them, he'll be a dead fucker."

Mines? I don't bother asking where Pyro can get his hands on them.

"Nowhere near the gym, I fuckin' hope," Ink mumbles, his brow creased in concern. But he's got a woman too. I guess if he has to start his project from the ground up again in order to keep Beth safe, it will be a small sacrifice.

"You," Pyro points at Ink, "are going to fuckin' help."

Yeah. Ink's handy with explosives too.

"Good idea." Cad is nodding. "As soon as a wire or mine is triggered, we can set off the rest. Take out anyone who's approaching or give them something to think about."

"Two lines," I put in. "They might get over the first, then think they're safe and be less vigilant. If they're mercs, they won't stop to bury their dead."

Yeah, as the likelihood is, they'll be looking at their individual paychecks, and won't necessarily be friends with the man who's just lost his life.

"No women, dogs or kids to leave the clubhouse," Prez announces.

"Max will need to shit, Prez," Beef puts in. "Pyro will have to set up the explosives beyond our fence line."

That will work. Beef prepared the rear of the compound to be safe for his blind wife. The flattened area is fenced to keep both her and Theo away from the dangerous parts. like the remains of the furnace where they used to smelt down trains. It's big enough to take half a locomotive at a time, a death-trap for anyone who doesn't know it's there.

"I'll set up more cameras, Prez, so we know what's happening at all times."

"I'll keep the drone up," puts in Paladin. "I got spare batteries in, it's just a matter of keeping them charged and swapping them out."

Prez is nodding. "Pyro's defence line isn't just early warning of an attack from the rear, it allows us to focus our manpower on the front line. The gates, as we know, are our vulnerable point."

Conversation continues for a while, concentrating on ammunition, guns and where we'll be positioned.

Eventually, Ink stares at Mace and asks, "Shayla got a golden pussy or something?"

When Mace growls and looks like he's going to launch himself over the table, Ink holds up his hands. "Hey, man. Just wondering why Major's willing to pay such a price to get her back. Surely, his normal MO would be to take another girl off the street."

Bomber supplies an answer which I think is right. "Doubt it's the woman herself, just the principle of the matter. By taking us on, he's sending a message, *'don't fuck with me, or I'll hit you hard.'*"

"What about Esme?" I wonder aloud. "If he's so keen to get his hands on his property, won't he go after her too?"

Demon nods. "You're right. I was in touch with her dad earlier on tonight. He's assured me he's got Esme covered."

"He can't have a clue what he's up against." I shake my head.

"Oh, I think he does." Prez grins as if he knows something we don't. "And don't forget, he's got the law on his side."

Which we haven't. I can just imagine the laughs we'd get were we to ask the cops for assistance.

Prez bangs the gavel. "Okay. We'll meet again tomorrow. I want plans fuckin' A, B and C worked out, so we all know what we're doing."

At last I'm free to go to see my wife and son. Mace calls me back as I'm about to leave. "Your fuckin' son." He shakes his head. "Chip off the old Jarhead's block."

I stare at him, then grin. "You better fuckin' believe it, Army Dog."

"What's happening, Liz?" Vanna stands as soon as I emerge into the clubroom, as if she's been waiting on me to come out. I beckon her and Cas over to a quiet table in the corner, making the split-second decision to include my son in anything I'm going to tell her. Kid proved he was a fucking man tonight.

I wait until they're seated. Without asking, Dirt runs over and puts a beer into my hand. I take it, then sit, leaning with my elbows on the table. "We're on lockdown," I tell them. "Which means you two, and every other man, woman, and child will be here on the compound."

"Major's coming for me."

"He's coming for Shayla," I correct my son. "But yeah, can't deny it. If he breaks through our defences, he'll take anyone he can get his hands on."

"We have to leave," Vanna says fast.

A corner of my mouth turns up. "Safest here, darlin'. I'm a Marine, Ink too. Mace, Pyro, Dirt and Nails are Army. A lot of men here have served, or if they haven't, they been dragged up in the school of hard knocks. Major has no fuckin' idea of what he's taking on. No one fuckin' messes with the Satan's Devils."

At that moment, Ink walks over and speaks into my ear. I nod at the news, and a full smile arrives on my face. As he moves off to spread the news, I turn to Vanna whose head's tilted to the side.

"RIP, he's the prez of the local chapter of the Wretched Soulz, well, it seems they haven't had fun for a while, so he's sending some boys to the clubhouse. It will be a bit crowded, but hell, we won't be turning a few more guns away."

"The Wretched Soulz?" Cas's eyes have gone wide. "Hell, yeah."

Hell, yeah is right. I grin at my son. They're certainly not afraid of getting their hands dirty and will be good to have on our side. Put it this way, rather they had our backs than were the ones gunning for us.

I notice the room has become emptier than it was before, and out of the window, a slight lightening of the sky. Well fuck, we've been up and talking most of the night. We're probably all running on fumes.

I pull my stick toward me and get to my feet. "Let's go to bed. Cas, you're sleeping with us tonight."

Vanna sends a look of relief my way. It was obvious mother and son didn't want to be parted. And this dad wasn't going to be missing out.

CHAPTER FORTY-EIGHT

Lizard

*B*ang, bang, bang, bang, bang.

Having emptied the chamber, I reload.

"Getting faster, Liz." Mace nods approvingly, then smirks. "Even hit the target a couple of times."

"Couple of fuckin' times?" I growl. "Every one of those last bullets was a bull's-eye."

"Lucky shots."

He's not going to give up giving me hell, but I really don't mind. Seems now my brain has decided to start cooperating, my recovery's speeding up all the time. That pistol is in my right hand, and while I'm still slow getting a new magazine in, whatever Mace has said, my accuracy is fine. If Major steps into my sights, he's going down.

"We better get back, Liz."

Yeah, we had. We'd gotten the okay from Demon to come out to our range for a while to see if I could handle a gun in my right hand, but he didn't want us gone for long. If Major wasn't the fucking reason I was pushing myself so hard, I'd be more pleased than I am that I'm steadily returning to normal.

"Joking apart, Brother," Mace tells me seriously as we walk back down, "you're coming along in leaps and bounds."

I think the need to protect my family has kicked my brain into gear and made me stop fucking around. I may walk with a slight limp, but at least I'm getting around without that damn stick which I hate.

"Cas doing okay?"

"Yeah." I glance at the enforcer. "With all the comings and goings, all the people around, I don't think he's yet come down. With everyone telling him how good he did to escape, he's still on a fuckin' high."

The clubhouse is full to overflowing. RIP, his VP Charmer and the Wretched Soulz sergeant-at-arms, Bam Bam, have taken over Demon's and Shayla's old rooms, both Cas and Vanna are in with me—my son might be cramping my style, but I'll not complain and rather he be close—and Shayla's in with Mace. Along with the officers, three other Wretched Soulz have come to help us, and are camping out in our clubroom.

"It's going to hit him hard at some point," Mace observes as we near the clubhouse, giving a wave to Pyro and Wills who are trailing wire along the ground. "But we're all going to be here for him when it does, Brother. Lots of us coped with that shit and are still around."

First time you take a man's life, whatever the reason, whether it was him or you, it's always difficult to come to terms when you realise the blood you have on your hands. "Just got to keep him knowing there was no other way." I nod at Mace, appreciating the support he's offering.

"If he wants to prospect for us in a few years' time, you going to be alright with that, Brother?"

I wouldn't be at all surprised if that's the way the wind would be blowing. "I wouldn't mind, but I think Vanna might have other plans." Like Cas going to college and getting an education. I'm still lagging behind, trying to catch up with how to help shape a youth's hopes and dreams so he can have the best life he can.

"You and Vanna tight?"

We've reached the back door of the clubhouse. Opening it, I step inside, and Mace gets his response without me having to say a word. As soon as she sees me, Vanna has come across, and she's in my arms.

"How did it go, Liz?"

Mace winks at me as he walks off.

I answer her, but also my Prez who's standing behind her, one eyebrow raised. "I can fire, reload, and hit a target."

"Your hand?"

I flex it and show her. "Almost good as new, babe."

"Good fuckin' news, Brother." Demon slaps my back as he walks past.

The kitchen is filled to overflowing. Jeannie and Mo are having a loud discussion about food and supplies they need to get in. Vi is rolling her eyes at them and making a list of her own. Steph and Beth are chatting at the table, and Mel's pulling something delicious smelling out of the oven. Jayden's got Theo in her arms, and Sindy's emptying the dishwasher. The club whores are, as usual, noticeably absent while there's work to be done. Mind you, they usually sleep through the day anyway.

"Where's Cas?"

Vanna rolls her eyes. "They've got *Call of Duty* set up on a big screen in the clubroom. Last thing I saw, he was beating everyone's ass."

Sounds like my son, I smirk. "Got a few minutes, Vanna?" I lean in closer and speak directly into her ear. "I, er, want to show you what I can now do with my hand."

"Your hand?" She bumps my hip with hers. "What if I wanted another part of your anatomy?"

She's speaking quietly, but as I've found out before, Beef's woman may not have the use of her eyes, but her other senses make up for that. At her barked laugh, I look down to see her sightless eyes staring at me, crease lines around them. "You and Vanna go fuck, I'll keep an eye on your son. Make sure you're not interrupted."

"What if he was standing behind you right now?"

Steph rolls her sightless eyes. "He's not."

He isn't. *How the fuck does she do that?* I didn't even see her sniff the air.

Vanna goes bright red as everyone turns and looks at us knowingly, but I don't give a fuck. I grab her hand and all but drag her out of the kitchen. On my way to the stairs, I stop for a moment, seeing exactly whose ass Cas is currently whipping at the game he's too young to play—only the Wretched Soulz prez and his sergeant-at-arms. Jeez. I continue on my way, shaking my head.

While I'd previously objected to him playing an adult game, I've revised my opinion. Seeing what Cas had to do to escape Major, if that game taught him any skills he needed to bring into play, I'm not going to be saying one more word.

"Liz." Vanna's puffing beside me. "Eager, much?"

Again I chuckle, pausing only to lock the door of my room once we're on the other side of it. "Gotta take our chances when we can."

"You're getting the hang of being a dad," she laughs back. "Be worse if we have a baby. You sure you want that?"

"So fuckin' sure, Vanna," I tell her, seriously. "And this time I want to be a part of it and remember every fuckin' thing about it until the day I die."

She's already taking off her top and letting her bra fall to the ground. My eyes flare as I see the body I'll never get tired off.

"You're fuckin' perfect, Vanna."

"You'd be perfect too, if you got the goods out."

Oh, this wife of mine. "I'll show you my fuckin' goods," I warn, stripping out of my t-shirt and unbuckling my belt. "I'll more than show you." I toe off my boots and step out of my jeans, handling my cock and pumping it. "Gonna fuck you hard, Vanna."

"Do your worst, big man."

I stalk her, pushing her down on the bed. "Tell me if it gets too much."

"Pretty sure I can take whatever you want to give me," she gasps. "Just get on with it, Lizard."

A flash of memory comes into my mind of a young Marine and his new bride. I handled her like fucking porcelain, never wanting to hurt her. Now she has more meat on her bones and somehow the independence that's been forced on her over the years has made her more confident in bed. She takes everything I want to give and even asks for more.

"On your stomach, ass up. Want to see my property patch."

She obeys, and as normal, all the blood in my body seems to rush to my cock as my name is revealed in all its glory. She's wet, ready for me.

Gotta slow this down. I reach around for her clit.

"Just fuck me," she instructs.

Oh hell. She's taunting me, wiggling that ass. I don't wait to be asked twice, just enter her already wet pussy in one long stroke, both of us gasping at the feeling. I swear her cunt tries to draw me in.

Then I start thrusting, hammering into her, my fingers finding her clit and strumming it.

I'd love to say I fucked her for hours, but once she starts clenching, I'm a goner, and I'm gone with her.

I roll over, pulling her with me, still semi-hard inside her. "Fuck, Vanna. Sorry, babe. That was fast…"

"I came," she giggles. "What's the problem?"

"No problem," I tell her. "No fuckin' problem at all. But we didn't use a condom, babe."

"So?"

I chuckle softly. If she's got no issues with that, I certainly haven't.

"Liz? You finished in there?"

I'm going to fucking kill Ink.

"Whatcha want, asshole?" I yell back, nuzzling my woman's hair.

"Prez wants us."

Vanna's giggling again. "Only one thing wrong with this clubhouse," she tells me. "No privacy."

"We are so getting our own place, babe," I tell her, dragging my jeans back on, knowing the dick I'm stuffing into my pants is sticky with her juices and mine, and relishing the feeling of taking her with me. "Soon as Major's no longer a threat, we'll find somewhere where no fucker will bother us."

My wife immediately grows serious. "Take care, Lizard. Please, take care." She pulls herself up, slipping into the robe she'd left by the bed. "I'm so scared I've found you just to lose you again."

Crossing the room, I curl my hand around the back of her head, forcing her to look up at me. "Can't make promises I might not be able to keep, but I'll do everything I can to ensure you and Cas are safe, Van. I'll walk through the fires of hell to come back to you." I feel like I already have. I've been in hell for twelve years. Now I've got my slice of heaven, I'll do whatever it takes to hang onto it.

Moments later, I'm walking into church. I'm not the last. Mace comes in behind me, the red flush to his face suggesting he too had taken the opportunity to get close to his woman.

"Okay," Prez starts. "Cad has some info."

"From the unknown fucker in Utah?"

Cad nods. "The same. Still no closer to knowing who he is, oh, and he's now shielded his IP address. Obviously was an error letting me know where he was from."

"Or her," observes Pal.

"Or her," agrees Cad.

Demon growls. "Don't care what sex he, she or it is, just tell us the info, Cad."

Our computer expert nods. "Major's on the move. Looks like

the hits coming sooner rather than later. He's been spotted heading for Pueblo."

"How far out?"

"Two hours' drive if he gets a move on."

"So we wrap this up fast and get into position."

"Who the fuck is this informant? How's he," RIP glances at the Prez, "she or they getting their info? Is it legit?"

"If it's not," snaps Thunder, "we lose nothing."

Bam Bam nods toward Thunder, two sergeant-at-arms on the same wavelength. "Would rather we prepared for nothing, than we're caught with our fingers up our asses."

Charmer bumps fists with his prez. "Could do with a good fight."

Good men these. Glad they're on our side.

The women, including the club girls, along with Cas and Theo, and the two dogs, Max and Bagel, are quickly gathered up and sent down into the basement. Christ knows where Bitch is, but as she's still got a couple of her nine lives remaining, hopefully she can look after herself.

Beth's hesitant to leave Ink. Shayla and Vanna, the other newest old ladies are also reticent, but Mo quickly hurries them up. I sense Vanna's reluctant because she'll be forced into close proximity with girls she's too well aware I've fucked. I hate to have it thrown in her face, but right now there's little to be done. We need to keep everyone safe. I send a message to her with my eyes, mouthing, *I love you.*

While Mo prefers to keep her life separate from the club, when necessary she can take charge, and at times like these her brusque approach works well. She eyes the three lingering at the top of the stairs. "If you don't let your men go and prepare, you're not helping them. Jeannie's got a few bottles of wine, Fireball and she's mixing up some margaritas down there. Mel's brought a few tubs of cakes and muffins."

I wink at Vanna. "Seems like we might have drunk sex later."

"Dad!"

Whoops. One of the drawbacks of having a son. But when I look at him, he's grinning.

"Don't forget, I'm sharing your room," he reminds me, laughing at the look on my face.

I chuckle, then grow serious, speaking to him man-to-man. "Keep your mom safe, Son." Heaven forbid anyone should get through our lines, but if they do? Well, I think I can depend on him.

"I'll look after them, Liz," Wills, who's staying down there with them, assures me.

I know he will.

CHAPTER FORTY-NINE

Mace

I'd thought I was going to have to tie Shayla up at one point. Seeing our preparations had made her want to give herself up and let Major take her. I'd explained and explained that a man like him wouldn't back down, even if he got what he came for. We've poked the hornet's nest, now we've got to grind the emerging insects into the ground.

Cas had killed at least one of his men, we'd sheltered Shayla. Once he'd found that out and who had her—and we'd still no idea how he'd done that—our fate, as far as he was concerned, had been sealed. He was coming for us whether he had her in his hands or not. He might even have gotten a yearning to get Cas back.

When talking hadn't worked, I'd fucked her. Hopefully, I've worn her out.

Wills has got strict instructions to protect the women, Cas, and Theo with his life. Knowing the measure of the man, he'd die before he'd let anything happen to them. I had a quick word with him and told him to watch Shayla carefully, in case she tried to get out in the incorrect belief sacrificing herself would save everyone else. At least the basement is soundproofed so they shouldn't hear bullets flying.

Sindy and Jeannie are also armed and so ready to protect themselves, I actually pity anyone who tries to get down into our basement.

Once the final 'goodbyes' and 'be carefuls' have been said, the door is locked and bolted from the inside. Judge is standing guard at the top, and I'm hidden outside with the rest of my brothers.

"Hate this waiting," Ink speaks softly from my side.

"Me too. Used to it, though."

"Yeah, well you're just a bullet sponge."

"Asshole." I know only too well what Marines call Army. Cannon fodder, that's the rep we've got. But I'll admire any man who puts one foot in front of the other heading into a firefight.

"Dogface," another voice sounds in my ear.

"You can shut the fuck up as well, Leatherneck," I respond to Ink.

But trading insults with men I'm proud to call brothers is our way of bonding. Whatever arm of the forces we were in, we're yet again facing a common enemy which unites us all.

Waiting might get on my nerves, but it is what I was trained for. Hours, days, of waiting, doing nothing, keeping still while the enemy was on the advance, knowing at some point we'd jump into action. Sometimes it would be us on the offensive, at other times like these, defending from a protected position.

I resist the urge to take out my phone to see just how long we've been waiting. I push down the desire to move, trying to calm my breathing, keeping my hand on my gun.

A glint of sunlight reflecting, it's Pal's drone, circling again.

"Looks like something's happening," a voice sounds in my earpiece. "Got camera's picking shit up."

"Trucks approaching. Got them coming up the track to the rear of the compound," Pal confirms, presumably from the drone footage.

"Need more men at the rear?" asks Beef.

"Nah," replies Demon. "Looks like we've got the same number who will be hitting the front.

"What I'd do," I say to Ink and Liz, "is hit us from the rear, then wait and attack from the front as soon as we're all headed out back."

"Camera feed is going down," Cad says. "Switching to back up. Damn. Right. Looks like the trucks at the front are hanging back."

"They can't know we're expecting them, can they?" asks Liz.

I doubt it, but who the fuck knows? Same fucker informing us could have been speaking to them. Don't trust someone when I don't know a name, but his info does seem to be checking out.

Suddenly there's an explosion, followed by another.

"Men down. Not ours. They've hit a couple of the land mines. Moving more cautiously now."

I notice Liz wince beside me. His hands are over his head, and the blood has drained from his face.

"Liz, not now, fucker. Stay here," I snap, recognising the signs of the onset of PTSD. He needs to stay in the here and now if he's going to be of any use to us.

"I'm okay," Liz growls, shaking his head as if to clear it.

The sound of rapid gunfire comes from our rear.

"Casualties?" Demon's voice snarls in my earpiece.

"A bullet scraped Beaver, but everyone else is okay. RIP and his men are chasing the fuckers down. They're fuckin' lunatics."

And indeed, war cries are coming through my earpiece. Yup, seems like the Wretched Soulz are eager to fight hand-to-hand.

"Coming our way now," Pal shouts. "Truck approaching the gate, fast."

We replaced the gates when the mafia knocked them down. Unfortunately, it seems they're still not strong enough. As they take the full force of the truck, they twist and allow the truck to wedge them open.

"Grappling fuckin' hooks. They're climbing the walls."

"Christ, how many of the fuckers are there?"

I try to line up a shot but cover my head as a grenade explodes close to us.

"Jesus!" shouts Ink, but I can hardly hear him as my ears are ringing.

Stun and gas grenades are landing all around us. Fuck it! We thought we'd planned for everything but haven't got masks. I pull my bandana up over my nose, but my eyes are stinging, and I can hardly see where I'm shooting. I get off a few more rounds, but then Lizard rolls into me.

"Stop." He knocks my gun out of my hand. "You might shoot one of us. Retreat, into the clubhouse."

Trying to peer through my watering eyes, I notice brothers stumbling around in their haste to get inside and away from the debilitating gas. A man's being dragged, *fuck, who's down?* I pick up my gun then I'm running, keeping low to the ground, trying to identify a target to shoot at.

Inside, men are doubled up and coughing, frantically wiping eyes.

"Water, wash them," shouts Dirt.

But we've no time.

A voice comes over a bullhorn, "Give the girl up. That's all we want."

I go to the window. My head is seen, a bullet breaks the glass and I feel the wind of it go past my cheek. *Close. Too fucking close.* I duck back down.

"Casualty report," yells Demon.

"Bomber's down," calls back Rusty.

"Need to get back out," shouts Beef.

"Not until that gas dies down, can't fucking see anything," shouts back Hellfire.

"Mace?" Demon must see where I am. "What's going on?"

I risk raising my head again. "Hard to see a fuckin' thing. Hold on. The truck's backing up. Trying to push the gate back."

"They're not fucking breaking down our door again." Demon sounds furious. "Man the windows. Covering fire."

I hear the cracking of rifles from upstairs and through the smoke see men falling down.

"Someone's got the driver," I call out, taking a shot myself. "The truck is revving but going nowhere."

"Rear is cleared. We're coming around," Pyro calls out.

"Watch yourself. There's gas and smoke. Starting to clear now."

Which is good. Now able to see, brothers upstairs are picking the invaders off one by one.

"All those who can still see, together now."

Most of us head over to Demon. I see Nails with a wet rag to his face, but Dirt shakes his head. "He's okay, but he was pretty close to a canister when it went off."

Rusty is crouched by Bomber. When he goes to stand, Demon waves him back down. "How is he?"

"Doesn't look good. I'm trying to stop the bleeding. We'll have to get him to the hospital as soon as we can."

"Ink, Lizard, Mace. You okay?" At our nods and as our bodies stand to attention, he issues his orders, "Get out and give cover to Pyro and his team coming around the building."

We don't hesitate. Outside, there are bodies, injured men, but enough live ones still to cause trouble. I load, fire, reload and fire again, emptying my gun time after time. Eventually, I realise I've no targets to aim at, or those I can, are standing with raised hands.

Pyro's already going around disarming them one by one.

"Jeez, move this fuckin' truck out of the way." RIP's voice comes from the front of the compound, the other side of the gates.

I see his face appear, and I hastily jump into the truck and try to back it out onto the road. It takes me a few goes of back and forth before it's free of the twisted metal.

"Thought you'd like this." He pushes a man forward with his hand. "Was waiting in a fuckin' limousine down the road."

For a moment, none of us move. My eyes go from the man I can't wait to kill and then back to the Wretched Soulz' prez.

Demon's the first to recover from the shock and steps up, his face twisting in distaste. "Major, I presume?"

The man tries to shrug off the men holding him, but Bam Bam's got him held tight on one side, and Charmer's got a tight grip on his other arm. Realising he's no chance of freeing himself, Major stops struggling. As his expression changes from bluff to concern, it's dawning on him what trouble he's in. "Look, you can keep the girl. Just let me go. I'll let you have her and leave your club alone."

"Keeping the girl anyway," Demon tells him, lazily.

My ears still ring with the sounds so recently died down, my nostrils breathe in the smell of cordite, but the breeze has luckily blown the tear gas away. I'll let Demon have his words with Major, then I'll take him down to the basement, once the girls have been given the all clear and allowed up into the light of day of course. Then I'll put the basement to the use it was really soundproofed for. I can almost smell the blood I'm about to spill. Major will be screaming for weeks and no one in the clubroom above will be any the wiser as I question him in my own enforcer style. For now, I'll let him try and bluster his way out of it.

Major's not put off. "I've got money. I've got girls, boys, you name it. How about you and I go into partnership? You could run a new arm of the business in Colorado. I'd give you a good—"

Major droops in the arms of the Wretched Soulz holding him, a distant crack sounding momentarily after he does so. Stunned, Bam Bam and Charmer let his body drop to the ground. There's a perfect round hole in the back of his head, the type of which means there's no chance of recovery.

What the…?

"What the fuck?" Demon growls, then more loudly, "Who the fuck?" His eyes glare accusingly at the men standing around, then at those still covering us from the top floor of our club-house. "Who the fuck did this?" he yells.

"Prez." I step forward, if possible angrier than him. Seeing Major die in front of me was not good enough. Too quick, too merciful. He should have died by my hands. "The shot must have come from outside the compound." I turn and indicate the wide-open gates.

"Sure did," Charmer confirms, shading his eyes and looking into the far distance behind him. "There, look? See that glint?"

Now I see where he's pointing. It could be the glint off a windshield or window as it appears to be moving. There's not a chance in hell of us getting close to intercept it, whatever it is, is driving off-road and fast getting away.

"You got a sniper I don't know about?" Prez accuses his counterpart, RIP.

RIP, turns and gives a disdainful stare at Prez. "If I did, I'd be fuckin' proud of him for such an accurate shot at that distance, but no, I can't take credit for this."

"Could Major have set himself up?" I ask, wonderingly. "Rather be dead than captured?"

"Makes no fuckin' sense." RIP is right, it doesn't.

"He's dead." Demon seems to have realised he won't be able to question him. "Which is the outcome I wanted, though I'd rather have drawn it out." Him and me both.

"Prez?" Pyro gets his attention. "We've got ten bodies out back. Six here in the front, plus injured and captured. What are we going to do about them?"

"You got a burial ground?" RIP asks.

"That's a fuckin' lot to bury," says Charmer.

"Rusty wants to know if he can get Bomber to the hospital?"

"Yeah, Judge. Tell him to go now."

Fuck. I hope Bomber's going to make it. Can't imagine what Jeannie would do if her man was taken from her.

RIP, chewing on a piece of grass, looks thoughtful. "Don't know how you're set here, but you take a gunshot wound into the hospital, cops would use it as an excuse to come to my club."

Demon nods slowly. Chances are they'd use it as an excuse to visit us.

"Shame we can't heat the furnace and burn the bodies in there. If it could melt half a train, then a few bodies should burn up okay."

I turn to look at the VP, at the same time as Charmer says seriously, "You'd have to heat it to fourteen hundred degrees Fahrenheit. You able to do that?"

At that moment, Rusty and Judge drive up in a truck. "Managed to get Bomber in the back," Rusty calls out of the window. I notice he's looking grave and drawn. Bomber and he go back nearly forty years.

"How is he?" Demon asks, leaning in the window. "Hi, Jeannie, love, you okay?"

Rusty makes a see-saw motion with his hands. "I've tried to stem the bleeding, not much else I can do."

"Just get to the hospital fast," comes Jeannie's voice.

We all step back so they can drive through the gap which once held our gates.

"So," RIP reminds us. "Bodies…?"

"Get them in a truck. One of theirs preferably. I'll get the prospects to drive them out. Can't think what else to do with them but put them in the ground."

"Need help? I've got prospects could do with some practice."

That's an offer from the Wretched Soulz that we're not going to turn down.

CHAPTER FIFTY

Lizard

"So who killed him?" Vanna asks, shaking her head and reaching for her glass of wine.

It's a question we've all been asking. The most logical conclusion is someone wanted Major out of the way as badly as we did ourselves. But there's also the notion that Major had information someone didn't want him sharing. I know Mace felt cheated that he hadn't been able to question him.

I'd given a shrug as my answer to Vanna, there was nothing else I could tell her, nor had been able to for the past couple of days since it had happened. We're all wondering exactly the same thing. Cad had tried to reconnect with his contact on the dark web, but he'd done a disappearing act, and Cad couldn't locate him again.

Gradually things are returning to normal. We had, indeed, had a visit from the police checking on the story that Bomber had somehow accidentally shot himself in the side, awkward as fuck, but that was what we were all going with. By the time they'd arrived, with assistance from the Wretched Soulz' prospects, the bodies had been loaded and taken away, and a pressure washer had removed most of the blood. Without a warrant, they couldn't search further and luckily hadn't checked on the rear line of our property which looked like a war zone.

We'd been outnumbered but had come out the victors. The mercenaries Major had employed had given up once their paymaster was dead. Mace got his way and was able to question a couple of those uninjured, but both told him the same. They were in it for the pay and had no allegiance. No personal beef with us, and no reason to come for us again. They'd all joined up individually, so no prior friendships or loyalty between them.

Interestingly, Major was paying them in cash, and the money was found in his limousine. The numbers to share it had reduced dramatically, so while we took half for our damages, the men left alive agreed to take their own injured away as they'd each taken a bounty greater than expected.

I'd been happy with the solution and the promise elicited that they'd never show their faces in Pueblo again. It's one thing to shoot a man in the heat of battle, quite another in the cold light of day.

A couple had grudgingly admitted they'd no idea what they'd be walking into that day, having been told it was a simple extraction from men unprepared and who had no idea the mercenaries were headed our way. That we were a bunch of wannabe bikers who, when not riding our bikes, sat around drinking and fucking all day. They hadn't expected to come up against experienced men armed and prepared to put their lives on the line for their club.

I was happy to see the last of them, which coincided with the news that Bomber was awake, grumpy and having been sewn up and given blood to replace that which he'd lost, would make a full recovery.

"Dad? I like this one."

I look down when he passes me his tablet. "Huh. Well think again. That's a little out of our price range." Way out of it, truth be told. Little shit has just shown me a house with an indoor pool and a gym.

"That one's more like it." Vanna, leaning over me, is scrolling down the page.

Yeah, a modest house with four bedrooms and seems in a good neighbourhood. Vanna wanted three, but I pushed her to look for something larger, wanting to fulfil her dream of having a big family.

"It's okay," Cas says sullenly. I presume he's noticed it doesn't have a pool.

"I'll make arrangements for us to go and see it." I stand, stretch, and take my phone out of my pocket.

"Liz?" I pause and turn around at my wife's voice who's staring down at her tablet. "Lindy's emailed. She wants to come visit. Says she wants to see Cas with her own eyes to make sure he's okay. Is it alright if she comes this weekend?"

Vanna's friend had been beside herself when Cas went missing. We were a bit vague about where he'd been, but Vanna had come up with something to calm her. There's no doubt she's been a good friend to my wife, so I can't see a visit would be a problem, I've not met the woman myself, but feel I should thank her. Not only had she let Cas stay, she'd been Vanna's support ever since she'd moved to Denver.

"Yeah, I'll have to run it past Demon, but it should be fine."

Her wide smile shows it was the right answer. I continue my interrupted journey out of the noisy clubroom.

As I walk out into the warmth of the summer's day, I stare before making my phone call. We've already got a new reinforced gate on the way, and the prospects have shored up the old one the best that they can.

I'm a lucky bastard, things could so easily have gone differently. This club is my life and family, but if my wife and kid hadn't fitted in as they have, I'd have given it all up and moved to Denver. That they wanted to stay has made my life perfect. I'll miss living at the club but can't wait to make a new start in our new home with Vanna, even though it means I'll have to deal with Cas every day.

He's easy to love, but a lot of the time he has me wanting to pull my slowly growing-back hair out. *Babies grow into teenagers,* I remind myself, *and here I am planning more.*

Idly, I wonder whether Cas would have turned out anything other than the Devil's spawn if I'd been there to shape him growing up. I scoff at myself, no fucking chance. Although I'd like to deny it, he reminds me of my much younger self, or what I would have been had I been brought up by a loving mom. I'd have bucked the rules too, hell, being a biker, I'm constantly holding up my middle finger to the world. I may not have had a hand in his upbringing, but he's so like me it's uncanny.

He's now talking about joining the Marines when he's old enough, and I'm not sure how I feel about that, knowing only too well how dangerous it is. Fuck, the injury I suffered had affected three lives—mine, his and his mother's. Part of me wonders whether he's seeking revenge on the enemy that caused my injury, but it wouldn't be the same war he'd be fighting.

He's already taken another man's life, but though I've been watching him carefully, he seems to have compartmentalised that. It was a desperate but necessary action. Had he not done what he had, I might have lost him forever. I shudder just thinking about it.

I came out here for a reason, I remind myself. To take that first step into our future and do something I'd never thought about before I had Vanna back in my life. To buy a house with my wife, move her and my son into it, and hopefully add more kids into the mix.

I'm Lizard, otherwise known as Norton James. I'm thirty-eight years old and I ride with the Satan's Devils MC. I'm a tattoo artist... or will be, if I get the full use of my hand back—no one wants a tattoo artist whose hand shakes, but as it's improving every day, I've every hope of getting there eventually.

I repeat my mantra which I haven't thought about for weeks. Vanna's not worried about my brain playing tricks on me, so why the fuck should I? But I add something that I'll always want to remember. *I'm a happily married family man.*

CHAPTER FIFTY-ONE

Mace

I glance down at the woman lying beside me, trustingly resting her head on my shoulder. Her mouth is open and she's snoring gently. I grin, knowing she'd refuse to believe me if I told her. Apparently, women don't snore or fart. I suppress a snort, knowing it's a lie on both counts.

I never thought I'd find someone I wanted to settle down with, but now can't understand how I ever thought I was contented with the club girls. Each time Shayla and I fuck, it gets better to the point I'll be satisfied with just her for life.

It's been a week now since the death of Major was taken out of my hands, my only regret is that I couldn't make him hurt and give him a death which was prolonged and painful. That one bullet to the head had been so much more than he deserved.

Shayla grunts softly and snuggles closer into me, as trusting in sleep as she is awake. She knows I'll never hurt her and would die before I let anything harm her.

I think about the meeting last night in church.

"I got a phone call from Red earlier," Demon had told us. "Big news story down in Vegas. Women and boys had been found held captive in a mansion. They'd been pimped out and used against their will. Each one branded with a tattoo. Everything points to it having

been Major's operation that had been brought down, though the police haven't made his name public. Rope, Cuff, and Twister identified it was their contacts who'd been arrested."

I breathed out. "Thank fuck." There was always the possibility Major could have been taken out to prevent that happening so a partner could continue the business. Major was killed before he spilled the details of his operation.

"It appears whoever killed Major knew he could die with his info intact, as they had it anyway. Or that's what Red and I surmise. Police got a firm tip-off and they followed up with a raid. Twenty women and four young boys who'd been forced into sexual servitude now saved and given a new chance in life."

Sounds simple, but if they're damaged like Shayla, I could only hope they're getting the support that they need.

We'd discussed it for a bit longer, but it was the ending of a chapter. Major's dead, his operation in tatters. Of course, someone else would undoubtably step up and take his place. Where there were men willing to pay to feed their depraved appetites, someone will step up and provide what they wanted. But the player who'd come into our lives is gone. He's now dead, buried and rotting out in the desert.

"Any other business?"

I raised my hand. "Prez, I want to put something on the table." At his nod, I'd continued, "Our bylaws state all old ladies should get a property patch tattoo. I propose we remove that rule." I pause and grimace. "After what happened to Shayla, my view of property patches has become tainted. Shay's my woman, but I don't need my name on her to know that I own her, and she doesn't want hers on me."

"Agreed," Beef said fast. "Never got around to putting mine on Steph. She's not keen on the idea of tattoos. Tucson got rid of that requirement years back."

For some reason, everyone looked down the table at Hellfire. He'd thought for a moment, then shrugged. "The regulation was there from the time the club was started, pre-dated even my time at the table. I was a prospect then and not part of the decision making."

"The club was wilder and more likely to go head-to-head with our *enemies, and other clubs tended to take something that wasn't owned. I agree, now, there's little need for it."* Bomber shifted a little, trying to get comfortable. We'd already agreed not to prolong this session as it was the day he'd been let out of the hospital. He'd insisted on coming to church, fucker didn't want to miss anything.

"I'm okay with removing the tattoo requirement, but old ladies would still need to wear their 'Property of' cuts though." Demon sounded adamant. *"It's protection if someone's sniffing around. Not taking a woman who looks unclaimed to a different chapter, or when the Wretched Soulz are around. A property cut saves a lot of time and argument."*

"That's a choice though, isn't it?" offered Pal. *"Why not leave it up to the couple to decide what's best for them?"*

Demon stared at him for a moment. *"Ok. Let's vote on it."*

The vote passed. The regulation was removed. I, for one, was very happy with that outcome.

I reach for my phone and notice the time.

"Hey, sleepyhead. Time to get moving."

She moans, coming awake slowly. I roll my body on top of hers, plant a quick kiss on her lips, then slide down under the covers.

"Mace!" Her voice is less sleepy, and her hands try to grip my short hair as I start eating her pussy.

When she comes, I move up the bed, my cock finding her cunt immediately. Now fully awake, she clutches at me.

It's a quickie as we've things we need to be doing, but no less satisfying than any other time I've fucked her. While I've just had a release, I'm sure my cock will be hard as iron once she's seated behind me on my bike. It's just the effect she has on me, and I know being close to me will have the same effect on her. But as soon as we reach Albuquerque, I'll find a motel and take her to bed.

Which, of course, is exactly what happens.

The next day we arrive at Flagstaff, and I use the GPS to find the house we need. Neither of us are certain of our welcome.

From the parents, I know we'll get a warm one—they'd extended an invitation as soon as I mentioned it—but neither of us are certain whether Esme will remember us, or whether seeing us again will cause her problems as the sight of Shayla might hold bad connotations for her.

I needn't have worried. Esme flies out of the house as soon as I cut the engine and launches herself into Shayla's arms.

"You came! Mommy and Daddy told me you would. You came!"

Her voice is strong and steady, and absolute music to my ears. It's how I always imagined it would be, more childlike than that of a teenage girls'.

"How are you Esme?"

"Good." She turns to me and holds out her arms. "Mace!"

"Hi, sweetie." I pick her up and swing her around. "We came to show something to you." I'm as eager as a kid myself as I put her down, leaving my arm around her, and turn her to face my bike. "Look."

Any thoughts that she wouldn't remember are blown away when her eyes open wide as they settle on the rearing stallion that she'd drawn, and Ink had painted on my bike.

"It's my picture!" She points to it, her hand covering her mouth, then looking up at me with wide eyes. "My picture's on your bike!"

"Come in and freshen up. I'm sure you've had a long journey. I don't know what you liked, but I've been doing some cooking."

So taken up with Esme's reaction to my bike, I hadn't noticed her parents coming outside, but should have guessed they would be right behind her. I turn to give them chin lifts now.

"You didn't have to go to any trouble for us," Shayla tells Esme's mother.

It's when Brett, her father is staring at Shayla, I realise the two had never actually met. He's got tears in his eyes as he hesitantly steps forward to her.

"Ms Yonovich, I'm, we're, so pleased to meet you at last. And nothing, *nothing* is too much trouble for the people who brought Esme back to us."

"Call me Shayla, please." Shay reaches out, takes his hand and squeezes it. "I'm just so pleased I got her out."

He looks like he's going to break down, so I quickly ask, "How's Esme doing?"

Brett slowly takes his eyes away from the woman who sacrificed so much to rescue his daughter and ruffles Esme's hair. "Esme's doing fine, aren't you?"

"Daddy, look at Mace's bike." Proudly she points to my gas tank.

"I can see, sweetheart. You draw that?"

She nods so hard I think she's in danger of her head falling off.

Maisie calls us to follow her inside, where she's prepared a feast fit for a king, far more than we'd ever be able to eat.

Just as we're remarking on it, a man appears. I've never met him before in my life, but I immediately know all about him.

"Uncle Paul!" Esme runs over and hugs the tall, well-built and rough-looking man, while wary eyes return my scrutiny.

"Army," I tell him, answering his unspoken question.

He smirks. "Navy. Retired."

Brett explains, "Paul's been living with us. He's a firefighter. His teammates and cops that he knows have been taking turns making sure Esme's kept safe."

Now I can better understand why Brett thought he was able to protect his daughter with the likes of him around.

Paul, it turns out, is Maisie's brother and a beloved uncle. I update him and Brett with the headlines, not going into details, but letting them know Major's no longer a threat. Esme pouts when hearing her Uncle Paul is now going to be moving out.

It's an enjoyable visit, and we stay longer than I'd expected, Esme wanting to show Shayla her room which is painted pink and decorated with unicorns. In pride of place on her bed is a shaggy dog toy, the colour of a bagel and, unsurprisingly, called

Bagel. A toy cat, less torn and tattered lies alongside it. When Esme opens her mouth to tell me its name, I hold my breath until she says she's called Bitsy.

"We're getting a puppy," Maisie tells us, grinning at our reaction to the cat's name. "We're getting it trained as a support dog for Esme. She's already named it."

"Max," Shayla and I say together, then both of us laugh.

A dog is a good idea. While on the surface Esme seems happy and settled, I'm sure she can't be totally unscathed by her experience, which her father confirms when he confides she never lets go of his hand when they go out. I suspect it's half and half though, and that he doesn't want to let go of hers.

She's lucky she's got a loving family, as what she is now is about where she'll ever get to. She won't get her GED or be able to work. But he confides they're looking into where her talent at art might take her.

I ask him about her tattoo. It's a sore subject.

He grimaces and drags his hands through his hair. "It bothers me, it bothers Maisie, it's there as a permanent reminder. But the one person it doesn't bother is *her*. Esme's not really aware of it as she doesn't see it like we do. Laser treatment might be painful, another tattoo would hurt. What good would it do her to put her through something just to make us feel easier?"

He's got a point. I raise my chin to show I can see it.

His hands tighten until they form fists. "For now, we'll leave it alone. It's a reminder of how we nearly lost her, and how precious she is to us. Maybe in time, when she's older, we'll rethink and get it covered, but for now? I'm not going to hurt her."

We leave with promises to visit again and turn down offers of money, neither of us wanted payment for doing something any halfway decent person would do.

Then, it already being early evening, I suggest we find a motel and head back to Albuquerque in the morning. With Shayla and my bike with me, I've all that I need.

We find a suitable place where we can park right outside, and I present the key card to the lock which turns green immediately. Then, once inside, I throw the saddlebags down on the bed.

"She's doing well."

"She is," I agree.

Shayla shudders. "What if I had failed, Mace? What if I hadn't been able to escape with her? What if Major had found us?"

I wrap my arms around her, holding her face to my chest. I knew seeing Esme would bring everything back to her. I'd had to weigh the benefits of her being satisfied that the girl she rescued was being well cared for with the downside of it dredging up memories of her time as a captive and what she'd had to do to survive after.

"I love you," I tell her. "I want to marry you. I want to settle down, get a house, have a family with you if that's what you want too."

She looks up, wipes away tears, and her eyes open wide. "Marry me? Are you actually asking me?"

"If you're ready to hear it as a question, then yes. But I'm willing to give you all the time you need before I come looking for your answer. Thing is, Shayla, there I was, a single man, fulfilled that way until you stormed into my life and upset everything. I thought my life satisfied me, never knew there was a piece of me missing, until you showed me there was. I was content, but not happy. I thought I wanted to be single, but that was because I was waiting for you. I want everything with you, Shayla. I just fucking hope it's what you want too." If she doesn't, I'd be lost, cast adrift with no anchor.

"I wish you hadn't gone through what you had to, to get to me, baby. I'd never wish that on anyone, and it hurts to know it happened to you. But we'd never have found each other if you hadn't."

It's only now she speaks. "We met because I wanted to get rid of his tattoo."

"Which is gone now." Vi did the last session last week. An intricate bouquet of flowers now covers his name, with a rainbow background. It's beautiful, something good from the bad.

She's still staring up at me. "I would never have found you. I can't say it was worth it, nothing is worth the suffering I incurred, and you know that I'm still working through it. But if you're willing to take me with all the baggage I carry, then one day I'm pretty sure I'm going to give you the answer you're looking for. It's just, right now, I'm not ready to."

I kiss her gently, then raising my mouth from her soft luscious lips, smile. "I know, and that's fine with me. Just wanted to let you know where I stood, baby. That nothing about your past bothers me, except that you had to live it. When you are ready, just know, I'll be here, waiting for you." In the meantime, she'll be in my bed, in my life, and fuck it, working alongside me too.

Her hands come to rest either side of my head, and for the first time I hear her tell me, "Mace, I love you."

EPILOGUE

"I saw their faces through my sight." I grin. "They were not happy." That is an understatement—shocked, confused, and furious.

"Stormy," he admonishes lightly, "you could have left it to them."

"Nah, Pip. I did what I needed to do. Couldn't risk that motherfucker getting free."

He raises his whisky, takes a sip, then asks, "You think he might have cut a deal with them?"

I shake my head, putting my beer bottle to my mouth and swallowing. "Who knows what people will do if the price is right?"

Pip snorts. "You don't trust many people, do you?"

"Nah," I agree. "I trust me and my rifle. Oh, and you."

"Then I'm honoured." He grins. "Oh, and I have another job for you."

"Someone else in the same business?"

"Trafficking this time." He chucks a folder across to me.

Opening it, I skim through it. "Ah," I exclaim after a moment. "This will have me crossing state boundaries again."

"Why do you think I've given it to you, Stormy? You're a loner, you get itchy feet staying in one place too long."

"And I live to remove scum from this earth."

"That you do." He chuckles softly. "Wish I could have seen their faces when Major hit the ground. They have no fuckin' idea who took him out. Their mysterious contact has disappeared as well."

Giving him a sheepish look. "Sorry about that."

"Fuckin' schoolboy error, forgetting to cloak your IP address."

"It won't happen again," I promise.

"See that it doesn't."

"I know the score, Pip. What we do only works if we keep underground."

OTHER WORKS BY MANDA MELLETT

Blood Brothers – A series about sexy dominant sheikhs and their bodyguards

Stolen Lives (#1) Nijad and Cara

Close Protection (#2) Jon and Mia

Second Chances (#3) Kadar and Zoe

Identity Crisis (#4) Sean and Vanessa

Dark Horses (#5) Jasim and Janna

Hard Choices (#6) Aiza

Satan's Devils MC - Arizona Chapter

Turning Wheels (Blood Brothers #3.5, Satan's Devils #1) Wraith and Sophie

Drummer's Beat (#2) Drummer and Sam

Slick Running (#3) Slick and Ella

Targeting Dart (#4) Dart and Alex

Heart Broken (#5) Heart and Marc

Peg's Stand (#6) Peg and Darcy

Rock Bottom (#7) Rock and Becca

Joker's Fool (#8) Joker and Lady

Mouse Trapped (#9) Mouse and Mariana

Blade's Edge (#10) Blade and Tash

Truck Stopped (#11) Truck & Allie

Satan's Devils MC - Colorado Chapter

Paladin's Hell (#1) Paladin and Jayden

Demon's Angel (#2) Demon and Violet

Devil's Due (#3) Beef and Steph

Devil's Dilemma (#4) Pyro and Mel

Ink's Devil (#5) Ink and Beth

Satan's Devils MC - Next Generation

Amy's Santa (#1) Wizard and Amy

ACKNOWLEDGMENTS

This book is dedicated to David 'Stormy' Haill for good reason.

A week before his eighty-fifth birthday, my father-in-law collapsed and was rushed to the hospital. By the time he arrived, he was unconscious. The doctors diagnosed a massive bleed in his brain, one from which he'd never recover. They offered no treatment whatsoever, not even a saline drip, and put him in a side room to die.

The close family assembled and stayed vigil at his bedside all night, waiting for him to pass. He was still breathing the next morning, but in a coma state.

That day, family assembled from far and wide, and as Dad was so close to death, the hospital didn't limit the number of visitors. A pattern developed. A new person would enter, pay their sad respects, but then see someone they hadn't seen for possibly years, and started catching up with each other's lives. As well as tears, there was laughter as anecdotes were shared, everyone had a funny story to tell. As the hours passed, people grew hungry, so teas and coffees arrived, and a table was commandeered to hold buffet food. There were up to twenty people at one time in the room.

Still Dad breathed on.

Night came, most said their last goodbyes, and left, now as sad as when they had arrived, as they left Dad for what they thought was the last time. His wife, of over sixty years with a card from the Queen to prove it, of course, stayed.

I had arranged to go visit him with my son the next lunchtime, but didn't expect to have to make the drive to the hospital. I certainly didn't expect the call mid-morning to say he was awake. His awakening kicked the doctors into action, he'd been without sustenance or fluids for two days.

His recovery was slow, he needed to be transferred to another hospital for a brain operation to stem another, smaller, bleed. When he first came around, he couldn't recognise anybody or talk. But slowly his brain began to mend.

Six weeks after he entered the hospital unconscious, and against doctors' expectations, he came home. Our medical miracle.

He's now one of my biggest fans and reads all my books. At the time of writing, he's approaching his eighty-ninth birthday and I hope he has many more.

Dad proved the impossible was possible. Mind you, we all think he woke up as he was annoyed he was missing out on the party we'd had in his room that first day. Or, it could show the power of hope and prayer.

Many years ago, I studied psychology, my course concentrated on how the brain worked. I was fascinated by memory. My son has also gained his degree in psychology much more recently. So I talked through any latest research with him, as well as doing reading online. It seems we're no further forward than we were forty years ago, theories come and go about memory, then someone's experience shows something else.

What happened to Lizard in Devil's Spawn is fanciful and based on no actual case study. But my research showed it wasn't impossible. What is fact is that there is a link between a serious brain injury and a tumour appearing later in life, some benign, some not so. There have also been instances when people who've forgotten their identity begin to remember who they are many years later.

So I've taken poetic licence to bring you this story, and I hope it's given you an enjoyable read. That, after all, is the point of fiction.

Now on to the thank yous. Thank you, Dad, first and foremost for being the inspiration for this story. I'm also nicking your Navy name for a character as, if you've reached the end, you'll already know. We'll be reading more about Stormy in later books.

Thank you, Michael, for letting me bounce ideas off of you. Love discussing my books with you and getting your insight. I am privileged to be your mum.

Thank you to my beta readers, and the comments elicited from you. You didn't wait for the end but messaged saying 'I didn't expect that!' while reading the story, which is the exact reaction I was looking for. Thank you, Tami, for checking the location details. Thank you to Danena and Sheri as always, and to Zoe, Alex and a new beta, Emma. I hoped this book would hit the spot, and according to you, it did.

Thank you to my cover designer, Dar of Wicked Smart Designs. I love what you did with the image I sent you and love how responsive you are. I'm really enjoying working with you.

Mary, my soul sister and editor. What can I say that hasn't already been said? When I said Devil's Spawn was too long, what did you say? That it needed two more chapters. You were right, even if it means this is the longest Satan's Devils' book to date. But this time, at least, I didn't set out to write a novella. Loved your insight and comments as normal.

Thanks again to Melanie for the quick turnaround on the proofreading. Love that you're part of my team now.

Last but not least, thank you to all my readers, old and new, who take a chance on my books. I'm always happy to talk about my stories, so if you've got questions or just want to connect, please do so via Messenger or email. I appreciate any and all reviews left and read every one. Reviews raise the profile of an author, so even one sentence is valuable.

You can keep in touch with what I'm up to in a number of ways. Follow me on social media or sign up for my newsletter.

There are exciting things coming in the future. The next book will take us to San Diego and reconnect with Lost and Dart, the prez and VP in southern California. That will set us up for Road Tripped, which will include a brief return to Tucson. I'm also planning a further Second Generation book. Have I finished with the Colorado chapter? Probably not. And what about Red and his boys in Vegas? I wish I could write faster, as I've lots of ideas in my head.

I better get back to writing now else there won't be any more books.

Love, as always,
Manda

ABOUT THE AUTHOR

Manda's life's always seemed a bit weird, starting with a childhood that even today she's still trying to make sense of, then losing her parents in the late teens. Going from the tragic to the bizarre, who else could be unlucky enough to have had two car accidents, neither her fault, one involving a nun, and another involving a police woman?

There isn't enough space to list everything that's happened to Manda, or what she's learned from it. But by using the rich fabric of her personal life, psychology degree, varied work experiences, and amazing characters she's met, Manda is able to populate her books with believable in-depth characters and enjoys pitting them against situations which challenge them. Her books are full of suspense, twists and turns and the unexpected.

Manda lives in the beautiful countryside of Essex in the UK, the area's claim to fame being the Wilkin's Jam Factory at nearby Tiptree. She can usually find jars of jam which remind her of home wherever she goes. As well as writing books and reading, Manda loves walking her dogs and keeping fit. She lives with her husband of over 30 years, who, along with her son, is her greatest fan and supporter.

Manda is thankful that one of the more unusual, and at the time unpleasant, turns her life took, now enables her to spend her time writing. Confirming, in her view, every cloud has a silver lining.

Photo by Carmel Jane Photography